I0596356

VIVATERA

CANDACE J. THOMAS

SHADESILK
PRESS

Paperback Edition 2020
Shadesilk Press, LLC

Edited by Elizabeth Gilliland

Published in the United States of America
Cover Design/Inside Graphics
by Monika MacFarland
Ampersand Book Covers
BISAC
Fantasy; High Fantasy; Magical: Adventure; Coming-of-age
ISBN
978-1-7335011-4-9
Library of Congress
2 0 1 9 9 1 9 1 0 0

To Kevin, my favorite

THE VIVATERA SERIES

VIVATERA

CONJECTRIX

EVERSTAR

VIVATERA

IGNIS MOUNTAINS
LUX LUCIS
THE NORTH
NETHERFIELDS
TRISTUS RIVER
BLACK WOOD
SHARLOT
MUSUNGU MARSHES
SOUTHWIC
PARBRAVEN
UND

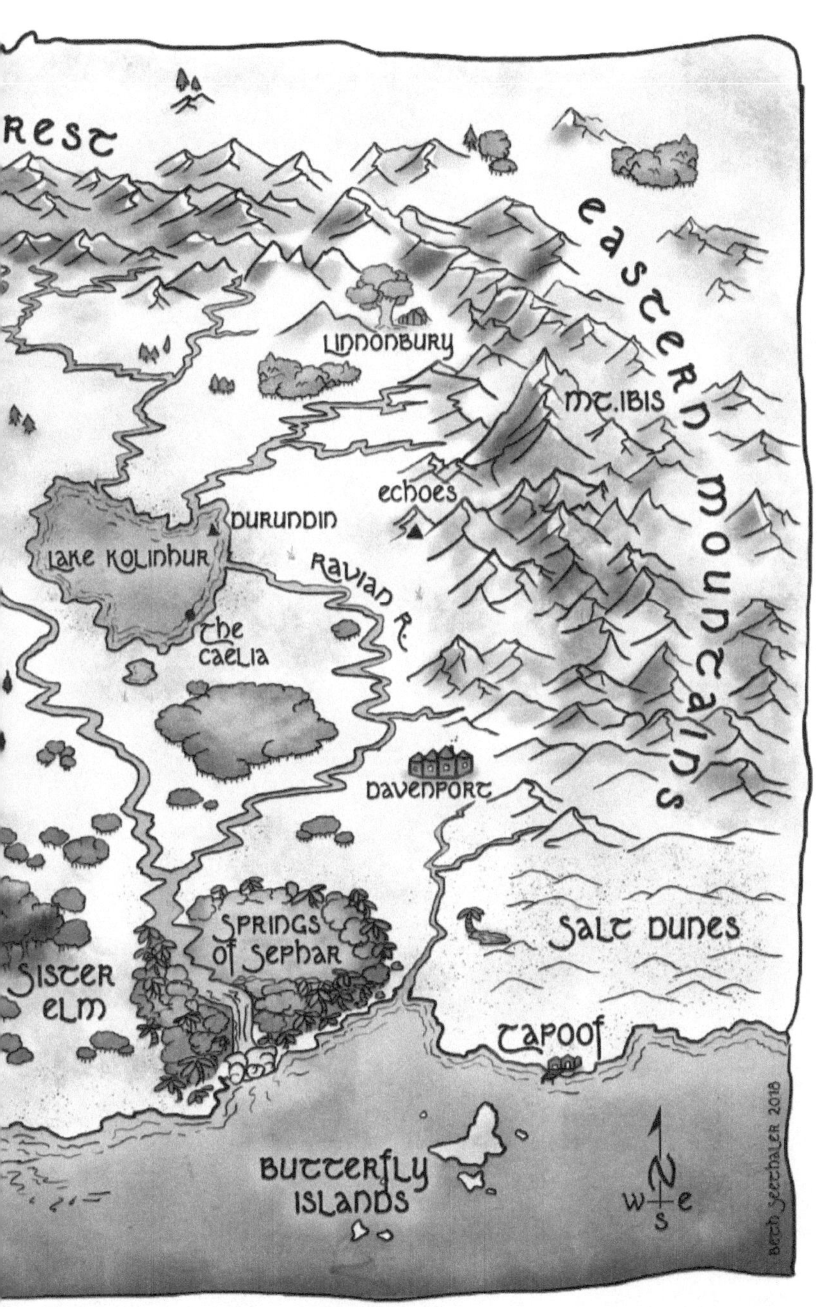

rest
eastern mountains
Linnonbury
Mt. Ibis
echoes
Durundin
Lake Kolinhur
Ravian R.
the Caelia
Davenport
Salt Dunes
Springs of Sephar
Sister Elm
Tapoof
Butterfly Islands
Beth Seethaler 2018
N
W E
S

PROLOGUE

The wide hall echoed with his footsteps. An unsettling quiet filled the palace. The only sounds Reyn heard came from the quick clips of his boots on the hard stone and the thumping of his young heart.

Most of court would be at the ceremony. The king rarely invited so many to come, but that special occurrence marked a crowning achievement in his reign. Only adults would be there, all except for the young princesses.

The impatient boy dashed from his family's quarters toward the palace apothecary. As apprentice to the king's healer, Lytte, Reyn knew he would find it empty. He needed the crucible for his experiment; Lytte wouldn't allow it if he knew. Tonight, an opportunity opened up. The ceremony provided the perfect cover.

The small figure of Taren stood tucked away in a quiet corner of the passage, waiting just as he'd promised he would. His age made him too young to understand the risk but old enough to keep quiet—innocent, naïve, and motivated, an ideal accomplice. If Taren wanted to be included, Reyn needed proof he could handle it.

"Come, Taren."

Taren hesitated. "Reyn, I think this is a bad idea."

"I don't care what you think."

"I don't think you should touch the magic— "

Reyn loomed over him, nearly a head taller than his toady. "You agreed, Taren. A promise for a promise. I need a second pair of hands for this to work."

The little boy swallowed his words and followed.

On and on the two traveled through the empty hallways, down stone paths and under intricate archways as they ventured to the apothecary.

The knapsack Reyn slung over his shoulder carried his precious treasures. Six jumbled jars clinked together from his hurried steps. His mind worked out everything he needed to do with the leftover stone pieces he had carefully collected and protected in secret——the discarded shards Lytte ordered him to destroy. But his curiosity wouldn't allow it. The possibilities his plan presented sent thrills throughout his body, down to his fingertips. He hardly contained the adrenaline racing in his veins.

They found the apothecary unoccupied, as expected.

"Start the fire," he ordered. "We need it really hot."

Taren did as asked. The flames grew bright.

Reyn took out each jar and placed it very carefully on the table. The magic glowed in its measure, curious and wonderful. Out of his pocket, he pulled the beautiful gold medallion, its center hollowed and empty. His fingers brushed over the intricate hawk symbol. Pride swelled at his own accomplishment.

It had started as a piece of scrap he used for practice. His father allowed him to make it—a project they worked on together when the trusted forge-master created others as a favor for the king. It belonged to him, and so would the stone.

Taren stared, completely distracted by the colorful magic sparkling in the jars. "What will you do?" he asked.

"Nothing wrong."

"I didn't say—"

"Yes, but I know what you meant."

Taren stared at the containers. He prepared to say more but thought better of it.

Reyn turned to face him. "You can't say a word to anyone, got it? Nothing that you see here. Nothing. Not to anyone."

The little one nodded.

"Swear it!"

A look of loathing crossed the child's face. "I swear."

Good enough. Reyn didn't have time to worry about the loyalties of the younger boy.

Now to heat the minerals.

Even at the age of nine, he knew much of the trade for which he was apprenticed to his grandfather. He grabbed the tongs and a small metal cup. They would have to do.

Each jar drew in an audible gasp as Reyn opened it, like the magic needed to breathe. The unexpected reaction provided a quick reminder of the danger, but he had no time to think about it.

Reyn softly tipped each jar until the pieces dropped out, careful not to touch them. The large pieces would work. Not everything would fit in the cup, so he left the small pieces in the jar. Too precious to waste, he would keep them for something special.

Whispers of magic floated above the top of the cup as each stone touched its brother. A strange sizzling started around the edge.

"Grab the tongs," Reyn ordered his assistant.

Taren watched the minerals move and crack in the small container, mesmerized by the thin wisps of magic escaping the rim. The hot sparks shot out in different directions, dangerously close to where they stood.

"Quick!"

"I don't like this," Taren complained.

"I don't care! Now, grab me the tongs."

Taren just stared at the magic, petrified.

Reyn's patience ran thin, and he grabbed the tongs himself. He slid the metal around the cylinder in a firm grip.

"Reyn, don't do it! It's not stable."

"And what do you understand about the magic?"

"Don't force it together. Bad things will happen."

Reyn didn't care to hear anything else. It took a long time to get to that point. He knew everything he needed to know. He felt the anticipation. He would create a stone just as amazing as the others—maybe more. It would be brilliant.

As he moved the tongs closer to the fire, the sizzling increased. He just needed to get the cup into the heat. The minerals would soften and the magic would release. Reyn thought of the splendor of what would happen. After seeing what each mineral could do—even the small taste he had witnessed—his wonder ignited.

"Reyn! Don't!"

Just a few more inches. The flames licked around the cup; the sizzling continued.

A spark . . . a crackle.

Just a little more.

The iron tongs grew scalding. He didn't want to drop it. Just a few more seconds.

Colors inside the cup turned to flame. Blue ribbons moved upward, mixing with the heat. Green sparks flashed out. Thick, purple liquid spiraled around the iron, like a snake wrapping around its prey. Sparks flew.

The tongs began to shake.

Just a little longer.

He couldn't hold on.

The tongs slipped out of his hands and the tiny cup dropped into the fire.

Boom!

The blast hurled both boys against the opposite wall.

Ringing . . . vision blurred . . . head aching . . . What had happened? Flames crept near him. The sizzling mixed with the ringing in his ears.

Then Reyn felt burning. *He* was burning. The purple flame reached around his chest. Moving quickly, he rolled over, smothering the fire that singed his skin.

Across the room, Reyn saw Taren. He lay still against the stone, his face and chest covered with sparks, his eyes closed against the pain.

Reyn stood and ran to the younger boy, smacking at the sparks with his hands. "Oh, no. Can you hear me?"

Cuts covered Taren's face. Fresh blood streaked down his forehead and around his ears. For Reyn, panic set in. What had he done?

Reyn grabbed some of the strips of cloth near the medical cabinet and placed it around Taren's head. He didn't care about his own burns. They were nothing.

What had happened? He did everything right. It should have worked. His mind raced on what to do.

The dust settled around the stone hearth. Within the fire, as it died into ash, a glinting shimmer of light attracted his eye.

Reyn watched as a small stone rolled out of the overturned cup and onto the floor. The mysterious magic secured inside. He crawled through the rubble, completely captivated by the beauty of his creation. With a tiny cloth, he picked up the delicate stone. A greedy smile covered his face.

He was right. It worked.

CHAPTER ONE
LIGHTSEER

Those in shadow watch through gentle cracks of cedar,
upon a young woman
with hair, silver as moonlight, running down her back.
She knows she will die and she waits.

Naomi sat straight up. Sun streamed through the leaves above her. How late was it? Disoriented, she looked around. The branches beneath her feet swayed along with the wind. The worn pages of her journal fluttered gently back and forth. She hadn't expected to fall asleep here, just to get some peace.

"Girl!" The yelling felt far away because of the muffling wind through the trees. She knew it was for her.

"Naomi, you lazy girl!"

Looking through the hollow, she saw Ferrell, mad as ever, his red skin nearly purple with anger. The sun high in the sky, it had to be late morning, which made her late for the market and left poor Zander all alone. The boy might get in trouble for her sake. Best not get caught.

Naomi gathered her dream journal in her knapsack and swung it over her middle. She looked down the tree and saw her boots at the base of the trunk. Well, she couldn't take those now. Climbing down would risk Ferrell seeing her. She hated the boots anyway. She loved the feeling of her toes in the grass.

Nimble as a cat, she moved along the branches to the next trees. She could hear distant yells with her name thrown in here and there. The further away she got, the better she felt. Ferrell would forgive her if she sold as much meat as he sent.

She followed along the great oak trees lining the rarely traveled road to the town of Sharlot, jumping when needed, but always with grace. She enjoyed testing her limits bounce after bounce. She could see through the trees, along the grass to the village. Not much farther to go.

Naomi rubbed the nape of her neck out of habit, tracing the scar she seldom thought about anymore. The scarf still wound around her throat, secure, just how Malindra taught her to wear it. The feel of the smooth fabric comforted her, reminding her of Malindra's love. Naomi smiled at the memory of her beloved caregiver.

With a few climbs and a small hop, Naomi's bare feet slid into the grass, which tickled her legs and toes. The soft ground yielded to her feather-light frame. Naomi cinched her hood tight around her face, her hair concealed beneath. She let the morning air fill her lungs before she sprinted off to town.

⁓⚬⁓

"Where h-have you . . . ?" Zander stuttered. The words always rushed out when he hadn't talked to anyone for a while, making him seem much younger than his twelve years.

"No worries, Zan," Naomi said as she approached the cart. "I'm here now. How are you this morning?"

"Okay," he mumbled. He looked embarrassed, maybe frightened to say anything more on the subject. "Where . . . do . . . you go?"

"The tree," she said without a thought. "I couldn't sleep last night."

"D-did you d-dream again?"

Naomi couldn't hide things from Zander. Her dream still sat in slim awareness near the surface of thought: the girl with the amazing silver hair, the lightning outside of the tiny space she hid, something or someone hunting her. She looked terrified, but not of the lightning. The lightning protected her.

Naomi blinked back to reality and looked at Zander. She nodded and patted her sack over her shoulder. "You want to look?"

Zander smiled as Naomi handed over her dream journal. It didn't look special in any way, just a small, insignificant parchment of scribbles. She'd added to it over the years with scrap pages and spare twine. It really didn't look important to anyone, but she liked it that way. It gave it character.

Naomi watched Zander carefully as he looked at her newest entry. A worry came over her. "How is your back?"

He looked up embarrassed, afraid to speak.

"May I see?" she asked.

Zander turned and slowly lifted his tunic. The whip marks were completely healed over, no oozing welts or bloody scabs, but smooth and clean. Naomi always liked to check. She had rubbed it the previous night with cornflower oil and it always worked.

"I'm sorry that happened," Naomi said, thinking of his father's tirade. "I hate it when he's in a bad temper."

Zander shrugged it off and forgot about it. "I'm g-glad I have . . . you."

Naomi rubbed his shoulder and smiled.

"I've only sold . . . a few . . . chops. Some people came to look and asked me a question, b-but I . . ."

"Oh, Zander," Naomi said with love. She reached her arm all the way around him in a mothering way and squeezed. "I don't want you to worry about it, okay?"

The boy nodded in relief.

Naomi looked over the crowd. Many people filled the streets and alleys. Women in fancy dresses and masks with ornate, jeweled wraps and men in headdresses with feathers peppered the street with color, like peacocks prancing for approval.

"I don't know why your father thinks we can sell more meat today than any other day," she said.

Zander shrugged his shoulders. "I did . . . see a man breathing f-f-fire."

Naomi scoped the street. She saw no fire-eater, but she did notice more blue than normal: men dressed in blue cloaks, swords strapped to their side. "Who are the men in uniform?"

"G-guards from Southwick," he stated. "The prince is c-coming."

"A prince . . ." Naomi repeated, perplexed.

Far from the village, Southwick stood near the sea. Sharlot served as a skipping stone to other, greater cities of Parbraven. Naomi knew very little about this prince, the son of the king. He must have a handsome face, she assumed, to draw such a crowd. She witnessed a glowing review of the monarchy in the faces all around her. An air of hope to a sad people.

In her assessment of the crowd, Naomi spotted someone in a dark-green cloak in a corner alley. She felt something familiar about him, like in the dreams she had scrawled on her parchment. He seemed interested in the crowd as well. He held very still, observing the people, not joining in or carrying on like the others.

The crowd wouldn't have noticed him, but Naomi sensed a deeper purpose for his presence. She surveyed the street and the guards. When her eyes wandered back to the alley, he had disappeared.

"Zan?" she asked. "Did you see someone in the corner in a green cloak?"

Zander shook his head.

They risked wasting the day with their wandering distractions. She didn't want Zander hurt because of her curiosity, and restored her focus. "Sorry. Let's see what we can sell."

Naomi pulled back her hood. Her hair glinted in shades of honey, seeming to take its energy directly from the sun. The fluid blonde curls attracted attention immediately. The color didn't appear commonly in Sharlot—or in Parbraven, for that matter.

Zander's father knew it caught attention of crowds and used it to sell his cargo. People would sometimes ask to touch it for good luck. They wondered where she came from, or where she got such a blessing. Sadly, she didn't know. It remained a mystery unlikely to be solved. While in town, and when not selling, Naomi covered her hair with a hood.

With her cloak down, trading started immediately. She drew customers without trying. Zander had a hard time keeping up with all the orders. Selling went well for a time, until the crowd erupted.

"The prince comes!" someone yelled. Girls throughout the crowd began giggling. All interest in buying disappeared.

Naomi reached for Zander's hand as she conceded defeat. "Have you ever seen a prince?" she asked.

Zander shook his head.

"Nor I," Naomi sighed, reminded of her small existence. "I don't know much of him. What do you think?"

Zander looked toward the crowd. "I don't know . . ." he started. "I've heard good things . . ."

"Can you tell me?"

Zander merely shrugged. Naomi understood his silence. He hadn't heard good things, but he hoped for good things, much as others in the town . . . much like herself.

"Can you see down there?" she asked as the crowd moved around them. "Come here."

Both small, neither could see over the crowd, so Naomi stepped gingerly onto the cart, pulling Zander up with her. From that vantage, they could see everything happening on the street.

"But, the meats—Father?" Zander mumbled.

Naomi hushed him. "He's coming, Zan. Look!" She pointed into the crowd.

A caravan of animals and performers paraded down the street to the awe of the crowd. Peculiar beasts appeared that neither Naomi nor Zander could recollect seeing before: horses of all sizes, huge cats lying in cages, and an enormous, lumbering, gray creature carrying travelers on its back.

Naomi smiled in spite of her dislike of the whole business. Seeing the animals filled her with joy and amazement. Finally, following behind an oversized, white cat with long, dark, vertical stripes, she saw a large, silver carriage.

She glanced at Zander, who watched, totally absorbed in the spectacle. Smiling, she looked toward the carriage. Sure enough, inside sat a very handsome gentleman waving at the crowd, sometimes blowing kisses to the girls. Dark, brown locks curled around his face and highlighted his bright, blue eyes. Without realizing it, Naomi found herself staring at him, transfixed, like all the rest of the women.

And then she caught his eye.

Blood began to pump faster as she gazed at him. Her cheeks became flushed, her hands sweaty, yet she could not escape. After a few uncomfortable seconds, he looked away to the waving females. Naomi stood embarrassed, her thoughts scattered.

What a stupid thing to do, she thought as she crouched down out of sight. *Why did I just stare at him?*

"Naomi?" Zander mumbled, confused. "I d-don't understand."

Naomi stood back up. "What is it, Zander?"

"Look," he said pointing, "at the woman in the back."

Naomi searched and found the woman Zander talked about: a thin, beautiful creature with wonderful features. Her short black hair swept along her cheeks in sweet curls, highlighting her heart-shaped face and pointed chin. Her flowing, gray gown looked like mist as the carriage approached. She sat stone-faced and emotionless, an unreal creature.

"I think I see her, Zander. She looks familiar, maybe."

"That's not what I . . ." he stumbled. ". . . look at her neck." His confusion could hardly find words. He grabbed her hand and pointed it toward the girl.

The carriage traveled right before them at that moment. Without any mistake, without a question or a doubt, Naomi saw what Zander had seen: the scar—the star symbol burned on the nape of the woman's neck.

Exactly like Naomi's.

Everything moved in slow motion, registering what she saw. The peculiar scar stood out, clear as day, on the girl's creamy skin: the lines of the six-star symbol intertwined. Naomi reached for her neck under the scarf which tingled as she rubbed the scar.

A spark of recognition. The young woman—she had seen her before. She knew her. The brief glimpse flashed in memory. White . . . maybe snow . . . cold. Pieces of an intricate puzzle. She needed to know more.

Every fiber inside Naomi yearned to understand what importance this young woman had in her life. She had so many questions—why she looked different than anyone she had ever met, what happened to her parents. Everything remained a mystery. Perhaps this woman held a clue, a key that could unlock where Naomi came from, maybe family, everything.

As the caravan passed, she stood frozen in place. The mystery of her own existence paraded before her very eyes. She felt paralyzed, unable to move under her own power. Precious time slipped by as the carriage moved away from her. She had to act.

Zander looked frightened as he glanced at Naomi's intense expression.

"Zander, I have to find out who she is."

"No," Zander warned. "The g-guards!"

Completely forgetting about the meat, Naomi hopped down from the cart.

"Excuse me!" she pushed her way through the crowd. Her heart pumped hard in her chest. She didn't care about anything else. She had to get to the carriage. She rushed forward like a salmon swimming upstream.

It only took a moment for the prince to take notice. With a snap of his fingers, the guards were on the move.

"Na—!!" Zander yelled, practically falling from the cart to the ground. "The g-g-gua— " he started, but fear choked him to silence.

Naomi saw the blue cloaks coming from every direction. The swarm of bodies following the procession smothered her, smashing together in a mass of heat and sweat, confusion and chaos.

"No! Stop!!" Zander yelled.

Even amidst the chaos, Naomi recognized the cry for help. She had heard it so much in the last few years: Zander in trouble. She had become jumbled in the sea of people. With a glance to her side, she saw Zander still on the cart, the blue cloaks surrounding him.

"Leave him!" she shouted at the guards.

A guard grabbed her arm. Naomi struggled away from his grip. Being small, she slipped underneath the large man's arm and around another cloak.

The crowd became hostile with the pushing and shoving. Her heart pounded and her mind raced. *Please, let me get to him.* In her peripheral vision, she saw the blue uniforms mixing in the mass of people. The blue headed toward her, she knew it. They had Zander. In another moment, they would have her, too. She had to save him. She had to try.

Suddenly, a strong arm grabbed her and everything went black; she felt herself covered by a thick cloak. A hand held her mouth tightly, preventing a scream. Feeling a swift motion around her waist, she was lifted off the ground and whisked away.

~—◈—~

Darkness and motion. The hand over Naomi's mouth moved a fraction to allow her breathing, but it did not keep her heart from pounding. The movements created dizziness, and she lost complete perspective of the world under the thick cloak.

Uncomfortable heat from the man's body smothered any breath she stole through his tight grip. Who was this person? She thought she had been caught by a Southwick guard, but the singular sound of his footsteps against the stone told her differently.

Other little clues made her more curious. His heart beat just as fast as hers. His strength gripped her like iron; she felt so small compared to him as he carried her. She felt a metal blade swing in its sheath; the weapons he wore around his waist clanked next to her body. The complete arsenal of weaponry alarmed her.

The progress finally slowed to a stop, and her feet touched the ground.

"Not a word," a voice whispered in her ear. The soft plea in his voice caught her off guard.

Naomi nodded her head slowly and felt the hand come off her mouth. The man lifted the draping cloak but still held her arms tight.

The deserted street they had entered looked different from the craziness of the town: an outcropping of homes built tightly together, all in shambles of straw and wood. Clotheslines strung between the houses and connected them intimately. It was quiet. Smoke rose from a few of the humble chimneys, filling the air with the smell of burned wood and grass.

Dread consumed her. Naomi thought she knew the town well, but she did not recognize this side at all. If only she knew how to get back to the street—she felt lost and afraid, with a stranger who had spirited her away from the crowd.

She looked at the man who had captured her. He, towering over her by a foot, and was not as old as she had imagined he might be but no longer a youth—perhaps five and twenty. His shaggy hair hung around his face in untidy waves, getting into his eyes. His skin under the dark green cloak looked browned by the sun.

"Who are you?" she asked. Afraid of the answer, her voice quivered.

He wagged his finger slightly. Confused at the gentle gesture, Naomi's mind filled with even more questions. But before she could speak, he tugged on her arm, guiding her down the rocky, unused path.

The closer she got to the homes, the worse they looked. Aging wood splintered on the outside of the cylindrical huts. Cotton curtains, tattered by the wind, hung in the dirty windows. The smell of rotting apples, mixed with moldering soil, swirled around. Bones of dead birds lay about the ground, crunching like twigs under her feet.

Naomi's heart had never thumped so hard.

The stranger led her between the houses and down a small alley just wide enough for the two of them. He stopped, brushed the ground, and uncovered a door under the dirt and a tangle of overgrown weeds.

"Down here," he whispered.

Naomi hesitated. "No, please," she begged. Strangely, her thoughts focused not of herself at the moment, but the boy she had left behind. "Please, I can't leave Zander. I can't."

His grip only tightened as he carried her like a rag doll down the steps to the cellar.

Panic filled her. "I have to find him!" She tried to remove her wrist from his iron grip. His other hand closed the door tight.

Darkness consumed them. The cellar stank of rotten apples and damp wood. The earth felt chilly, freezing Naomi to the bone. The warm hand of the stranger guided her backward. She stumbled, but landed in a soft pile of straw. She curled up in the corner, holding her ankles. She shivered all over; her nerves worked outwardly in the chilly cellar. She hadn't her cloak, which she left near the cart.

"I have to go back for him," she pleaded.

"I can't save the boy right now. You were all I could carry."

Naomi took a deep breath at the word. "Save?"

"Here." The man wrapped his cloak around Naomi to keep her warm.

His kindness felt out of place. "Thank you."

The man stood and began pacing the room. His steely grey eyes reflected like deep, shiny onyx from the little bit of light streaming through the old wood slats of the cellar door. Without the cloak, his frame looked fit and strong; not an inch of him appeared unused. He confused her. His natural bearing projected sensibilities—something she hadn't expected from a kidnapper. She didn't know what to think of him.

"Can I ask a question?"

An enigmatic smile crossed his face. "I expected that."

"Are you going to kill me?"

"That's your question?" A small laugh escaped him. "No. Quite the opposite."

She sat up, curious instead of fearful. "You said you saved me—from what?"

"A better question would be, from whom? And that I couldn't tell you specifically." He stabbed a rotten apple with his small blade and flung it. "The last thing I want is Southwick finding you."

"What's wrong with Southwick?"

He laughed softly again. "They don't like me much down there."

"What about Zander?"

The man knelt before her, his eyes suddenly solemn. "We can't go back for the boy. I don't believe he is in danger."

"Only because you don't see it." A nervous knot formed in her stomach for the boy's safety.

"It's not him who is in danger, it's you." The look in his eyes indicated that he wished he hadn't said the words.

Naomi didn't know what to make of him. "The prince's guard doesn't scare me."

The man sat in quiet contemplation. "Naomi Everstar, you are a conundrum. Do you not care for your own life? Don't you think the Guard wanted *you*? They swim in a pond with many bigger fish."

Naomi lost her voice. Shivers ran through her as the word 'Everstar' echoed in her mind. She hadn't heard it in years; Malindra had been the only other person to call her that. "How do you know my name?" She nearly bit her lip with her question. "Who are you?"

He stroked his untidy, unshaven face, contemplating his answer. "My name is Reynolds Fairborne. Some call me Hawk. Does it sound familiar to you?"

Naomi had to admit she did not know the name. But like many things in this world, he did seem familiar, like a whiff of tobacco or change of season. She shook her head. "I'm sorry, no."

"Just as well," he replied. "I try not to know many people. Though . . ." He trailed off as he moved next to her and crouched down in the straw. He lowered his voice. "Does it help that I have known you all your life?"

"Me?" Naomi immediately retreated. Her brain tried to make a connection and failed. "I don't believe you."

Reynolds took a breath. "Would you believe that I knew Malindra?"

Naomi froze. Speaking those words felt like walking over a grave; Malindra had died years ago. Naomi had only lived eleven summers when it happened; she had now passed seventeen. "But, how? I've never seen you before."

"Somebody had to keep you safe."

The conversation unsettled her. Naomi huddled in the dark corner, suspended in thought. She didn't like being watched, but the idea of being protected made her blush. "But why would I need—?"

Reynolds quickly pressed his hand back to her mouth to prevent her from talking, angling his head around the darkness for a better view. Then, swiftly he rose and disappeared into the dark.

Naomi's heart jumped.

He returned, pulling Naomi to her feet. "She has come. Hold tight to me."

He led her forward into the dark toward a faint glimmer of color. A light purple glow fell on the back corner of the cellar, behind a maze of crates and barrels.

There, between the high barriers, stood a small, ancient woman, shawled and patched. The purplish light fell around a glowing orb which she cupped in her withered, crippled hands. Her hair resembled white-spun cotton, softly flowing down her back. *Not much substance to her*, Naomi thought. Spindly legs and spider-web arms. She could blow away with the wind. But her eyes stood out the most: peculiar and white like her hair.

The old lady reached forward. "Hawk?"

"I'm here." Reynolds stepped out of the shadows. He embraced her, speaking words Naomi could not hear and pointing in Naomi's direction.

"Let me look at her," the old woman said, confirming she wasn't blind. Naomi felt exposed, as if this woman could see right through her. "Come here, Goldie."

Naomi did as she was asked, although tentatively.

The woman reached toward Naomi's neck. "May I?" she asked as she slipped off the silk scarf. Naomi put her hand up to her scar and tried to cover it—a self-conscious habit. The old woman rubbed and smelled the fabric, wrapping it around her own hand several times. The scarf shimmered with flecks of dazzling color, shone brilliant in the pale cellar light, highlighting the intricate patterns of gold and pearl. "This was Malindra's," she muttered, "made of Shadesilk. Still as beautiful as I remember." She gently placed the scarf back on Naomi.

"How did you know that?" Naomi asked, amazed.

"I was there when Malindra acquired it. I always liked it, you know." Her thoughts seemed to drift back to the girl. "And you are Naomi," she finished, matter-of-factly.

Naomi stood perplexed, not knowing what to say or do. "Yes. How do you know me?"

"I don't," the old woman laughed. "I only know of you, and that is enough." Her eiderdown hair waved in the air as she chuckled to herself. "Do you have any memories of your parents?"

Naomi was stunned. She hadn't expected this. "No, nothing."

"Only Malindra?"

"Yes," she whispered solemnly.

"Oh, child." The woman's raspy voice tinged with sadness. "How sad to lose the only family you've known. Come," she beckoned her forward. "It may be safe for now, but the magic will be discovered soon. We have little time." She turned to Reynolds. "Hawk, lead me."

Reynolds held out his arm. The cotton-haired woman held to him tightly as they walked. Naomi, though still apprehensive, followed behind. He led them to a back corner of the cellar and removed a stack of crates which led to a barren, cold tunnel. Roots in the earth hung down in the passage, blocking the view of what lay deep beyond. Reynolds reached into his pocket and pulled out something black and small. As he snapped his fingers, a light appeared above his hand. Without saying a word, he led them down the earthen trail.

Creeping softly over the earth, Naomi followed the two along the long path. The claustrophobic atmosphere almost became too much. The air smelled of mustiness and decay. Past the roots, there lay a small room which had sunk down into the ground. Beyond it, from the light above Reynolds' fingertips, she could barely see what might be a staircase.

Storage of all kinds lay inside the room: crates, barrels, and woven blankets sat about in piles, rotting from the dark earth. The smell overpowered, and rested in the back of Naomi's throat, prompting her to gag.

Reynolds quickly started to pack gear and food from the barrels.

The old woman turned and grabbed Naomi's hand. "Help me, Goldie. I cannot see down here."

Naomi steadied herself and looked back at the woman, confused by her comment. But she led the woman to a crate where she could rest, which creaked as she sat. To calm her stomach, Naomi began breathing through her mouth.

"I'm sorry," Naomi started. "I'm really confused. How did you know Malindra?"

"She was my sister," the old woman explained, taking a breath to steady herself. "My name is Jeanus. Some call me Lightseer."

Naomi's heart erupted in joy. "I never knew Malindra had a sister. She never said. Why didn't she tell me?"

The old woman laughed, heartier than before. "There are many things left for the world to reveal to us. You are no exception. Reynolds has shouldered his responsibility well."

"How do you know him?"

"He is my eyes." Jeanus smiled in his direction. "I cannot see the world of men very well. Years have taken a toll on my sight, but I can see you just fine, bright as the sun. Men sometimes cannot see the world as it is—making up silly explanations for the unexplainable. But you saw the magic today while others did not. Yes?"

Naomi didn't understand. "Magic? I'm not sure I understand."

"I am talking about the girl," the old woman whispered.

"The girl? The girl with the scar?"

"This girl has magic. Do you understand magic?"

Naomi thought about it. She had watched a few of the magicians while with the Travelers as a child. She had watched Malindra make potions, and she'd taught her the cards, but that wasn't magic at all, just understanding the signs. "No," she concluded.

Jeanus's eyes wandered off to something distant. "Magic is brought forth by the elements of the earth itself. There are very few who clearly understand that." She smiled as she turned back to Naomi. "Do you believe it exists?"

Naomi wasn't sure what to believe. She had seen no evidence to support the existence of magic, but in her heart, she had always hoped there was. Malindra had used crystals and powders to help her create the illusion, but deep down Naomi knew the old woman's tricks held no magic, rather illusions for the eyes to pleasure the heart.

Jeanus bent her head as if she had read Naomi's mind. Her fragile fingers lifted, and, with a twirling motion, she whirled both hands in opposite directions. Streams of ribboning blue light curled around in excited strains, moving together to form a delicate wheel.

Breathless, Naomi watched the magic dance before her. How she wanted to touch it, to be one with it, to manipulate its power. Her finger stretched forward and touched it delicately. The magic moved about her fingers, tickling with gentle kisses.

Then it disappeared, fading away with a wisp of wind.

Reynolds appeared behind her. "I'm ready. Where do we go?"

Jeanus stood up again, urgent. "The camp will be the safest place."

Reynolds hesitated. His lips pursed in contemplation. "Are you sure?"

"Be careful of the Blackwoods. They will snatch her." Jeanus looked through Reynolds. "Don't be tempted, even though it is shorter."

Reynolds slowly agreed.

She turned to Naomi and fussed with her scarf. "There are spies everywhere. Malindra's scarf will give you protection. Do not take it off. Trust in your strengths and abilities; they are great. Do not doubt."

Strengths and abilities, Naomi thought. She didn't do anything particularly well. If luck constituted talent she would count it, maybe her sense of balance, and her innate ability to trust others—which also counted as a weakness.

"Also, be careful of your friends. They are both a strength and a curse." Jeanus smiled sweetly at her. "It is sad Malindra did not live to see how beautiful you have become." She kissed Naomi lightly on the cheek. Her finger stroked the side of Naomi's face. "How much you look like your mother."

Naomi stared, shocked. "Did you know her?"

The answer never came.

"Quick, put these on." Reynolds threw her a pair of old, crusty boots, hitting her in the chest.

Naomi stared at the boots—ugly, black things stinking and rotting with mildew. Somehow, she feared the boots almost more than she feared the danger she was in.

"And this," Reynolds urged, handing her a well-draped cloak and a pack full of gear.

Naomi did what was asked of her, but a small grumble escaped when she felt the weight of the pack. Shifting her body a bit, she could feel the uncomfortable squeeze around her toes. She longed to stretch them out on the cool ground.

"Jeanus, promise me. Stick with the plan," Reynolds said behind her.

The old woman waved goodbye. "It is not me who needs to worry. You talk to me like I'm an old fool." She smiled at Naomi. "Sounds like he doesn't trust me."

Reynolds bent down and kissed the woman on the cheek. "Sorry. My trust is something you haven't earned." He winked at her.

"Now, go," she ushered them out. "Go! There is little time."

Strange emotions seeped into Naomi's heart: feelings she hid deep inside that she didn't fully understand. Longing rose within her, to be with Jeanus, to know her better. The wetness that formed in the corner of her eyes felt foreign. She didn't like crying.

"Will I see you again?" she asked.

"In time, my dear."

A clanking sound came from the entrance to the cellar, like something hard was trying to pry open the door.

Jeanus turned sternly, her white eyes nearly red. "You must go! Now!"

Reynolds pulled Naomi with him across the room to where an ancient staircase climbed high to the surface. He extinguished his light and stopped at the eaves, listening.

Naomi heard men's voices shouting. "What about Jeanus—?" Naomi began, but was quickly silenced by Reynolds's hand.

"Go. Climb," he said in a hurried whisper. "At the top of the stairs, there is a storage chamber. It will lead us out. I'll be right behind you. Now, go."

Naomi did not hesitate. She climbed as quickly as she could in the pitch black. The dirt stairs were worn smooth by time. Once she climbed thirty feet, they tapered off more like a tunnel, winding this way and that in a confusing maze. Though stumbling a few times, Naomi moved forward, feeling around for a grip from the roots and crevasses.

Bang! She found the door with her head, not realizing it was going to be above her. Naomi went into it full force. She found a ring and used it to lift the hatch, which did not give way easily. But it opened with some effort.

Sunlight streamed into the stairway, blinding her. She crawled out, squinting, to find herself in a small room surrounded by walls of stone. Crates and barrels lined the room, cramming it with goods and clothing. Reynolds appeared in a matter of seconds. The hidden door slid back into place and became impossible to detect against the dirt and stone.

"Where are we?" Naomi asked.

"A Prolian Church," he answered. "It's a good escape if you need it. No one looks in a church. I made the tunnel myself."

"I've never been here," she recalled.

"I don't think Ferrell Bucklingdown is a religious man."

"How did you . . . ?" Naomi started, but stopped herself. "You really have been watching me."

Reynolds looked at her up and down. "You're a mess," he said, dusting some of the dirt off her head.

Naomi didn't care. Working on a pig farm for the last few years made her used to dirt. "Will Jeanus be okay?"

"I wouldn't worry about her," Reynolds said. "She can get home all right, resilient little bird."

"Why did she come here?"

Reynolds looked at her, his eyes speaking to her soul. "I asked her to. Earning your trust wouldn't be easy, and I need your trust."

Naomi couldn't hide her smile. It had worked.

"Come." He beckoned her forward, and together they slipped out of the room.

They entered a room among many hallways, interconnected in a labyrinth of stone. Naomi lost her perspective, but Reynolds smoothly navigated his way, guiding her.

The grand cathedral echoed like a silent tomb with every footstep the two travelers made. Not a soul stood inside the church, and no one to find them. "It's a good thing no one's here," Reynolds remarked. "I'm not sure they would let someone so dirty on hallowed ground."

Naomi stared, trying to catch his meaning. Was he joking with her? She hadn't expected that. His mouth curled into a smile. But just then, they heard footsteps on the stone floor; rushing footsteps coming from the back passages.

"Go, go, go!"

As fast as they could, Naomi and Reynolds ran from the church. The outside streets were empty but for a few wandering souls. Down they ran, taking a few turns to lose their pursuers, all the while hearing their trackers following close behind.

The wall of the city appeared in sight—but no gate.

"Can you climb?"

"Of course."

"Show me."

Naomi continued to run. The rush of being chased urged her forward. Reynolds's footsteps followed behind, but she never turned to look. Upon reaching the wall, Naomi spied a tall tree and quickly climbed up the branches that stretched out over the edge. As she shimmied herself across, she glanced back to Reynolds.

Worry overcame her, but the sounds of the guards reminded her of the danger. He had led the guards away from her, away from the tree. The men in blue followed his lead—his movements smart and agile, like he could predict the moments of the others.

He turned again and led the guards down another alley. A flash of light followed.

Naomi reached for the edge of the wall and dropped down. She strained to listen to what happened on the other side, but the adrenaline pumping in her veins made her tremble. She couldn't focus.

Take off the boots, she thought. *Feel the earth under your feet.* She sat near the tree and slipped off the boots, tied them together, and slid them over her shoulder. Her toes stretched deep into the grass and the feel of the cool blades helped her relax.

The tree branches rattled. Naomi looked up to see Reynolds shimmying across the limbs to a safe drop.

"The boots are off already?" he joked.

Naomi didn't know what to say.

"Come on," he pulled her up. "I know somewhere safe."

CHAPTER TWO
MEMORIES

The wind moved through the trees and branches, down the steep slopes of the deep ravine they walked beside. Boulders stuck deep in the ground from ancient ice flows. Roots of trees lay sideways, exposed to natural elements. Most people would find the height daunting, but Naomi found it exhilarating.

The boots her feet found so uncomfortable now flopped around on her pack as she walked. Her toes moved easily in the grass and dirt, negotiating the boulders with ease, and helping to hasten the journey.

Every so often, she stumbled, but Reynolds steadied her. She hadn't been around any men so casually before; it felt strange and intriguing. Reynolds would protect her at the cost of his own life. Goose bumps raised on her arms at the flattering thought.

The ravine looked dark and dangerous from above, but they scrambled down. Caves lined the sides of exposed rock, with networking connections of arches and alcoves.

Naomi hadn't seen anything so interesting as the descending framework of caverns.

Soon, Reynolds headed in the direction of their intended hideout. The mouth of the cave hung open, like a gapping maw, with a huge hollow inside—perfect for hiding.

The hike had consumed the day. It wasn't late, but Naomi felt drained as they finally settled inside their den.

"Rest awhile," Reynolds suggested. "Have some food."

Naomi didn't want to eat, though she knew she should.

"I want to check something." He pulled some cheese from his pack and handed it to her. "You'll be safe. I promise."

Reynolds left the cave—and left her alone.

She stared at the cheese in her hand, hardly believing her circumstances. What was she doing there? Just the day before, she prepared meat to sell and nursed the wounds cut into Zander by his brutal father and his whip.

After a few nibbles, Naomi leaned her head against the cave wall in thought, wondering about Zander's safety. She had abandoned him. Of all the times she'd thought of leaving, she never would have—not without him. The heartache of the separation caught her unprepared, her stomach churning at the thought of what might happen to him without her protection.

Despair emptied any other feeling she had, and she lay still for an immeasurable time. Darkness crept into the cave as the lulling sounds of nocturne came alive around her. She curled into a ball and cried silently.

Blue . . . All Blue . . .

      A Sea of cloaks . . . Blue as midnight.

      A Crest of Arms!

            March . . . March . . .

. . . Where is Zander?

The wheels turn in mud slick from rain.

. . . Where is Zander?

A man, broad, stern,

            . . . leads the army

            . . . the parade.

   A man recognized.

The soft patter of rain pelted the ground outside the cave as Naomi awoke. It took her a moment to remember what had happened and where she was. She looked around. *Reynolds?* She tried to slide over to the cave opening, only to bump into someone beside her. In the dark, Reynolds's gray eyes reflected the cloud cover outside.

"How long have you been here?" she asked without moving another muscle.

"Long enough." Reynolds groaned with protest at being disturbed. "Do you always have fitful dreams?"

"Possibly." Naomi blushed. "Sometimes I dream about people or places." Embarrassment washed over her, though it was nothing to be ashamed of. "It doesn't matter."

"It might matter more than you think. It sounds like you have a gift."

Naomi sat up against the wall, thinking about her most recent dream. Someone else had mentioned her dreams as a gift—Malindra.

"Do you think my dreams are dangerous?"

"Could be."

"Is that why you took me away?"

Reynolds continued to lie on the ground, still and quiet. "Well, I can't prevent you from dreaming."

"That's not an answer."

"You're safe tonight. How's that answer?" Reynolds turned and looked directly into her eyes, hiding a smile behind his lips. "Naomi, I promised you, there is nothing I wouldn't do to protect you. I know if you didn't trust me, you wouldn't be here."

"I don't know if I like that answer." Her voice had fallen quiet. "Why would you risk your life for mine?"

"My reasoning doesn't matter right now."

He lay back and looked away.

Naomi felt his silence, and her own growing sense of frustration. "Well, how is this fair? You haven't answered anything."

Reynolds closed his eyes, ignoring her.

"Can I at least ask where you're taking me?"

"North, to a place called the Willows. You will be safe there for a while."

"How long is 'a while'?"

"We'll see." He sat up and reached into his bag to pull out some bread, breaking off a piece and handing it to her. Their hands brushed and he recoiled, like he was ashamed in some way.

Composing himself, he continued, "I think you will find it much more to your liking than Ferrell Bucklingdown's pig farm."

"And what about Zander?"

"Once you're safe, I'll try to find him." He rested against the cold rock surface of the cave wall and closed his eyes. "Get some rest, little Naomi."

Naomi sat in the stillness, thinking. Hours passed before she fell asleep again.

A gentle nudge on her shoulder, and Naomi woke. She shrugged a little to lift the dream from her mind. Looking around, she could see gray light visible on the eastern horizon.

"We must hurry." Reynolds pulled out some food for her. "Here, eat this."

Naomi took it without question.

Reynolds packed what he could, a look of worry on his face. "I think we're being tracked."

"Someone is following us?"

"It appears that way, but I'm not quite sure. We must be creative in our choices. Here." He threw her the heavy green cloak. "You'll need to keep your hood up. Your hair will give us away."

Naomi did as she was asked, sweeping her hair from around her face and tying it in an untidy knot on the back of her head. The cloak weighed heavy and felt scratchy on her already-sore body. Straps from her pack rubbed raw on her delicate skin, unprepared for the force exerted upon it.

The two followed along a small brook that traveled down into the ravine. The scrub oak thickened near the water, and cattails bent in the gentle breeze. The boots Reynolds had generously offered Naomi, removed the moment he wasn't looking, hung around her belt. The feel of the soft earth between her toes made her feel more at ease.

The morning smells of deep earth and wet foliage brought memories to the surface. Her dream still fresh in her mind, she could not shake it away, like walking the fine line of reality. So much bothered her; all of her anxiety came back—the man in her dream who led the guards, who went by the name Lockwood.

Even remembering his name brought chills. Guilt filled her soul at the thought. If only she could have warned Malindra. She'd had a dream the night before it happened, a premonition of her caregiver's fate. But she dismissed it much like many other dreams. Only eleven at the time, Naomi remembered the details but was still too young to comprehend what everything meant or how her life would change.

She remembered the man approaching, just as she had seen in a dream. He came for Malindra. She still didn't know why; Malindra stayed away from the authorities and liked simple things, quiet living.

That day, Naomi saw him approaching with two others, down by the river bridge. She only had seconds to warn Malindra, and ran as fast as her bare feet could take her.

Naomi found her sitting in peaceful meditation in the small cottage. With tears streaming down her face, she spoke of the men coming, tripping over her words as the panic set in.

Malindra looked surprised but calm. Sweat beaded on her weathered brow. She came and caressed Naomi's cheek. "Do not be afraid. It is time to be brave. But I must hide you." She kissed her forehead. "Quick!"

"But what about you?"

"Whatever happens to me, they must not know you are here."

She reached down and lifted up a small mat. Underneath it appeared nothing but floor. The old woman rubbed the planks softly with the palm of her hand, and lines began to appear in the wood. Suddenly, as if by magic, a hidden door appeared in the floorboards. "Down here." She pulled the silk scarf tight around Naomi. "Do not take this off, whatever you do. It will always protect you. Promise me."

Without any hesitation, Naomi nodded and slipped down to the secret room. It was not much more than a dug-out dirt crawlspace, only good to hide someone. Malindra replaced the door, small slivers of light seeping through the cracks; Naomi could still see her guardian, but only slightly.

"Silence, little Naomi," Malindra whispered. "My love will always be with you, my little Everstar—my star that shines forever."

Fear overcame every impulse; Naomi didn't move an inch.

Very little explanation given . . . very few words exchanged.

"The illusive Malindra. Thief! Coward! I demand you hand over what you have stolen."

"You are the thief, Lockwood! You have stolen precious lives from this world."

"The stones were traced back to you, old woman. Prolius had contact with you in his last days. We have a witness."

"You have no witness. Prolius gave a gift and you will never have a witness of that!"

"You are so pitiful, woman. Still hiding secrets, but we know all and nothing can save you."

"Do what you must. In the end, you will still lose. Search out your secrets, but one you will never discover."

Blue powder illuminated the room. Naomi heard the scuffling: shouts and cries from every direction, clanging of metal on metal, then the crash. The smoke cleared. Naomi could see the face of Malindra's attacker standing tall over her body.

"Malindra." His voice was hard and sharp with pain; she had hurt him, Naomi could tell. "You are useless to me." With that, he stabbed her deep with his blade. Blood soaked through her clothes and saturated the floorboards.

Silent, dirty tears stung and streaked down Naomi's face. She tightened her knees to her chest as she watched blood slowly drip down the wall and puddle in the dirt.

"Search everywhere!"

Naomi couldn't remember much of what happened next: a lot of noise, emptying of drawers, boxes, everything turned out. She clung to her scarf and imagined them away.

Hours went by while the murderer rifled through all the old woman had owned. Naomi sat stiffly and silently, waiting, as she pressed her hands to her eyes and sobbed.

⁓◦❈◦⁓

"Naomi?" A voice awoke her to her senses. "Naomi? What's wrong?"

Naomi, her face lined with tears, saw Reynolds staring at her in the daylight. Quickly coming back to reality, she wiped her eyes and stepped back to the pace of the hike. "Sorry."

"Wait." He stopped her with his arm. "What happened? Tell me, please."

Naomi closed her eyes, embarrassed to have been caught crying. She glanced back to Reynolds's face and sighed. "I saw . . ." She changed her mind. "Just memories."

"Memories?" Reynolds leaned back. "Huh . . . memories." He turned around, quickening his pace, but then stopped. "And where are your boots?"

Naomi felt caught.

He turned, shaking his head. "It's slippery; you might want them on."

Naomi feared putting her wet feet in those old crusty boots, so she slipped them in her pack and silently followed.

They had progressed deeper along the side of the ravine a few miles or so. Traveling grew hard, but Reynolds kept a fast pace. Thistles and briars bunched together, scraping her skin and blocking what natural path existed. Slick stone walls dotted with caves of all sizes hemmed them in. The wind whipped around, making an eerie whistle, unsettling Naomi's already shaken nerves.

They went on and on. The sun did not penetrate the depths where the two fugitives hiked. The sky grayed and large clouds mixed together, threatening a storm, swelling with energy. Tiny trickles of rain fell, penetrating the dry ground. Within minutes, drops pelted down on them, saturating their cloaks and slowing their travel.

Naomi felt miserable. The rocks of the canyon became slippery under her feet; the dirt changed to mud and filled the cracks between the rocks, and Naomi's bare toes felt the squish of it. Maybe she should have listened to Reynolds and worn the boots.

Then she slipped but grabbed a branch of scrub oak. Beneath her—a gaping drop of smooth rock. She stretched her hands for a better hold but slipped more, her balance precarious as she clung to the smooth stone.

Reynolds kept moving forward, not realizing her difficulty. Naomi slipped off the rock and fell into the abyss below, her scream silenced by the pelting rain.

~⁂~

Reynolds knew they were being followed, and unfortunately, he knew who, and why. He had feared this for the past few months—that she might search for him.

They had left the prince's glorious procession far behind. No soldiers would ever venture through the ravine, not even to find Naomi. But having a Louving tracker following—a dangerous one, too—brought a new level of trouble.

He had known the day would come when he would take Naomi away, but he hadn't expected it yesterday. He had been unprepared . . . for everything.

Energy surrounded Naomi—a pull so strong it caught him off-guard, like a magnetic force gripping all his secrets. Why did she have to ask him questions he couldn't answer? Not now. He hoped not ever.

The rain provided a good cover; he could mask their tracks, their scent. The continual pelting soaked through the layers of clothes, and the travel became miserable. He only hoped Naomi could withstand it.

A faint cry came from behind him. Reynolds turned, his stomach dropping. Naomi was gone.

His eyes went wild. He had lost her.

Forcing through his panic, he closed his eyes and searched for the magic. He could perceive it all around him. She had to be close. He saw her as bright as the sun in his mind and knew where she had fallen.

Reynolds ran back, searching high and low, his heart pumping in a rhythm he didn't understand, fast and intense. A patch of ground looked as if it collapsed under the saturation of the rain. His eyes followed the mud trail down to the bottom of a sink hole. There he found Naomi looking stunned but aware.

"Naomi!" Reynolds yelled, waving his arms.

The fall was daunting: nearly fifty feet. It should have killed her.

She flagged back, alive and unhurt. How could she be okay? This girl became more confusing by the minute.

Reynolds took off running, evaluating the breaks in the landscape. The wind had carved away layers of stone, exposing the natural beauty underneath. Hollow pocket caves wove in and out of catacombs, but there were no breaks, nothing that would take him down.

Further along, cracks formed from a rock slide down the ravine. A particular slice looked promising. Reynolds took it and began to work his way to her. The crack opened up to a wide chasm, and he knew he could get to her from there.

Keeping her hidden within a solid location proved easy; traveling through a waking magical world with her at his side became insanely challenging.

But he had to keep the secret.

Inside the deep cavern, puddles of water swelled around the exposed walls, and the air felt humid from the lack of circulation. The sound of the beating rain amplified in the rock, and its drumming filled the air like tribal music. Reynolds pulled out sunsparks and lit them at his fingertips, guiding his way through the narrow paths.

"Naomi!" he yelled, his voice echoing off the red sandstone a dozen different ways.

Reynolds followed the light in and out of different tunnels. Holes, created over years of exposure to water, followed down the entire length of the cavern, and every so often a filtering cascade slipped in from the rain.

"I'm here!" he heard her voice resounding down a large opening.

At last, he found her, curled up in a small muddy bundle, a brown crust covering her skin and hair. She sat quietly near a wall, picking pieces of dried mud from her arm. No harm had come to her—nothing broken, nothing bleeding.

"Naomi." Reynolds exhaled her name, relief washing over his face. He looked at her state and shook his head. "I hardly believe it. Are you all right?"

Naomi didn't respond, just looked at him with a humiliated expression; the mud had even caked on her eyelashes.

"You're quite a sight." He grabbed a cloth from his cloak and soaked it in a stream of rainwater. "Here." He handed it over.

"Thanks," she muttered. She rubbed it over her face and body, removing the dirt and freshening up her skin. A few good wrings in the water and she started to look like herself.

Reynolds took a moment and found suitable brush for burning. His fire provided little warmth but helped dry Naomi's soggy, muddy clothes. Naomi stood and tried to rinse out some of the mud in the dripping rain before coming near the fire.

"There's no sense in trying to get out until the rain stops," Reynolds said. "This place is nice and secret. Hungry?"

"Yes, please." He threw her some bread to munch on. "Thank you for the fire. I like fire."

"Do you?" Her comment made him wander in the deep recesses of thought. He felt her pull again, like filling his lungs with sweet air.

"I like the sun. I like being warm."

The pull relaxed a little, yet she didn't seem to feel it. She probably didn't even recognize that she did it. Reynolds looked at her, amused.

She stared back. "Are you laughing at me?"

Reynolds returned his eyes to the fire. "No. I promise, I'm not laughing at you."

"Is there something wrong with me?"

"No. Really. You're just fine. . . . But, did you ever figure you have a . . . charm?"

"Charm?"

"Yes." Reynolds hated himself for saying it. A flush of stupidity covered his face. "Just forget it."

Naomi's mouth turned into a little wry smile. "You're confusing," she said, moving closer to the blaze.

Reynolds ruffled his hair again. "So are you. Any regular person would have died falling from that height."

"Yes, I know."

"You've fallen before?"

"Of course. But I like trees. I like to climb. There is a hazard to that."

"Did you get hurt?"

Naomi's cheeks turned pink. "Why don't we talk about you instead of me?"

She withheld telling him something, a new twist. He thought he kept all the secrets. He couldn't help but be impressed. "What do you want to know?"

"What are you hiding?"

A queer smile crept into the corners of his mouth. "Everything!"

"Why? What's the danger? You never answered that question."

Reynolds mused. "You're right, I never did."

"And . . . ?"

"You're keeping things from me, so it seems fair."

"Like what?"

"You know a lot more than me. Your dreams can tell you anything."

"But most of the time I don't know what I'm seeing until later. That's hardly helpful."

"You should work on that." Reynolds sighed. "You should know that I keep things from you for your protection. Does that make sense?"

Naomi nodded. "It's best that I don't know that there are dangerous dragons, and monsters, and things that might hurt me."

"Yes."

"But I'm not afraid of getting hurt."

This girl is persistent. Thoughts ran through his mind and he questioned if he should speak them aloud, but her charm held him again and he started saying things he shouldn't. "But there is a difference between *hurt* you and *hunt* you."

Naomi stiffened. "Hunt?"

"You don't understand anything about hurting. What does it matter, if you've never gotten hurt? But being hunted has serious consequences."

Naomi looked astonished. "So, that's the danger you wouldn't tell me?"

"Possibly."

"But if it's my life, shouldn't I have the right to know why I would be hunted?"

"But that's the thing." Reynolds carefully selected his words before responding. "Are we only talking about your life or lives of others connected to you?"

"Are you talking about Zander?"

"He's not the only one."

Naomi looked more confused. "But I don't know anyone else."

"Not yet, but that will change." Reynolds didn't mean to flinch when he said the words. The idea of taking her to the Willows still felt dangerous. "Do you know anything about elemental magic?"

Naomi's hands went up to her face. Worry covered her brow, and she shook her head.

Reynolds took a deep breath and whipped a hand through his brown hair, thinking of what he should say, what he should tell her. "That's what you'll see at the Willows—the difference between the illusions and realities to each magic."

"Well, that doesn't sound so dangerous."

Reynolds blinked at how naïve she was. "Illusions of magic are brought out by being touched by something magical—some kind of element that leaves what is called a Stain of Magic. Jeanus showed you this kind of magic."

He lifted up the stick he had been working around the fire. The tip seared red hot and mesmerizing, Naomi's face lost in the light. "There are realities of magic: pure elemental reactions. Many cannot tell the difference, but there is a big difference. If you could imagine spark next to lightning, you'd know."

Then the spell disappeared. Reynolds smarted at the girl across from him. She had done it, charmed out the information. He sat back in wonder, unable to hide the astonishment on his face, though Naomi didn't look like she knew she had done anything at all.

"So, what does that have to do with me?"

Reynolds thought about what to say. He felt like he would tell her everything but abruptly stopped. A small rumbling interrupted his thoughts.

"What is that?" Naomi asked.

Reynolds got to his feet, scoping the cavern floor. He swore under his breath and ran to her. "Quick!" he yelled, and grabbed her arm.

They moved lightning-fast through the hollowed tunnels. Reynolds knew he pushed Naomi to her physical limits. She didn't know what rushed behind them, but he did.

The water started very small, running like a little river around the ground, but it came fast and high. Mud and debris mixed with the water like a cauldron of mire—an unstoppable force.

Naomi saw the rising water and panicked; her fingers wrapped tighter around Reynolds' arm.

Reynolds moved up a ledge and lifted her up effortlessly. "Climb!"

Naomi looked at the wall of rock above her, blinking a few times to understand what he wanted her to do. There were only tiny lipped ledges to stand on. "I can't." She shook her head. "I can't, Reynolds."

"Trust me," he repeated. "You can. Just like climbing a tree. Hurry! Go!"

The water came through the tunnels at an unimaginable speed. The force it moved could hollow out the cavern in its entirety.

Reynolds stayed close but watched from below as Naomi took hold of a ledge and tried to lift herself up. Her feet dangled for a hold, but soon found one, though very small. He could see the panic as she moved from one to the next. Her hand slid to another hold as she swung her leg up, catching another foothold. Only one more ledge.

The span between the ledges was wider and trickier than the others. He watched as Naomi held onto the wall like a spider caught in the daylight. It would take a leap to reach it, and he could see her fear. But not much could be done. He sent up words of encouragement, climbing like a monkey as quickly as he could to help her.

Naomi's grip began to slip. She jumped, but her hands hit the ledge. She missed and began to fall.

Reynolds reacted, quick as a cat. As the water rushed underneath them, rising higher and higher, he wrapped his arms around her waist, holding her inches from the water. "Hold on to me!" he yelled over the torrent. He moved her onto his back and she held on with a grip of iron.

Reynolds moved swiftly up the rock face, gripping holds no one else would dream of using. Naomi gripped so tightly she nearly choked him.

They reached the ledge and continued upward, not stopping until they saw the trees. Not until then did Naomi loosen her grasp.

Reynolds slid her off his back. "Are you all right?"

Naomi didn't speak, still in shock. She started to sob.

Reynolds wrapped around her like a security blanket, pulling her little frame close.

Her force over him intensified and sent his mind swimming. It felt like invisible tendrils gripping his chest, wrapping tighter and tighter. Its hold grew stronger than in the cavern, the binding hold fastening around them as he held her near. He felt he would snap if he let go. Such dangerous magic exuded from her tiny frame, and Naomi didn't even know she had done anything to him.

Reynolds released her and stood back.

Naomi just stared at him.

He shook himself and swore again. Glancing back at Naomi, he sighed deeply and closed his eyes. "The light is almost gone. We need to hurry." He glanced at the girl and walked away, only to turn back to ask, "Do you have your boots?"

Naomi shook her head, glancing toward the mudslide.

Reynolds hung his head and grimaced. "Come on." He held out his hand to her. She grabbed it, and together they walked carefully through the ravine.

CHAPTER THREE
AN INVITATION

Naomi had created a disturbance. The parade continued, but the prince looked agitated. From the height of the cart, Zander could see the plan of action as the blue hoods went after Naomi.

But why? Why her, and not anyone else?

It had to be the scar. The prince sat with the other girl behind him, the mark visible on her neck, clear as anything. It had to be linked. This girl must be special for him to be protecting her . . .

. . . but Naomi would get hurt.

Zander thought in those few seconds of what he had to do.

"Sto . . . p!" he tried to shout. But no one would listen to him. No one ever did.

He looked around. The meat. He grabbed the salted jerky nearest him and threw it. A few of the pieces hit the guards, but none cared.

Something bigger, he thought.

Zander grabbed some of the larger pieces. His father might be mad, but compared to losing Naomi, it didn't matter. A few of the pieces hit the guards. One looked upset, but seeing the scrawny boy who had thrown it, he turned without reacting.

He would have to find something harder.

On the cart sat a sack of walnuts, which he had picked up off the ground on his way there and had planned to share with Naomi. He grabbed a handful and threw one at a guard close by, hitting his head with a sharp *thwack*. It worked. Zander steadied his aim and fired one walnut after another. More guards turned to see what had hit them.

Before Zander could react, the guards were upon him, ripping him down from the cart. Someone punched him in the stomach. The blow took his breath and he fell to his knees. Hands came down upon him, pulling, pushing, grabbing.

Something smacked his head and everything went black.

⌒⊶✿⊷⌒

Zander awoke to the splash of water on his face. He sputtered, shivering in the cold air. Mocking laughter surrounded him. Head spinning, he lifted his eyes to see his attackers.

The guards of the cold, stone prison were not a kind lot, especially the head of the guard, a strong, burly man who wore a steel mask everywhere he went. Zander feared him most of all. The past few days had changed him, had altered his perception of humanity.

He'd lost Naomi, who left behind only the bundle of papers she treasured. He held them close to his chest, a sweet remembrance of his old life with her.

He hardly remembered the journey to the prison, having been gagged and blinded with a bag over his head as the guards shoved him into the corner of a dark, covered wagon and carried him off. In the prison yard, he had been kicked and beaten. It came as a relief when he finally reached the dungeons, but there he soon discovered what real cruelty could be. Subjected to inexcusable torture— more sport than anything else—Zander wished it would all go away, that he could go back to the fantasy that had once been his life.

The guards approached him, the head guard in the center, all laughing as Zander cowered in a small corner of his cell. He knew what awaited him; his eyes closed tight, bracing himself for the beating to commence. But it never came.

"Haggar, you've had enough fun, now leave him!" a voice shouted. Zander still kept his eyes closed. It must be a trick. But still, nothing came. Opening his eyes, he saw torchlight flicker on the wall as guards disappear out of the cell, leaving behind a man, dressed head to foot in midnight blue, standing at the doorway.

The man walked toward Zander and examined him. "Ouch. Looks like they cut you good there." He snapped his fingers to some outside presence. Soon, a little maid dressed all in white came forward, carrying a small basket full of medical supplies. He whispered in her ear and she began to dress Zander's cuts and bruises, dabbing on ointments and creams and securing bandages.

As she did so, the man sat on the ground and lowered his hood. Leaning against the stone wall, he rested his gaze on Zander. "You're a lucky boy. Haggar would love to see you dead if he had the chance, bloodthirsty maggot that he is."

Zander tried to form words but could not. His recent experiences had heightened his stuttering, so he simply remained silent.

It only took a few moments for Zander to recognize the man, though he looked kinder than at the festival. His manners and demeanor befitted an heir to the throne. The recognition must have read on Zander's face, for the man smiled.

"So, you think you know me, do you?" He laughed. "I'm Bryant, just Bryant, and there is no need to be afraid of me. Understand?"

Zander slowly nodded his head but more out of fear than trust.

"That will do," Bryant ordered the maid dressing the wounds. She finished in a hurry, grabbed the medical basket, and left.

Silence fell in the cold, stone cell.

Bryant stood and paced back and forth, examining the living quarters: the poor condition of the bed, no more than a board with a thin layer of straw. The bucket provided for waste—the general stench. "Disgusting," he pronounced.

Zander sat in the corner, not daring to move but wondering why in the world a prince had come to visit him.

Finally, Bryant sat down on the bed and rested his elbow on his knee. "How are you?"

Zander only stared at him.

"I hear your name is Zander Bucklingdown, yes?"

Zander nodded.

Bryant's smooth brow furrowed with worry. "I'm sorry to tell you this . . . your father is dead."

A lump grew in Zander's throat. He had suspected something like this might happen, but he didn't like hearing the words. Nothing made sense to him anymore. Tears wanted to form but didn't. He wanted to mourn but couldn't. Overwhelmed with emotion, he put his head down on his knees.

"So sorry, my dear boy." Bryant's expression looked pained. "How unfortunate. It sounded like he got in a confrontation with some of the guards."

Zander didn't want to hear the details. He didn't particularly like his father, but he hadn't wanted him to die. With Naomi gone, he had nothing to do and nowhere to go. Despair took over and the tears finally came; he sobbed.

Bryant ran his hand across his chin, like he didn't know how to comfort him. After a moment, he knelt by Zander's side, placing a firm arm around his shoulder. "I'm sorry I had to be the one to tell you."

He lifted the boy up and brought him back to the bed, waiting a few moments before speaking again. "I hear that you don't talk much and that's too bad, because I have some questions for you." Dirty tracks of tears streaming down his face, Zander met Bryant's gaze. He hadn't dared look at the prince until now; the older man seemed sincere but guarded.

"I sent the guards after a girl, not you. You were trying to save her."

The memory stood out in Zander's mind as the worst day in his life.

Bryant placed his arm on Zander's shoulder. "Do you happen to know where she might have gone?"

Zander felt an empty void without Naomi. He remained silent.

Bryant sighed. "Sorry to ask, but here's the dilemma: the guards brought you here—which was not my idea, by the way. You're now an orphan, without family, without a home. Did the girl know of relatives or someone who could take care of you?"

Zander heard the lies in the words. Did this man think because he didn't talk, that he couldn't think? He tried to say the words, but only "mmmmmuhh," came out.

"So you *can* speak after all!" Bryant clapped his hands together. "Good news; I have no need for a mute." He laughed a little, though Zander did not know why.

The Prince stood and began pacing again. "So, the question begs—what should we do with you? And I've had an idea."

Zander looked down, not wanting to meet the prince's eyes or hear his charming words. He wanted Naomi.

"I need a page, and you would be perfect for the job. Since you have no family, there's really no need for you to reject my offer." Bryant stopped for a second and lifted up Zander's chin. "Unless you don't trust me."

Zander pulled away. He didn't mean to, but the reaction came naturally.

"Ah!" exclaimed Bryant. "Now I'm getting somewhere. You think I'm not trustworthy. You think it's a trick. How could you possibly trust me, after all?"

Zander huddled back into himself, hugging his knees tightly.

Bryant sighed and smoothed his hair with his hands. "Listen . . ." His tone came out differently—weaker, filled with remorse. "I'm trying my hardest to rectify this situation." He heaved another big sigh. "You're here now, and I'd rather not see you die in a prison when all you did was throw some harmless walnuts at a few lousy guards."

Zander liked hearing the prince call the guards 'lousy' and couldn't help but let a gentle smile creep around his mouth.

Bryant knelt down before the boy. "I feel responsible for your placement here and . . ." he hesitated, "and your father's death. I sought after the girl, more out of curiosity than anything. I didn't want to hurt her. You got in the way of things. And . . . and I am trying to make things better."

"My father . . . dead." The words came out clear and articulate. Somehow, Zander scarcely noticed, but he could no longer stand to be silent.

Bryant leaned back on his heels, seemingly astonished to hear Zander speak. "I'm sorry."

Zander unfolded his limbs, taking in the prince's words. "I don't know . . . wh-where . . . N-Nnn . . ." He stopped. He couldn't form Naomi's name.

"I know you've lost her," said Bryant. "There are men trying to find her now."

"W-why?"

"Someone is looking for her. I don't know why, honest! Lockwood, my father's head general, is looking for something."

"Will . . . they k-k-kill her?"

"Oh, I hope not." Bryant shook his head. "Such a rare creature shouldn't be murdered like that."

Zander felt the anger rise in his body as he stared down the other man. He still didn't trust Bryant, but what other choice did he have? If he stayed in this prison, he would surely die.

"Think about my offer, boy." Bryant waved over the gatekeeper as he moved to the cell door. "The guards don't care about you. You'll be forgotten, until you don't even remember your own name. They care nothing for the life of someone like you. You'll die in here. But I am trying to save you, give you a life that means something. Don't you see that?"

Zander sat in silence, wiping the tears from his cheek.

"This is all too much for you today." Bryant brushed the straw off his clothing. "I will return for your decision in a day or two."

Bryant whirled around, his big cloak sweeping the dust on the floor as he exited.

The door swung shut, plunging Zander again in to darkness. He curled up his knees and cried.

CHAPTER FOUR
THE BLACKWOODS

The devastation of the mudslide had bent many of the trees down and cluttered the path with broken limbs. Reynolds picked Naomi up and carried her through most of the tricky parts, until the grass returned and she had steadier footing. They traveled in silence. The rain slowed, and a tiny sliver of sun hung around the horizon, slipping in and out of the thunderheads.

Slowly, things started to improve. Ahead lay a large grove of shady trees. And toward the top of the hill stood a strange forest with tall, black-trunked trees, their large, dark green leaves stretching from their branches. They had reached the Blackwoods.

Reynolds remembered the advice Jeanus had given in the cellar and altered his course, walking the other direction.

"What's wrong with those trees?" he heard Naomi ask from behind him.

"Those are the Blackwoods. The Willows are on the other side."

"They look sick."

"You would be right. Contaminated magic—waste—has poisoned the wood." Reynolds stopped to look at the forest again, contemplating. "It would be much shorter taking you through there, but Jeanus warned me not to risk it."

Naomi looked sad, even horrified by the state of the trees. "Magic did that? Illusion or real?"

Reynolds stood, impressed. "You were listening." Naomi didn't look amused. "It's a dumping ground for residual magic. It has mutated the animals that live inside into hideous creatures and other things. I'd rather not have them following us."

Naomi swallowed. "What *other* things?

Reynolds looked right into her face. "Ghosts. The place is haunted by Stains."

Naomi's voice quivered a little. "Do I want to know what Stains are?"

"I'm surprised you don't. The souls of those touched by real magic, trapped to haunt this world—they are Stains. The ones affecting the Blackwoods are more like a virus, infecting those who live in it. The elements need to live and breathe, just like us. Something else from the world has to die in order for them to survive." Reynolds stopped in thought. "Why don't you know about Stains?"

"Why would I?"

Reynolds shrugged. "Well, I don't know. I figured being around Malindra . . ."

"We didn't get out much." Naomi pressed her hand gently against her ribs. "I think I would have to see the Stains to really understand, but don't take that as a hint that we should go in there, because I don't like the idea of ghosts. We've had enough scares today."

"Agreed. Though I think you could charm any Stain in there."

Naomi blushed. "No, I doubt they would be interested in a little thing like me."

A laugh burst from his lips. He knew the truth: those creatures would feel her charm, just as he did. The pull had started again. He cleared his head and travelled onward.

The light faded, and they needed a place to stop. Reynolds surveyed the area, then froze. Off in the distance, a figure stood in a dark cloak near the ridgeline of the trees, long hair billowing from the hood.

The tracker.

Reynolds seized Naomi's arm. "Quick! Down!" he whispered as he flung his cloak over her, covering her completely. "We've been spotted."

He made a quick decision. Reynolds grabbed her hand and practically dragged her up the hill. "We need to make for the woods."

Naomi huffed. "After all your talk of ghosts?"

He hurried, pulling her faster. "We don't have a choice."

Naomi couldn't know the trouble they were in, but Reynolds did. It wouldn't be long before the bloodthirsty Louving reached them.

The exertion spent from the flash flood made for a hard run to the trees. He looked back once, only to see the dark image of the tracker darting after them. It wouldn't take her long to find them in the woods. He had to confuse her, mix up the trail—lose her in the snarled tangles of the Blackwoods.

The tree line loomed before them, and soon they were enveloped in thick darkness. Reynolds' eyes adjusted quickly to the black shield as he led Naomi through the dense, eerie stillness.

They ran swiftly, darting this way and that, flying over the broken tree branches and small shrubs littering the ground. Massive black shadows came and went as they moved between small pathways and cracks within rocks. The gloom of the hovering Blackwoods chilled every sense and crept like a plague onto everything it touched.

Although the forest appeared to be dead, it definitely lived. Reynolds could feel the curiosity of the woods, and the overwhelming craving for what had just entered. He knew their hunger, a desperate yearning for home. The Stains felt Naomi's magic as a saving grace, a beautiful unspoiled wish for their salvation.

Naomi's hand gripped tighter in his. Reynolds held it, firm and reassuring. He wished he hadn't scared her with the talk of ghosts and Stains.

The Blackwoods manipulated thoughts. Reynolds knew how to handle it, but Naomi would have no idea. Strange moaning came from one direction, then straight in front of them, and then disappeared altogether. Human shapes appeared but quickly vanished. Every fiber of

Reynolds' body warned him of the danger Jeanus mentioned. He should not have brought Naomi here.

The dizzying depth of the Blackwoods kept him guessing at their location. Had he lost the tracker? He wouldn't know until he figured out where they were. His reassuring grip on Naomi's hand tightened. Their pace slowed to a trot, and finally Reynolds stopped to listen again in the wind. Naomi breathed in exhaustion.

"We need to rest, but we can't stay long."

"Can you see in the dark?" The question came out more like a complaint. "I can't see anything."

"I can. There was a time in my life when I lived underground."

"Like a rabbit?"

"Not exactly." He smirked. "Come." And with that he grabbed her hand once again and they began working their way through the darkness. "I see a grassy clearing not far from here. It should make a more comfortable bed for us tonight."

"You're telling me we're sleeping here?" Naomi sounded panicked.

"We're resting," he explained. "I don't think I can find the Willows tonight. Entering is tricky, even for me."

The clearing looked more dry and bare than he'd anticipated. Reynolds brought her around and sat her next to a rock.

"I don't think I can sleep here."

Reynolds understood her fear. He tried to be positive, but he knew the Stains were watching. He squeezed her hand again, trying to reassure her. Then he ran his fingers over the knuckles on her hand.

What am I doing? He had been charmed by her once again. He released her and stood. He needed to clear his head, so he paced.

"Rest. I'll be close."

"Don't leave me."

Her pull felt different this time, filled with desperation. It held him tight. He didn't know how to act. Just a little distance would help. "No worries. I'm too invested to leave."

Reynolds perched himself on a rock ledge where he could see all around the clearing. The tracker would find their trail. He feared her more than the Stains.

Images appeared and disappeared in the clearing, each curious about the strange girl he had brought with him. He knew they smelled her magic, pulled mystically to her.

Movement alerted his attention.

Reynolds unsheathed his broadsword. Images moved from his sight . . . right side . . . left side . . . then vanished. He blinked. Did he see anything? He shook his head to keep alert. A clicking sound moved through the trees, circling, and then disappeared. He jumped down from the ledge, his sword ready. His ears perked up, listening for footsteps or breathing. He felt he'd lost his mind.

Mist moved into the area, chilly and iridescent. It glided in a solid form, an undefined mass of grey cloud creeping toward him.

Reynolds froze and narrowed his eyes. He held his sword firmly. Sweat dripped from his forehead. The clicking came again, louder and stronger. Reynolds moved slowly in a circle. The mist moved forward, and then stopped right before him. Weird light slowly began to condense and form into the resemblance of a man.

Cold sweat ran down Reynolds's back as he coiled, ready to strike. His eyes followed the floating image.

The form before him stood tall and floated gently in the slight breeze. Reynolds could see the crown still on his head, the wrinkles still prominent on his face and brow. Gray hair streaked down his back, flowing into the silvery robes he wore.

The sword moved fast through the misty form.

"Trying to kill a dead man?" a voice mocked from behind him.

Hands came around his throat. His quick reaction jerked his body away. The hands lost their grip as he twirled around to see his tracker face to face.

A coy smile curled along her lips. "Hello, Reyn." She waved a little with her fingers near her mouth. "Thought you could lose me?"

Reynolds gripped his sword tightly. "Easy mistake it seems, Browneyes."

"Funny, I thought I'm the only girl for you?"

"There is that problem with you wanting to kill me and drink my blood." Reynolds' words stayed playful but cautious, still considering his options.

Her smile widened and her eyes lit up at the remark. She loved this kind of mischief. "Pish, pish."

"What do you want?"

"I want to know about your girl." She attempted to hide the hurt in her voice. "You were very careful before. After all the work it took to mislead me like that, this move is careless, don't you think? I wouldn't chance bringing in something so . . . delicate."

"And what do you know about anything delicate?"

Browneyes reacted, moving aerially, curling around the trees to fly directly at his side, a knife to his throat.

Reynolds held very still, waiting for his opportunity.

Browneyes moved her lips very close to his ear. "You don't have to lose. I don't have to kill you, you know. It will be our little secret."

She loosened her grip. Reynolds grabbed the knife and twisted it out of her hand, pointing it back at her.

"I always liked you, Reyn."

"I'm flattered. Poor timing, though."

"I'll find out who she is. I think I have the right to know who replaced me."

"No, you don't."

A small sinister smile crept across her face. "We'll see."

A long snarl echoed through the hollow.

Browneyes disappeared from sight.

⁓ ✽ ⁓

Reynolds looked to Naomi but couldn't see her. He searched for her around the clearing as the mist dissipated. She'd vanished.

Bad idea. Jeanus had been right. Completely right. He immediately thought of Browneyes, how she had disappeared so quickly, but she couldn't have taken Naomi. Something had gotten to her first.

He fought off his mounting panic. That wouldn't help Naomi now.

The rock where Naomi had lain turned into a mullshroon, a large fungus that could alter its shape to lure in prey. He saw the evidence it had tried to wrap itself around her—but something didn't look right. The mullshroon had bite marks on it. Not even Browneyes would go so far as to bite a mullshroon.

Listening closely, Reynolds could hear the chittering sounds moving through the forest. He followed, not sure what he would find. Browneyes could still be up to her old tricks.

As he followed the tracks and sounds, he concluded it must be knarls.

The strange mutant creatures had been altered through time and magic, with large teeth and strange white eyes, big and bug-like. The fur left on them was patchy and gray; the rest of the body covered with red scales. They traveled in packs like wolves, extremely dangerous, even deadly when they attacked as a group.

But the knarls had both a weakness and a strength— their vision. The years of darkness made them almost blind. Their hearing had sharpened to compensate, and their other senses grew stronger.

Knowing his enemy, Reynolds knew what to do. He had a plan.

Placing his sword back in its sheath, Reynolds followed their trail in silence. With one hand, he reached into his pocket and grabbed a small pouch of dust; with the other he grabbed his knife from his boot. Quietly as he could, he opened the pouch full of white dust.

Something moved ahead of him, like the forest floor had shifted. And he saw her. Naomi lay tangled within bands wrapped tight around her body and mouth, panic-stricken and helpless, the knarls dragging her deeper into the woods. His mind raced. He needed time, something he didn't have.

The chittering slowed, and suddenly the knarls changed direction—coming for him. The creatures jumped on his legs and chest, biting and scratching, tearing his clothing and ripping into his flesh.

Reynolds struggled, stabbing what he could and throwing off the rest. He ran to Naomi, whose eyes were wide with horror. The knarls jumped over her to reach him, scratching her skin on their way. Her eyes swelled with tears.

"Hold still," he yelled, taking a pinch of powder and snapping his fingers. A brilliant white light emanated from his hand and lit the forest.

Then he saw what they were really against.

Behind the cluster of hideous creatures, a large foreboding form rose ominously: a snarling warlock troll, drool oozing from his mouth.

The light repelled the knarls, who fell back, stunned. Reynolds acted quickly, slicing the tangles that held Naomi trapped.

"Go! Go!" he yelled. Grabbing Naomi's hand, they ran.

Through the darkness, they darted back and forth. The chitters followed them closely, along with the lumbering thud of the troll. A few knarls caught up to them, wrapping around Naomi's legs and biting. She screamed and fell to the ground. Reynolds turned back and slashed at the creatures, making them scatter.

A giant wooden club swung down, smashing the trees next to them. The roar of the giant beast ripped through the air like a savage call to the forest, waking all that lived within.

For a brief moment, time stopped. Reynolds tried to force his magic to calm the excited creatures, but the troll's roar had created a frenzy. Squeals, chitters, and shrieks ramped forward toward where Naomi lay.

She screamed.

Reynolds hacked his blade left and right, dicing animals to pieces, but still some got past and found Naomi.

Their claws sliced through her, leaving deep cuts and gashes in her legs where the animals bit and gnawed. The troll eyed her with a panicked hunger. His long yellowed teeth were sharp, ready for her blood.

Reynolds had never seen such violence, such insanity, in the Blackwoods. He picked up Naomi and ran.

Naomi screamed in agony.

Her allure surrounded Reynolds now, stronger than ever before, pushing him forward, helping him stretch further and faster. He only thought of her.

CHAPTER FIVE
THE WILLOWS

Morning broke in a haze of swirling fog. Freezing mist filled the valley with the thick, strange frost. The sky looked iridescent through the icy clouds as the waking sun bridged the horizon. The willow trees swayed from side to side under a light breeze, vulnerable to the slightest movement.

With the tip of his knife, Taren flicked at the carved wood of one of the branches, already covered with hacks and marks in several areas, the result of boredom. The clustered branches hid his presence; there, he could watch the others; there, he could collect information, like a fly on the wall; and there, he planned his escape, if ever he could find the exit.

Taren liked the seclusion of the willows, the cluster of trees and long bending branches well-covered from the outside—his own hideaway overlooking the small camp and its circle of tents and buildings.

Not far below him stood the barracks, with the entrance near the base of the tree. The building looked like a small cabin left abandoned, full of bunks for the boys to sleep in, though Taren preferred to sleep outside. The less time he spent in there the better. Cramming everyone into one place to sleep infringed on his privacy, and he preferred the solitude.

He watched the morning sky turn from gray to a greenish fog, which made flecks of the morning light in the cold air. He didn't mind the cold; he liked mornings like this, bracing himself for the chill. He would win over it. He would always win.

Just below him, a slender red-head stood at the door. *Katia*, he thought—the lone girl in the entire camp, though not much of a girl. With what limited knowledge he had of females, he knew Katia wasn't a good representation.

Sitting back, he watched her walk to Aristatolis' hut, as she often did in the morning, though no one knew what she did there—meditate, he thought. Or possibly complain about her sad stories to the crotchety old fool. He went back to carving at the tree, not caring to find out.

Even Aristatolis really didn't know what to do with the menace. Her magic had great potential, from what Taren had read from her, but she couldn't figure it out.

Something beneath him rustled in the trees—too strong to be the wind. He thought it might be some kind of animal, but his mind sharpened to the presence of magic. Someone had entered the camp.

He stood, looking and feeling for the change. Few knew the secrets of the camp and how to get in and out, including himself. He, too, had yet to find the passageway—the one and only failing of his talent. Closing his eyes, Taren tried to listen to the magic. The fibers of his gift weaved in and out of the branches, searching, the aura clear and perfect . . . searching . . .

Nothing.

He opened his eyes again, a curse passing through his mind. He'd missed it again, and would continue to be stuck in this hell with no possible escape, imprisoned like a caged rat. Anger pulsed through his body. The knife in his hand came down fast, stabbing the branch and splitting the wood.

The rustling in the brush below turned into fast-paced footsteps as someone raced into the camp. Fearing it might be a troll broken in from the Blackwoods, Taren held his knife tight in his hand. How he wished to use his magic instead of waste away in the camp, day after day.

The magic circled inside him, erratic and untamed. The heat of it blistered his fingertips. He hoped it would be one of those beasts, giving him a chance to burn off some steam, but instead of the trampling of trolls, he heard a voice shouting.

Others had heard it, too. A few of the boys in the barracks lined the door to watch. Katia came running out, followed by the withering Aristatolis.

"Lytte! Where is your healer?" the voice screamed. "Your healer! Where is Lytte?"

Finally, someone came into view: a man running into the clearing in the center of camp, his dark cloak and tunic soaked in scarlet blood, carrying what looked like a child. The bundle did not stir. Taren wondered if it was alive—the crumpled figure limp and hanging as if dead. His heartbeat quickened at the sight; adrenaline pumped through his veins. This had just become exciting.

Aristatolis hailed the man as he approached. "Come! We will fetch him." The man followed Aristatolis back into the hut with his precious cargo.

Having heard the yelling, the eccentric healer, Lytte, reached the hut, his silken robes tangled around his long, cotton-like beard as he ran. He carried a small box full of vials filled with colorful liquids. When he reached the small dwelling, Lytte snagged Katia for help.

Taren couldn't help but be amused by Lytte's decision to ask Katia for assistance. No good would come from her aid. Still, he felt a little envy that she would see firsthand the bloodstained, wounded creature, and the stranger who had carried it into camp.

"Did you get a good view, Taren?" someone shouted at him from below. He looked down to see Landon standing near the bottom of the trunk.

Taren didn't feel like sharing his secrets. "No," he remarked as he climbed down. "Not much to see."

Landon met his eyes when he reached the bottom. Although Taren had never thought of Landon as a friend, he could see no point in making him an enemy. Well-liked by all the boys, with strong charisma and a charming nature, Landon would be a good ally if needed, so Taren didn't want to offend him—at least, not too much. "Looks like your girlfriend might know more."

Landon's face steamed. "She's not my girlfriend."

Taren shrugged. "Whatever you say."

"Micah's the one in love with her, not me," Landon persisted. "He could get more information."

The little ground-dweller, Micah, served as the other misfit of the camp, a small, dark mystic with crazy white hair. Amusing enough just to look at, when Micah opened his mouth, sheer buffoonery emerged. Still, he somehow managed to get answers that others couldn't.

Aristatolis led Reynolds to the middle of the hut where he placed Naomi down on a mat. Trying to comprehend how it had all happened still proved too horrific for Reynolds. The consequence lay quiet and still.

Guilt flooded every part of him. How could he have been so unwise to disobey Jeanus' instructions and take Naomi into the Blackwoods? His heart ached from the foolishness of his decision. Only *he* understood Naomi's condition. The woods had tricked him, leading him through a powerful mind game to get what they wanted—Naomi's blood.

Browneyes had followed them, practically forcing them in, understanding full well the dangers. At least she hadn't left with what she wanted, unless . . .

He felt the trick, the trap . . . Unless she had been searching for a way into the Willows. Was she using him to find the entrance? She knew what lay inside: the elusive magic only spoken of in whispers.

Another mistake. They kept piling up.

"Jeanus told me to avoid the Blackwoods." He fell onto his knees, crumbling in his despair. "I don't know what I was thinking . . ."

Aristatolis checked Naomi's heartbeat. "It is weak. In shock, I imagine." The old mystic's hands moved over her in small rotations, using the earth as a guide to understand her needs. His wrinkled hands sliced the air, cutting through kinetic disturbance, his eyes closed in meditation.

Lytte entered the hut a moment later, accompanied by a girl from the camp. "My boy, my boy," Lytte greeted, patting Reynolds on the back. The wizened white-haired healer saw the scarlet blood, soaked in the shredded fabric of Naomi's cloak. "What's this we have here?" His manner remained calm and immediate for the job at hand; despite the fact that Naomi's body couldn't be more still. "Katia, please hand me the eucalyptus root."

Katia stood, mesmerized by the situation. She stopped and blinked at Lytte, connecting what he had just asked her. "Oh, right. Sorry." She fumbled through Lytte's bottles, and found a white powder. The healer took it and lifted the bloody cloth covering Naomi's body.

Reynolds froze, confronted by the unexplainable. Naomi's fair legs looked as if they had never been touched. The scrapes and scratches from the knarls had disappeared, with only some dried blood left behind in spare patches.

"This can't be," he said in disbelief. "I saw the creatures tear into her. The blood—that's her blood." He flipped his hand through his hair, not understanding.

Lytte examined the girl's fragile legs. "It was right to bring her here, Reynolds."

"But I don't understand. She bled all over—I still have the blood on me. I've never seen the Blackwoods as angry. The knarls left two big bites, here and here."

"Wrapping her legs was the right thing to do. Precious as she is, if her blood hit the ground . . ."

Aristatolis moved his hands above her heart in circling motions. "There is energy around her. I feel it."

"You only just met her," Reynolds mumbled. "I've been with her for two days and I already feel like she's controlling my every impulse." He slid back with his hand to his forehead, his thoughts spilling out of his mouth, beyond his control. "It's unlike every high and low I've ever had."

Katia stumbled and dropped some of the bottles. "Sorry, so sorry."

Reynolds looked up in surprise, having forgotten about the girl listening to their every word.

"Thank you, Katia." Lytte took the bottles from her hands. "I think it is best that you go for a bit of breakfast, dear."

Katia, clearly embarrassed, nodded and left without another word.

Lytte watched Reynolds with tenderness. "Let's take Naomi to my tent where I can better treat her."

Reynolds picked her up again. She weighed barely anything, and he held his precious cargo close as he walked out of the hut and across the camp to the healer's tent. Several eyes followed them—inevitable when a stranger arrived in a place where no one ever entered.

Aristatolis stayed back to manage the others, giving them some privacy.

Reynolds couldn't help peering over his shoulder, feeling someone watching him. Recognizing the presence, he held on a little tighter to Naomi.

Lytte's tent seemed enormous, cluttered with tapestries and silks, boxes of books, and crates filled to the ceiling with unknown pots and powders—a whole apothecary within the small space, as if he had been living in transit and never unpacked. The comforting draperies made it much warmer than the cool morning air outside. Enchanting scents burned around in smoky ringlets, the smell bringing back childhood memories of time spent with the healer.

"Set her here." Lytte motioned to a small cot laden with furs.

Reynolds placed her down with care, resting her hands on her chest. She looked even paler than usual; he knew she had lost a lot of blood. "What are you going to do now?"

Lytte fiddled around with some of his healing medallions until he found the right one—the Blood Medallion. "Ah, this will work," he said to himself. He came and knelt near the sleeping girl. "She needs to rest and heal."

Reynolds looked at the old man. "How did she do it?"

Lytte started muttering chants in a very low voice. When he finished, he looked up. "My dear boy," he said, just as he had with Reynolds as a child, "why do you wear so much guilt? I think this is wonderful."

"Wonderful? I nearly killed her."

Lytte smiled his gentle smile. "Yes. She is wonderful." His enigmatic outlook of life had always differed from others, with a sweetness and respect for the beauty of simplicity.

"What do I do now?"

"Face your fears, I expect. I will place her in deep sleep for a few days so her body heals completely."

Face his fears. Reynolds's eyes moved to the medallion. "Is it still safe?"

"Yes, very." Lytte responded, though clearly preoccupied with Naomi to fully process the question. "Reyn, my boy, I need Aristatolis to visit me. Her heart rhythm distresses me. Please find him."

~◈~

Taren went back in the barrack which had emptied with all the excitement, and lay down on his bunk. He would have to wait to learn about the newcomers until

Katia or the stranger who had aroused so much curiosity left the hut.

Minutes passed in complete peace. Maybe they wouldn't have to do their warm-up or duties today. Maybe Aristatolis would be too preoccupied. One could only hope.

The echo of footsteps on the stone floor broke the silence. Taren lifted the hat he had placed over his head to see Katia returning. She lay on her bunk with her back towards him, unaware of his presence.

Soon Taren heard a voice interrupting the quiet.

"Hey, Red. Quit sulking."

Landon. Taren held still, listening in on the conversation.

"What do you want, Landon?" Katia complained. "Couldn't wait to insult me today?"

"Exactly. You know, I plan my whole day around your attitude."

"Do you have to be so rude all the time?"

"I don't have to, but it's just so easy. You take teasing so poorly."

"Somehow, you don't seem to get the hint that I don't like you."

"No, I get that. I rather enjoy it."

Taren lost interest in their banter. Their constant arguing bordered on flirting and quickly became irritating. Craning his head a little, Taren saw the two standing in between the bunks by the door. Katia started storming away. "Wait." Landon grabbed her arm. "I was hoping to ask you a question."

"Forget it."

"Come on." Landon continued to hold her back. "I promise I'll be nicer."

Katia stopped and sighed. "What is it?"

"You saw the girl today."

"Yeah, so?"

"I'm just curious about her, that's all."

"Well, I don't know anything."

"You know more than the rest of us."

Katia huffed and started walking again.

"Come on, Kat. Any information."

"I guess she got hurt, but I couldn't tell how badly. There was blood all over, but from what Lytte could tell, she wasn't hurt that much. And she's blond. I'd only ever *heard* of blond before; never seen it. Wore a scarf—a really pretty one."

"I'm not interested in her clothing," Landon snapped. "I want to know about the person who brought her here."

"I don't know him. His name is Reynolds."

Taren stopped listening. Heat rose to his ears; all the blood in his body turned cold. Of course Reynolds would be behind this. Taren's mind raced back through his memories, his hatred burning through all his rational thoughts.

Silence returned. Katia and Landon had left the barracks.

Now he had some investigating of his own to do.

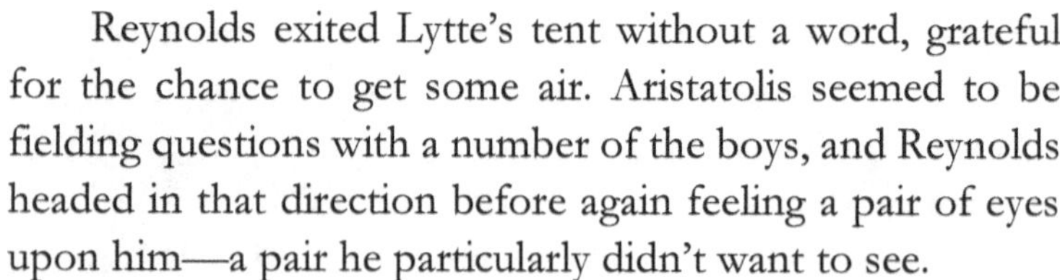

Reynolds exited Lytte's tent without a word, grateful for the chance to get some air. Aristatolis seemed to be fielding questions with a number of the boys, and Reynolds headed in that direction before again feeling a pair of eyes upon him—a pair he particularly didn't want to see.

Taren.

The cold eyes weighed like heavy stones tied to Reynolds's feet, preventing any movement as Taren's hard expression bore him down with hatred.

The plan would have to change.

Heading to Aristatolis, Reynolds delivered his message. As he moved back toward the tent, he felt Taren's eyes following him.

Reynolds ducked into the tent after Aristatolis, who began discussing with Lytte some of the particulars of Naomi's condition. He could hear them speak, but hardly registered what they said, too busy thinking of what he needed to do next.

Lytte would keep her safer than anyone. Jeanus had been right, and he trusted her word. But that didn't stop him from worrying. The place couldn't be safe for her, not when it had Taren, a very dangerous problem.

As much as he wished he could keep Naomi a secret, he feared having Taren there made that impossible. Taren would read her magic and understand everything. But Jeanus had been right about the Blackwoods. She would be right about the village, too.

He couldn't stay. In doing so, he would betray Naomi. She bound him so strongly, the thought of leaving her caused physical pain, but he had no other option. He should go find the boy Zander, as he had promised. It would be a nice diversion, a chance to clear his head and help him remember why Naomi had to be there in the first place, though the thought stung on the inside.

And what of Browneyes? She needed to be reckoned with before she unraveled everything he had tried so hard to keep safe.

"Lytte, I can't stay," he finally spoke.

Lytte understood without further explanation, Reynolds knew the healer comprehended deeper meanings he could not see.

"I'm turning over my promise to you. I'll be back. Watch Taren."

Both Lytte and Aristatolis nodded, understanding well their most dangerous tenant.

~·❖·~

Within a few minutes, Reynolds had packed some supplies, ready to leave again. But first, he faced Naomi. The hold she had over him felt stronger than ever. She lay so still and peaceful, though her soft expression remained a bitter reminder.

This is my fault . . . everything. He turned away. He wouldn't say goodbye, not yet.

He thought it would be safest to leave through the back of Lytte's tent, not attracting attention as he had that morning. But his trek didn't take him far before someone stopped him cold.

"Bringing more people to this hell?" Taren's voice came from somewhere above him.

Reynolds saw him in the trees. The younger man had been waiting for him, predicting his moves. He walked on.

"That's what you do: bring them in and drop them off. Leave them here to rot." Taren dropped to the ground and began following Reynolds' tracks.

"But this one is different. Why bring a girl? What's so special about her? Adding another butterfly to your collection?"

Reynolds didn't want to hear any more. He swung as he turned, catching Taren off-guard and connecting with his side. Taren retaliated with a blow toward his middle, knocking the wind out of him.

Reynolds' wits were sharp. He blocked the next punch easily and deflected two more before Taren calmed down.

"Who is she?" Taren demanded, readying himself again. "You know I'll find out."

Reynolds flinched, his anger growing, his concentration wavering. "Just try. I dare you. You'll be affected just like the others." Another swing and miss. Reynolds, so in tune to his adversary, could predict the movement now. "I'm warning you. Stay away from her."

Taren's blow hit Reynolds square in the jaw, knocking him back into a tree. His lip cracked and bled.

Taren looked satisfied. "I want out. Get me out of here."

Reynolds wiped his lip on his sleeve and stood back up. "Why should I do that?"

"You owe me and you know it."

The guilt treatment wouldn't work on Reynolds. "It's simple magic. I'm surprised you haven't figured it out."

"I'm not simple," Taren spat. "You would know."

"Then I'll leave you to figure it out if you can." Reynolds stared him down a long moment to see if Taren would accept the challenge.

He took off running.

Taren followed close behind—faster and faster, pushing Reynolds to his limits. He knew where to find the apex, but also knew Taren couldn't figure out the puzzle. It took more than brains and magic to get out of the camp. It took something beyond Taren's capability.

Reynolds ran through the willow trees.

Behind him, Taren lost the trail.

CHAPTER SIX
SOUTHWICK

A few days passed without any trace of Prince Bryant. Zander understood that he would be a fool if he did not take Bryant's offer. He regretted not telling him yes when he could. The opportunity to live a clean, cared-for life had seemed too unreal to him at first—but even if it proved to be a trick, the option of staying in the grimy, rotting cell, being beaten daily, left him begging for the chance to leave.

Being in the service of the king would be better than begging in the streets or wandering the world in search for something better.

Curled up in the corner of his cell, Zander watched the bugs crawl in and out between the stone cracks, which had proved to be more interesting than examining the fibers of straw in his bedding. His eyes drifted to the bundle of Naomi's papers wadded together under the mattress. He tried to make patterns out of the wrinkled papers, matching lines to lines.

The door swung open without him noticing.

"You!" A large rumbling growl startled him. Zander's hand grabbed the bundle and stuffed it quickly under his shirt as he turned to stare at the menacing helmet-clad guardsman. "Come!"

Feeling weak and fatigued, Zander's adrenaline soon kicked in as the guardsman stepped toward him. He scrambled to his feet, his muscles sore from lack of use and malnutrition. Marching forward, the guardsman grabbed Zander's shrinking wrists and chained them with heavy cuffs meant for a man, not someone his size. He struggled to hold them up.

"No trouble," the guardsman grumbled. Shrinking in his presence, Zander followed him out of the cell in silence.

A series of tunnels spread out before them, lined with dirt and stone, dimly lit with torches in brackets. Zander glanced into a few of the other cells, looking for any human connection, but only darkness greeted him. All remained silent and still, unlike those fearful days of mocking when he first arrived.

They ascended several flights of stairs. The bulky guardsman knew the climb, but it made Zander's legs burn and tighten. The wheezing in his chest accelerated to an outward gasp, but the guardsman gave it no mind, just pulled on the chains tighter than before.

On and on they climbed, turning this way and that in a dizzying progression. Zander felt glad he had never tried to escape. He certainly would have died, lost in the labyrinth of this dungeon. He could not fathom how the guardsman knew where to go.

Suddenly, the corridors looked very different. Zander turned a corner at the top of a stairway and walked down a long hall lined with polished granite walls. Finally, he felt they had traveled above ground.

After the torturous hike, Zander stopped for a moment, taking the opportunity to breathe the good air. The guardsman pounded a few times on a thick wooden door at the end of the pathway, followed by the sound of many locks clicking on the other side. The door creaked open, and Zander blinked and squinted as the guardsman pulled him into the light.

Before his eyes could adjust, the guardsman pushed him from behind, knocking him off balance. Landing awkwardly in a chair, he felt large hands holding him down. He struggled to free himself but his weak muscles proved useless. The guardsman removed the chains and replaced them with a hard coarse rope on both his hands and his feet.

Several men loomed over him, each with sword and armor, dressed uniformly in tunics and dark purple cloaks with a large woven crest stitched in the front. The intricacy of the design grabbed Zander's attention. He had never seen it before but could tell this said a lot about the importance of the men.

He looked around to see if he could find the prince, but with all the helmeted faces, the search proved pointless. Voices echoed from an adjoining hallway, and the men quickly lined up away from him.

Zander tried to focus on the men as they began marching forward, but the enormous room sparkled with white marble and beautifully polished stone, which distracted him. Wide columns ran from the floor to the ceiling, large windows covered with intricately patterned glass and sent rainbows cascading onto the floor.

It felt so unreal to have come up from a place so foul, so horrible, to a place so remarkably beautiful. How could the two co-exist?

Two men came forward and stopped in front of Zander—one very familiar. He didn't know whether to smile or cry at the sight of Prince Bryant.

"You look like hell," Bryant's voice rang around the giant room. ". . . and you don't smell too good, either. I think the bucket got the best of you, boy."

Zander didn't speak, but sighed with relief.

"Curt, I need him presentable for the upcoming festivities." Bryant's hand swept over his brow in contemplation. "Keep him close to the kitchens. Mildred will take care of him."

"Yes, Highness," the man next to him answered, his silky voice slithering about him like oil.

"Boy," Bryant addressed Zander again. "This is Curtis, my Primitus. He will take charge of you until you understand your role and get used to this place. We have quarters for you with the other servants by the kitchens. It will be pleasant enough, I'm sure." He evaluated Zander's bound arms and legs. "Did you really think that necessary?"

A man standing next to Zander—who in fact, held onto his shirt collar—spoke up. "My lord, he came from the deepest part of the dungeon, from the isolation chamber. We did not know what to expect when he arrived, so I had my men take every precaution."

Bryant snapped back, "Well, he is no threat. Good glory—he's a boy! Untie him at once!"

The men scrambled to cut the bindings, and Zander fell forward from the unexpected imbalance.

"Steady!" yelled Bryant, reaching out to catch him. "I do hope you aren't always this much trouble." He smiled. "I need you healthy."

Zander attempted a grin.

"Can you walk?"

Zander opened his mouth, but no sound came out. Instead, he nodded his head.

"Good, because you really do smell awful. No offense." Bryant released him from his grasp, then wiped his hands off.

Zander nodded in agreement.

"All right, Curtis, he's yours." The prince evaluated Zander's face, his expression tender and sincere—as if he truly intended to help him. "I hope you'll find everything to your liking." He patted him tentatively on the shoulder before turning to walk away, then paused. "I expect our conversation will be more stimulating next time."

～-●-～

Zander remained with the man named Curtis, who seemed too tall and freakishly slender. He wore all black, interwoven with ornate threads and swirling patterns that mesmerized the eye. A peculiar, pointed, hat of intricate design sat atop his head, which made him resemble an arrow. At first impression, Zander didn't like the intimidating man.

"Let us get you clean," Curtis said in low silky tones. "This filth is burning my nostrils." The comment came out rather dryly. Zander couldn't interpret the real meaning but followed him just the same.

After his much-needed bath, Curtis provided him with clean clothes, simple but elegant wear: a white tunic, a camel leather vest that laced in the front, and leather pants that fastened at the knee. It felt like a costume, but Zander recognized it to be the uniform of the servants, having seen others in similar attire wandering about. His hair had also been cut and cleaned, revealing tan lines that came from farm life and the hot summer sun.

"Here is your room." Curtis pointed down a corridor of doors lined back to back, each marked with a circular window in the front of the door. The window bent around like a fisheye and had the color of a shiny pearl. Curtis ushered Zander into the chamber at the end of the hall. "I will be by later, at the prince's request."

The small room stood simple, clean, and private; a wondrous improvement over his cell. The bed pushed up next to the wall looked more comfortable than even his pallet on the farm. An iron-thatched window let in the sunlight, and a large chest sat across from it. He found extra clothes, similar uniforms, and a nightshirt within. What an unfamiliar life he had entered: a life without possessions or debt, just service. He bounced on the bed.

I could get use to this.

Outside, he could hear a muffled roar but didn't recognize it. By the third shove, the stubborn window finally opened and sunlight poured in. A strong smell swelled in his nostrils.

Zander did not expect what he saw.

Steep cliffs of sliced, smooth rock dropped from his window hundreds of yards down. Below, the sea rolled, wide as the horizon, with its waves rushing wildly toward the rocks. Far beyond, the clouds played with the sun in mixed golds and pinks. The bird cries blended beautifully with the crashing of the waves against the rocks far beneath his feet.

"Beautiful, huh?" a voice whispered close to his ear. Startled, he jumped away from the window and turned to face the intruder. A slim, girlish figure backed away, laughing at his reaction.

Still startled, he took in the presence of this stranger. The girl couldn't have been much older than he, maybe fourteen. She appeared unlike anyone he'd ever met but strangely pretty. Her hair fell long about her shoulders, like flowing copper reflecting in the sunlight, and she'd pulled it back behind her pointy ears. She wore a dress similar to Zander's uniform, but slightly more formal-looking, with a cinched waste at the skirt. She had a willowy frame and good muscle tone. But, her most distinguishing feature, her emerald eyes stood out and made her pale skin seem almost transparent.

"Easy, easy," she started. "I was just curious who Curtis would bring down to this room, that's all."

Zander just stared at her, too dumb to speak.

"My name's Audra Thornhollow, and don't stare at my ears."

Zander looked down, not realizing he'd been doing just that.

"Aw." Audra waved her arm, dismissing the innocent reaction. "I'm a Louving. There aren't many of us and people are always curious. So I have pointy ears and a good sense of direction. That's all you need to know. Happy?"

Zander liked her instantly. He enjoyed her carefree expressions and honesty.

Audra stared out at the sea and no longer seemed to care what Zander might think about her. "You really do have an incredible view, though. If I could open my window, I wouldn't have such a good view; it looks out over the sewer drainage."

She walked back to the window and breathed deeply. "Don't you just love that smell?"

"I . . . never . . ." Zander stuttered, then shook his head.

Audra looked back at him. "Not much of a talker, are you?" She smiled and turned her gaze back to the sea. "That will go over very well here. The quieter you are, the more they like you. I tend to talk a lot so they stick me in the back of the kitchens. But seriously, haven't you ever seen the sea?"

"I . . . don't know where . . . whe . . ."

"Please, don't kill yourself trying to speak. You're at Southwick."

"Wh—?"

"Do you really not know Southwick? It's where the grand palace is. That's where we are. Every king of Parbraven has lived here since the old times." She turned to face him. "So, where are you from?"

"Sh . . . Sharlot . . ."

Audra laughed. "That filthy, beggar-ridden town? Yikes. You're in worse shape than I thought."

"Why?"

"Southwick will seem like heaven compared to Sharlot. Your view doesn't even show it, but I should take you to see the city. It's so wonderful. The lights at night sparkle like the sky and there's singing you can hear from far in the streets. It's so calm and peaceful and safe. That's why I stay here. It's hard to get work in the palace. You should feel privileged you're here."

Her attention turned to the room itself. She rummaged deep into the chest. "Where's all your stuff?"

"I don't . . . have . . ."

"Nothing? That's boring. How am I going to find out about you if you don't have anything with you?"

Zander grinned at his forward new friend.

"What's your name at least?" she asked.

"Z . . . ander."

"Well, Ander, I'm down the hallway and to the right, in the girls' quarters. I've got to get ready for dinner preparations, but we'll talk later." She gave him an awkward smack on the shoulder, knocking him off balance, and walked to the door. As she reached the archway, she looked back, winked, then disappeared.

He went back to his window and the beautiful view, drawn in by the smell of the salty sea. He watched the waves continue on and on, the clouds moving slowly in the distance. He might have been there for hours and wouldn't have even known it.

"Boy! Here!" a harsh voice demanded. He turned to see a large, unpleasant-looking woman, very soggy and greasy, who smelled of fish. "Can't be wastin' time. Got work to do."

Zander blinked at the woman before moving forward.

"Pick up them feet," she barked. "I ain't runnin' a daisy farm. Hundreds of hungry people wantin' their food. On with ya!"

He moved as fast as he had ever gone before.

The woman tried to swat his behind but missed.

CHAPTER SEVEN
PRISON

Warmth covered Naomi's entire body. She felt safe and secure. How strange for Ferrell to let her sleep in this long.

She lay contemplating her dream, mulling over the details in her mind. As strange as this dream had been, it was not alarming like some of the others. Flashbacks of previous dreams came to her as painful memories: sharp pains, blood, and a handsome face carrying her through a dark forest . . .

Wait, Naomi thought. And then the reality of what had happened came rushing back: the prince, the escape, her fall into the ravine, the flood, the Blackwoods, the creatures, and Reynolds. She wasn't home on Ferrell's farm. Where was she?

Her eyes popped open, and the suddenness blinded her until she adjusted to the light in the room around her. The backdrop looked peculiar and disorienting. Fancy fabrics and tapestries of intricate craftsmanship created a canopy of free-flowing fabric, suspended by a polished wooden pole that stood in the middle.

She sat up, shaky and groggy from sleep, amidst piles and piles of brightly colored blankets. She still had her tattered clothing on. Dried splatters of blood stained her skirt.

Instinctively she rubbed the mark on her neck. Not until then did she feel something missing.

A lanky teenage girl entered the tent. With bizarre, red-colored hair standing up in untidy spikes, her boyish cut emphasized a pointed face and almond-shaped eyes. She dressed in what appeared to be boy's clothes: tan leather pants and a cotton tunic with a leather vest which didn't quite fit her proportions nor hide her girlish curves.

"Oh, you're awake," she said. "I promised not to leave, but I saw you stir and thought I should go get the others. They're waiting outside."

Naomi just stared, confused.

"Are you all right? You're as white as a ghost."

"I . . ." Naomi hesitated.

"I'll get Lytte . . . just a sec," and she stepped out the door.

A moment later, she returned, accompanied by two men.

An elderly man dressed in a long, flowing robe approached her. "Good afternoon. My name is Lytte. I am the healer here and Reynolds left you in my care. This is Aristatolis." He pointed to the other man. "He is a Whirler. We mean you no harm."

"Where is Reynolds?"

"In good time, my dear, in good time," said Lytte. "Now, let me take a look at your wounds, if you will permit me." Naomi felt uncomfortable but nodded. Lytte lifted the blankets from her legs and examined them thoroughly.

Naomi looked at her legs, too. She remembered the bites from the creatures in the Blackwoods—the searing pain and the blood soaking her clothes—but there were no scars or marks, not even scratches to be found. "We are told your name is Naomi."

"Yes," she returned, bewildered.

Aristatolis smiled and sat on a chair nearby. "You are a curiosity to us."

"You see, you possess magic we have never seen," Lytte added.

The reminder of the magic worried her. "Reynolds mentioned something like that. I think we should talk to him about it."

Aristatolis leaned on his staff. "Reynolds brought you here three days ago. You were covered with blood. The wounds healed within hours. Within a day, the scars were gone. Now, aside from your clothes, we have no evidence you were harmed at all. So, you see, you are a mystery."

Lytte gave an endearing smile. "I have never met anyone like you."

"I'd like to think that a good thing," she joked. "Reynolds said something similar. Can you get him for me? I think he would like to know I'm awake and okay."

"Reynolds has asked us to keep an eye on you," said Aristatolis, exchanging a glance with Lytte.

Naomi stared. "Are you saying he's not here?" A knot started in her stomach—an uncomfortable feeling she, at first, did not recognize. It sat in a funny place inside her—

in her stomach or in her throat, she could not tell, but the realization scared her for a moment even more than the forest. She had grown fond of Reynolds, trusting him with her life created something more, and suddenly she didn't want to part from him. She didn't want to be there without him. "Where did he go?"

"He does not tell us of such things and we do not ask," Aristatolis answered.

Lytte took his turn to speak. "We have set up a place for you to sleep, separate from the others, and I would like you to be under my stewardship as a healer."

Naomi nodded, but felt her anxiety grow without Reynolds near to guide her in this new environment. Her mind rattled with questions. The world had changed, and she didn't know how to view it.

"Katia!" Aristatolis called. The red-haired girl stepped forward from the back of the tent. "Please take Naomi to your new tent."

Lytte bent down and lifted the lid of a small basket. The long, familiar scarf seemed to move like fluid in his hands. "I believe this is yours." He draped it around her and winked, his voice a whisper. "You will need this." With that, he and Aristatolis left the tent.

Katia smiled widely, hopping up and down. "This is going to be so much fun. Are you all right?"

Naomi hesitated. "I'm a little disoriented. I'm not sure . . . I don't know where I am."

The girl looked around. "You're in Lytte's tent."

"Okay, but where is Lytte's tent? I mean geographically."

"Oh, sure," Katia returned. "At the edge of camp."

Naomi gave up. She wanted to know more about what happened to her, but this girl didn't have any answers.

"I'm Katia Ravenmoor, by the way," she said, waving. "Aristatolis put me in charge of you for now, until we know what to do. So, what's your name?"

"Naomi, uhh . . ." she hesitated. "Just Naomi." She rubbed her neck out of habit again. She could feel the smooth fabric of the scarf. It warmed her and hid her insecurities. She brushed her fingers over the silk, looking at the patterns.

"It's very pretty," said Katia. "The scarf, I mean."

"Thanks."

An awkward pause followed before Katia spoke. "Sorry. I just have to say this. I am so excited that you are here. Really! The boys give me an awful time, being the only girl and all, but now we can be friends and I no longer have to deal with it—well, not as much, probably. They like to pick on me, I guess. They really don't know what to do with me. My magic is a little different than theirs. I'm trying to figure it out, but it kind of explodes out of me and then I freeze everything."

Naomi just smiled and nodded. She had nothing to say. Her anxiety hadn't let up one bit and this girl's rambling conversation only confirmed how much she needed Reynolds.

"Oh, sorry about the clothes," Katia continued. "I have clean ones, but I didn't know what would fit."

Naomi looked at the state of her clothing, dirty from mud, bloody from her wounds, then to the pile of boy's clothes Katia handed her. She held up the trousers. They looked enormous. "Uh, okay, I think."

Naomi slipped the tunic and trousers on. She felt ridiculous.

"I'll try to find something that fits later," Katia apologized, and they exited the tent.

~·◆·~

Katia led Naomi down a worn dirt path. The camp looked small and narrow. A grove of willow trees surrounded it, covering the ground with shade. Sun streaked in through branches, slicing the thickness and littering the ground with patterns. A few other small huts were strung along the dirt paths that led to a small wood cabin at the far end. Various boys could be seen sparring with sticks.

As her anxieties continued to rise, she tried to focus her thoughts on other more important issues. Zander wasn't here and she worried about him. She half expected him to walk up to her from the sparring ground. Her heart ached. She missed him tremendously.

That might be why Reynolds left, she concluded. She had been annoyed at first, and then hope replaced the feeling. Her thoughts drifted off, and she felt as if he were standing next to her. Her stomach tied in knots at the memory of his hand in hers, running his fingers along her knuckles . . . *Stop it!* These thoughts were destructive and unnecessary.

She saw a lot more people as they moved deeper in the camp: boys in tents meditating, eating under a large thatch canopy, fighting amongst themselves. Everything ground to a halt as Naomi passed, the camp slowly quieting until every eye focused on her. She felt extremely self-conscious and grabbed hold of Katia.

"How much farther?"

"Not much," said Katia. "We have to go around the barracks. That's where all the boys sleep. I did, too, but now with you here, we get to have our own tent. I'm so excited." She made a strange pumping motion with her fists and squeezed Naomi's arm.

"We have to go past all these . . . ?" Naomi looked out into the camp at all the faces watching her pass. She didn't dare meet anyone's gaze directly.

"Yeah, but no problem. We're by Aristatolis' hut right over there." She pointed down the path. "Just stay close."

And Naomi did, holding tight to Katia's elbow. Time seemed to stop. Everyone stared at her like a foreign creature.

"Oh, great!" Katia mumbled under her breath.

Two out of the crowd approached them. "Katia, oh lovely Katia," one squeaked, hailing them. "The rabbit is out of its hole. So glad to see you this fine, fine day."

"Hi, Micah. This really isn't a good time." Katia's voice was calm but focused.

"Any time is good—good for time!"

"Whatever, Micah. I've got to get Naomi to our tent, if you please."

"Naomi, is it?" The tall boy with the smooth voice stepped in, halting their progress.

"Yes, Landon. But could we do introductions later? It's a little cold out here."

"No time like the present. Hi, I'm Landon Rhees." He stuck out his hand. "My rhyming friend here is Micah Shadower."

Naomi smiled and tightened her grip on Katia's arm.

"Now's not the time for introductions, Rhees," Katia muttered. Naomi flushed beet-red but remained silent. "So, could we please get past?"

Landon smiled widely and stepped aside.

Katia and Naomi walked swiftly towards their shelter. Naomi glanced back and wondered about the tall one with the smooth voice.

The gentle trees and shrubs surrounded the shelter, making it secluded and private. The warm air inside felt good. Two cots flanked the inside of the tent, covered with piles of soft furs and blankets. Deep in the shady wood, the sun couldn't filter in.

Katia grabbed a lantern, reached into her pocket, and pulled out a little dust on her fingers. She snapped them together, producing a spark, and gently blew it into the lantern. Instantly the tent lit up. The light grew greater than Naomi had imagined, almost as if the sun shone in through a window.

"How do you do that?" Naomi asked.

"Sunsparks." She lifted a small pouch out of her pocket to show her. A fine powder filled it, bright white with strange flecks of gold mixed well together.

"I'll try to remember that."

"Can I ask you a question?" Katia asked. "Don't be offended by it."

"Okay."

"What is that star thing on your neck?"

Naomi choked. She hadn't thought anyone had seen it. "Just a scar I got when I was little—a birthmark, I guess."

"It's very pretty," Katia said wistfully. "Wish I had something like that."

Naomi didn't have a response. She didn't think she should be flattered by the compliment, since she had tried to hide it all her life.

An awkward silence filled the space.

"Why don't you tell me more about you?" Naomi asked.

Katia perked up at these words. "You want to know about me? No one here has ever asked about me." She smiled brightly. "Well, there's not much to tell. I grew up in the Salt Peaks, a place called Tapoof, near the edge of the south sea. It's beautiful, but very hot.

"My father was a fisherman and my mother was a pattern maker. She was from the Butterfly Islands and we traveled there all the time. I miss those days sometimes. The feel of the sea and the ship, the rocking and motion . . .

"My first memories were of the sea. We lived on the boat until I was around nine. But when my mother found out she was pregnant, she couldn't go out on the water anymore. When my brother came, everything changed. She's dead now, along with my brother." Katia's voice fell away.

Naomi realized she might have hit a soreness that had never healed properly. "Sorry. I didn't mean . . ."

Katia shrugged. "It happened years ago. Near the end of her life, my mother went mad. She forced me to drink something she got from a mystic. Said it would make me beautiful. That worked, didn't it?"

She laughed at her own joke, but then sighed at the seriousness of it. "My mother killed herself and the baby. My father had a hard time dealing with my mother's death. I look like her, you see."

"How did you get here?"

Katia's tone darkened. "My father talked to the fishmongers about me—about the magic my mother forced on me. I got packed up and shipped away, just like that."

A bell echoed through the tent from somewhere outside. Katia's mood seemed to immediately improve. "Wow, dinner. I bet you're hungry."

Naomi thought about it, and food—real food—sounded like the best idea in the world.

"Come on, then." Katia grabbed Naomi's arm and pulled her out the door.

The mess hall lived up to its name—a mess. The unstable structure rose in the corner of the camp like an eyesore. Wood planks hung together with rusted nails. A fraying rope and weathered reeds thatched together the roof. Inside, round tables filled the room wall to wall, each one crowded with noisy, disgusting boys laughing and talking loudly. Filth and grime covered the tables and chairs, along with old, crusted food. The place smelled of dried meat and sour milk.

Naomi's appetite began to wane, and not because of the lack of cleanliness. Her stomach lurched with uncomfortable hunger pains, weak from her days in the tent, and knew she had to eat. She just wished she didn't have to do it with everyone staring at her.

"Oh, my ladies, my ladies . . ." a voice squealed at their approach. The boy called Micah stood and gave an unnecessary bow. "I am honored with your presence."

Naomi stared. He stood out, his appearance unique but not alarming: striking white hair over dark skin, with eyes of vivid blue.

"I'll be back." Katia headed in the direction of the food.

"You have no need to be afraid of me. Sit, sit," Micah said in his hypnotic voice, motioning to the empty chairs at the table. "Fear is good, healthy, wise, but the fearless need extra eyes, don't you think?"

Naomi simply nodded. *What?*

"I am Micah Shadower. I come from Feather Downs in the east. Do you know it?"

Naomi shook her head. "Sorry, no."

"I am of a people descended from the Great Mountains. We were once earth and then became trees, and now we are men searching for our way back to the earth. Sharing space and time with the elements which make us and the legends that bring us as one—"

"Whoa, whoa . . ." a voice called from the side of the table. "Micah, don't scare the girl." The tall, dark Landon Rhees slid over next to them. "None of that kind of talk. She just got here."

Micah didn't lose his smile. "My heritage should be shared and known."

"Not on the first day." Landon smiled at Naomi. "Don't worry about him. He just wants his shot at knowing you first, but clearly I got that with our introductions earlier today."

Naomi raised an eyebrow. "I didn't know about a competition."

Landon grimaced a little but returned a bright smile. "There are a lot of others who want a chance to know you, but I felt it my duty to get here first, just to warn you. You know, for your protection."

"How noble."

"Thank you. I try to watch out for the girls here. Katia and I have been friends from the beginning."

Naomi stared down his dark eyes. "That surprises me. I got the impression that no one liked her here."

"Well, to be honest, she is a little odd, but in a sweet way. We go way back, Kat and me. I'm sure she didn't mention that I traveled with her when she arrived." He leaned closer, his expression intense. "I got to know her pretty well on that trip. I'm one of the best friends she has here, whether she knows it or not. I have faithfully defended her for years."

"How?"

"I understand a little about girls and the way they work."

"Really? A lifetime couldn't give you that much knowledge. How old are you?"

"You lose track of time in this place. Eighteen or so."

"And Katia is the only girl? Then where did you get all your wisdom?"

Landon's mouth twisted into a smile. "I think you'd call it charm. There are only a few older than me. There were only a handful or so here when I arrived." He began pointing some out as he talked. "Justis, Pollack and Leto over there, Derron, Taren over there in the corner, Nathaniel—all of them were here. Kat and I arrived, then Micah showed up—what, a year later?"

Micah nodded in approval.

Naomi liked that he pointed others out, glad to know something about the people who surrounded her. Landon certainly charmed her with his likeable qualities, even if he masked something. "So, where is home?"

"He has traveled the Salt Seas, across the forest that has no name, to the tallest rivers and highest peaks . . ." Micah chimed in.

"Please, Micah—you're making me sound better than I deserve." Landon laughed in spite of himself. "I'm originally from the Springs of Sephar, south of the Ravian River, but I left there long ago, so long I hardly remember it. Both my parents were killed in the Great War. I fell in with travelers for a while, and then came here."

Naomi gaped. "Travelers?"

"Yeah. Not a fabulous life, I know, but I learned a thing or two from those mystics." Landon moved his hands up and down, and a strange image of light danced through the air, then disappeared.

"Wait, wait, wait . . ." Naomi stopped him. "You say you traveled around like a gypsy?" A new image of Landon came to her mind. "So did I! I traveled with an old gypsy woman when I was a child."

"Seriously?" Landon jumped up out of his chair raising his fists in the air. The entire room silenced at his declaration. "I win! I win! I win!" He finally settled down. "I think I remember you! I do!"

"What?"

He leaned toward her. "The enchanting little girl with the blonde hair who would dance around the fires. I can't believe I missed it!"

"I don't remember you," Naomi returned, suspicious.

"I followed a family named Pipkin. A father, two boys and a girl. They taught me illusions and crowd pleasers, only us for the most part, but I remember grouping with others, sometimes. But you were unforgettable! I remember first seeing you, on the plains of the Sacred Ties Festival." He laughed at the memory. "You must have been really young, maybe six, waving the streamers in the air. Even then, you were mesmerizing."

Naomi blushed a little at his words, but remained silent in amazement.

"Well, I found it more profitable to become a thief and left. I met Katia, and there you go." He finished abruptly, not seeming to need to say any more.

"That's incredible!"

"What is?" Katia asked, carrying the plates of food to the table.

Naomi turned to her. "We know each other."

"Well, sort of," Landon interjected.

"What?" Katia stared in horror. "No! You can't!"

Landon grinned widely.

"You already know her? That trumps the fact that I'm a girl." Katia looked defeated, slumping into her chair.

Overwhelmed watching the two argue over her attention, Naomi quickly changed the subject. "Reh . . . someone said this place had magic."

Landon studied her. "No, it's not like that." He downed his stew. "We're trying to improve our natural abilities, not just use magic."

"Natural abilities?"

"Well, I'm really good at magic, but not real magic. Just little illusions and such, something to distract a person long enough to pick their pocket. It's a good and useful skill. Say there's someone trying to kill you. You distract him, steal the daggers from his back pocket, and replace them with carrots. Before he's even aware of it, he goes to throw the daggers, and bam! A face full of carrots."

Katia smirked. "Now that you mention it, Landon, it sounds kind of dumb."

Landon glared at her. "I'm sure it sounds dumb coming from you, Miss I'm-Going-To-Freeze-Everyone-With-My-Feelings."

"Shut up! You don't have any idea of what I can do!"

"You're right." He pointed his stew-covered fork in her direction. "I've never seen you actually do anything right!"

"I've done things right!"

"Yes, but nothing deliberately. You're always at your best when someone makes you cry."

Katia glared at Landon and his accusations but stayed silent.

"What about you, Micah?" Naomi asked, trying to lighten the mood. "What are your natural abilities?"

"Mine are complicated."

Katia brightened. "Micah's skills are amazing. He can move stuff around, like wind and things, right?"

Micah hesitated at her description. "Not exactly. You see, the earth and dust are my arms as we are one, and they help me if I need it. Also, I am very sensitive to movement; I can feel vibrations, even heartbeats long distances away."

"That's unique."

Micah shrugged. "It is not special or uncommon in my heritage."

Landon glared at Katia. "How can you think Micah's abilities are amazing and mine are rubbish?"

"Micah's are traced back centuries."

"So are mine," Landon snapped, and then reconsidered. "Well, maybe not, but it doesn't mean I'm not as useful. 'Oh, Micah's *so* wonderful' . . ."

"Oh, just stop it, Landon. Naomi will see for herself in the yard. You can impress her there with your 'illusions'."

The two continued to glare at each other, seeming to have forgotten Naomi and Micah were there. She cleared her throat. "So, why did you choose to come here?"

Katia looked up at her. "No one chooses to come."

"Then why do you choose to stay?"

"We don't," Micah answered. His voice fell to a quiet whisper.

Naomi froze. "You can't leave?"

"We're not criminals," Landon clarified. "Well, mostly. There are a few here that I can't vouch for."

Again Naomi wondered why Reynolds had left her there. "I don't like the idea of being trapped."

Landon slid forward. "You can trust me."

"Trust us!" Katia added.

"Is this why he brought me here?" Naomi thought out loud. "Because he knew I couldn't get out? I don't understand . . ."

"Try me," Katia said.

"Try us!" Landon insisted.

Naomi thought carefully about what she should say before she spoke. "There's something dangerous about this place. I'm not sure how I feel about staying here."

Katia frowned. "That's normal. Everyone feels that way when they come, but you'll get used to it."

Naomi thought about Katia's words, but they didn't ring true. This place didn't feel right. An uneasy feeling crept around her insides. She felt trapped—like she stood at the edge of the world, ready to tip, and something unseen pushed her off-balance.

CHAPTER EIGHT
CURIOSITY

The girl entered the mess hall with Katia. Taren didn't spend much time in the mess hall, but he knew Naomi would be there tonight, and it would be an opportunity to find out more about her.

Just observing her, he could see why Reynolds fought to keep her away from him. He could feel her presence when she entered the room like an unexpected warm wind, surrounding her with protective arms. He found her peculiar.

The conversation she had with Landon and Micah wasn't interesting. He pushed his magic to see what he could find out about her.

Taren held very still and searched for the magic surrounding her.

Cold . . . ice blue . . . dancing . . . The boundless energy from Katia's magic read easily because of her complete lack of confidence and control. It hovered close to the surface but never fulfilled its potential. She could be a threat if she knew how to use it.

He pushed further.

Patterns . . . erratic flashes . . . reflection . . . Landon's magic was useless. It only worked if used with something else. What a waste.

Tiny specks moving fast . . . a cyclone . . . Typical ground-dweller magic. Micah was only a duplicate of his people—all the same earth-matter conjuring, nothing varied.

Come on, he pushed. *Find the girl . . .*

He blocked all other magic around him; their insignificance didn't affect him. Further and further . . . He could be wrong. Maybe Naomi didn't have any magic. But Reynolds wouldn't risk her being here if she didn't. There had to be something, anything . . .

Black . . . a wall . . . thick . . . Nothing. He could find nothing.

Naomi looked around her. Landon talked on and on about nothing important. He pointed to Taren's direction. Taren glared.

He made eye contact. Quick! Act now.

Taren pushed his magic. His sight intensified, searching for weakness within the invisible shield; his neck strained as he threw forward his telepathic invasion.

Pain . . . shock . . . sting!

Taren blinked. Pain everywhere, like fire burning his insides. A breath, a gasp for air escaped. *Calm down.* She talked with the others as if nothing happened. The sting still resonated in his body. His nerves pulsed in raging, throbbing pains. He tried to clear his mind to get rid of the feeling. *Out! Out! Out!*

He had to leave. Taren left his food untouched on his plate, stumbled toward the door without intending to draw attention, and left as quickly as he could.

That night he didn't stay in the barracks. Instead he lay in his tree, suffering. The pain still pulsed with every thump in his heart. She had magic, the most powerful he had ever experienced. The truth constricted all his muscles and pulsed in his blood.

He had never experienced anything like that before. Magic of others expressed itself as easy to read, easy to feel, especially for him. He could read anything—except her. He wasn't going to risk his mind by invading hers again.

After breakfast, Taren resurfaced in the camp. Lytte and Aristatolis never made him labor like the others. Being the oldest there, he resented the confinement. Others thought it a unique environment to grow and learn, but Taren knew full well they were caught in a trap that caged them like animals.

Aristatolis prepared the yard for meditation, a good exercise for the unskilled and unfamiliar. Taren had no need of it. He hadn't joined in a long time, so for him to show up today might look suspicious. He hung back by the trees to watch.

The crowd started to plant themselves around the grounds. The small group consisting of Landon, Katia, Micah, and Naomi came out of the mess hall.

Rows formed and everyone sat cross-legged on the grass, except for Naomi, who continued to walk towards the back rows. Micah grabbed Naomi and sat her down not far from where Taren stood.

"Stay by me, little Naomi," he said. "Do not be afraid. I will listen."

Aristatolis stood before the group and called everyone to order. Everyone silenced, immediately ready for instruction. A calm humming noise covered the yard like a thin blanket. The hum—the calling of the magic.

Inside Taren's body, the resonating began. Even though he wasn't participating, his body knew how to respond. Naomi looked around, watching the others. Taren wondered if she felt it, if her magic wanted to come out, or could be forced.

Aristatolis sat before the group, cross-legged and focused, his arms moving motion upon motion, up and down in large circles, adding complexity to the patterns.

Naomi didn't move with the others but watched the strange actions.

Aristatolis brought his hands to his lap and began rubbing them together, feeling the friction and the energy. It didn't take long until the palms of his hands began to glow.

"This creates the energy," Micah narrated. "Try."

Taren grew anxious as Naomi started to rub her hands together. The noise around them sought out the humming and fused together with the low chants, building a harmonious sound. The rubbing slowed as the hands glowed around her. Everyone raised their palms high into the sky, and then with a sharp sound, smacked them down to the earth. The ground rumbled.

Naomi looked startled but curious. This ritual went on a few more times: rubbing, humming, and slapping the ground.

Taren held back, cautious not to push his magic too far, remembering the sting from last night. His body wasn't quick to forget, and the pain still lingered in his system—alarming, yet dangerously compelling.

Several of the others' hands glowed—red, green, white—to reflect their magic. Micah's hands were bright red and rested softly on the ground, tiny curls of dust swirling around his fingers. Landon sat in the middle near the front, his hands and arms bluish-white, little sparks dancing away from his fingers. Katia sat close to Landon. Her hands didn't emit much glow but tiny ice crystals had formed around her fingertips.

"Please, try," Micah encouraged Naomi.

Naomi started with her hands, rubbing them gently together as if washing them. She raised them with the others, and then smacked them to the ground.

Nothing happened.

Taren's curiosity rose. Her magic inside didn't want to be found. *But why?*

Naomi tried again. Still the same, no magic—at least, nothing Taren could read.

"Is there something wrong with me?" Naomi asked Micah. "Am I doing it wrong?"

"You need to free your mind of this world. Separate body, mind, and magic. You need to believe in the abilities and focus on bringing out the fibers of magic."

Sound logic, Taren thought.

"Concentrate, feel it, believe it . . ." Micah muttered as dust came up from the ground in tight, neat spirals around his hands.

Naomi took in a deep breath and tried again.

Taren wasn't the only one who took notice of her frustration. Aristatolis looked over and saw the struggle to connect to her magic. A small wave of greedy anticipation crossed through Taren's thoughts. If anyone could get the magic to respond, it would be Aristatolis.

Several of the others stopped to watch what was happening, even her friends.

"Child, look at me," Aristatolis said, as he sat quietly in front of her.

Naomi looked nervous. "I don't know if I like this."

Aristatolis grabbed Naomi's hands. "Relax, dear one." He started to rub her hands together.

It started slowly, her hands turning the color of a magnificent opal. Different colors mixed together like the underlining of a seashell. The hum in the air changed its tone—higher and more intense. Aristatolis didn't stop but kept going, probably as greedy as Taren felt. The yard fell silent while everyone watched.

Naomi held Aristatolis' gaze, looking terrified.

Taren pushed his magic and read what Aristatolis could feel.

Aristatolis had sight of the magic within her, and Taren's own greediness envied him the closeness, wanting it for his own.

Then he saw it—a stream of light coming from her hands, wrapping around her fingers, purple and blue. Ribbons weaved out and around each other—a spark, a green flash from her fingertips.

"Stop it! Stop it!" Naomi cried.

The light spread up from her hands, brighter and brighter, moving past her hands to Aristatolis'. Swirling fingers of light wrapped upward.

Aristatolis, still grasping her hands, raised them into the air. Naomi fought the motion.

Her hands, still held in Aristatolis' grip, smacked the ground. The earth shook violently. The wooden structures swayed as if in an earthquake.

Taren watched in shock.

Katia ran to Naomi's side. "Aristatolis! Stop!" She grasped his hands, trying to pull him off. Landon soon arrived, helping free Naomi from the energy force that bound the two together. Aristatolis succumbed and lost his grip, falling to the ground, silent.

No one seemed to know what to do. Taren's greed compelled him to act. He ran to Aristatolis and pressed down on his heart. The rapid beats weren't normal. He looked up at Landon.

"Go get Lytte!"

Several of the boys ran towards Lytte's tent. Landon turned his attention to Aristatolis, touching his face and trying to feel his breathing.

"What happened?"

Taren didn't answer, but listened to the violent pulsing in Aristatolis, the familiar pain it created, the poison spreading through his body.

Behind them, Katia glanced at Naomi. "Are you okay?"

Naomi didn't answer but turned and ran away.

~⁕~

. . . surging power.

. . . blinding light.

Naomi went straight to her tent. She couldn't believe what had just happened. The greed pulsing through her body, the screaming invasion. Reynolds had meant well when he left her here, but she shouldn't be around the others.

. . . continual pounding
. . . throbbing
. . . roaring inside.

Thump . . . Thump . . .

She couldn't calm down. It terrified her, what her body wanted to do. The residue still filled her veins, coursing through her system like an addictive drug. She wanted more, though she knew of the hidden danger. She had to leave, get out before she did something she would regret. Innocent people could be hurt because of the unbridled magic she had and didn't know how to control.

She grabbed what she could in a moment—just the bare essentials, her cloak, a little food.

Naomi heard voices coming. She had no time. She ran out the door and down into the forest.

. . . Warm tingles on her bare feet.

Push . . . run!

It didn't matter how far she went. She didn't care as long as she got away safely. She heard her name called again and again—sometimes close, sometimes far away. Farther and farther she ran, till her heart thumped loudly in her chest.

. . . He wants us.

. . . Forcing us from safety.

. . . Stealing the light!

If she had to, she would go back through the Blackwoods. The horror of what she had done to Aristatolis in the yard seemed much worse than the monsters in the woods.

At a clearing of trees, she slowed down, not believing what lay before her. The Willows come back into view, but she approached the other side of the camp, by Lytte's tent.

She could see a few boys in the yard, talking fast, excited about her interruption of the peace.

She took off in the opposite direction as fast as she could. All she had to do was run away, but she watched the small thatched roof of the mess hall come into view.

. . . No!

Get us away!

She felt the trap, the continual circling and never escaping. So this was the prison the others mentioned. She quickly turned and ran back into the woods, searching for an exit. The forest thickened. She had difficulty maneuvering through tangles and trees. Voices approached not far from her. She stopped and hid behind some shrubbery.

"It doesn't matter," the voice called out; Katia, arguing with Landon again.

"Are you kidding?" Landon exclaimed. "She has to be the most powerful person I've ever seen. Honestly, you think she didn't know that?"

"Yes. But it doesn't matter. We have to find her before she does something stupid."

"Like what? Trying to kill one of the greatest teachers I've ever met? Is that what you mean by stupid?"

"It wasn't her fault!"

"Maybe not, but I don't understand how you can live all your life without the faintest knowledge you possess power like that."

"I don't know. I never got to ask her."

"She is close," Micah squeaked from nearby. "Quiet, I hear her heart fluttering."

Naomi grimaced. Of course. She had forgotten Micah could hear heartbeats. Regardless of how far she might travel, they would find her anyway. She looked up and saw the three looking down at her as she huddled under a bush.

"What are you doing?" Katia asked.

Embarrassed at having been found so easily, Naomi sat up. "Trying to get out of here."

Katia smiled. "Nice try. I think my first attempt I circled the camp twelve times before I gave up."

"What do you mean?"

"We can't leave," Landon informed her. "We're trapped here like prisoners. Every pathway out leads you right back in."

"So, if every way I go leads the way back, how did I get in the camp in the first place?"

"Oh, there is a way out," Micah spoke up. "We just have not found it yet."

Despair ran through her. She couldn't do anything. She had to go back and face the reality of what had happened.

"Come on." Landon stuck out his hand to help her up. "Let's get back before they start hunting us."

"Have you really never seen anything like . . . I mean, what I did to . . . ?" She trailed off, afraid of what the answer might be.

All three shook their heads.

"What is wrong with me?" she uttered more to herself than to anyone else.

Katia sat next to her. "Are you kidding me? Naomi, I have been working for years on my magic, waiting for something like that to happen with me, and you did it on your first day. It was incredible!"

Landon agreed. "It wasn't just what happened, but more the possibility of what could happen. You know?"

Naomi shook her head.

Micah approached, lifting her chin so she could see into his deep sapphire blue eyes. "You are more than what you believe." His voice no longer squeaked with unbridled enthusiasm but was calm and soothing, more grown-up and fatherly. "I can feel the same fibers of your magic that are in mine, but, also different, much more complex."

Frustration overwhelmed her. "I don't know how to use it. I didn't even know I had it!"

"Aristatolis will know," Katia spoke up.

"No. I almost killed him today."

"Not on purpose. He'll overlook that. I think you might've even impressed him."

Naomi just glared. How absurd. No one in their right mind would want anything to do with her, Aristatolis more than anyone.

Micah frowned, looking into the distance. "I hear shouting. We need to go. Bad things can happen when the truth is not there to speak."

Landon explained. "Rumors will start about you, and that could be bad."

He helped Naomi up, then attempted to help Katia, but she was already standing. "Too late. Maybe next time."

"Which way is camp?" Naomi called after her.

"It really doesn't matter, does it?" She walked off in a huff.

Landon leaned closer to Naomi. "What's wrong with her?"

Naomi half-smiled. She knew; it was one of the unwritten laws between girls that boys would never understand.

Landon stood out. His chiseled dark features would make any girl look twice. His devoting so much time and care to Naomi must be driving Katia mad. Of course, she liked the attention, too, but Katia didn't need to worry. Naomi's interests lay elsewhere.

They walked back to the camp, entering through the south side by the mess hall. Some of the boys saw them return and called to the others. A commotion of voices began, some accusing, some curious.

As they approached the yard, packs of boys watched her pass. Naomi stiffened. They already thought she was strange enough; this certainly wouldn't help.

The shouting and pointing toward the crew soon became hostile.

"Shut it!" Landon shouted. "All of you!!"

Most of the boys settled down. Only a few kept pointing and murmuring.

"Naomi is just like us! She is still human. It's time to grow up and stop looking at her like she's not. If everyone is warmed up, you should be doing your movements now."

Lytte appeared out of nowhere and stood like a statue, his hands raised high, and the crowd quieted.

"Landon will lead you for the time being," Lytte spoke, his voice commanding and deep, unusual for him. "Movements!"

Shaken back to their senses, the boys formed into groups to practice sparring with each other.

"Naomi, come with me. Micah, you, too." Lytte stopped and turned to the group. "Taren! I need you also."

One of the boys came forward. Naomi's insides twisted as he approached. Tall, lean, brooding, with an intimidating presence, he wore an unreadable expression.

"What about me?" Katia pleaded, turning to Lytte.

"I believe you have Movements."

Katia sulked.

Naomi lowered her head and walked next to Lytte, with Micah and Taren trailing behind. This couldn't be good. It was Aristatolis' fault, in all honesty. She could see his thoughts now: the hunger, the greed in his soul that wanted her magic. She hadn't been able to break the bond, and believed Aristatolis was to blame for that, too.

The inside of Lytte's tent felt stiflingly warm on such a day. Aristatolis lay where Naomi had been only the day before—on the cot, layered with blankets. His eyes open, he watched her every movement, captivated by her presence. His body did not move.

"Naomi," Lytte gestured to a seat next to Aristatolis. "Please sit. Aristatolis is very weak but needs to ask you a few questions."

Naomi obeyed. Micah and Taren stood silently in the background, watching.

The color in Aristatolis' eyes had changed a little, like two colors mixed into one; the emerald green flashed with pale light, glinting and piercing. He looked frightening, as if possessed. His already frail frame appeared withered, glistening with sweat.

"I am sorry." Aristatolis' expression intensified. He lunged toward her, a roar erupting from his chest.

Lytte reacted instantly. He placed his palms on Aristatolis' head and sent him back into unconsciousness.

Naomi felt the tears well up in her eyes. "What did I do to him?"

"I am not sure. I do not think that you have the answers he was looking for." Lytte smiled, trying to help her feel more comfortable. "Can you tell me about your experience with the magic?"

Naomi's tears ran silently. She wasn't sure where to start. "I honestly didn't know I had magic. Please, believe me. I always knew I was different, but I never believed this kind of magic existed. And I definitely didn't think I could do this."

"Do not blame yourself." Lytte placed his aging hand on her shoulder. "Please, tell me what happened."

Naomi told him what she could. The magic didn't do anything at first—it kept quiet—but when Aristatolis approached, something stirred, like a monster awakening inside her. She described how it felt, the pulsing and hunger, crawling its way to the surface of her skin, its safety now compromised. Naomi had been given a vision into Aristatolis's magic—its desires and the curiosity about her own. She'd reacted with the tiniest defense, just to get him to leave her alone—not with the incredible shock that forced its way out. Naomi filled in all the details, not leaving anything out. She wanted to reveal anything that might help save his life.

Lytte turned to Micah. "What did you see, Micah Shadower?"

Micah stepped forward. "Truth is its own weapon. She speaks it."

"How did it make you feel?"

Micah smiled. "It filled me completely, a warm incredible sensation. It felt familiar. Like a relative. A lovely reunion . . ." His thoughts seemed to drift into a different realm of thought.

"Taren. What did you see?"

The tall man stepped forward, moving his gaze to Naomi, his eyes pulsing with intensity. He looked puzzled as he took in her face. Naomi felt an unexplainable fear under his scrutiny, tunneling to find her secrets. With the same intensity, he turned to Lytte.

"Aristatolis was curious about the magic. Her first appearance with it appealed to him. He attempted to pierce through to her soul, trying to get to the mysteries. He found none."

"What of Naomi? What do you see?'

Taren again turned to her, staring in silence for a moment longer. "I don't know," he answered finally. "I . . . it's hard to communicate. I can see Aristatolis' side, however."

"Well, that is something." Lytte moved over to Naomi, stroking her hair again. He touched her arms and examined her more closely than before, then shook his head. "My dear, I am at a loss. The same bitter conclusion."

Naomi searched for the meaning in his words.

"I have no answers," Lytte smiled, his voice lightening again. "I know you are as curious about yourself as we are. But we may have to work out the mystery together. Taren, do you have a theory?"

"Aristatolis has been poisoned."

Naomi sat, stunned. "By me?"

"I believe," Lytte intervened, "that he was not prepared for your magic and let it penetrate deep within himself before letting go, leaving a lethal dose in his system. He seems possessed, and may even have cravings for more. Is that right?"

Taren agreed.

"Tell me about the magic, Taren?"

Taren flinched and turned his head back toward Naomi. "It's . . . very . . ." He tried again to concentrate. ". . . violent. Hostile to the host. Pure and complex. There is no stain, no illusion."

Reynolds had been completely right, Naomi realized bitterly. He had known of the dangers, but she hadn't realized it until she could see it for herself. "I had no idea. I don't know what to do."

Lytte carefully thought his answer through. "I think this will be your first lesson."

"Oh . . . no," Naomi stumbled back. "I'm too dangerous."

Lytte's voice filled with tenderness. "I'm sorry if you are uncomfortable with your newfound magic, but in order to save Aristatolis' life, you will need to believe in yourself, in your abilities, and in your magic."

"I can't . . ." She shook her head, scared and confused. "How am I supposed to do that? It exploded out of me today."

"That was not all your doing. As we have already discussed, it was Aristatolis' own fault."

"That doesn't help my confidence."

"I think that no one is in danger of your magic."

Taren's head lifted at the remark, as if he questioned the statement.

Naomi crumbled. "How can you say that? I don't know what will happen if I use it."

Lytte looked deeply into her eyes. "I want to help you become a healer. Your ability to heal yourself is fascinating. If any of that power could be put forth to help others, I think it will console the monster within you."

Naomi heaved, her breath stuck somewhere in her chest. "I don't know how."

"I want you to try and think about what the magic wants to do. Now that you know it is in you, you have the power to control it. But the magic is limited in its understanding of control. You must learn to communicate with it and befriend it in order to use it. It did not want to come out of hiding today, but was forced out. That is why it showed its power of destruction. Now, let's try to use it in a way it wants to be used."

Naomi had no words. Tears trickled down her face.

Micah came forward and placed his little hand on hers. A spark of energy surged through her body. The magic alive within her purred at the touch. "Try. Find the fibers. Find the source."

Naomi stood up and paced the tent, taking deep breaths. "Okay," she said to herself. "I can do this."

Her eyes closed, her body began to relax, her heart eased, the knot in her stomach unraveled, and her brain cleared. Her thoughts traveled her recent memories—through past dreams and realms of thought. She heaved another deep sigh and she thought of her tree: her happiness and the contentment she found there, soaking in the smells of the wet wood and gently swaying in the branches, the sounds of the wind rustling the leaves, whipping around like fingers in flight.

. . . it was there . . .

She could see it—a star dazzling in the corners of her mind, calm and peaceful. Beautiful streams of light danced about it in a playful manner. She could smell it, like sweet winter roses bursting with fragrance as the season ended. She stretched her hand to touch it. The tickling fibers wrapped around her, and a sensation of completeness coursed through her.

Naomi felt enchanted, content, and happy. She could stay there in wonderment for the rest of time. But the thoughts of reality slipped in, and she didn't know what to do.

"Help me," she whispered, hoping to somehow understand.

We are here.' The voice seemed distant, like a whisper. The communication came not from talking, but feeling. Naomi fed from the pulsing energy, weaving in and out of the fibers of the star. She knew what she must do. She knew how she could help.

Naomi opened her eyes, the magic still close behind her eyelids. Silently, she walked back to Aristatolis and placed one hand on his neck, rubbing gently as she had for so many years on her own neck, on her own mark. She asked the magic to retrieve the poison and become whole, to take what was stolen and return it to itself.

It did so instantly. A light spark emitted from her fingers as she rubbed gently. She felt it surge back into herself and disappear.

Aristatolis awoke. His breathing and eye color had returned to normal. He blinked, adjusting to the light in the room. Then his eyes locked on Naomi, a look of peculiar speculation covering his face. Not knowing how to take it, Naomi backed away toward the tapestries.

"Incredible!" Micah yelled. "Connection!"

Taren's expression remained intense and unreadable.

Lytte's eyes swelled with tears. "Come here, child." Naomi rushed to him, like the father she'd never known. "You are indeed special."

Naomi just sobbed in his arms.

"From now on," Lytte whispered, "let us have you meditate in here and not in the yard, shall we?"

CHAPTER NINE
CHANGE OF PLANS

Reynolds moved as fast as he could away from the Willows, traveling east instead of south. He saw the Apex—the meeting of the enclosure of the camp and the outside world—before him. Taren didn't have a chance of finding it; its clever design had proven itself again. A pang shot across his heart as he exited, knowing he was deserting Naomi, but the choice was clear: he couldn't stay.

Going through the Blackwoods again would be a gamble, so traveling east felt like a much better route. He had promised to check on the kid for Naomi, but going south was borderline suicidal. If the guards had taken Zander to Southwick, Reynolds wouldn't be able to rescue him without a grand escape plan.

Instead, Reynolds came up with a detour, traveling to Spotswood's home.

A great time had passed without a visit to Spotswood Shadower, the eccentric ground dweller—a friend to Lytte and Jeanus, and a trusted confidant of his own. He was an uncle to someone in the camp, a boy named Micah, who Reynolds remembered as a small child. Spotswood had been gracious enough to open his home to Reynolds and Lytte after their exodus from Southwick many years ago. Reynolds hoped Spotswood might have answers to his perplexing questions about Naomi.

In Reynolds' hastily thrown-together bag hid something he hoped Spotswood could tell him more about: a medallion, like the others safely hidden in Lytte's tent, but that one Spotswood had made particularly for him. The illusions it created looked real enough, and Reynolds hoped it might help him. Naomi's strong presence might make keeping her safe very difficult. He would need all the help he could find. The magic inside the medallion slept quietly, resting in his pocket, waiting to be used.

Reynolds traveled for days and days. East made for an easier journey than any other direction. In the west stood the Ignis Mountains and the deserts, so no one traveled that way; the same could be said of the Northern Crest and the continual cold that never melted. He'd stayed away from the rivers, as smugglers and travelers sent goods to the south. But before him lay the beautiful Mount Ibis and an intricate maze of caves—the framework to the underbelly of Parbraven.

Spotswood's home, the Durundin, was cleverly situated near Lake Kolindur in an underground pocket partially beneath the water, one of the safest places Reynolds could think of. He wished he had brought Naomi here instead of leaving her with Lytte and the dangers in the camp. His anger built inside any time he thought of it, so he cleared his mind and pressed on.

The hills rolled along. Groves of trees cropped up around small townships. Reynolds belonged in these hills. The closer he came to the mountains, the more at home he felt. Soon he would cross the Ravian River and draw close to the shoreline of the lake.

As the foothills grew closer, he thought he should look for the girl, the guardian of the mountain. The townsfolk around spoke of her as legend, but Reynolds knew the truth: a daughter of Prolius roamed the hills, though he didn't know which one. Her guardian—a large bear—patrolled along the river, keeping safe the entrance to the Echoes and those who roamed inside.

He couldn't see any sign of her, no distinct bear tracks to follow. Then he felt it—the quick movement behind him. His heightened awareness sensed magic. It moved fast, following, tracking. From what he knew of bears, that wasn't one.

Quick change of plans.

Reynolds darted for the river. The forest near the edge had many fallen trees. The crossing wouldn't be hard as long as he found one. His pace accelerated, and so did the presence behind. In fact, it gained. Only one conclusion: he was being tracked. Browneyes had found him, possibly changed forms. Ahead of him lay several fallen trees across the riverbank; a good crossing. He ran for it.

A low growl came from his right side. A large black wolf darted through the shrubs and trees, weaving in and out, finding footing through the brush.

Reynolds reached the fallen trees near the catacombs at the base of the mountain and nimbly crossed as fast as he could. One leap and he would be there. A growl snarled close behind him. Reynolds landed on the other side just before he felt the pressure of the animal crush him into the rocks.

Reynolds flipped out a knife and turned. The animal's paws pressed down on his chest, a low snarl escaping behind its sharp teeth. Reynolds slashed at the animal, but each time, it kept its paws pressing down, pushing the air out of his lungs. The animal bit his hand. His weapon dropped to the earth. Reynolds winced at the deep teeth marks cutting across his wrists. He lay there, waiting for its next move.

The animal began to shake as if wet. Long fur flipped from one side to the other until it no longer looked like an animal pelt, but hair—long black braids, blurs of fabric gathered together like strings of material stitching around her body. It took only a moment for Browneyes to appear before him, her grip now firm around his knife, digging at his throat.

"How long have you been trailing me?" Reynolds demanded, out of breath.

"Not long. You tricked me." She whipped her long braids off her shoulder like a wild animal.

"No, I changed my mind." He tried again to knock the knife out of her hand but failed.

"Where's your trophy?"

Reynolds kept his focus on his enemy, his voice even. "Safe."

"Now, come on, Reyn. Why can't we be friends about this?"

Reynolds stopped struggling and thought of a plan. "When you stop trying to kill her."

Browneyes hardened her stare. "It sounds easy, not killing her, but I don't think it's possible." She pressed the knife against his skin. "But you must know, I'm putting the pieces together. You tricked me into loving you. In fact, I don't think you even cared about me. You just wanted to keep me away from her."

Reynolds didn't respond.

"I'll take it by your silence that I'm right." She smiled a wicked grin and gripped his injured wrist with her free hand. He winced as the pain shot up through his arm. "I don't think I should ever come second.

"I saw what happened to that poor girl in the Blackwoods. I saw the blood dripping down her legs. I could smell the magic. Smell it, Reynolds. Wouldn't her blood be a great addition to my collection?"

"Doesn't mean anything," he tried to say through the pain.

Browneyes twisted the blade in a circle. It bored into his skin and blood trickled down his throat. "It does when you know how to get in."

Reynolds' anger built up. With a jerk to his side, he escaped her hold. Browneyes jolted forward, still with the knife in hand. She kneed him in the back, but Reynolds rebounded off a boulder and stood on his feet, facing her.

"Fronzi!" she yelled.

He knew Browneyes might inflict minor injuries, but never seriously hurt him; she loved him too much. But her sister Fronzi hated him, and would destroy him if she could. He needed to play to his strengths.

"Why here, Browneyes?" Reynolds probed her while he still had time. He knew where he stood; the entrance to the Echoes and the caves below couldn't be far. "You wouldn't chase me here unless you had business with the underlord."

Browneyes stiffened at his accusations. "Harrow is looking for something. Something you made and hid, maybe something you stole."

Reynolds knew exactly what she meant, his secret treasure hidden safe in the Willows. "Tell your underlord I don't know anything about it."

"But I watched you exit the camp."

Reynolds played down his anxiety. "That means nothing."

"Doesn't it?" Browneyes slid slightly forward like a snake ready to strike. "I know how to enter. I could go any time I wanted. I could find your treasure and your girlfriend."

She's bluffing.

Heat flushed her cheeks. "I could destroy your whole world. I could murder your girl, take her blood, and use it however I wanted. You wouldn't know she was dead. I would be such a convincing replacement." Her words pierced Reynolds's heart; overwhelmed him with guilt for his decision to lead her on as he had. "Just watch me do it."

Reynolds evaluated her expression. She was serious. He'd known the consequences of hurting her, and at the time, he hadn't cared. But Browneyes could never be near Naomi. The risk was too great.

"You know I wouldn't hurt you, Browneyes. I never meant to." "Reynolds searched for mercy in her eyes. "There's no need to take out your revenge on her for my mistakes. I'll do what you ask."

A tall silhouette appeared in the shadows, her long braids highlighted against the rock—so like her sister's.

Browneyes heaved a breath before she spoke again. "You're wrong. I think I do have the right to exact my revenge." Her head jerked to the side—a signal to act.

Reynolds knew they were going to do something unpleasant, but his mind was made up. He had to go graciously or he would never reclaim the advantage.

"I'm sorry," he whispered as he got down on his knees—the words audible to Browneyes, but intended for Naomi.

CHAPTER TEN

SILEXA

The next few weeks passed quickly for Zander. The palace ran like an enormous clockwork. Zander struggled with the pace; everyone moved so quickly. Audra stayed close to him and made sure he wasn't lost in the flurry of work around them.

His days as a servant in Southwick were filled with duty and honor. Each servant knew the importance of his job, and pride of place swelled within them. A busy hive of activity, nothing got missed or overlooked.

The lifestyle fit Zander quite well. He got used to the steadiness of the kitchen. His duties consisted of washing dishes and serving. Mildred, the head cook, also became a better friend. Under her hard, callused skin lurked a consummate professional with total devotion to her work.

She took to mothering Zander like he was a baby bird fallen out of its nest, sometimes to the point of smothering him. He liked her attention, reminiscent of how Naomi had cared for him, but he liked the quiet moments by himself, something he'd never had before.

His room became a comforting retreat. The sea had a calming effect and lulled him to sleep. He had never felt such peace as in his room, watching the waves roll back and forth. His one frequent disturbance to the calm was Audra.

After completing her routine in the kitchens, Audra began a nightly habit of visiting him before venturing to bed. Zander liked the company but was reticent to answer her probing questions.

"Ander?" she started one night, "I always feel like I'm the one talking. I really wish you would get over that speech thing of yours. Is it something you've always had?"

Zander had moved his trunk just below his window so that he could sit and watch the sea. He sat motionless, barely listening to Audra but understanding her completely. "I d-don't know."

"You must know all about me by now."

That was true. Zander had learned of her exile from her family, her sea adventures as a stowaway, the nightly raiding of the liquor from the brew house on the edge of Southwick's walls. She always had a story, and it was great entertainment.

"Are you going to tell me more about your life before here?" she prodded.

"I'm not s-s-sure," he returned. He didn't like the question. Everything was still so close to the surface and he grew sad at the thought of his old life with Naomi. Every night, Audra brought up questions about his past. He couldn't figure out her interest, and he wasn't sure if he could trust her. Maybe he could talk about something that didn't have to do with Naomi. It might satisfy her curiosity.

"My f-father is dead."

"So is mine," Audra returned. "So, what? How did he die?"

Zander shrugged his shoulders, his answer methodical. "I think he was mur . . . murdered."

Audra raised her head to look at him. "Sorry about that. Not that my father deserved to die either, but he was a stupid man. He should have known better than to trust me."

Zander's insides twisted uncomfortably. He wasn't sure how to take that response.

She began again to talk about her father and family. Zander slowly wandered back into his own world of thought, watching the sea ripple back and forth. The sun hung low on the horizon, giving off incredible colors as it set. He found the view much more interesting than what Audra prattled on about—until he heard a name that caught his attention.

"Who did y—?"

"Prince Bryant. Have you met him?"

"Briefly." Zander's mind wandered to the elusive prince, and wondered where he had been. "What did you say . . . about him?"

"He's crazy. Ever since he returned from the north, he's been acting so funny. Kender, who works out in the gardens, says he goes out there all the time, talking to himself." Audra shifted herself on his bed and kicked up her feet in the air in a playful manner. "Well, I have never liked the prince. He's completely worthless. The king doesn't care for him either."

"W-why?"

"Oh, you know, he uses people to get what he wants. It's a typical story. Of course, he's very attractive and he knows it, so he swindles and abuses others at his leisure. And he never notices all the work we do for him."

"Excuse me."

The unexpected sound of Curtis' voice startled them. He stood in the doorway. Audra gasped.

"Come now, boy," he said. "The prince would like to meet with you."

Audra smiled and stood up. "See ya." As she waved goodbye, she winked.

Zander stood and followed the tall man down the hall.

***

"Well, little squire," Curtis said, velvet and smooth. "Did you find a girlfriend?"

Zander winced at the word as he trailed behind the tall figure. His stomach tied itself in knots in his anxiety at meeting the prince again.

They traveled through a maze of hallways and grand staircases, around courtyards and through many wonderful rooms. On and on they went. Finally, they reached an enormous chamber filled wall-to-wall with pictures. Light filtered through colored glass panes in the ceiling. Beautiful rainbows reflected off the paintings hung about the room. It didn't take long for Zander to realize they were portraits of kings of long ago. He wondered about the lives they lived and the kind of rulers they were.

A long window opened up at the end of the room, revealing the silhouette of a figure whose broad shoulders stood out unmistakably. "Thank you, Curtis," Bryant said, more to the window than to anyone else. "You may leave."

"Sire," Curtis answered, his tone low and serious, "I think you may need my counsel."

"No, I don't think so." Bryant turned to face them. "The business I have with the lad does not concern my business with you. I wish to be alone with him."

"Excuse me, sire, but I think—"

"Alone, Curtis." The command had an uncomfortable sharpness to it, clearly communicating his desires.

Curtis bowed low, the tip of his long hat nearly touching the ground. As he rose up, he glared briefly at Zander before leaving the room.

Bryant turned back to the window. Zander took in his appearance: finely dressed in rich jewels and fabrics, including a long, blue cloak—similar to one he wore when Zander first met him in the dungeons, draped from the embroidered collar of his silk-spun tunic.

Silence filled the room as Zander waited for direction.

"Please, come here, boy."

Zander walked forward until he stood next to him, not sure what the prince had been looking at until he pressed his forehead to the glass.

The view of the city looked incredible from that height. Like a sea of gold, winding streets lined with lampposts wrapped the glorious buildings with their tiled roofs and cobblestone streets, and ornate gardens with pathways of green foliage and colored flowers of all kinds. From that height, people looked like ants, scurrying to their destinations.

"Wow . . ." escaped Zander's lips.

"Well," Bryant stated, impressed. "I knew you would rediscover your voice after a while. I didn't expect so soon. Must have been the bath."

Zander looked away from the city to glance at his new master. It confused him why the prince took such an interest in him.

The smile on Bryant's face faded after a moment. "So, how do you like your home so far? I tried to get you one of the nicer rooms, but there isn't much of a choice down there."

Zander fitted on a smile and nodded. "V-very n-nice. Thank you."

Bryant's big hand gave his shoulder a playful smack. "You like the view? This is Southwick, home of the kings of Parbraven. When the fires are lit at night, it looks like the starry sky reflecting on the water. Have you ever been to Southwick before?"

Zander shook his head.

"That doesn't surprise me," he muttered under his breath. "Sharlot is a waste of a town in my opinion." He heaved a sigh and turned away from the window. "Come over here, boy."

He led Zander to a set of finely carved benches facing a portrait of a tall, thin, severe-looking man. "I am glad we are alone now." The prince's words sounded unnatural and hurried. "There are a few things of grave importance that I want to talk to you about. First . . ."

He paused as if making a decision at the spur of the moment.

"Zander, know that I had nothing to do with your father's death. The fires were lit to get his attention, but I never imagined the man would be so insane as to lock himself inside."

Zander did not like hearing this. The inside of his chest hurt.

"We weren't there for him anyway. We were looking for a girl. What was her name again? Naomi? I am positive you know something about her. Tell me."

Zander considered the question. What would he want to know? A quick sear of pain crossed his heart every time he thought of her. "I," he started. "I m-miss her."

"Please, that is not what I asked."

Zander swallowed the lump in his throat. "She took c-care of me. I loved being by . . . h-her. Knowing h-her."

A half-smile appeared on Bryant's face. "She is interesting to me, in more ways than one. You will understand why over time."

He smoothed the ends of his hair. "Zander, I brought you up from the dungeons for a special purpose. That day in Sharlot, the day my guards captured you, I was riding in the caravan with a very special girl. Most people cannot see her, but you did. And this is very important." He leaned over so his voice did not carry across the hall. "She is here with me. Her name is Silexa, and I need you to be her special attendant."

Zander froze. "M-me?" he stammered. He remembered the girl all too well, almost like a dream, ethereal and enchanting, with a short, black moppet of hair and a star exactly like the one Naomi had on her neck.

"As I said, not everyone can see her, but some can, and I don't know who. It's not safe for her out in the palace anymore. She needs company."

Zander's heart quickened as he considered what had been asked of him. He liked the kitchens and didn't feel qualified for an important assignment.

Bryant watched the boy's reaction carefully. "There will be a big feast soon, and she is one of our special guests. Those who have been invited to this feast can see her, like you can. I want you to stay with her and attend to her every wish. You do not need to speak to her. Don't disappoint me."

Zander looked up. He nodded obediently, and the prince smiled.

"Good, that's settled." He stood up. "Come with me, my boy. I will introduce you."

~--*--~

Bryant led Zander through the palace. All the while, the prince looked focused, yet nervous.

They turned a corner and wound up a flight of narrow stairs. This part of the palace looked different, not as ornate as the other halls and rooms Zander had seen. No artwork hung on the walls and no fancy flowers filled the air with fragrance. It seemed small and forgotten.

"Silexa's security is my highest priority, so everything about her, including your duty to her, must be kept a secret. Tell anyone and you're back to your life in the dungeon, understand?"

Zander nodded, although his insides twisted around, making him feel slightly nauseous.

"I do not want you talking to her," Bryant continued. "I'm sure you may have many questions you want to ask, but don't." He stopped at the top of the staircase and turned to face Zander. "Only people who have been exposed to powerful magic can recognize who she is. Was your mother a sorcerer, or did she possess any magical ability?"

Zander's thoughts confused him. "I don't . . . She d-died when I . . ."

"Hmm." The prince stroked his chin, thinking. "Ah, well, never mind." He started down a hallway which led to a wide, wooden door with steel hinges on either side.

The door opened to another corridor, darker and smelling of dust. Old tapestries, forgotten and torn, lined the walls. The hall looked so majestic, it seemed hard to believe no one used it, but the dust indicated a hideaway long forgotten.

"Where are . . .?" Zander started but lost his voice.

"This is the forgotten end of Southwick. I used to love sneaking here when I was younger," Bryant reminisced. "When my father became king and we moved into the palace, I was determined to explore every bit of it. I found a room that I made my own, and I put all my treasures there."

Bryant stopped, narrowing his eyes toward Zander. "Not a word of this to anyone," he demanded. But the tone of his voice softened. "I trust you, Zan. I know you will be loyal. Do you think you can find your way here?"

Zander didn't know if he could, but he obediently nodded.

"Here we are." Bryant stopped at the third tapestry and drew it to one side, revealing a secret passageway.

Behind the drapery hid the opening to a tunnel, small and narrow. Broken cobwebs clung to Zander and Bryant as they passed through, one behind the other. The end of the tunnel opened into a long room, filled with covered windows on the ceiling, allowing very little light to enter, like muted sunlight on a cloudy day. A door stood at the end of the room—and before it, a withered, small man.

The bizarre figure at the door stood at attention as they approached.

"Good evening, Matlock. How is she today?"

"Very well, your lordship." The man answered in a hissing voice, adding to his strange appearance. Zander didn't want to look at him; fresh, visible scars and sores covered the man's face, the deep puss pockets terrifying and disturbing.

"Good, thank you." Bryant clapped his hand on his shoulder. "We won't be long. Just a night cap, that's all."

"Very well." With scarred, deformed hands, Matlock opened the intricate locks on the door—very extensive, for someone intended to be a guest. Zander wondered whether she was a prisoner, hidden away in secret.

Entering the room beyond the door revealed a dramatic contrast. Zander gazed at the stunning chamber, with large, wooden carvings in every crevice and corner—masterpieces from a former age. Fine silks draped the walls, strung floor to ceiling, filling the space with color and warmth. Tiny lit candles sparkled around a large chandelier hanging in the center of the room. Even the air felt different, filled with the sweetest aromas.

And there she was.

Zander recognized the girl from the market. She sat in the middle of a curtain-draped bed with her knees tucked to her chin, revealing her delicate feet. Her dress wrapped about her slender figure, while her hair, short and black, swirled neatly around her head. The ice-blue tones of the dress complemented her fresh white skin and eyes, blue as the palest sky. She watched them in silence from the bed.

"Good evening, my lady," Bryant's voice brightened at the sight of her. "I trust you are well."

"I am," she said, her voice soothing like warm milk.

The prince smiled before speaking again. "Here he is, just like you requested."

The girl slid her feet down the bed and sat on the edge. "I'm not sure what you mean. I did not ask for a boy."

"Zander Bucklingdown, this is Silexa. Zander is my new page and will be attending you during your stay. He will keep you company."

This time Silexa laughed. "This is your solution to my loneliness?"

Zander didn't know what to do next, so he gave an awkward bow to the lady.

She made no movement to greet him, but it seemed her eyes smiled back. "You can see me?" she asked, melting him with her voice.

"Sadly, he is a mute, but very obedient." Bryant eyed Zander, who swallowed hard. "I'd like Zander to accompany you to the Autumnal Feast."

"Why do I need accompanying, Bryant? Matlock is good enough."

"Matlock will not be attending. He is not dressed for the occasion."

Her musical laugh, endearing and lovely, filled the room with warmth.

"My lady." The tone in Bryant's voice changed, surprising Zander greatly—no longer sharp or harsh, but gentle. He left Zander's side and walked to where Silexa sat with her feet dangling off the bed. "Aren't your feet cold?"

"There is not much point in slippers if you cannot walk the palace." Silexa smiled playfully.

Bryant picked up her delicate hand and stroked it. "My father is here. He returned this afternoon. Sharrod will soon follow. I did as I promised, but I fear for your safety."

Silexa said nothing to this, simply moved her other hand to his face. "I am not worried."

"But I am. I cannot tell you what Sharrod will do, but I am sure he knows who you are. I can only blame myself for that."

Zander watched the gentle play between them before Silexa rested her eyes on him, making him blush. "Thank you for Zander."

"He will be loyal to you, I promise." Bryant lifted her head, giving her a sweet kiss on her lips.

Zander now understood at least part of Bryant's anxieties. He was in love with this girl, but it had to be a secret. The responsibility weighed on his shoulders.

"I must go talk with Curtis." Bryant stood again, still holding Silexa's hand. "I will be back soon. That should give the two of you enough time to get acquainted." He kissed her palm, and then turned back to Zander.

"Not a word," he whispered, pointing directly at Zander's lips.

Zander shook his head in reply.

Bryant smiled and rubbed Zander's head as he left.

An uncomfortable silence settled on Zander and Silexa. She stared at him. Sliding back into the middle of the bed, she laid her head on a cushion, still looking at him.

"Bryant is worried people will find out about us," she said after a moment. "But I am curious about you. You are not a mute, and I wouldn't want you to go against your word. So, if you will not speak to me, will you at least nod?"

Zander thought about it for a moment, not wanting to break trust with Bryant, but considered her words. He slowly nodded.

"Good." She smiled. "Please, come sit by me." She held out her arms and he approached at her invitation.

The soft bed lay covered with intricate embroidery that spiraled around the silk blankets. Zander had never known such elaborate luxury. He felt his dirty servant hands unworthy to touch anything so fine.

"Please, come up. I am not someone to be afraid of."

He climbed on the bed and sat across from her.

"Now," she started, sitting up to better look at him. "How old are you Zander? Twelve?"

He nodded his head.

"You are not from around here, are you?"

He shook his head.

"I can't say I am either." Silexa took his hand, calming him. "Not really. I lived here when I was very young, but I do not remember much. I feel like a stranger here. We can both be strangers together."

Zander felt awkward having the girl's skin against his. Only Naomi had shown him such kindness. He yearned to have her here with him.

Silexa saw his discomfort and let go. "I won't hurt you. I want us to be friends."

In spite of his best efforts, his eyes welled up.

"You have been through a lot."

Zander nodded his head.

She reached over and enveloped him with her arms, "You are safe here with me, Zander. I will take care of you."

He silently sobbed on her shoulder. She cradled him in her arms, and the warmth of her skin comforted him.

Though wet with tears, Zander's eyes didn't miss Silexa's scar as it sparkled like diamonds, glowing white on her neck. He gasped, lifting his head in surprise.

Silexa smiled. "Please don't be frightened." The white light began to fade, vanishing completely.

Zander pointed to the scar on her neck.

"Don't worry about that. It's just a scar."

Zander recognized the mark—exactly like Naomi's. The madness of the last few weeks flooded his memory.

She looked down, sadness filling her face. "I do wonder how you can see me, but I'm so glad." She raised her eyes to him in an innocent way, stealing Zander's heart immediately.

"I must get ready for bed." She stood, somehow even more beautiful at her full height. "Will you wait for me here?"

Zander nodded and waited as Silexa slipped behind a screen. Her appearance rendered him speechless.

Not only did the lovely nightgown in silks of blue and purple catch his eye, but she *glowed*, her light robe radiating in words he couldn't describe.

"You look beautiful." The voice came from behind Zander, echoing his thoughts. Bryant walked to Silexa and they embraced, as he stroked her hair.

"Come, Zan." Bryant sounded disheartened. "I will return you."

"Before you leave, Zander, I'd like to give you something." Silexa walked to her bed, unwrapping a long, slender piece of her silken bed hangings. "This is a special gift for you." Draping it around his neck, she kissed him on the cheek. "Shadesilk. It will help protect you, keep the bad men from finding you. We will meet again tomorrow."

Confusion flooded Zander's brain. The material, the silk, was so familiar. Naomi's face flashed back into his mind: she had always worn a scarf, just like this one.

Zander remained quiet during their stroll back to his quarters. Bryant led him along until they arrived in a courtyard, surrounded by high stone archways. Tropical trees of the south filled the air with sweet fragrances of orange and sandalwood. A light breeze made its merry way down the long path and wound around the palace wall, swirling dainty fallen leaves near Bryant's feet—who made no move to take a confused Zander any further.

"She is in danger here," Bryant said suddenly, his even voice filled with worry. "My father is not a good man. He is being used by a man named Sharrod who wants his power. Do you know Sharrod?"

Surprised at having secured the prince's confidence, Zander slowly shook his head.

Bryant paced back and forth, apparently deep in thought. "Sharrod is searching for stones. There was a story of a girl who lived in the snowy tundra with a wolf, and she was said to have one. So they sent me to the Northern Crest to find it."

Bryant stopped, distracted by the wind as it picked up again, blowing the leaves in sweeping circles.

"I found wolf tracks," he continued. "They were so large. Many different times I thought I saw her, but I found myself wandering around in the snow—lost, running out of food, slowly freezing to death." He took a breath. "And then she found me. She saved my life. The wolf is her guardian, and it brought us food. I owe her my life, and this is what I have done to her."

Zander watched and listened, knowing Bryant's tender recollections required a moment to recover.

"My father was right. She does carry one of the stones—all of her sisters do. But it's not something they can hand over to Sharrod. They're bound to them. If they separate from the stones, they slowly die."

"What . . ." Zander started. Bryant stopped his pacing to listen. "What does Sha . . . rod wa-want with the stones?"

"Each one has some element that it can control." Bryant looked up at the sky. Zander followed his gaze, noticing for the first time the cloudy, stormy sky.

"There is a girl here," Bryant continued. "A sister of Silexa's—I don't know her name. She is coming to the feast but not as a guest. I think Sharrod already has her stone."

"The w-wind?" Zander guessed, remembering the strange turbulence of the skies.

Bryant sunk helpless. "I didn't expect to fall in love with Silexa, and now I have sentenced her to die. She knows it. She is prepared." Bryant's head turned sharply to face Zander. "I can't be around her. My father knows she's here and knows I am keeping her hidden. I have to keep her safe. When the feast comes, we'll figure out what to do. But we can't let her die."

Bryant stood again. "I trust you. I know your heart. You've met her. You love her, too, I know. Say you will protect her."

Zander nodded, uncertain about the huge task before him, but knowing he would do anything for Silexa.

Bryant grabbed him by the shoulders, his emotions barely controlled. "You are a valiant servant. I knew you would do me good."

CHAPTER ELEVEN
OVERHEARD

Sweeping . . .

Traveling . . .

Flying over clouds . . .

. . . to the tops of the mountains.
The winds push!
Change and move direction
. . . Erratic
. . . Harsh
. . . Uncontrolled

Move down through the mountains.

. . . through tunnels and caves

Little people . . .
. . . Dressed in white
. . . blue eyes pierce the darkness
Shield from the approaching light.

"Where is Harrow?"

A woman, long braids down her back
. . . pointed ears.

Stops before an ancient man.
. . . Black matted hair
. . . sunken white eyes
. . . deteriorating bones
"I am here."

. . . Surprise! . . .

"Well, done, Browneyes, I am impressed.
"Have you brought me a present?"
"As you requested."

Cruel laughter . . .
"Truth cannot hide from my eyes."
"The girl is not there. Only him."

"No matter.
"He is the perfect bait.
"Bring him forward."

Another emerges, gripping a prisoner.

"Glad to see you well, Hawk.
"Perhaps you can finally return to me what you have stolen."

"I am not a thief, Harrow."
"Then where is my medallion?"
"I do not know."
. . . Thwack! . . .
. . . Laughter . . .

The man falls to his knees.
Hands bound.

"It makes no difference.
"That is not what I brought you here for.
"Spies informed me of the girl."

Heaving . . .
"What girl?"

"Do not take me for a fool, Reynolds Fairborne.
"I know all about your encounter in the Blackwoods.
"What value is she to you, thief?
"Tell me!"

Silence . . .

"Oh, I believe we have found a sore spot."
Another blow to the head . . .
Cringe in pain!

"I have my own theory of who she may be."
Gasping . . .
"What do you want from me?"

"Not from you. Her."
The ancient wizard stops.
. . . sniff . . . sniff . . .
Eyes searching . . .
A peculiar smile . . .
"Ah, through space and earth,
"I feel the magic is here . . . watching."
"What do you mean?"

"I think she has found you."

. . . Strange, white eyes pierce directly into the sight . . .

Reynolds struggles . . . searching
Turns into darkness . . .

Whisper . . .
". . . Naomi . . ."

. . . Blackness . . .

Naomi sat up, sweating, her heart pounding hard, the vision of Reynolds' smooth features still visible in her head. The dream looked real, like when the men had come for Malindra. She watched it happen right before her very eyes.

Reynolds was in danger. The pain of his decision to leave stung sharp in her chest. Just the sight of him hurt. He had left her here protected in the trees, but she didn't feel safe without him. Now his life was in danger because of her, and she had no way to save him. She had thought of him every day since he left—days, weeks, she couldn't remember. Time no longer held relevance there.

Naomi glanced around. Everything in the tent looked the same, but somehow she felt she was in a foreign place. Katia slept soundly across from her. Her deep breathing broke the silence and made the confusion of reality even stranger than before.

Naomi's connection with Reynolds might have cost him his life; her heart skipped at the notion. Her mind drifted to him often, imagining a relationship that grew stronger with every thought. Reynolds filled an empty space she never knew she had, and she couldn't allow it to disappear.

Cool night air bit near her ears and cheeks before Naomi lay back down, covering herself with thick animal skins, and deciphered the dream—or rather, the vision she had witnessed. She pictured Reynolds's face: in a deep mountain, surrounded by little people dressed in white; a decrepit sorcerer surging with magic, holding a staff of light, his eyes white as snow.

People surrounded Reynolds, dragging him; she hadn't missed the strange pointed tip of their ears. The wizard knew of her magic. He called Reynolds a thief, claiming he had stolen a medallion. Naomi's stomach turned with nervous anxiety.

Naomi placed the pillow over her head and tried to erase the images she created in her mind: the torture Reynolds might suffer, the brutality at the hand of his captors. She would normally have written the dream down in her journal.

She closed her eyes and saw Reynolds again. He fascinated her—mysterious, maybe dangerous, but in her thoughts, he stood courageous. Every time she thought of his face, he grew more handsome, not just how he looked, but his countenance drew her in and made him more appealing.

Time passed slowly with the pillow covering her head. Her anxiety built with every breath. She lost the battle, got dressed, and left the tent, heading for some answers.

She walked down the now familiar dirt paths leading to Lytte's tent. The cool ground felt good on her bare feet. The wind picked up; her silk scarf blew gently around her neck, and she subconsciously rubbed the smooth fabric between her fingertips as she walked.

Naomi stopped just outside the opening of the tent, breathing deeply, trying to clear her head. Everything was quiet. He might be sleeping. Back and forth she paced before the entrance. So many questions flowed through her brain. Maybe she should just wander around the camp a little and check back later. But the questions were eating her away inside. She drew in a breath and stepped through the tent door.

"Why did it take you so long?" a voice called. Lytte sat cross-legged at a small, round table, looking at runes and ancient stones. A little lamp burned nearby, keeping only the table and his face lit.

Naomi stared, surprised to find Lytte awake so late. "How long have you been up?"

"I am connected with the outside world, much like you." His voice felt comforting. "Come, sit."

Naomi crossed the room and knelt across from her mentor. "So, you know about my dream?"

"Dream? No." Lytte's piercing, steely, gray eyes seeming to peer into her soul.

Naomi sat, confused. "Then how did you know I would come?"

"I think we will cross that bridge eventually." Lytte continued to examine the stones thrown haphazardly around a dark, red cloth. "I am very curious about your dream. Please, tell me."

Naomi told Lytte what she remembered. The old man named Harrow, Reynolds, the pointy-eared people, the weird ones in white, and the conversation that plagued her.

Lytte lifted his head, listening.

"What you saw was indeed real, not merely a dream," he explained as soon as she finished. "I believe you saw the Ibis Mountains in the east. They are filled with hollow caves and caverns. Many call them the Echoes. The little ones in white you speak of are the Arenmas, or Echo People. Their home is Mount Ibis. They have lived there for centuries and have adapted their life to the darkness, knowing very little of the outside world." Lytte measured Naomi's expressions before he continued. "Does that sound right?"

"Yes."

Lytte smiled. "Your friend Micah is a descendent of the Arenmas. His uncle, Spotswood Shadower, is a friend of mine, and they are the only surviving Shadowers. They left Ibis for a life on the surface. Their skin color is a reaction to the elements they had never encountered before."

"How sad." Naomi sighed, wrapping her finger in her scarf as she listened to the wind blow around the tent. "Do you think Reynolds is in danger?"

Lytte stopped and scratched his beard in thought. He glanced back at Naomi. "I think it might be wise to look at why he's in danger."

Naomi knew Lytte's style now; he always pushed her to find the answers to her own questions with logic and reason. "He is captured. They think he's a thief."

"Do you think he's a thief?"

"Of course not."

"But do you know Reynolds well enough to make a judgment?"

Lytte's question tested her trust. "If Reynolds needed something like food, he might pilfer, but this was different. I saw the greediness. This was something important."

Lytte's face lit with her understanding. "Harrow is looking for something important he thinks Reynolds has. What do you think that could be?"

Naomi gulped. "Is it me?"

A small chuckled escaped from Lytte's lips. "Harrow knows about the incident in the Blackwoods. He has spies, sweet one."

Naomi sat in resignation. "It's because of me. Reynolds is in trouble because of me, and I don't even know why he kept me safe."

"The evidence is in the dream," Lytte evaluated. "Your magic is precious and he knows this. I think he is still trying to protect you from afar."

Naomi put her head down, keeping focus on the dream and not her own feelings for Reynolds, though Lytte's words felt comforting. "Can you tell me who the man is with the staff?"

"Harrow, an underlord of Parbraven . . . a keeper of secrets." Lytte shuffled in his seat to better look at Naomi. "Harrow is a worry, but not as much as others. The real concern isn't Harrow—it's the wind."

"The wind?"

Lytte lifted his head, listening to the outside world. "You talked about the wind and rain sweeping through the cave. That is what frightens me. The winds have changed."

"What do you mean?"

"This is a sign that confirms my fears." Lytte's eyes shifted in a peculiar manner. "One of the stones has been found."

Naomi sat back. "The stones?"

"Yes. Harrow is looking for the stones, but not for himself, for someone else. He may think you have something to do with it."

"Can I ask about the stone?"

"Not tonight," Lytte assumed in his usual enigmatic manner, and returned to reading the runes.

Nobody mentioned the difference in the direction of the wind or the gloomy skies, although everyone felt the shift. The air even smelled different. The changing breeze swirled throughout the camp, whipping down and around and through every tree and branch. The conflict with the winds and the trees displayed the evidence that the struggle between power and control had begun.

Landon, Katia, and Micah found Naomi, who sat in pensive thought near a tree in the corner of the yard, all alone. Naomi hadn't gone back to sleep. She'd stayed awake, thinking until morning, her mind made up. Still, the words froze in her mouth as they sat before her, waiting for her to explain her decision.

"Do you think we'll have activities in the yard today?" Landon asked. "I know Aristatolis is anxious to get us back to full strength since his absence. Though, I still think I've done pretty well on my own."

Naomi felt conflicted whether she should involve her friends or go alone. Her internal crisis took over every other thought. Even if she could hear their mundane conversation, she wasn't really listening. Here she had a great opportunity to bring up her plans, but the words stuck in her mouth. *Do it now*, she told herself. Her mouth went dry and her palms started to sweat.

Katia groaned. "Landon, pull-ups in the barracks doesn't make your magic better."

"Couldn't hurt."

"I'd rather not be in the rain. My ice crystals melt so much faster."

"Say," Naomi spoke up, finally getting her mouth to function, "have any of you been east?"

"I've never crossed the river," Landon returned, hardly listening. "I wouldn't even know what direction it is from here."

Katia sprawled out on the ground, looking up. "I heard a story once when I was young about a banished sorcerer who lives in the eastern mountains. He traps people in the web of caves and slowly sucks out their souls so he will never die."

"Like a spider?" Landon suggested.

"I guess."

Naomi pressed her questions further. "Have you heard of the Echoes? Lytte mentioned the place this morning, and I wondered where it was."

Micah gave a huge smile, his mood altered by the change of topic. "The Echoes! My happy heart returns there in the best of dreams."

Naomi had hoped Micah would have the information she wanted. "Do you know where it is?"

"No." Micah sighed. "I have never entered, not allowed, but my body yearns for the comfort of it."

"But how far is it from here?"

Landon eyed her. "Wait, Nam, what's going on? You're up to something."

Naomi felt her cheeks flush. "Well, I had a dream last night."

"A dream? Sister, you're getting yourself worked up over nothing."

"Dreams can be very important, you know," Katia argued.

"Dreams are nothing but delusions of our own imagination. Good luck with that." He ripped a piece of jerky apart with his teeth—the remains of breakfast.

Naomi knew Landon didn't mean any offense, but she couldn't help feeling confused. "Haven't you ever thought dreams had meanings?"

"Maybe," Katia thought out loud, "when I first was poisoned."

"That's different," Landon returned. "Those were hallucinations."

"I see this kind of thing all the time," Naomi explained, slightly embarrassed. "Some are horrible, dangerous warnings for people I love. This one bothers me and I need to find out what it means."

Micah beamed with excitement. "You want to get out."

"Seriously?" Landon looked impressed.

Naomi's cheeks colored as she slowly nodded.

The others looked shocked.

A sly grin crossed Micah's face. "The timing must be right. It is not yet. We need to be prepared."

"I don't know if I can wait," Naomi muttered in a whisper. "It's not that simple. Someone's in danger and I think I might be the reason. I'm the only one that knows."

"We're not leaving. I've tried. There's no way out." Katia whispered.

"This is suicide," Landon protested. "I'm not leaving the camp until I really know the details."

Naomi realized the grounds were filling with the others who had finished their breakfast. "Not now. Later, I promise."

Aristatolis, though still recovering from Naomi's violent magic, stood in the center of the yard. Landon, Katia, and Micah joined the others. Naomi, still shy about her experience with Aristatolis, leaned out of sight behind Landon's tall frame.

Aristatolis' voice sounded muffled under the thick trees and the swollen thunderclouds. "I have tried to teach you how to harness your own power. Today, we will warm up as a group and practice using our forces with each other. Depending on each person's specialized magic, the results will be considerably different. Combining our strengths will both confuse the enemy and make us stronger."

Groups of twos and threes began forming as Aristatolis hobbled through the crowd, instructing each on methods and dynamics.

Katia bumped her in the shoulder. "Naomi, come partner with me."

Naomi, who had decided not to join the exercise, shook her head, afraid of the monster inside her.

"We may need to know this, especially if we plan on . . . *escaping*." Katia mouthed the ending.

Naomi thought about it. Katia did have a point. She would soon need better control of her magic, whether it was here or somewhere else.

"Please?" Katia bounced on her heels like a puppy.

Naomi looked to see if Lytte had joined the activities, but he hadn't. Her insecurity escalated. She hadn't warmed up with the others since her first day in the yard. The way Lytte taught differed greatly from the grand spectacle of the yard meditations: individuals shouting and pounding until the magic felt comfortable in the circulating air.

Naomi watched Katia doing her own outlandish meditations. It looked so silly, Naomi almost laughed, but kept it to herself.

To reach her magic, Naomi talked to it, found it inside her, and persuaded it to help. She discovered very early that her magic was specialized. It wouldn't do everything she asked—it would not harm things, and it could not be used for destruction unless Naomi stood in harm's way.

A thought occurred to her: maybe Katia needed the same kind of instruction. Maybe her magic didn't like the way it awoke or was forced out. She wasn't a boy, yet she had been trained like one. Naomi's emotions controlled her magic. Maybe Katia's needed to be reached in the same way.

Naomi interrupted the other girl's concentration. "Katia? Have you ever tried talking to your magic?"

"What are you talking about?" Katia laughed.

Naomi crouched down on the ground next to where Katia sat. "I want you to try and find your magic inside yourself."

"I don't know how to do that. Aristatolis taught me to channel it through movement."

"Trust me," Naomi said again. "Close your eyes and see if you can find it."

"Okay. I'll try."

Naomi sat cross-legged across from her and settled Katia's hands together, pointing up. "Relax. Close your eyes and tell me what you can see."

Katia did as instructed. "What am I supposed to be seeing?"

"The magic is hiding somewhere inside. Can you find it?"

Katia wiggled her shoulders and tried again. She sighed a few times with no progress.

Naomi could sense Katia's frustration. Her emotions were always so close to the surface. Naomi looked at her friend's face and saw the tears forming. *Come on*, she urged. *It's near the surface*. Naomi reached over and placed her palm on the top of Katia's hands.

Then it happened—a flash of light, blinding—before it disappeared.

Katia opened her eyes, surprised. "Whoa! I saw it!"

Naomi, still touching her hands, pulled back. "So did I. Was that supposed to happen?"

"I have no idea."

"Channel again." This time Naomi did not touch her. "Do you need my help?"

Katia closed her eyes again, searching. Moments passed with nothing happening. "Come on."

She opened her eyes. "It won't stay."

"Ask it to stay."

Katia seemed skeptical. "Like it's a person?"

"Yes," Naomi answered. "It's alive and it wants to play. Ask it to stay, ask it what it wants. Be nice."

After five good attempts, Katia made a connection with her magic. "I don't know how to communicate."

"Let me see if I can help." Naomi hated seeing her friend struggle. "I will only support. It is your magic and needs to talk to you, not me. Understand?"

"Yes," Katia whispered like a little girl.

Naomi rested her palms on Katia's already cupped hands.

Behind her eyes sat her magic, waiting for her.

White, like endless fog drifting thickly around cool waters; its cool sting froze every fiber—numbed senses and tingled toes. It kissed the skin and lifted the hair on her arms and head.

The tears that threatened to come out did, and stained her face, stinging with the coolness of the air. The magic, excited by the emotion, swirled happily in a blizzarding wind.

The movement took Katia aback, but Naomi's hands tightened and urged her to continue.

Speak, Naomi instructed through her magic.

Katia calmed herself. "Thank you."

The mist seemed to smile, though thick and shapeless. It swirled again, playfully, not threatening. Katia seemed to enjoy it. "You want to play?"

Naomi's magic stood near the back, watching as a welcomed guest. The coolness encircled Katia and kissed her lightly on the cheek.

Katia's expression showed she couldn't believe it. "What should we play?"

The mist danced lightly through her hair and back down to the tip of her nose.

"Will you show me?"

The mist swirled away from her again, happy and smiling.

Naomi opened her eyes and saw Katia's tears on her face, forming small crystals. "So, what do we do?"

"Let it show us."

Katia began rubbing her hands as she always had. A light formed instantly and crystals crept from her fingertips, lacing an intricate pattern. Snowflake shapes formed and grew, weaving in and out and becoming more recognizable: legs and a body and a head. A face with wonderful, glassy eyes and soft flowing features, smiled. The woman was beautiful.

The sounds in the yard had stopped, all attention on the mesmerizing sight of the lady of ice emerging from the tips of Katia's fingers.

She stood before Katia, beaming with happiness, her eyes focused only on her; nothing and no one else existed. She mouthed, "Thank you," silently as she stretched and moved her gently flowing limbs.

Katia's tears kept flowing, washing some of the crystals away.

The Ice Queen moved gracefully, twirling and playfully lifting the sweeping dress Katia had created, seeming pleased with the air and the beauty of the world, like a young child tasting snowflakes for the first time.

The dance lasted but a moment before she bent low and kissed Katia on her forehead. The Ice Queen shattered at the touch and fell into a million crystals, showering both Katia and Naomi with tiny ice shards. Silence hovered for a few seconds before the boys began clapping with excitement.

Landon rushed over. "Amazing. How . . . It's so different." Seemingly at a loss, he hugged Katia, then immediately let go, embarrassed. "Uh, good job," he said, and quickly walked away.

Micah rushed right behind. "Katia! The earth smiles in delight of the life you have made."

Naomi blinked a few times before brushing the ice from her body. She was surprised. First, at what she had witnessed and second, that she had been right about the magic. Katia needed to understand it on an emotional level.

Katia smiled wickedly. "You were right, you know," she called to Landon.

Landon grimaced. "What are you talking about?"

She laughed. "I do freeze with my feelings."

~⊷❋⊷~

Taren watched two hooded figures creep out of the barracks after the others fell asleep. A wide grin crossed his face; he expected this. The little group of misfits had acted differently today—suspicious and secretive—ever since the incredible magic Katia displayed. Taren, who'd become very familiar with reading the patterns of her magic, watched in surprise.

He'd never seen anything like it before in the patterns; it couldn't be her magic. Naomi must have helped her. A little touch from her hand released magic Katia didn't even know she possessed. The magic read as happy—not like anything he'd felt through Katia before.

And yet, Taren felt anger in Naomi's magic, and for it to help Katia like this didn't make sense. His taste for Naomi's magic grew with every encounter.

When it was safe, Taren dropped from the tree and crept down the paths to find the group's secret meeting. The wind would be the perfect cover if anyone heard him sneaking in the dark—but he wouldn't get caught. He was too smart.

The girls' tent remained silent, aside from the sound of leaves swirling on the ground and the wind tapping quietly on the fabric. It whispered of a presence nearby. He ducked behind branches to watch. Ahead, the door flap lifted, Katia's hair reflecting a deep purple in the dull, gray light as she poked her head into the darkness. She spoke, but the distance was too great for Taren to hear what she said. He must get closer. The figures entered the tent, the flap secured tightly behind them. Small flickers of candlelight illuminated the inside.

Quickly, he slipped around the other side. Finding a small, weak spot in the canvass, he slit it with his knife enough to see a part of the group in their conversation.

"Nice place you got," Landon exclaimed. "This is downright lovely."

"I have brought some of my trinkets that might be of interest," Micah's squeak resonated.

"Is that what took you so long?" Katia sounded irritated.

"Some of the others took a while to wind down," Landon explained before Micah had a chance to talk. "Today was very exciting for them. But we can get to that later. I want to know more about this dream, Naomi.

Something must have happened—and it's something big, isn't it?"

"I didn't understand the consequence until I went to Lytte for advice. He has so much knowledge about the world."

"Did he advise you to leave?"

"No, that was my decision. He doesn't know."

Taren stiffened. He suspected they might be discussing escaping. Naomi could get him out.

"Getting out of this place isn't like picking a lock. Did your dream explain how to do it?"

"Well . . . no."

"Then what *did* your dream show you?"

Katia interrupted. "What's wrong with you? It's not like Naomi's lying to us."

"Well, maybe she is."

Taren could make out Naomi's expression in the flame. She looked affronted.

Landon continued. "How do we know? We don't see what she sees, and I think she's holding something back. I can sense it."

"Oh, you're jealous that you didn't get anywhere with your magic today," Katia retorted. "Your magic is so hard to combine with. Nothing you did today produced any success. Your illusions have no substance."

Taren smiled as the argument heated up.

"It doesn't have anything to do with that!"

"He's right." Naomi's declaration made everyone quiet.

"I am?"

"He is?"

"Yes," Naomi answered, looking fed up with the debate. "Let me explain. The dream has something to do with a man named Reynolds."

Taren's temper heated at the mention of his name.

Naomi told her companions her dream of a place called the Echoes, a strange people called Arenmas, and Harrow the underlord of Mount Ibis. She talked about the changing of the winds and how that was somehow connected to her—concepts that stretched what Taren understood about the capabilities of his own magic.

After the telling, Landon sank down next to Naomi, his face expressionless. "That's not what I expected at all."

"Were you expecting something more sensational?" Katia quipped.

"Maybe."

"The Echoes are the place of my heritage and the Arenmas, my people," Micah spoke up. "They hold a sacred place in the earth. Only something very powerful would be able to enter and direct you into the mountain. Did Lytte suggest the stones?"

"Yes, but I don't know anything about them."

"Wait! What stones?" Landon interrupted. "That wasn't in the dream."

"The winds!" Micah continued. "The Atmos stone can control storms. Someone must have found it."

"But Naomi doesn't have a stone, do you?" Katia asked.

"No."

"But this Harrow thinks one might be in the camp."

"Maybe." Naomi shook her head. "I don't know. I wish I understood the importance of the stones and what they have to do with me, but I don't. Trust me. To find the answers, I have to go to the Echoes."

"But it's a trap."

"If it's a trap, I'll need help from all of you."

"It's because of the man who rescued you, isn't it?" Katia realized aloud. "He's in the cave. That's who we need to save, right?"

Anxiety washed over Naomi's face like a fresh wound. "His name is Reynolds, and he rescued me in Sharlot and risked his life to save mine several times. I'm the only one that knows he's in danger, and I feel helpless here. I must do something."

Taren sat back, considering what he just heard. Just the mention of Reynolds clouded his thinking. He took a few breaths to level his temper before he could look back.

"That's all I needed to know," Landon broke the silence. "I'm in."

Katia smiled. "That wasn't too hard."

"So, we are agreed?" Micah pulled out items from his pocket. "Let me show you my treasures. I have a map of the outside."

"Where'd you get that?" Landon asked in surprise.

"I nicked it from someone while they were sleeping."

"Nicely done."

"Mount Ibis is there. If we're prepared, it might take us seven days; unprepared will be longer. And this," Micah continued, holding out his palm, "is my compass stone. It belongs in the Echoes and will always point to its home."

Naomi leaned over to look more closely. "How does it work?"

"Cup it in your hands and rub it gently with your thumbs."

Naomi did as he directed. The peculiar stone circled around until it pointed in a direction. "Fantastic," Naomi breathed.

"So, what about this last one?" Katia asked.

Micah hopped up with excitement. "Ah. This is my sacred treasure. The Percipus Amulet. Let me show you how it works."

Taren watched the little ground dweller place the amulet over his head and disappear.

"Let me try," Landon exclaimed.

Taren envied the magic he didn't have, craving the object so he could better understand it.

Micah reappeared as the shield of his magic lifted from around his neck. "I have never shown this to anyone before. My uncle created a few different medallions in his life. Some Lytte carries in his keeping. Of this stone, he made a brother; the other he gave away long ago. But there are flaws. Those who have seen the object or know of its power can see through it. Also, it does not work for everyone, so it can be very risky to use."

"Okay." Landon wrung his hands with anticipation. "We'll take a few days to start collecting provisions. I don't want anyone else to start suspecting anything, so we'll have to be careful. Naomi, can you find out how to get out of the camp?"

"I think so."

Taren had heard enough. Soon the two boys would be heading back to the barracks, and he needed to make a plan of his own.

CHAPTER TWELVE
INTERLOPER

Zander worked diligently the next day. From the corner of his eye, the sight of Audra made him weary. He avoided contact, knowing she would ask about last night. He was sworn to secrecy and would keep it safe, for Bryant, and for Silexa.

Promises, promises.

Zander visited Silexa every evening when he could. The conversations were light, and he kept his promise to not talk. Silexa obeyed Bryant's wish to a certain extent, but was also slightly, sweetly rebellious, asking gentle questions about his upbringing. He didn't respond verbally but nodded when she got things right. She knew he'd lived on a farm and that he loved tending to the piglets when they were born, as well as his love for picking wild strawberries.

Zander contemplated his situation one night while lying in his room. A different secret ate at him, not Bryant's or Silexa's, but his own: the secret about Naomi. She bore the same scar on her neck as Silexa. He knew there must be a connection, though he didn't know what. Someday, the question would creep to the surface, and he would deal with the consequences when it did.

In the kitchen, he and everyone else were kept busy, working furiously to prepare for an upcoming feast, still a week away. Zander didn't know much about it, but he honored his responsibility and did his best to perform his duties.

Zander had found a moment to have a small lunch when Audra caught up to him—alone with his thoughts in the corner pantry, quietly eating his soup.

She slid down next to him and smiled.

"I've been trying to talk to you all day," she started, her whisper hissing next to his ear. "But it's been so busy."

"Yes," he agreed.

"Tell me," she started with a flirtatious tone, "what has the prince got you doing every night?"

"What?"

"I'll have to start looking at you differently if you're friends with the prince."

"Not exactly f-friends."

Audra shifted her legs to a more comfortable position. "Prince Bryant has a lot of enemies, but he usually doesn't seek them out at the end of the day."

Zander thought carefully before he answered. "He gave me a sp-special a-assign-ment."

Audra's face lit up. "Ander, this is so big. You have no idea. What kind of assignment?"

"Uh . . ." He wasn't sure what to say and he had no experience thinking quickly. "Secret."

Audra's smile fell a little. "But surely you can share it with me. I won't tell anyone. You can trust me."

"I . . ." he started, then stopped. Audra looked at him pleadingly. "Sorry."

Audra didn't like that answer.

Zander wasn't sure if he was seeing things right, but he thought he saw her eyes flash black, then back to green.

"Ander," she said, smiling as if nothing had happened, "I want you to be careful about trusting the prince. Whatever he has asked of you could be dangerous. It could cost you. I'm serious when I say he has many enemies. A few of them may be here for the feast. You have to be careful. I don't want you to be used in some devious plot he's woven."

Zander sat very still, thinking.

"If you tell me, at least one other person will know if anything happens to you."

That explanation made sense to him. It was a backup plan; in case anything happened, she would know. "Okay," he said, looking around to ensure their seclusion. "He has asked f-for my help pr . . . protecting something."

Audra's face contorted into an intense expression. She leaned in very close to him. "Do you have it? Can I see it?"

"What?"

"Is it with you?"

"No."

Her expression changed. "What is it?"

"Well," he started, "it's . . . S . . . " he couldn't spit it out. He tried again but struggled.

"Yeah, you there!" Mildred hailed him from the hall. "Master Curtis wants ya," she said in her gravely tone. "He's to have ya go tur your room and dress. He'll pick ya up there."

Zander set off, glancing back at Audra, who did not look pleased.

When he arrived in his room, he found a uniform lying on his bed. He looked through the clothing. Pieces upon pieces layered each other; he wasn't sure how the whole look fit together. Quickly throwing off his clothes, he slipped the uniform over his undergarment. He fumbled a little with the bulky buttons, but it looked quite put together. His favorite part was the cloak made from a blue velvet material, much like the prince's. The soft, fine fabric was nicer than anything Zander had ever owned. He planned to sleep in it every night from now on.

"Well, well, nice suit," Curtis said, coming into the room. His long body filled the room to the ceiling, smothering Zander's light mood.

The way Curtis looked at him made Zander's insides twist. There was no trusting the tall obelisk. But he was Bryant's Primitus, and he would trust Bryant to the ends of the earth for saving his life and treating him so well.

Curtis' stone-cold eyes scanned the room before coming back to Zander's. "Nice view you have," he said snidely. "It was smart of Bryant to keep you as far from the city as possible. We wouldn't want our little bird to fly."

Zander's cheeks felt hot as embarrassment rose inside him. He turned, but Curtis left without him down the corridor, so Zander headed in the direction which made the most sense. All he needed to do was to find the grand hallway. If he found that, surely he could make it back to Silexa's private room.

On his way, he glanced toward Audra's room. All was quiet, which secretly made him happier. He had been afraid Audra would see him or want to follow, but he was safe for the moment.

Zander eventually made it to the grand hall with the winding staircase and the door of many locks. The cogs were heavy and aged, and he had trouble unfastening and fastening them again. But with persistence, the door hinge squeaked and opened.

Matlock wasn't standing at the entrance of the secret room; the missing guard caused a flutter in Zander's beating heart. Something must be wrong.

But then the door opened from the other side, and the pock-faced Matlock came out, accompanying the beautiful Silexa.

"Oh, Zander," she exclaimed with joy. "Look at you, so sharp in your uniform."

Zander lost all thought at the mere sight of her. The flowing gown was flecked with gray and blue, dazzling to the eye. Her hair was shaped back into a sweet curl, with white flowers setting it delicately in place. As she walked forward, the air moved out of her way, leaving ribbons of magic in her wake. A lovely shawl made from silk flowed freely about her shoulders.

"I guess you approve." She grabbed the edge of her dress and curtsied. "Bryant picked it out for me."

Zander smiled, though his cheeks felt hot from blushing.

Silexa turned her attention to the strange guard. "Matlock, thank you."

"I will be back, my lady," he said in his cracked, haggard voice. Setting his eyes on the boy, he winked before exiting, leaving the two together just outside her bedchamber.

Silexa flung her arms around Zander. The warmth of the embrace helped ease the tension he felt, loosening his thoughts and feelings. He embraced her back.

She pulled away to look at him, "How do you like your suit? I picked out the colors myself. I love any shade of blue, and I thought it would go so well with your hair."

Zander had forgotten about his fiery red head, and felt embarrassed.

Silexa squeezed him again with a little giggle. "I love your hair. But if you ever need to hide it, the cloak has a hood." She smiled. "I'm glad we have a chance to talk."

Zander's heart beat very fast. He, too, wanted to talk to her, but fear stopped his speech.

Silexa took his hand and sat down with him on the steps before the threshold of the doorway, looking into the passage. She seemed suddenly more serious, her voice dropping to a faint whisper. "I'm terribly afraid for you. We still have a few days and I thought I should warn you about what might happen." She stopped and looked into his eyes. "Do you understand, or am I just rambling?"

Zander smiled even though he didn't.

Silexa reached into a cloth bag and brought out two items, a small dagger and a lustrous blue stone. "I have some things to help protect you. This,"—she handed him the dagger—"is for protection, in case you need it." She helped him place it by his hip, under his cloak, before turning to the other item. "This other one is a little different, and I will need your help with it."

Zander nodded, but didn't like the direction she was headed.

"This stone is very special. My father gave it to me. I am the sole guardian of its power. This stone is why I am in so much trouble and why we are in danger." Her voice fell to the tiniest whisper. "I need you to keep it safe for me. I fear people will kill me if they find it."

Zander choked at the words. He remembered Bryant's warning: the separation from the stone would kill her. He hadn't expected this kind of responsibility. Of anyone in the entire world, he was probably the worst choice.

Silexa handed it to him. He was reluctant to touch it, but she pressed the cool stone in his hands. "It gives the bearer unusual powers and will protect you. But it also carries a burden. I need you to keep it safe until I find a hiding place. The palace will not be safe for long. Bryant has already found infiltrators in the court, which is what has made him suspicious of everyone, and is why he's kept me here."

Zander felt the moment coming—his moment to speak. He mouthed words, but no sound came out.

"I have an idea," she said without noticing. "I don't know if it will work, but it could be the key to saving our lives."

"Yes . . ." The word escaped his lips.

Silexa smiled, raising her hands to her heart then brushed his lips with her fingertip. "Sshh," she whispered. "I don't want you to break your promise."

"Ple-ee-ase."

Silexa removed her hand, listening.

Now that he had her attention, he wasn't sure what to say, so he started with what he knew. "Na . . . omi."

Silexa looked confused. "Who is she?"

A sound echoed in the empty room, like footsteps sliding across the tunnel. Zander and Silexa stopped their conversation and stood up.

Silexa placed a finger to her mouth and motioned for Zander to be silent. Taking his hand, she guided him behind the door. Removing the shawl from around her arms, she flung it gently about them, covering their bodies.

The silk cloth material was sheer enough to see through, but hardly covered both of them. Zander's heart pounded loudly inside his chest as he waited for the footsteps to reach them.

Within seconds, a figure emerged from the stairs: a small person covered in a dark plum cloak, who paused at the threshold. The hooded figure moved through the door with caution, searching.

Silexa crouched and tightened her grip around Zander, her fists clenching hard around his collar. She hardly moved or breathed.

The interloper entered the room, moving carefully toward the bed. A slight turn and he would be standing where Silexa and Zander clung to each other.

As the cloaked figure approached the bed, he moved his head back and forth, searching for sound.

Zander, against his better judgment, moved his hand which held the blue crystal stone, and smoothed it safely out of sight, deep into his pocket. The hooded figure stiffened and lowered the hood.

He bit his lip. Audra's ears raised and fell. So fast no one would have imagined it possible, she grabbed him from beneath the shawl and threw him to the floor, a knife blade pressed against his throat.

"Nice hiding place, Ander. But nothing can escape my ears."

Zander lay very still, his heart beating fast.

"Who are . . . ?" he started.

Audra smiled but didn't loosen her grip. "I was very honest with you, Ander. I never lied to you. I'm a

Louving—a hunter and an assassin. And I didn't come to kill you, though I wouldn't care if I did."

Zander gulped, the lump in his throat coming dangerously close to the blade.

"I was hired to find something that's hidden within this palace, and you gave me the key to it today."

Zander froze, confused.

Audra leaned very close to his ear. "So, here we are, Ander." Her voice hissed in his ear and down his spine. "Where is the girl?"

Zander shuddered, too terrified to speak. His mind flashed with different ideas of how to escape, but his arms wouldn't work. He held still, frozen in fear.

She angled the sharp tip of the knife. "I know the girl has the stone. You can't hide her from me. I need that stone, and you're going to get it."

Zander didn't even see what happened next. One moment, Audra stood over him, and the next she had collapsed in a heap on the floor.

Silexa lifted off her shawl, a metal vase in her hand. She went to the girl and checked her breathing. "She's still alive, just knocked out." She looked at Zander. "Come on, we've got to find Bryant."

~⊰❈⊱~

Zander walked casually into the hall, as if he had nothing better to do. The sun was going down, but it was hard to detect with the clouds brewing over the mountains. He stalled a little, but Silexa—hiding underneath her cloak—pushed him forward.

They passed chambers he had never ventured near before, up more stairs, and around more corners. Finally, a hall opened behind two large double doors. Without hesitation, Silexa walked through.

The room looked much like a large library, housing books of every kind. Dark, velvet curtains blocked the large windows that overlooked the city of Southwick. Passing through a different door, they entered the bedchamber, just as grand as the other room, but completely lined with uncovered windows.

From this perspective, Zander was finally able to look at the strange sky. Though he hadn't known of them earlier, he saw the clouds, frightening and dark. A green tint covered them, and they hovered instead of moving with a breeze as expected.

"What is that?" he asked.

"That," Silexa answered, "is why we have to get out of here."

She began to search the room, pulling out clothes, packs, supplies—as if she had put them there in the first place.

"Quickly. Help me."

Zander obeyed and began cramming the packs with miscellaneous gear she threw about. Through the rummaging, he noticed a collection of rocks and gemstones on a shelf. Each gleamed in its own way, though one peculiar stone looked almost exactly like Silexa's. It seemed a little dull and was round and fist-sized, with a blue tint.

Silexa turned and saw the stone in his hand. "Perfect, Zander. Good idea—just in case."

Zander smiled, knowing that he had done something good.

"Bring me both stones, Zander." He did as she asked, digging the original stone from his pocket. Looking at both together, he realized there was no comparison to the one he'd found.

Silexa placed one hand on the top of the stone. Instantly it lit, dazzling his eyes. She moved her other hand to the one Zander found. A pulsating beam of light went through her to the new stone, transforming it to resemble the original. Within seconds, it was complete.

"There is no magic in this one," Silexa explained. "It is only a copy. Please, you keep the real stone, just in case I get caught."

Zander nodded and hid the stone, this time in a better hiding place—a deep pocket inside his cloak.

Suddenly, they heard the sound of approaching voices.

"Quick! Hide!" Zander slung one pack on his back and moved to a hiding place near the tall curtains. He was so slight it would be hard to detect him. Silexa threw the shawl back over herself and slid behind a chair.

"In here," a voice shouted.

Two pairs of footsteps marched into the room, carrying the limp form of the prince to his bed, a small groan escaping as he was thrown down.

"Father," Bryant pleaded in a raspy whisper, "please."

"Enough!" the king yelled. "You are useless to me. If you won't give me the stone, we will find the girl ourselves."

A third voice entered the conversation. "Should we ask the oracle to find her?" Curtis' greasy voice inquired.

King Reinoh sighed before he spoke. "Yes. How soon will Sharrod be here?"

"Not long. I believe he has one of the sisters with him, a girl named Ymber. He plans to sacrifice her after the feast in the Ritual Room, as you requested."

"What is her stone?"

"The Atmos, I believe."

"And Bryant's girl?"

"She protects Silicis—stone, rocks, dirt, and mountains. Not as powerful as weather, of course. But remember, my lord, without all of the stones, the circle cannot be complete."

"Yes, yes," the king said. "Let us consult the oracle."

"What do you want done with your son?"

A brief pause. "He is a traitor and no longer my son," the King muttered finally.

The sound of footsteps faded, and the doors slammed shut.

Confirming that both men had left the room, Zander ran to Bryant. He had no visible bleeding, and nothing seemed to be broken. His skin felt warm to the touch, his pulse slow, while his eyes rolled to the back of his head.

Silexa emerged from her hiding but stayed frozen in place, looking fearful.

"Alive," Zander assured her. "But, I don't know . . . He's s-strange."

Silexa regained her composure. There was still a chance to save him.

Zander tried valiantly to lift his body.

"The stone will help you," Silexa whispered. "Place your hand on it and use it."

Zander did just that. He felt inside his cloak to the stone and by touching it, either the prince became lighter or he became stronger. He slung one of Bryant's arms over his own shoulders to prop him up. "How do we . . . ?"

"Get out?" Silexa finished. "There is a tunnel, not far, that is hidden. It is our only chance."

"What about Audra?" Zander asked.

A glaze of confusion crossed Silexa's face. "The Louving? I don't think there is anything we can do about her now. I'm more worried about the oracle they talked about."

True. In either case, they would be hunted no matter what they decided to do.

"We need to get out, Zander." Silexa draped the shawl back over herself, and with Bryant hanging limply between them, they left the chamber.

Not as many people lingered in the hallways at that time. The sounds of soldiers marching on the marble floors echoed throughout the palace walls, but soon the footsteps could no longer be heard.

Silexa's stone made Zander feel invincible.

"We're very close. It's down here," Silexa whispered. But before they turned the corner, they heard rhythmic footfalls entering the hall, growing louder and louder. Zander, still supporting Bryant, hid behind a pillar, while Silexa crouched behind a statue. A tiny crack gave him the chance to see the disturbance. His heart skipped as he watched line upon line of soldiers marching directly past the small hallway where they hid. He tried to make himself as small as possible.

In that instant, the atmosphere changed. The world slowed to a moment; edges blurred, and Zander's vision faded.

The heartbeat of the march hit as hard in his ears as a pulse, thudding and ringing. His vision focused on something that resembled the nightmare lingering in the back corner of every dream.

A dark figure walked forward, flowing robes draping his tall frame. A sneer of malice curled on his lips, and a fathomless evil shone in his hollow black eyes. He could only be called a monster—too large to be a man, yet too human to be a beast. He appeared to be the devil himself.

Shock went through Zander's tender heart at what he saw—not the appearance of the demon, but the sight of a slight, fair girl who trailed behind him. Like Silexa, she reminded him of Naomi with her small frame and tender expressions, but her straight, smooth hair looked silver in the hall light, unlike Naomi's strands of gold.

The parade passed, and the footfall rhythm quieted.

Zander turned to stunned Silexa, who appeared frozen in place. He stepped toward her, but she was again slow to respond.

"No . . . no . . ." she muttered, rocking back and forth.

"Silexa," Zander stammered, "please . . ."

She did not want to move, but seeing the panic in his eyes and the unconscious Bryant he supported, her determination returned. As the hallways cleared, they made their way to the secret tunnel hidden beneath stairs. She rubbed her palms together, and a doorway appeared in the lines of marble. They entered, and the door sealed shut behind them.

Silexa reached in her pocket and pulled out the fake stone she'd made. She rubbed it until it began to glow, filling the tunnel with small fibers of light.

Zander put Bryant down and checked on him once more. His condition had not changed.

Silexa knelt close to Bryant, laying her head on his chest and weeping. "I do not want to live without him." She sobbed for a moment before looking into Zander's face again. "The girl . . . is my sister. They are going to kill her."

The adrenaline in Zander's veins obliterated any clear and rational thought. He embraced Silexa as she wept, the tears staining his new cloak as he came to one conclusion: three lives needed saving, but he wasn't sure how he could do it.

CHAPTER THIRTEEN
THE VIVATERA

Naomi's time with Lytte felt pointless. She spent all day with him, trying desperately to learn what she could about an exit to the Willows. Every time she thought about bringing up the question, their lessons got in the way. Anxiety grew with every passing moment. She had not accomplished anything.

By the third day, she began to panic and found it increasingly difficult to hide her emotions. There had to be something that could distract her and keep her from telling Lytte the entire plan.

But when she entered Lytte's tent that day, she found there was no need; the distraction presented itself.

Lytte whistled as he lit candles around the tent. He noticed Naomi at once and gave her a pleased smile. "Our lesson will be special today."

Naomi noticed various objects lying on his small, velvet-draped table: five sparkling gold medallions, each unique in design and size, placed in symmetry. She examined them closely. Intricate markings wove in and out on the sides, with a stone set in the middle of each piece.

Lytte moved about the room, minimizing the outside light, leaving only the candle light and the oil lamps. "Today, I would like to show you the Healing Medallions." He knelt close to her, excitement on his face. "The Healing Medallions are very special and sacred. I rarely let them out of my possession. But I want you to learn how to use them."

Enraptured by the beauty of the medallions, Naomi completely forgot about her mission. She wondered about Lytte's collection after Micah mentioned them the other night. These must be what his uncle had made so long ago—and what Harrow was after.

"This first one is the Blood Medallion." Lytte held it to Naomi, gently placing the heavy object in her hands. The stone within swirled about like wispy clouds in various shades of red. "It helps heal blood wounds and such." He gestured to the others on the table. "The Bone Medallion." He pointed to one with a crusty white stone which Naomi assumed must be actual bone. "Poison and Burn Medallions." He pointed to the next two, one acidic green and the other fiery orange.

"How were they made?" Naomi asked.

"These particular stones were from a family collection of the Shadowers. Micah's uncle is an alchemist and ingenious craftsman. He is the creator—an ironsmith of great talent."

Naomi's eye flashed past the others to the fifth in the line of medallions—by far the most dazzling of them all, and most peculiar. "What about this one?"

"I knew you would want to know." Lytte scooped it from the cloth. "This sweet one is different than the others.

It was not crafted the same way, nor was it crafted by Micah's uncle."

Lytte handed the medallion to her. Naomi gasped as she handled it, surprised how much more fragile it seemed. What a wonderful creation! The pale, pink stone rested within the metal fasteners, seeming to dance within the surrounding gold. The faint light sparkled off delicate inlays of tiny stones, reflecting shimmers of rainbows around her fingertips. It was breathtaking.

"Please tell me about it," Naomi asked in a whisper, breaking the silence surrounding them as she held the beautiful object.

Lytte uttered words Naomi didn't understand, then looked at her softly, lovingly. "Life. This is the Vivatera or 'Life' medallion. Its qualities are peculiar and widely misunderstood."

Comprehension flooded through Naomi, and she gasped. "Wait—is this the . . . ?" But words failed her. She could remember it in her dream, the vivid memory dancing around her head. This was what Harrow wanted—what he accused Reynolds of stealing.

"This is the medallion mentioned in your dream."

Naomi's face went pale. "Did Reynolds really steal this?"

Lytte smiled. "It is more complicated than simple theft. But, yes, this is the very medallion he was accused of stealing."

"How could it . . . ?" she began, but so many questions filled her mind she couldn't begin to ask.

"I cannot explain without getting into detail about Reynolds's life I'm not sure he would like anyone to know."

"Please," Naomi begged. The information felt crucial. It would put everything into perspective, and Reynolds' fate might very well rely on it. "Please, Lytte, I need to know."

Lytte rested his elbows on the table, his hands clasped at his chin. "I will share with you what I know, though it is not everything. I do not think anyone knows the entire story."

Naomi glanced at the wonderful stone and pressed it lightly with her fingers. It was warm to the touch. She smiled, intrigued by its connection to Reynolds.

Lytte sat down on the floor next to her. "The medallion casing was in possession of a man named Cornwallis. You can tell by the engravings on the back— the family crest. He was a man of honor and great courage and led the royal armies into many great battles, which eventually cost him his life. Reynolds is his son."

Naomi raised her head to meet Lytte's gaze. *Reynolds' father?* Reynolds had not stolen the medallion—it belonged to him. She bent again to look more closely at the artwork, noticing the intricacies of the craftsmanship. Symbols and engravings spiraled in gold, gemstones lining the outer edge, lifting impressions that were delicately inlaid. It looked unrefined, almost as if it wasn't finished. She liked the raw talent and amateur charm of it. Knowing it was his, she admired it more, rubbing it softly in her hands.

Lytte continued, "His mother died when he was a baby and he was raised at court, a regular nuisance." He laughed at the memory. "But as he grew older, he showed me great respect. His little mind filled with so many things at such a young age that he hardly seemed a child, rather a smaller version of his father."

He gave a deep sigh before pressing on. "I believe Reynolds was nine or ten years old when his father was killed and everything changed. A new king took reign, and we became traitors and refugees. From that point I do not know much more."

"But how did it get here? With you?" Naomi asked.

"He had it with him the whole time he traveled. Rumor of its existence went through Southwick and the monarchy, although I do not understand how anyone learned of it. Where it came from and what it really does, I do not know. I have never used it. I only provide its safety."

"So, he *did* know where it was." Naomi remembered her dream again, and Reynolds' denial.

"Of course he knew, but I wouldn't go telling people of its existence."

Naomi smiled, unable to help herself. She felt closer to Reynolds. These simple truths about his life made him more interesting. Her eyes fell back to the warm medallion in her hand, and she evaluated the markings. "What can you tell me about it?"

Lytte picked the medallion out of Naomi's hand to examine it again. "It is a very special item, though not all the uses are known. The power which flows through it pulses like a living thing. It can act on its own, or persuade others to act for it. It is speculated that this medallion is more desirable then others because it can raise someone from the dead."

Naomi gasped. "Everyone would want this!"

"Look at this marking." Lytte pointed to the top of the medallion—a carving of a wide-winged hawk stretching out across mountains. "This is the sign of the Accipitor. In its legend, the sign of the Accipitor speaks of the return of life, life continuing after life. That is why so many believe it has this power. I have not yet seen the Vivatera confirm it."

Naomi tried to understand, but like much of Lytte's explanations, she felt out of her depth. She looked at the marking again. "Hawk . . ." She had also heard that before.

Lytte shifted his attention toward the other medallions again. "Let us move on."

"What about Reynolds? Do you think he's in danger?"

Lytte thought about it. "I do not believe Reynolds is in a situation he cannot handle."

"Do you think he will come back?"

"He comes now and again. But he will be back for you."

He kissed Naomi's cheeks as she blushed. "But how is he the only one that gets in?"

Lytte looked at her, seeming to study her expression. "The magic is simple, but you do not need the magic to enter. It's all in here." He pointed to her heart.

Her brain swirled with questions and unresolved answers. "If it's so simple, why can't anyone leave?"

"We keep everyone in camp for their own safety. If anyone from the monarchy knew what we were doing, serious consequences would befall us. Many have tried to leave—even you, if I recall—but they are not asking the right questions."

"So, it's a question?"

"No, it is an answer—the answer that will save your life. None of the boys can leave because they have never experienced it."

What Lytte said made absolutely no sense to her, and it seemed even more impossible to get out of there. But maybe the others could understand his words.

"Now, which medallion would you like to try first?"

Naomi smiled. "This one," she said, holding up the Vivatera.

"I thought you might." Lytte glanced at the other medallions. "As I said, with these other medallions, their uses are quite self-explanatory, and the medallion guides you to what you need to do. This one," he pointed back to the Vivatera, "is a mystery. Please, put it on."

Naomi did as he asked. The medallion dangled around her neck from a long chain. So light, she could have easily dismissed it and forgotten she wore it, but for its unearthly beauty.

"The Vivatera reacts to the person wearing it. Unlike your magic, which you had to befriend, this will work for everyone. But what it creates is different for every user."

"Anyone can use it?"

Lytte shook his head. "Yes and no. It may react toward everyone, showing diversity in taste toward the wearer. What do you see in it?"

Naomi took the Vivatera in her hand and studied the milky-pink stone. The substance swirled in different patterns, forming a confusing shape.

"What do you see?"

"I'm not sure." Naomi stared harder than before. "I think it's a tree?"

"Does the tree look familiar to you in any way?"

"Not really." Naomi responded, thoughtfully inspecting the image. "I like trees. I feel safest in a tree. What do you see?"

Lytte sighed, his face covered with years of grief and wear. "When I wear it, I see a part of myself that I had forgotten." The sadness in his voice matched the pain in his eyes. "It displays for me the happiest time in my life—the time I spent in the service of King Prolius."

Naomi thought about the image she saw. Was this stone displaying the time in her tree in Sharlot, by the

Bucklingdown farm? Naomi lost herself in memory—the time by herself, feeling the life of the tree which she so loved, the solitude and seclusion she tried to keep secret. All the times she spent filling her journal with her dreams.

How had she forgotten so easily? She loved those moments in the high branches of the tree when she felt whole and complete. Was that what the Vivatera was trying to communicate with her?

Lytte's voice called her back to the moment, his tone filled with intense anticipation. "Please hold the medallion to the light."

Naomi held it to the flickering candlelight. The stone absorbed its rays. A bright beam shot out, quick and powerful, breaking a glass beaker on the stool table across the room.

Lytte gasped in surprise. "You are amazing, truly."

Naomi dropped the medallion and looked at Lytte in horror. "What did I do?"

"It is what you are. Everything you touch is remarkable." Tears filled Lytte's eyes. "I wish I could explain."

Naomi gazed at her mentor, dumbfounded by his reaction. "What does it do for you?"

"Let me show you," Lytte whispered, holding out his hand.

The medallion did not like leaving her neck and she did not like taking it off, but she handed it back to Lytte, who placed it over his head. He smoothed it for a moment with his fingers before holding it to the light.

A delicate, enchanting ribbon of light streamed out of the stone as sweet music began to sound. Naomi couldn't help herself and reached out a finger, allowing a stream to wrap around it.

Lytte looked on in astonishment. "I have never seen it act in such a way before."

The stream moved up her arm, dancing and playful, but the magic soon changed. Its grip tightened and began to squeeze Naomi, its direction and intent clear as it slid up her shoulder, heading for her throat. The band throbbed and pulsed uncomfortably.

Noticing the change, Lytte lowered the Vivatera from the light. The medallion reacted harshly, sending a shock through Lytte's body that knocked him, convulsing, to the floor. Naomi screamed as it tightened its grip on her.

Reacting quickly, Naomi grabbed the Vivatera from around Lytte's neck and placed it back around her own. The music still hummed in the air, reminding her of its power.

"Oh, please—Lytte, wake up!"

She bent low to the ground, listening to Lytte's heart. It was beating very fast. Rubbing her fingers together, she circled them over his chest. The fibers of her magic began slowing the rapid beating and returned his heart's rhythm to normal.

Lytte stopped shaking, and his color gradually returned. His eyes opened slowly. "Where is it?" he whispered, as if afraid the Vivatera might hear him.

"I have it," Naomi whispered back.

"Please, put it away, out of sight. I can't . . ." He could not finish. "It saw me . . . It threatened me . . ."

Naomi examined the Vivatera closely. It was such a beautiful thing. The music still called to her seductively. She ran her fingertips over the hawk emblem. It looked as if it were moving closer to her. She held very still, watching. A pulling, tugging sensation filled her. She wanted this. Its danger fueled her desire.

"Please put the medallions away," Lytte begged meekly. "This is far too dangerous."

Naomi nodded.

Still lined with pain, Lytte's face turned to her. "In the trunk." He pointed in its general direction, too weak to be more specific.

Naomi gathered the other medallions, none as warm and wonderful as the Vivatera. Opening the trunk, she put the precious medallions away, each one in its delicate case.

All but one. The Vivatera still hung around her neck. She grasped the chain to lift, but the weight suddenly felt impossible. Bowing her head, she let the medallion sink close to her skin. Inside her, the magic stirred with greed and wanting. But she couldn't steal it; it needed to be there.

Heat moved up her fingers, burning her where she held the chain. She dropped it, letting it lay against her chest. Naomi began to panic. She couldn't get it off, and she didn't want to. She had no choice. She was a thief.

That would be the day. She would not be back. They would leave tonight.

Lytte lay down, exhausted, and soon fell asleep. Naomi pulled out a parchment and penned a brief note to her mentor, placing it in the empty case where the Vivatera had once sat.

Lytte,

Please forgive me. The Vivatera wants me. I don't know why, but it has persuaded me. I stole it and we're leaving to find its owner. Please don't look for me. I don't want anything to happen to you. I will keep the Vivatera safe and secret. It needs protection.

I'm sorry.

Naomi

The hour grew later, and Naomi dozed in and out of consciousness until awakened by a whisper in her ear.

"Time to go." Landon grinned at her.

Outside, clouds filled the air with the energy of an untamed storm.

The food supply they'd gathered would be sufficient to get them to their destination—the home of Spotswood Shadower. As long as they reached it within a week's time, they would be in good shape. Micah's crude map and compass stone would be helpful, but every eventuality couldn't be predicted.

The little company traveled through the scant trees, battling against the icy wind. When the trees thickened and the inner camp disappeared, Landon turned to face the others.

"Before we leave, I want to make sure we stick together. Micah has the compass stone and I've got the map. Once we get to a safe distance in the forest, hopefully it can help direct us out. Naomi? Do you know how to get out?"

Naomi nervously gritted her teeth. "Don't worry, I have all the information. Lytte told me all he could."

"Good. Micah, listen closely for anyone following us."

"Can I do anything?" Katia asked.

"Not really." Landon grinned at her from the lead. "Just stay out of trouble."

Katia glared at Landon's smug expression. "You don't need to be so rude."

Micah placed a hand on Katia's arm. "There will be plenty for you to do after we get out, I promise."

Deeper and deeper they ventured into the thickness of the trees. Darkness enveloped them. Naomi bumped Landon's shoulder, confirming she was still on track. He patted her head reassuringly.

Micah pulled out his compass stone. The odd rock spun in his hand until it pointed the way to its home—the direction in which the company must travel.

Micah took lead, and the others followed. Within a few paces, the stone began to turn in his palm, back toward the direction from which they came. "Stop," he whispered.

"Why?"

"We're heading back to camp. We have reached the Apex." Micah looked up toward the heavens. "The trickery starts here."

Naomi took a deep breath. "Then, this is it. Time to solve the riddle."

She thought again of her discussion earlier that day, back at Lytte's tent. The Vivatera spoke to her, comforting her heart.

"It's a question, I think," Naomi started, then shook her head. "Wait, no! Lytte said you have to ask the right question to get the answer."

Silence fell as everyone pondered the puzzle. Naomi, after serious contemplation, broke the silence. "Lytte mentioned something about the safety of the camp and that was why no one could leave."

"But it's a question?" Landon asked. "What question?"

"He didn't say," Naomi answered. "Just that the question was more important than the answer." She thought of Lytte pointing to her heart. *It's all in here.* Confusion surrounded her like the swirling leaves at her feet.

Micah's hand touched Naomi's shoulder, breaking her train of thought. "I sense someone."

Everyone fell silent.

Micah concentrated. "Back at the camp. Someone knows. He is looking for us."

Naomi's heart quickened; the beats moved from her chest to her throat as her thoughts turned immediately to Lytte and her stolen prize. She slipped a hand in her cloak and felt the warmth of the Vivatera against her skin. An irrational fear ran down her spine—mixed with sadness for her mentor and friend.

Landon's voice dropped to a whisper. "Who?"

"I cannot tell. I only hear the heartbeat. It's fast. He's in a hurry."

None of them moved, too fearful to make noise. The air thickened, the wind blowing and whistling through the forest.

"What do we do?" Katia whispered. "Should we hide?"

Micah seemed to be searching the air through the darkness. "Yes. Hide behind the plants and cover yourself with your cloaks. I will climb so I can hear more clearly."

With some difficulty, Landon and Naomi managed to hide behind shrubs near Katia as Micah scaled a nearby willow.

Naomi's breathing quickened as memories of the Blackwoods resurfaced, consuming her; but Reynolds would not save her this time. She reflexively placed her hand on the Vivatera, and let her terror melt into the medallion.

Time passed slowly in the dark and eerie quiet. Nothing moved—not animals or leaves; even the wind kept silent, frozen at the knowledge that someone attempted an escape.

Naomi's calves began to cramp and burn. She grew more agitated with every second. The dawn would break soon, and they would still be in this forest, trapped by their stalker.

"I can hear him," Micah whispered in the dark. "Prepare yourselves."

They readied themselves as best they could, straining their ears for any sound. Naomi placed her head on her folded knees, and suddenly heard the crunch of footsteps on leaves.

Though she could not see Katia's face, Naomi felt the frost building at her friend's fingertips; the coolness surrounding Katia increased with her heightening emotions.

The footsteps traveled in and out of hearing range. Whoever followed them knew how to be careful.

Naomi wondered who would follow them here. Her mind drew a blank. The steps were light and nimble; neither Aristatolis nor Lytte could move like that. She feared the tracker from the Blackwoods had found her. As the presence moved closer, her heart pounded. Suddenly, something popped, accompanied by red sparks.

Light flashed, illuminating the shadows and a young man, tall and lean, whom Naomi recognized from the camp. Landon stood and pulled out his sword.

"Landon!" the boy yelled. "I know you're here."

Landon did not move but stood motionless above Katia and Naomi, waiting.

"I have a proposition for you, Landon. That's all." The presence came closer and Naomi grew more nervous.

"I know you better than that, Taren," Landon shouted. "What do you want?"

"I could ask you the same thing, Rhees," Taren returned, slick as an eel. "You don't care for her. You've never cared for anyone. But we both knew the moment we saw her, she was the one we were waiting for. The girl who could get us out of here. All I want is a way out."

The exchange surprised Naomi, motivating her to shove Landon in the gut.

"It's not true!" Landon shouted back. He leaned toward Naomi to reassure her. "It's not."

"I mean no harm to any of you," Taren continued. "I'm a tracker. I could be useful."

"You spied on us."

"I had to."

She had heard enough. Naomi stood up next to a stunned Landon. "I will lead you."

Taren stood still. "Thank you."

She turned to Landon. "Is he dangerous?"

"Possibly."

Naomi bit her lip as she considered her options. "Well then, I would rather have him out of the camp than hurting anyone inside."

"I am unarmed," Taren returned. "Tie me if you have to."

Katia stood up, whispering so only Naomi could hear. "This is stupid, Naomi. I don't like this idea."

Naomi weighed the information she heard, but feared for the safety of others if Taren stayed. "There's no choice."

Landon whistled for Micah who returned in a flash. "Do you think you can do this, Micah?"

"Sure as ever," Micah responded, his strange eyes flashing blue in the darkness. As he moved his hands in rapid, fluid movements, dust and dirt from the ground gathered in a billowing cloud and whipped into a tight rope around Taren's wrists.

"That should work for a while." Micah smiled, holding the rope tightly, though Taren made no effort to escape.

Landon turned back to Naomi. "It's now or never."

Naomi's mind raced. A feeling came over her, overwhelming and pure; she needed to ask her magic. She closed her eyes. *Help me.*

Light!

The bold patterns of her magic emanated light in every direction, intricately woven, both surprising and dazzling her, the streams of blue floating just as before.

"Please, help me," she whispered.

We are here, it returned, echoing loudly in the caverns of her thoughts.

"What is the question I need to know?"

The magic danced about her arms and fingers before spinning off in wild directions. *"Where is your heart?"*

Naomi considered it. Was that the question? She glanced down. Was the question literal or metaphorical? If not inside her chest, then where else could it be?

. . . That was the answer.

Tears came quickly at the relief of knowing.

Naomi opened her eyes. "I know the answer," she whispered. "Micah, grab the compass."

"Done, my lady."

"I don't know how this will work, so keep an eye on it. Everyone hold on to each other so we can all make it."

Naomi reached out her hands and walked forward. *Where is your heart?* She knew the answer—not inside but outside, and not within the camp, but far away, trapped.

A wave of new emotions overcame her, feelings she had never experienced. The truth stood clear in her mind— her heart belonged to someone else, and the reality weighed heavy in her chest.

She knew love when the others didn't—such a simple answer to a complicated question. She needed to keep his heart beating. Her life depended on his life. She knew how to leave the camp.

She continued to walk in the darkness, dragging the line of people behind her, still not sure what to do, but continuing as she thought of Reynolds's plight and her need to save him.

A faint light began filling the forest as the breaking dawn crept upon them. Naomi could see distant rolling hills, grassy knolls, and in the far distance, mountains. They'd done it. They'd left the camp. She took hold of the Vivatera hidden beneath her robes and caressed it. They were free.

Everyone felt the exhilaration. Years of anticipation ended. Together they reached a small clearing, where Naomi finally stopped.

Exclamations erupted from the company, but Naomi quieted them. "It's not over. We're not safe. We have to be careful. These forests can't be trusted."

Taren turned to her. "Let me travel with you."

Landon stepped forward, guarding Naomi. "No. We got you out—that's enough."

Naomi took Landon's shoulder, pressing him back from Taren, relieving the tension between them. "We will stay together for a short distance," she said to Taren, "but then you'll need to leave us to our travels."

"Agreed."

Landon's face creased with worry. He leaned in toward her and whispered, "You don't know him like I do."

"Then you know what he is capable of." Naomi turned to Micah. "Untie him."

The rope turned back to dust. Taren stood straight and tall, wiping his eyes with his sleeves before facing her. His cold expression contained a strange familiarity. "My name is Taren," he informed her. "Taren Lockwood."

CHAPTER FOURTEEN
THE FEAST

Zander made up his mind. The girl needed to be saved.

Silexa had used her magic to find a tunnel that led outside into the city, but they were anything but safe. They could only get Bryant as far as a wine cellar near the palace wall.

In the days following the escape, Zander watched Silexa nurse her love back to health. Zander helped as much as was in his power, gathering small rations where he could. Silexa kept Bryant hidden in a dark corner, ready with her shadesilk covering, fearful that the guards would discover them. After three days, Bryant came around and started talking again. Although weak, he seemed in tolerable spirits.

Zander knew Silexa suspected his plans, though he never spoke to her about them. The feast approached and he prepared to the best of his abilities, cleaning the beautiful page uniform.

Silexa watched as he worked. "Here." She passed something into his hands—both stones, one real, one fake.

"I can't. You'll . . . die."

"*You* will if you don't take them." Silexa straightened his collar. "The stone knows your strengths, so follow your instincts. And remember, I'll be with you. I'm connected to the stone. If you lose your way, it will always find me."

Zander took the precious stones and placed each in a pocket to keep them separate. Right for real, left for fake. In his mind, he created a little tune to remember each.

Bryant fell asleep, which Zander counted as a blessing. If he knew what Zander had planned, he would probably try to stop him.

His cheeks reddened as Silexa kissed each one. "Come back to me." Her voice cracked. "Promise me you'll come back."

Zander lift his head, nodding before heading in the direction of the tunnel.

Finding the feast wasn't as easy as Zander thought. Instinct told him if he found the Grand Hall, he could find the courtyard, and from there, surely he could find the feast. Covering his hair with his hood gave him more confidence, and he moved with determination and purpose, holding his head high, like he belonged, like he knew what he was doing, although neither was true.

Once he got to the feast, he had no idea how he'd find the girl. And once he found her, how on earth would he get her out? Silexa had told him to follow his instincts and use his strengths, and he could pretend to have both. He really feared Audra. If he ran into her while in the palace, she could cause his downfall.

"Boy!" cried a voice from behind him. "Boy, where are you headed?"

Zander turned to see a man approaching, dressed in a tailored crimson jacket of marvelous workmanship. Zander bowed to play his part well.

"Are you heading to the feast?" Zander nodded. "I'm looking for Prince Bryant. I expected him here, but I haven't seen him tonight, and his chambers were empty." The young man smiled, scratching his head. "You don't think he ran away with that girl he mentioned? Sly devil . . ."

Zander sensed the man was lying. Bryant hadn't told anyone about Silexa. "I am sorry, sir." The words came out crystal clear with no stutters, surprising him.

"Could I at least accompany you back to the feast? I'm Vlad, by the way. Vlad Jonas. We attended school together as boys, Bryant and I. My father resides in the west, on the other side of the Crest."

The young man liked to chat, so Zander let him as they continued on the path. It didn't matter if the information was true. Zander knew nothing of Parbraven or geographical locations. The man prattled on while Zander did his best to act as if he knew where he was going.

A company of drunken men headed towards them, and Zander knew they had almost reached the feast. Gold and blue fabric draped several columns which led to lines and lines of tables that filled the courtyard. He didn't see anyone at the head table—no prince or king or demon or girl.

"Wait!" Vlad spoke up before Zander could leave. "I want to thank you for your help. What is your name? Are you part of the court?"

Zander thought quickly. "Ander. Ander Stone. I'm visiting with my sister."

"Your sister, you say?" Vlad grinned to himself. "She isn't that incredible creature I saw near the king, is she?" He sighed. "I've never seen silver hair like that, almost purple . . ."

Zander maintained his guard. Though he found Vlad charming, he knew he shouldn't trust him.

"Come, join me." Vlad pulled Zander next to him at a long, unkempt table. The feast had reached the point where civility lost all importance, the food scattered about as if ravenous dogs had dined there, which did nothing for Zander's already nervous stomach. His intensions were to arrive late, but he hadn't expected the event to get out of hand so quickly.

"You must tell me more of your sister." Vlad helped himself to some wine and offered some to Zander, who shook his head.

"Like what?"

"Why the devil would she come here? A lady shouldn't show up to some place so lacking in refinery."

Zander looked around. The crowd had become unruly and drunk, not what he'd expected. He swallowed. "Do you know where she might be?"

"Why, yes," Vlad answered. "She went down that passage with a few other guests, including Bryant's adviser. I couldn't tell you who the rest were, but I do remember a boy, smaller than you, traveling with them."

"Thanks." Zander stood to leave, bowing again. "I must go find her."

"If you don't mind, I think I will accompany you." Bold Vlad stood up beside him. "I'd like to find Bryant, and his advisor should know where he is."

Zander didn't think that sounded like a very good idea. But Vlad seemed quite determined, and it might look suspicious to argue too much.

Next to the elaborate courtyards stood many columned pathways, arched and lined with beautiful wisteria and other climbing vines. Wind picked up petals of tiny flowers and blew them across the colonnades.

Together they walked. Vlad's stride doubled that of Zander's, who had to skip into a run every few steps. His heart began to beat so fast he could feel the pounding in his throat. The vacant arcades wound further and further from the feast, and soon he felt overwhelmed with fear.

"Stop," he said.

Vlad turned in confusion.

"It's a trap."

"What? What trap?"

"I . . ." Zander couldn't speak. He looked around. They had reached a cobbled, old atrium, hidden in perfect seclusion.

Vlad folded his arms and smiled—not nearly as friendly as before, and much less charming. "I think you're right—we have traveled too far." Through his grin, his eyes flashed black.

Zander's heart sank.

"Did you bring the stone?" His voice sounded cold and familiar.

Zander sank back as the shadows in the atrium became more focused, more human-like.

"Nice work," a silky voice called as Curtis's shape became prominent amongst the others. "I think that performance should give you a raise."

Vlad laughed, whipping around in a cyclone that contorted his shape into the slender, feminine Audra. She looked at Zander and sighed. "You know, you really aren't that bad a kid, Ander. But my head still hurts and I can't forgive you for that." Curtis joined her.

"How did . . . ?" Zander started, but his impediment returned and he couldn't finish.

"Your simple heart is so easy to read," Curtis sneered. "You disappeared the same time Bryant did, and we all know he wouldn't leave his pet. Now you'll lead us to the girl and the stone."

Zander backed away from Curtis but stumbled to the ground. Other people emerged from the darkness. The king moved to Curtis' side, along with two others Zander didn't know: a burly man and a small boy, who looked no older than six, with strange, glowing, blue eyes and dark auburn hair.

"Where's Ym . . . ?" Zander couldn't finish.

"Oh, she's here. Quietly waiting for the end. Her death is only the beginning. Silexa will be next."

"No!" Zander shouted.

A laugh escaped Curtis' lips. "My young friend, I know the secrets of the stones. The silly girl gave you the stone, for whatever reason—your protection, perhaps. Her actions will kill her. Just like her sister."

Another rumble of laughter erupted from the shadowed witnesses.

"Enough, Curtis." A voice filled the atrium—low and booming—as a figure emerged from the darkness.

Zander knew who it would be. He didn't want to look but couldn't help himself.

Up close, he could see things he hadn't noticed before. The man looked more animal than human—his skin baked and brown, the deep hollows of his eyes shining with the color of blood. Though his body was massive and bulky, he moved like liquid—a mass that molded at will. In his arms, he carried the limp body of a girl wrapped in linen, bound and gagged. "Stop playing with the boy, Curtis. We have work to do."

Curtis' smile faded. "Let us kill them both and be done with it."

"Are you sure he has the stone?"

"Yes," the small boy answered, without any hint of emotion.

"So be it." Curtis raised his slender hand and pointed toward the linen bundle. The girl flew across the air and landed near where Zander had fallen.

He looked over at Ymber, seeing her eyes widen with fear. Reaching into his pockets, he felt the stones, both cool to the touch, one real . . . one fake.

Zander's heart felt like it would burst from his chest. His hands tightened around the stones. They felt different to the touch, so that he could instantly tell the real from the fake. His fist began to tingle, and the sensation traveled upward.

As he decided on a course of action, the magic wrapped itself around his arm, making it feel lighter and freer.

Curtis moved his long hands left to right in motions of uninterrupted precision, muttering the words of a spell.

Zander felt the pull immediately. The stone reacted in what felt like rage, but it did not move or give away its position. He lifted the fake stone out in the open and glanced at it. Suddenly, it lifted fast as lightning to Curtis' outstretched hand.

"Too easy," the king said in a tired voice.

From the background, the little boy looked at the stone, blank and emotionless. "There is deceit," he said in monotone.

Curtis glanced at the stone and sneered.

Zander's arm twisted against the stone he clenched in his right fist. He didn't want to give it away, but the magic was strong and angry. The tingling ran up his arm and tightened around his chest, stealing his breath. Zander's vision faded as the magic wrapped around him like a coiling snake.

Silexa's sister struggled violently to get out of the linen coverings.

The onlookers in the shadows sensed the fear and strength of the stone and backed away. Only the dark lord stood in front of Zander then.

"I have no patience for this, boy." He raised his arms and clapped.

Everything went dark. Screams and cries could be heard around the palace. A low rumbling rose as the foundation began to shake. Flames sparked at the sub-beast's fingertips and shot out at Zander and the girl.

Zander held the stone tighter. *Please save us*, his tiny plea called the magic for help.

White light illuminated around Zander. A shield, clear as glass, wrapped around him and the girl. The flames couldn't penetrate it, sizzling away from the light.

Zander felt the warmth of the fire but could not see it. Visions of streaming light crossed his vision. He fought to think, to be free, but the magic held him tight, consuming him.

The white light inside of him looked so familiar. He couldn't see anything but her face, the face he dreamed of every night. Her arms stretched out to hold him and take care of him.

She walked very slowly, glowing and ethereal. He watched her approach, yet he still couldn't move. *I'm dying. Naomi is taking me to paradise.*

"Zander," she whispered. "Hold my hand, Zander."

He reached out and she touched him, sending a shock of energy through him—not painful but powerful. "I will help you." Her voice echoed about him.

Another surge of flames shot out, trying to break the shield.

Someone else grabbed Zander's arm—the girl, Ymber. She stared at the vision of Naomi, allowing Naomi to take hold of them both.

The shield vanished . . .

. . . along with Zander and the lady he'd tried so hard to save.

CHAPTER FIFTEEN
TORTURE

Reynolds sat in his cell alone. Days had passed since he surrendered to Browneyes and the other Louvings, and that time had pushed him to his physical and mental limits. Every day, he felt his strength drain more.

His surrender gave Harrow the opportunity to find out his secrets. At first, Harrow attempted physical torture to force out the information, instructing the Louvings to use whatever method of persuasion they could design. Reynolds could bear the humiliation, but it wasn't until Fronzi brought out her whip that he actually felt the excruciating pain Harrow desired.

The first lash surprised him. He'd prepared for the throb on his back, but the end had a sting, a bite like teeth, sharp on his spine. Near the tip was fastened a silver spike resembling the tail of a dragon, designed to grab the skin and rip it to shreds. Throughout the torment, Reynolds kept his silence, swallowing back his screams.

Harrow didn't want him to die, apparently, but seemed to have given an invitation to push him to the limits of his tolerance.

Still, Fronzi's torture didn't compare to the mental games Harrow played. The underlord could search through memories and feelings, manipulating them as he wished and filling Reynolds with pure fear. The first time Harrow had done so, Reynolds hadn't been prepared for the intense onslaught of emotions:

> *. . . A dark room,*
> *His mother lying still.*
> *. . . His tiny fingers wrapped around her cold hand.*

Reynolds couldn't believe how real it felt. The memory of his mother's death he'd buried so deep within the recesses of his mind, Harrow had unearthed in a single moment.

> *. . . The smell of lavender,*
> *The flower wreath around her head.*
> *The maidens' song filled the air.*
> *. . His father walking away . . . alone.*

The images overwhelmed his every waking thought, making him helpless. The terrifying reality of what else Harrow could uncover helped motivate Reynolds to strengthen his mental fortress, but it created such an intense, internal exhaustion, he didn't know how long it would take before he broke.

The cell was nothing more than a hollow in the rock created by water and time. A door with an iron lock had been fitted over the opening. A peculiar wind would travel through the mountain and reverberate an eerie whistle around the walls of the cave. Darkness engulfed the small enclosure, and only a sliver of light found its way through a crack near one of the hinges—his only connection to the outside world.

An occasional Arenma would send in drink and small bits of food. The small people were of a quiet nature and never answered any of his questions.

The isolation gave him plenty of time to think. At times his sacrifice to keep Naomi safe felt futile, but Harrow's curiosity about her kept him alive. The underlord's attempts to unlock his memories had been Reynolds' greatest worry and caused his worst mental strain. So far, Harrow only knew that Reynolds protected something about her, and it spurred his interest.

Reynolds' wrists crossed in front of him, bound tight. Sore from the restraint, he limited his movement and tried to rest, his hand still healing from the wound Browneyes had inflicted what felt like ages ago. With all the time he had to think about his escape plans, much of it he wasted remembering Naomi's gentle face. His strength slowly sapped away. His best plan of action still lay hidden in his pocket—but how he would get to it with his hands tied, he hadn't yet figured out.

The locks clattered from the outside. Reynolds straightened up as much as he could bear with the bruised and torn flesh on his back. Although the Arenmas barely looked at him, the little company he received was still welcomed, even if it was silent.

The iron door screeched open, revealing the silhouette of a slender figure outlined in an arch of light.

"You're not who I expected." Reynolds squinted as the unmistakable dark brown braids came into view.

"I don't like to be expected."

Exhausted, Reynolds rested his head on the rock wall. "Why are you here?"

"I'm leaving. I thought I would see you before I did."

"And you decided to check on me? I'm flattered." Reynolds shifted his body carefully.

"You should be." Browneyes crept closer until she stood above him. "I spared your life. You can thank me for that."

"No."

"Fronzi wants to keep ripping right into you, but I told her you're not worth it."

Reynolds stared up at her. "I appreciate the thought. But why are you really here?"

She stooped down to his eye level, her slender finger sweeping across his jawbone. "Harrow has asked Fronzi and me to travel to the little hideout. What did you call it? The Willows? Harrow wants us to look for something there."

Reynolds flinched away from her hand. "That's not why you're going."

"You're right. I'd love to get a piece of that girl you hid there."

"You won't get in."

"Wrong again. You forget, I know the secret."

Reynolds felt exhausted just talking to Browneyes. "What do you want?"

"Help."

"And why would you think I would help you?"

"After all I did for you?"

"You chased me down like a dog."

Browneyes stood, no longer playing the game. "Harrow's going to kill you. He's tired of your mental stalemate. He's sending in Hughes to do it."

"Well, thank you for the kind words—"

"Hughes is irrational," she interrupted. "He never thinks things through before he acts. His behavior is, frankly, embarrassing. I hate him."

Browneyes fell silent, biting her fingernail. Reynolds recognized her nervous habit, indicating some deep, internal struggle. He searched in her dark eyes for some hint of reasoning in her behavior. Had she really only come there to taunt him, or was there another reason for her visit? After everything he had put her through, did she not want him to die?

Browneyes leaned down, her face only inches from his. "You owe me." She kissed him on the mouth, pressing with such force, it took him by surprise.

At almost the same moment, he felt the slice of the knife—right through the bands around his wrists.

She backed away without saying a word and shut him in, locking the cell door.

Reynolds lifted up his wrists, and the rope fell to the ground. He rubbed the raw skin with his fingers. She had freed him. He hadn't expected that. She had the knife; she could have taken his life.

The simple act caused his hope to surge. Perhaps there was still a chance.

Moments later, he heard the locks again. Reynolds returned to his original position and covered his wrists with the spare rope. The Arenma servant entered with a few scraps. But someone also accompanied him—a thin man with mousy hair and a wild expression, like a rabid animal.

"That'll do." He dismissed the little servant, then came over to Reynolds, crouching down before him, studying his expression. "You don't scare me. The others said I need to be aware of you, but . . . nah, I don't think so. You look easy to kill."

"Looks can be deceiving." Reynolds analyzed the stranger. "You're Hughes?"

The Louving tilted his head, studying him. "There's no satisfaction in gettin' the kill over with. I like to know how they feel and think while I'm pretendin' to be 'em."

"How do you intend on killing me?"

Hughes took out a sharp, angled dagger. "Slicing your throat might be fun, but I'll end with stabbing you in the heart. I need to get your energy while the heart's still beating."

Reynolds smirked "That's exactly what I thought."

Without warning, he sprang up and grabbed Hughes around the chest, trying to seize his arms. Startled, Hughes regained his bearings and fought back, swinging wildly with his dagger. Tightening his hold around Hughes and pinning him in place, Reynolds used all the strength he could summon to hurdle him into the rock wall.

Smack. Blood burst from the side of Hughes' head. He dropped his dagger.

Reynolds snatched it and pressed it to Hughes' throat. "Yell for help and I'll kill you."

Hughes sniveled as the blood dripped down his face, flinching away from the blade. "Don't kill me . . . please don't . . ."

"Get on your knees."

The Louving sank to the ground. Reynolds fastened the rope around his hands.

He pulled out the medallion he'd held onto for so long, a gift from Spotswood. Now he would finally see it work.

The center of the medallion held a porous, white rock, which he held under Hughes' face. A small trickle of blood slipped down the Louving's chin and landed in the center of the stone. As it soaked up the liquid, it began to change color. A vivid breath of life escaped as magic penetrated the core.

Hughes eyed the stone. "You won't get away with this."

"Watch me."

Abruptly, Hughes flipped his head backward, smashing into Reynolds' face and knocking him to the ground. He leapt toward the knife, trying to rip it out of Reynolds' hands.

Reynolds' vision blurred as he struggled through the pain. His tired muscles seized and throbbed. His mind raced to find some weakness in the other man. Images flashed before his eyes that he'd hidden from Harrow—a sliver of golden hair reflecting the sun, his reason to stay alive.

In an instant, Hughes tore the blade from his hands, driving it down toward his throat.

CHAPTER SIXTEEN
POSSESSION

Peaceful, Dreamy, Sensations
* . . . like warm milk drizzled with honey.*
* . . . Happiness.*

*   He stood there, safe, well.*
*   His touch. Warm. Real.*

*   . . . Embrace . . . Tender . . .*
*   . . . Tears on both faces . . .*

*   "You saved us. You saved us."*

*   Head buried.*
*   Content*
*   . . . Could be forever . . .*

A girl, bewildered . . .
* drained and colorless . . . panic, stepped forward.*

"He is searching."

Remembering . . . the Monster!

"Your magic cannot last much longer.
Please help us if you can."

Shielded,
Invisible barrier to the dangerous outsiders:
The unknown enemy revealed . . .
Hissing,
Snarling,
Searching for the missing.
"I will help you."

. . . Questions . . .

"Where? Where is safe? Where must I go?"

The boy moved away,
urgent.
"To Silexa."
"How do I find her?"
"She is connected to this."
He held out a hand.
A dark stone, blue, electric.

"Find her through the stone."

Touch . . . Surge . . . Sensations . . .
Happy! Joyful! Dancing!
. . . Connection with a person so close . . .

Power rushing into veins, pumping . . .

. . . pulsing . . . searching for an outlet.

The pull!

. . . swift rush of wind . . . moving to its home.

In secret,

A sobbing, tear-filled girl.

. . . a fallen prince.

The scar still evident on her neck . . . the girl from the parade!

She sees the magic.

Astonishment on her face!

The Pull!!

. . . flashing before her . . .

. . . a scream stuck inside!

Naomi gasped. She sat straight up, nearly knocking her head on a shelf. *No,* she thought. No. She needed to go back. Zander was there. He needed her. The dream mixed with reality, though the confusion abated when she saw the blurry outline of someone standing near.

"Naomi?" Katia's face came into focus. "She's awake." Two other figures came to her side. "Are you okay?"

Naomi's head dripped with sweat. She felt clammy and cold, bewildered by her experience, but physically there, alive.

"Yes." She lay back down. "Where am I?"

"We're in a storage room at the Silver Fox Inn." Katia looked around the room. "We didn't have money to pay for a room, but it's still raining and we needed a place to keep you safe. We can't escape the weather, it seems." Katia looked at her more closely. "Are you sure you're okay?

Naomi sighed. "I don't know. I feel drained."

"You went all glassy and just collapsed on us. Landon brought you in."

Landon's face came into view. "You weigh practically nothing."

"How long have I been out?"

"Not long. But you were shaking. Like something possessed. I was nervous. We all were."

Naomi sank back against the wall. The others quieted as the sounds of the rain outside filled the room with constant, musical patters. Naomi liked the noise. It numbed her thoughts, so her feelings wouldn't overwhelm her mind.

The dream had carried her through the wind and down to the scenic coast, to a beautiful city surrounding a huge palace. It could only be Southwick, the capital. Zander was there, in danger.

Angry and misused magic possessed him, overpowering him. But Naomi tamed it like an obedient dog. It recognized her. It trusted her. She reached her hand for Zander and pulled him to safety.

It seemed so real, even if it had happened hundreds of miles from Southwick. Zander and someone else—a young woman with silver hair—saved from danger. It somehow connected to the prince and the black-haired girl, her scar as visible as ever—the beginning of everything.

Katia broke the silence. "Well, we're staying hidden tonight. I think we all need to dry off. And I need some real sleep. Micah says his uncle's home is only a day's journey east."

Micah lowered his hood so Naomi could see his bright eyes. "Fine matters of fun for us. Spotswood will be pleased."

Naomi had given up trying to figure out Micah's meanings. The dream had drained her of all energy. She needed to rest.

But before the vision, something had happened, and only now did she remember. "Where's Taren?"

"We don't know," Landon answered. "He vanished when you collapsed."

"Taren disappeared?"

Landon straddled a vacant stool near her. "I think it's best. It's time for us to move ahead without him."

The thought of Taren suddenly made her insides hurt. Naomi had studied him closely during the last week of traveling with him. Quiet but intelligent, Taren kept to himself, observing everything with a serious eye. Even after days together, his magic remained an enigma. It made it hard to trust him. But, although Naomi hated to admit it to herself, Taren had an unmistakable appeal. Something about him left her searching for . . . more.

Despite his mysterious silence, he had unwittingly given one clue that haunted her, a terrifying revelation of his identity—his surname. He'd casually dispensed this information as if it had no meaning, but Naomi knew the name. She would never forget it.

Lockwood.

Right before her collapse, she'd been watching him closely as he walked ahead of her. He kept looking back, as if expecting something. Then, suddenly, an invisible force pressed against her, pushing her back.

At first, she couldn't tell what had happened, just stumbled a bit. But when she looked again at Taren, his eyes pierced through her like a knife.

She had felt a scream of violence inside. Her magic reacted, though she couldn't understand why—like an invisible shield had risen up to protect her. In an instant, the terror vanished, and Taren turned and walked ahead.

She couldn't remember anything more.

Lost in her thoughts, Naomi gradually regained awareness of the conversation going on without her.

"I guess you're right, but I never trusted him." Landon leaned back on his stool.

"There's no reason to think he's a threat. He said he would leave when we got to the mountains, and he did. So, I think we should stay."

"Bad idea, Kat. Just trust me on this."

"I never trusted you before Naomi came around. Why should I trust you now?"

Landon rose to his feet, staring down at Katia. "I always had faith in you. Where's your faith in me?" He held her stare, plain and serious. She didn't flinch.

Naomi looked back and forth between the two. "Why must you two always fight? It doesn't solve anything."

Landon broke his gaze from Katia, turning to Naomi. "Taren is trouble. I've seen the things that he can do—he used to demonstrate on the animals near the barracks. We shouldn't stay."

"Micah, what do you think?"

Micah smiled. "I don't think we have a choice. He will follow us whether we will it or not."

"What do you mean?"

"I think he can read thoughts—most peoples'. I know he cannot penetrate Naomi's."

Naomi puzzled through her memories, piecing it together. "He struggled the first time he met me. After I paralyzed Aristatolis."

"He is observing all of us. Curiosity drives him, creating a new reality between the thinker and the victim."

Katia squirmed on her seat. "I don't follow."

"Taren wants Naomi," Landon clarified. "Which means we need to protect her more than ever."

Micah beamed. "Spotswood's home will be very safe for you."

Naomi mulled the options and came to a painful conclusion. "I need a moment to think."

"No," Landon protested. "We aren't leaving you—"

"Please. Go get supplies." Naomi watched Landon's expression soften to her plea. "Nothing will happen to me."

Observing all of this, Katia glared at Landon. "Sure. Fine. I'll go look for some food." She left without a word to Naomi.

"We'll be back in just a moment." Landon grabbed Micah by the shoulder and directed him toward the door, shutting it behind him.

※

Naomi waited for the right moment, then jumped up and began searching the storage room for anything that might help her. Her small knapsack sat next to her, virtually empty. Inside the room stood barrels of ale and honey wine—nothing useful. Nearby lay a small knife, the one Katia had brought with her.

She had a rash thought. Taren wouldn't leave her alone. Her magic warned her of that. She knew he wanted something from her, though she didn't know what. But she couldn't bear to have the others risking their lives because of her. The time had come to save her friends.

She found a broken window lying against the side of a wall—enough of a mirror for her purposes. Gathering her long hair with a string, Naomi sliced clean through with a trembling hand. The weight lifted from her shoulders as the long tail of hair fell to the floor. She looked again in the glass. The transformation was drastic—almost into a different person.

Perfect.

The detached ponytail lay still in Naomi's hands, flecks of gold sparkling in the dancing flicker of light. She stroked it softly, saying goodbye.

Taking the band of hair, she placed it on the ground near a bundle of tarps, making it look as if she slept underneath. Then, grabbing her cloak, she pulled the hood over her head.

Before she could reach the door, the knob began to turn from the other side. Naomi slid behind a stack of barrels and watched as an unreasonable, indefinable fear shredded her nerves. "Naomi?" a voice called, but it wasn't who she expected. Landon walked over to the tarps. "We have everything."

Now what? Naomi held her breath as she watched Landon lift the canvass.

Landon looked bewildered. "Naomi?"

Naomi started to come out of hiding—then felt a hand clamp around her mouth. "Don't move," Taren hissed in her ear.

Picking the hair up from the ground, a bewildered Landon ran out of the room.

Strong arms seized Naomi's shoulders. She struggled, but Taren held tight, cradling her against his strong body. "I don't intend to hurt you. Just tell me what you are and I'll let you go." He uncovered her mouth.

"I don't know." The reality of the words stung Naomi. "You have to believe me."

His grip loosened. Naomi seized the chance and pulled away, whipping the dagger around to point directly at his chest.

Taren did not move but held her with his dark eyes.

"Leave."

"No." His focus remained on her, cool and unwavering. "I know you'll come with me."

Anger heated Naomi's face. "And why would you think that?"

He stood very still, but his expression did not change. "I can help find Reynolds. Your other friends can't."

Naomi stared, trying to read his expression in the dark shelter.

"I know that's the reason you left the Willows."

Naomi shifted her knife, calculating. Was it worth the risk?

Suddenly, Taren snatched her wrist and squeezed, hard. Naomi winced, and the knife clattered to the ground. "I don't have time to waste. You're coming with me."

Naomi met his gaze. "I'll come, but because I choose to."

"I'm not giving you a choice."

"You're wrong. I have something you want."

Taren squinted as if trying to read her expression, but she didn't flinch from his gaze. "And what's that?"

Against her better judgment, Naomi slowly lifted the chain around her neck, the warm light from the stone sending a flicker of magic into the darkness and catching Taren off-guard. "Looks like we both have secrets."

For a long moment, Taren simply stared. Then, still clutching her wrist, he dragged her to the door and out into the night.

Far from the Silver Fox Inn lay the ridgeline of Edenwake Forest. Crowded thistle bushes made for an uncomfortable passage, but Taren knew of a farmhouse not far off. He would take Naomi there until he knew the others hadn't followed.

He gripped her tiny wrist tight, increasing his pace to put distance between himself and Landon before the other boy figured out his plan.

The rain fell in heavy drop until they entered the canopy of the forest. The ground felt soft and marshy, covered with slippery ivy. Although night had fallen, an unearthly glow stretched across the forest floor. He continued through the misty patches hovering over pools of standing water.

Naomi began to lag; he pushed her to her limit.

"I have to stop, Taren," she finally insisted. "I can't . . ." She lost her breath and fell to the ground.

Taren stretched out his arms and scooped her up, carrying her as he ran. He moved much faster without her dragging behind across the vines covering the forest floor.

They reached the small farmhouse near a quiet spot on the river. Light gleamed from the windows. To the right of the house, a barn sat dark and still. It would be perfect.

Not many animals slept in the barn, so Taren found a stall in the back, stored with hay. The small piglets didn't mind sharing their home, too tired to squeal as he laid the exhausted Naomi on the soft bed. He couldn't risk her escaping, so he found a bit of rope and tied her to a post near the door, in case she woke and tried to run away.

Naomi looked peaceful, though the soggy clothes on her body couldn't be comfortable. His internal struggle returned. Naomi confused him. To him, she couldn't be more beautiful, and he understood why Reynolds protected her as he did. He didn't want her to hate him, to fear him, but he knew what must be done in the end.

Taren clapped his hands together and began rubbing them. The heat came immediately, like little smoke ringlets. He pressed his palms to her wet clothes until a light heat moved through the fabrics; steam rose as they dried.

The rest of the night Taren sat against the wall, drifting in and out of consciousness as he watched Naomi sleep.

Taren sat watch during the night as Naomi began to stir. She looked around and flinched as she saw the pigs nuzzled next to her.

"Careful," Taren warned from across the stall. "I'd rather you not wake them. Who knows what kind of sounds they would make?"

"You put me next to pigs?" Naomi whispered, her tone harsh.

"Yes. They kept you warm."

Naomi tried to slide away, but noticed the thick rope binding her hands. She held them up to him. "Is this really necessary?"

"It might be." Taren continued sharpening his knife against a stone. "I wasn't sure how you would react when we were alone. You're a smart girl, though a little too trusting."

"Why did you take me away?"

Taren smiled wickedly. "There are plenty of people looking for you, but probably not around here." He examined his knife again before continuing. "I know your little band of friends would fight a very valiant fight, but they would lose. You don't realize the kind of danger you're in, but I do."

"You lied to me."

"You were ready to believe." He shifted his focus. "I didn't say anything you hadn't accepted already. I think you wanted to believe someone chased you, to make you feel better about leading everyone on a meaningless quest. Actually, I deserve a thank you for saving you that embarrassment."

Naomi looked stunned. "A thank you? What do you know about me?" She struggled with the rope. The pigs rustled in the hay next to her and she stopped.

Taren watched. "It's only rope."

Her tone became a cutting whisper. "You think you know who I am and what I need just by being around me for a few days?"

Taren sat still, as calm as before. "People aren't that complicated, Naomi." He sounded out her name, rounding the vowels almost sweetly, which angered her. "Believe it or not, I care about what happens to you, and I don't trust the others. They're going to lead you into trouble."

"I know you have the ability to read other people, but I also know that you can't read me."

Taren sat back, evaluating her perception, impressed. "You're right . . . and wrong about my ability. I can't read minds, just magic." He felt a slight excitement at sharing the information he'd kept hidden from everyone. "Magic is different for everyone, and some are easier to communicate with. I'm curious about you, though. You puzzle me. I know you could be powerful if you had to, but your magic . . ." He trailed off, looking for the right words. "It's so unfriendly."

"Are you really that surprised?"

Taren remembered the shock he'd received when he first tried to read her magic. "I've never felt such boundaries around anyone. Usually I can get some communication."

Naomi examined her wrists. The rope had rubbed her skin red. She tried to flip it with her fingers, but could not reach.

"See?" Taren watched her struggle and almost laughed. "Why not try to use your magic?"

Naomi just stared.

"I have a theory about you."

"How could you know anything about me?" she asked. "You don't even know who I am."

Taren smiled, wickedly amused. "Well, you've got a good point. Maybe I should shed some light."

Naomi rolled back on her heels, indicating her readiness.

"I know Reynolds."

Naomi looked skeptical. "How?"

Taren noticed the color flush to her cheeks and waited for his jealousy to pass before he spoke again. "The real question isn't how I know Reynolds, it's how much do *you* know him?"

"Enough to trust him with my life."

Taren kept his temper in check. "You don't know what you're talking about. Saving you once doesn't make him a saint."

Naomi shifted, clearly uncomfortable. "How do you know Reynolds' character?"

Taren twisted his knife in the straw, his focus lost in memories. "I've known him all my life." He looked up to gauge her reaction before pressing on. "I grew up in Southwick with my father, who lived in the palace.

Everyone knew Reynolds Fairborne. He was everyone's favorite." A small, bitter smile crossed his face as he remembered. "Reyn had the run of the place. I was very young. I idolized him; every boy did.

"I was there in the palace with Reynolds when he first experimented with magic." Taren snapped his fingers and a spark of fire burned near the tips of his fingernails. He blew on it, giving it wings, and it took flight toward Naomi—an elegant fire sparrow that landed near her tied hands before fizzling out in a gentle puff of smoke. His favorite trick.

"Humans are not naturally born with magic. No one would choose this. It's a poison that saturates your body until it needs to breathe on its own. It possesses and controls you, and each element has its own way of seduction."

"How do you know this?"

"I wasn't always like this. Reyn wanted to experiment. It was his idea and he let the others mess around with the magic he collected—I don't know from where. He didn't want me touching it. He let the others, but not me. He said I was too young and that I was a pest." A bitter taste formed in his mouth. "He wouldn't show me, but I followed anyway. I saw what they were doing. I threatened to tell."

"So it wasn't his fault. It was yours."

"Wrong. He used me. He wanted to experiment. I agreed, because I wanted to be included. But the experiment went wrong. I have the scars all over my body to prove it." He pointed to a line near his temple. "That night changed everything."

Taren's hands started to fidget; emotion took over his body, sore from years of repression. "I aged overnight. There was no childhood left for me. Lytte didn't even know the magnitude of it until years later, when they brought me to the Willows."

He looked at Naomi, whose face turned pale; she bit her lip, seeming afraid to speak.

"I was only seven years old," he continued. "Seven! And already I could feel things about people that no one knew. I could make things burn if I wanted to."

"You can't blame Reynolds. It was an accident."

"I can and I will. The camp is not a place for special kids with special abilities like they want you to think. It's a decontamination ward for those exposed to magic."

"Maybe it was for your own protection."

"I don't need protection." He slammed his fist into the ground. "He persuaded us to go into hiding, but he was wrong. He took us away from our families and friends, trapped in that unforgiving environment where our magic remained bridled. Magic can't live that way. It needs to feed and breathe and live, just like us. To have it stifled inside is torture. And Reynolds knew and did nothing. He left me there."

"He did it for me," Naomi murmured as she clenched pieces of straw wrapped in her hand. "To make sure I was safe. To protect me."

Taren glared at her—such a naïve creature. "Haven't you figured it out yet? He cleans up his messes."

A look of recognition came over Naomi's face. "Do you think Reynolds did the same to me?" she whispered. "You think he poisoned me?"

Feeling a surge of unexpected pity, Taren moved close, cutting the rope from her hands. Naomi watched it fall but continued to sit there. "He doesn't love you, Naomi. Everything he does is to hide his own guilt."

He watched as her expression changed to horror and then resolution. Naomi believed him, every word. She breathed in and out, slowly. "He's responsible for me . . . for the way I am . . ."

Taren didn't answer.

Tears streaked down her face from unblinking eyes. Naomi fell back to the hay and lay in limp, disillusioned thought.

Taren thumbed the knife again, the one his father had given him. The warmth of the handle breathed a faint whisper to his mind. *I could do it*, he thought. *Now, while she cries and wastes tears on my enemy.*

He couldn't help but feel compassion, even as the magic spoke to him. It must be done. He must restore the magic—make it whole again. His knife could do it.

No. Not now. He would wait to see the reaction on Reynolds' face when he let the knife sink in softly, where it belonged.

CHAPTER SEVENTEEN
FERRA

Naomi felt something sticky covering her face and hair as she opened her eyes. The pigs, happy and awake, had decided to use her as their own personal saltlick. She squirmed and tried to move away, but strong arms held her in place.

Wide awake, Taren signaled for her to be quiet. Dark circles under his eyes evidenced his lack of sleep. He half-smiled at her—strangely refreshing, since she remembered all too well the anger he'd shown last night and the turmoil he'd caused inside.

"Relax," Taren whispered, though the feeling of his breath on her neck made her even tenser.

Soon she heard a door open, followed by the gruff voice of a farmer, calling to his animals to come and eat. The pigs scampered to the barn door, squealing with pleasure as they exited, leaving Taren and Naomi in quiet solitude. Once alone, Taren release her.

"Am I still your prisoner?" she whispered.

"Possibly." Taren sat up.

Naomi took a look at herself and felt embarrassed at how dirty she must appear. She brushed her clothes and rustled her short hair to a manageable state. Her hasty impulse to cut her hair rushed back like a smack to the face.

She eyed Taren, thinking of her next course of action. He looked peculiar in the half-light of morning—shady and wild.

His revealing history had changed her perception but not her intent. She still believed him a danger to her friends, possibly to Reynolds. Her action to leave with him might have very well spared their lives. Taren seemed to tell only fractions of the truth, leaving huge pieces missing—pieces she believed only Reynolds could put together.

"You look restless," Taren whispered. "Are you all right?"

"Fine," she lied.

Taren's dry smile returned. "I want to trust you, but I'm not convinced you trust me yet."

Naomi stood up. "Are you using me for revenge or just trying to win the prize?"

"I haven't made up my mind." Taren shifted his eyes. "Depends on how much you're worth."

Naomi stared at him. "To Reynolds or to you?"

Taren put his hands to his head and took in a sharp breath. "Naomi, he isn't what you think. He doesn't care about you or he wouldn't have left. I confronted him in the Willows, and he ran like a coward."

Naomi pressed her chest slightly and felt the warmth of the Vivatera against her skin. She knew that was real, even if Reynolds's regard for her might not be. She also knew that Taren's memories had been shaped by his lonely, bitter, seven-year-old self. "I can't know the truth until I see him," she said finally. "Every word you speak may be true, but I need to know it for myself."

"Who's there?" a yell bellowed from the entrance of the barn. Their argument had alerted the farmer outside. Taren seized her wrist in a grip so tight it hurt, pulling her through a gap in the planks and leading her to the back gate. They bounded toward the trees beyond.

A safe distance away, Naomi struggled to stop. "Where are you taking me?"

"I thought we would go find Reynolds and then you can see what he is for yourself." He pulled her onward, anger seething from his body. "You said he was in trouble. Where, exactly? Can you use your magic to locate him?"

Naomi stumbled. "How could I?"

Taren stopped, looking directly into her eyes. The closeness unnerved her. "I think you know. I'm not a fool."

Naomi wrenched away from him his grip. "I'll try." She took a deep breath and closed her eyes.

Her magic wouldn't play. She tried to relax, to channel, but it wouldn't cooperate. *Come on, please. I need to see Reynolds.*

It came fast, frantic. The usually calm spirit moved erratically, spinning in odd patterns about her.

Run, a voice echoed in her mind. *Get away.*

'What's wrong?' she thought to her magic.

He wants us. Save us.

'How?'

Protect us. Keep the secret.

Naomi began to panic. 'I need Reynolds. He will help.'

The magic spun around her even faster, at an almost blinding speed, little tendrils wrapping around her arms, holding her in place.

We cannot. He is seizing you. He has tricked you. Go now! He will find us and we will die. GO!

Naomi's eyes opened. She found herself lying on the ground with Taren hunched over her. She pushed away from him.

"What's wrong?" Taren asked. "What happened?"

Naomi scrambled to her feet, watching him closely and trying to understand the danger. "I . . ." She tried to think. "I'm no longer connected to him. I couldn't find him."

"There's something else." Taren's eyes hardened. "You pushed away from me. Why?"

"Just startled, that's all. I don't have much control when I . . ." She trailed off. Taren had tried to read her magic when she connected. Her magic always told the truth. "I can't find him."

Taren's eyes roamed over her. "Did you see anything else?"

Naomi looked straight at Taren. His hair whipped around in the wind and fell soft around his thick eyebrows, contrasting dramatically against his sharp jaw bone and dark eyes. She felt the danger of him, but also a thrill of excitement, wild and unhinged. A fire of interest sparked in his gaze.

Taren walked toward her, his hand outstretched.

Naomi hesitated before taking it. The magic pulsed through her veins, fast and frantic near her fingertips. She stumbled backward.

"Naomi, please. Let me help you."

Then everything changed.

She fell backward toward the earth, reaching out to catch her fall, but it didn't matter. Vines of tangled ivy caught her before she touched the ground. Naomi's eyes widened with amazement. She watched the tiny woven patterns yield to the pressure of her weight, cradling her from harm.

Naomi caressed the resting ivy between her fingers, her magic reacting to the touch. The plant acted like an obedient cat, purring at the attention of its master.

Taren loomed behind her. "What are you doing?"

Naomi turned to see him stop in bewilderment. The vines crept up slowly around his feet.

"Stop it, Naomi!"

"I'm not doing it."

The vines continued slithering around his boots in tight ringlets. Taren lifted his legs, trying to free himself. He whipped out his dagger.

The vines beneath Naomi lifted her back to her feet. She could see Taren's greed for her magic's knowledge, despite his attempts to hide it from her—like a thirsty leech, craving her lifeblood. He wanted her magic and would do anything to have it.

She turned and ran, her magic ready to help, narrowing the paths between the thick trunks and shrubs. Her naked feet moved nimbly over the ground.

Taren kept stride behind her, at the advantage for strength and height as he cut through the foliage. The vines continued to try and trap him, but he broke through their defenses.

Glancing back, Naomi saw him advancing. Ahead she heard water.

Run to the water.

Taren grabbed her from behind and pulled her down. She struggled to get away, but she couldn't match his strength as he pinned her wrists.

"Naomi, stop," he huffed, breathing hard from the run.

While Naomi struggled, the vines caught up to them and again began wrapping themselves around him. As he fought to free himself, Naomi slid from his grasp. Taren grabbed her by the ankle and she stumbled into a tree as he ripped off the remaining cords.

"No, don't run away!"

She couldn't escape him; he was too strong. "Why are you doing this?"

"I'm selfish." He leaned forward to kiss her.

It wasn't a kiss but an invasion. Taren's lips forced down on her, distracting her as his magic searched for information. A black, formless mass entered, spreading like a disease, fueled by a hatred that controlled Taren like a puppet. The destructive power knew where Naomi's magic hid and came with a force so strong that Naomi braced herself against it.

Whap!

The dark magic vanished.

Naomi opened her eyes. She stood, bewildered, free from her captor. Taren lay on the ground, knocked out cold by a branch of the large mulberry tree, its arm slowly moving back into place. Naomi couldn't believe it. The tree had saved her. She wrapped her arms around its trunk and hugged it. Energy flowed into her from the tree, filling her soul with hope.

Run to the water.

Feet light, she ran across the forest floor, drawing closer to the water. Large boulders replaced the small bushes of the forest.

The crashing river stretched before her. Naomi glanced over her shoulder, paranoid Taren would find her. The river, swollen from the rain, rushed down the cascading falls with tremendous force. Across the river rose a tall, slick mountain of rock. Alcoves of caves wound in and out like catacombs. She saw no bridge. She could not cross.

Not unless she asked for help.

Naomi looked to the tallest tree and pressed her hands against it. "I'm in danger," she whispered. "Please, help me."

But the tree remained silent. Naomi's hope waned until a small rustle of branches alerted her. The bottom limbs slowly lowered to her. Overjoyed, she grasped the nearest and hoisted herself up.

The long branches stretched themselves across the raging river as far as they could reach. Naomi walked across without wobbling until she reached the opposite bank, her feet touching the cold stone of the mountain base.

As she slipped down from the branches, she leaned over and kissed the tree in gratitude. It shivered in acknowledgement, like a gentle wind rustling through its leaves. As the branches moved back into place, she fled to the catacombs.

Hiding behind a rock wall, Naomi watched through a crack for Taren. It didn't take long for him to arrive at the edge of the riverbank. Panic filled her at the sight of him, his head still bloody from the blow. But, he soon left, unable to follow her trail.

Naomi moved closer to the rock. Although it was not as giving as the tree, she felt it move with her pressure. The discovery thrilled her as she began to understand her own abilities—a partnership of mutual understanding between the earth and herself. It felt wonderful.

She heard voices close by. Naomi curled up and shielded herself with her cloak. She tried to disappear, to stay hidden from view. But then she froze, listening closer.

It couldn't be. Naomi's heart burned, her lifeblood filling with energy as if her soul had returned home. Reynolds's firm voice reverberated like it had off the canyon wall after he rescued her from her fall. She wanted to stand and run to him, throw herself into his arms. But the voices of others mingled with his. It might not be safe. Just a glimpse was all she wanted, just to see his face.

Naomi lifted her hood to the slit in the rock and looked around. Not far from her hiding place stood two men—one dressed all in dark purple robes, the other in the unmistakable green cloak he'd worn the first time she met him.

Reynolds.

Naomi's heart leapt at the sight of his half-lit profile. A warning came from deep inside—that it was a trick or illusion. Things might not be as they seemed. She sank back into the shadows and observed.

The roaring river muffled the conversation. An idea whispered inside, calling her to press her ear to the rock and use it as a conductor for sound.

"Did you see where he went?" Reynolds asked. "I miss hearin' things with these ears."

"A man stood over the river just a moment ago," the man in the dark robes answered. His voice sounded strange to her—piercing and uncomfortable.

"Do you think Browneyes has it?"

"I don't see how she couldn't. From what Reynolds told us, the old man should be no match for them. Humans are nothing against the likes of us." Both men laughed.

Reynolds spoke again. "Oh, I hope they have it." He sounded unusually excited and silly, like a bully stealing pocket money. "I'd like to see it. It took all my strength to torture that information out of him. Can you imagine—a stone that can raise people from the dead?"

Everything felt wrong. Naomi shivered, but could not tear her ear away from the stone.

"That's only what he said. I'd like to see it with my own eyes," the other stated. "Hughes, why don't you change back into yourself?"

Reynolds laughed. "It's a badge of honor. This body is great, much better than my other one. Reynolds kept good care of himself. Really fit, too. I need to make the most of it."

The vibrations in the rock slowly faded as the two climbed out of hearing. Although she feared getting caught, Naomi couldn't help following at a distance, darting in and out of the catacombs that pocked the mountainside.

The two men reached a rickety ladder bridge crossing the river. Naomi watched as Reynolds leapt on top of the lashed rope and walked on it like the ridgepole of a roof, reckless.

As they crossed the river, two others emerged from the trees—two girls who Naomi recognized from her dream.

Reynolds jumped down in front of the crew. They exchanged words that Naomi couldn't hear. She tried her trick with the rock again.

". . . if you had just waited for me," snapped the girl with the long brown hair.

"Browneyes, all you do is play with fire."

"Shut up, Madden. What do you care?"

Reynolds started laughing. "He didn't care for you, you know."

The girl named Browneyes punched Reynolds in the gut. "Hughes, you're an idiot. You couldn't hold off your insatiable craving for once!" She shoved Reynolds directly in the chest, storming past the others on the bridge.

"So, tell me," the other girl started, "is Reynolds really dead?"

Hughes straightened up and gave a penetrating look at the blonde. "I killed him myself."

The world suddenly went foggy, like light drowning in water. Naomi lifted her ear from the stone, not wanting to hear any more. Pain surrounded her heart, as if it had stopped beating.

Tears came fast, flowing but silent. She didn't want to wipe them away. She wanted to feel them close to her, sliding down her cheek until they dripped from her chin. Her body curled over like she had received a punch to the stomach, the pain taking her breath and seizing her strength. Everything inside her snapped.

She had come too late.

Naomi curled in toward the rock. Tears stung as she rubbed her eyes with her dirty hands. The heat from the Vivatera hurt instead of comforted, a painful reminder that stabbed at her heart. Reynolds couldn't be dead, his blood used by shape-shifting monsters. She refused to believe it.

A resolution flashed through her mind; she would save him. The power resided in the warm stone around her neck. Lytte said the Vivatera could revive someone from the dead. The quest filled her with hope, something she desperately needed.

Her tears continued as the daylight faded. Her strength left her and she fell silent, cradled in the arms of the magically softened stone in one of the catacombs. The Vivatera, as sweet as breath to her lungs, pressed warm against her heart—filled with hope for the life she endeavored to save.

. . . Drifting . . .

. . . Drifting . . .

Searching with purpose . . .
Searching . . .

Following . . .
Bring the connection . . .

. . . Please.
Mind wandering uncontrolled . . .
Through trees . . .
Mountains . . .

Cave . . .
. . . catacomb

. . .an underground world.
Breathtaking ceilings of height unimaginable.
Crystals . . .
Carvings . . .
Sculptures of the lost world . . .
In a dark room among others surrounded in pain,
Crying for help . . .
The prisoner landed.
His white head stained by red blood.
His blue eyes visible in the dark . . .
Pain on the tender face.
Closer . . .

Searching . . .

. . . Find him.
Faces in the dark,

Strangers . . .

Strangers . . .
. . . but one.

It was he.
The searched!   The lost!
Glowing amid darkness!
Unreal and kindled!

> *His hair, untamed . . .*
> *His face . . . perfection!*

Magic swirling about him.
Swirling and frenzied.

> *Angry! Protected!*
> *The mask! The disguise! The façade!*

Whispers . . .
. . . Go! . . .
. . . Look no more . . .

———❖———

Naomi awoke in pitch dark to the echoing rustle of bats, taking off in sudden, startled flight.

As her gaze adjusted, she encountered something unexpected: two pairs of eyes, big and bright, staring at her. Hot breath filled the air with a putrid smell from the large, lumbering mass moving back and forth.

Naomi froze.

"Don't be alarmed," a voice broke the silence. "We won't harm you. I don't mean to frighten you, but it's dangerous here. I've come to protect you."

Through the darkness, Naomi could see the outline of a girl before her. She thought of the horrible people on the bridge who had stolen Reynolds's blood. "Who are you? Are you one of them?"

"No," the girl answered. "But they're near. Can you stand?"

"Yes." Naomi attempted to do so. A hand met hers, pulling her up. "Thank you. But who are you?"

"No time for that now," the girl answered. "Grab on!"

"To what?"

"To the bear."

"The what?" Naomi became suddenly aware of the great beast sitting only feet from her—a creature so immense Naomi would be an appetizer had he been hungry.

The strong girl grabbed Naomi's arm and flung it across the beast. As she grabbed tightly to the fur on its back, the bear began bounding over the rocks, climbing higher and higher, out of the cave and up the slippery cliffs. Naomi struggled to draw breath. The speed and strength of the animal felt incredible. She held on for dear life.

The bear dove into a wide cavern near the crest of a great peak, too high for any human to reach. As it slowed to a saunter, the girl let go. "It's okay," she reassured Naomi with a smile.

Naomi, too, loosened her hold and looked around in surprise. Before her stood enormous clear crystals, crisscrossing in a star-shaped pattern, reflecting light off one another. All the rock felt smooth, like river stone. In the middle of the cave, a pool of icy blue water reflected the gentle trickle from the melting snowcap carving a trail in the crystal walls.

The bear moseyed to the water and sank his muzzle in for a drink. Looking to Naomi, the stranger took her hand. "We will be safe up here. Please, come eat something."

Food sounded like a wonderful idea. "Thank you."

The girl led her to an area totally encased in purplish crystals, complete with ample provisions and a store of thick fur pelts. She pulled out some dried fruits and meat.

As Naomi ate, she contemplated her rescuer. The young woman looked to be around Naomi's age, maybe a year or two older. Beauty surrounded her. Her garments had been cleverly stitched using organic materials: leaves, sticks, mulch. Her chestnut-brown hair tangled in a nest of twigs and leaves, falling out in a wild yet elegant way.

"How are you feeling now?" she asked.

Naomi smiled. "Much better, thank you."

"Are you from the Northern Crest?"

"I've never been."

The girl motioned. "I thought maybe because of your hair color."

Naomi pulled at the hair around her neck, thinking.

"Where did you get your shadesilk?"

"My what?"

"Your scarf," the girl explained. "It is made of shadesilk. Am I right?"

Naomi stared at her. "You could be right. I've had it since I was a child."

The girl smiled, raising an eyebrow. "Do you know what it does?"

"It does something? I thought it just hung around my neck."

"You're charming, you know that?" She laughed before continuing, "It conceals magic. Which leads to my next question: what are you trying to hide?"

Naomi felt stunned. "You know about magic?"

"Oh, sure," she returned. "I hope I didn't offend you. I just wanted to know where you got yours."

"No, no . . ." Naomi waved her hands. "It's just that, I don't really know."

The girl grinned even brighter. "How delightful. A mystery. That puts every possibility before you. It is very intriguing, don't you think?"

"I guess." Naomi sighed. The question made her think of Reynolds and she didn't feel ready to answer. "I just breathe in and out every day and live through it."

The girl crossed her legs casually and hugged her knees. "I love the thrill of never knowing what's before me, of being reckless and daring and tested to the limits and surviving it. Have you ever experienced life like that?"

Naomi sat in awe. "Not if I can help it. For the past few months, I have been living daily with the fear of being killed at any moment. It wasn't exciting; I'd call it terrifying."

The girl's eyebrow rose again with a mischievous smile. "Would you?"

The green in her eyes seemed to swim forever. Naomi felt lost in the truth that lay behind them. Then, realizing she'd been staring, she cleared her throat. "My name is Naomi."

"Oh, good." The girl relaxed her legs and sighed. "I came across some people last night arguing about a person named Naomi and how they feared they would never find her. But here you are. I had Paolo sniff you out, and we watched from behind the rocks. I saw the tree help you across the river. It really thumped that guy chasing you. Who is he?"

Naomi didn't feel like revisiting Taren's horrifying magic. "I'd rather not talk about him."

"Did you ask the tree to do that?"

"Well, maybe," Naomi answered, still a little confused by the whole incident. "I knew it sensed my danger. Same with the ivy at my feet."

"I love that," the girl replied. "I think that's my favorite part." She extended her hand. "My name's Ferra. Sorry to ask so many questions, I just thought we might be related—cousins maybe. I have family from the Northern Crest, and you look like someone I know." She smiled wide again. "My mother."

"Your mother?" Naomi's curiosity peaked.

Ferra waved her hand as if it were nothing of importance. "I'm sure I'm wrong. No worries."

"Where is she now?"

"Dead." Ferra shrugged. "It's been many years now, so I don't mind talking about it."

"Who was she?"

Ferra smiled. "Her name was Andriana Levonmore, from the north. She was a good woman, and people hunted her down and . . . killed her."

"Do you know your father?" Naomi asked.

"He's dead, too. Both parents, dead." Ferra spilled the information like it was an everyday event. "He was a king, you know."

Naomi almost swallowed her tongue. "You're royalty?"

Ferra shook her head. "I wouldn't say that. My father's dead and his reign died with him. He had no sons to inherit the title, and it happened so long ago that I never knew that life. I would have made a terrible princess. Corsets and stuffy dresses and parades and such . . . Not really my thing. I'm so much happier living a life of freedom." She squinted a little, studying Naomi. "Most people know the stories of my family."

A glimmer of recognition passed through Naomi's mind. "You're one of the lost daughters of King Prolius."

"That I am." Ferra bowed—silly and unnecessary. "There are six of us: Sera's the oldest, then Vespa, Ymber, Silexa, Fontine, and then me, Ferra. I'm the youngest." Her faint smile faded as soon as it appeared.

Naomi contemplated everything Ferra told her. She recognized the names—as the girls in her dreams. A wave of cold washed over her. "Maybe I *am* related to you."

Ferra seemed confused. "Why would you say that?"

Taking in a deep breath, Naomi grabbed her scarf and slid it off her neck, exposing her scar.

Ferra stared at her, dumbfounded. "How did you . . ." But words failed her. She came closer and looked at the mark. As her fingers gently stroked it, it began to shimmer, and she gasped. "Where did you get that?"

Naomi trembled like a frightened kitten. "I told you, I don't know."

"I've only ever seen the scar on the six of us. I assumed we have it because we're stone bearers."

"I have no stone," Naomi returned nervously, "but I think I am linked to you and your sisters. I've seen you in my dreams."

Ferra's eyes grew large. "Do you know where any of my sisters are?"

"Yes." Naomi felt her excitement coursing through her body at finally being able to confide in someone. "I saw one of your sisters at a festival in Sharlot, with the scar on her neck in the same place."

"Was it Silexa? Please tell me it was Silexa," Ferra pleaded.

"Yes, I think so," Naomi returned. "I've seen her and another with silver hair together in Southwick palace."

Ferra looked astonished. "I thought they were both dead. The winds and rain have lost their control." She hugged Naomi spontaneously, and Naomi hugged back. It felt odd but good.

Ferra took the scarf and placed it again around Naomi's neck. "Let's try to keep that a secret for now—until we find out who you are."

A lump formed in Naomi's throat. "I fear the only one who would really know is dead."

"Who do you mean?"

"Reynolds Fairborne." Her heart skipped a beat. "Do you know him?"

"No," Ferra returned. "I am sorry. How do you know he's dead?"

"I saw a man who looked like him today. He said that he was a Louving and that he had killed Reynolds."

"Well, let's hope he didn't." Ferra contemplated the matter. "Can I tell you something? The stone I care for is for the living: creatures and such that feed upon the earth, plants and life within the soil. I can sense things like animals do—with smells and hearing—and one thing I know for sure: there is an imposter among the Louving. Don't lose hope."

Naomi sniffled. "Thanks."

Clapping her hands together, Ferra rose to her feet. "I've got a great idea. Tomorrow, we'll ask my father. He might have an idea if we're related."

Naomi blinked at her in confusion. "But I thought you said your father was dead?"

Mischief was printed all over Ferra's face. "Remember, not all is what it seems."

CHAPTER EIGHTEEN
UNDERELM

Zander sat in a quiet corner, watching the prince sit up. Silexa had attended him for the past few days with some success, but without a healer, her guesswork often came with a price.

"Ow!" Bryant yelped in pain. "Would you please stop doing that?"

"Sorry." Silexa moved away from Bryant's chest again.

"They're definitely broken," he complained, rubbing his chest. His breath came in ragged gasps as he tried to find a comfortable way to sit up. "I don't think your magic can do anything to help fix this."

"I still want to help." Silexa sank next to him.

Bryant smiled. "You did. You saved my life. So, please," he reached out to her through the pain, "*please,* don't try to save me again." He looked at her face. "And thank you."

The curse infecting Bryant's body acted like a poison and had worked its way very close to his heart. But Silexa managed to stop its progression with the little knowledge of healing minerals she had. Bryant had vomited a good many times in order to get it out of his system, which both pleased and disgusted everyone in the small confinement.

Silexa smiled before turning to Ymber, who also needed a medic. At the moment, she looked peaceful, lying on a wooden plank, but violent seizures often beset her without warning.

"I'm fine, Silexa," she said in a calm, even tone. "Just resting."

"Okay." Silexa faltered ever so slightly, but left her alone.

Loving and affectionate, Ymber always stayed close to her sister. She did not talk very much, but watched the relationship between Silexa and Bryant, scrutinizing the effortless care and affection between the two. She seemed to both love and hate it. One could almost have mistaken it for jealousy. Zander understood. He, too, was an extra wheel.

The shed sat on a vacant property on the outskirts of the city, near the wall, dirty and smelling of musty, rotting wood and filth. Guards invaded the wine storage where they had first hidden. Zander and the others escaped without detection. Silexa found the shelter, but they needed to get out of the city. Where they would go, Zander hadn't a clue.

On occasion, Kubla—Silexa's wolf companion, whom she ordered to stay close outside the city wall—would find them at night after foraging for food. Zander enjoyed having the beast come to visit. It reminded him of the animals he cared for on the farm.

Days passed as the small crew huddled in the shelter. Only Zander ventured outside to meet Kubla when she brought them food. It didn't take long before the new space felt crowded.

Zander decided to stretch his legs in the fresh air and give the others some peace. He sat outside the shed near a high stone wall and looked over the torchlight of the city. The huge wolf curled up beside him as he stroked its fur for comfort.

In the last few weeks, Zander's world had flipped upside-down. He found himself once again lost in his thoughts, wondering about Naomi, his angel who had rescued them.

The winds changed constantly. Rain would come and go, but the clouds never lifted.

The air felt good on his face. He enjoyed the breeze whipping through his hair and on his neck as the wolf's head rested on his lap. Kubla, though a wild creature, had grown tender toward him. Zander basked in the unconditional love of such a marvelous animal.

The city of Southwick sparkled in the distance, surrounded by a high wall that acted as a barrier of protection. The palace, built high above the city, towered over the rest. Zander remembered the dizzy feeling in his stomach when he'd first looked over the enclave with Bryant. He appreciated its height now. The streets went around and around, winding eventually to the palace walls.

He heard footsteps behind him and turned to see Ymber approaching. His insides flipped.

"May I sit by you, Zander?" she asked, her voice and manner soft and gentle.

He nodded. She sat on the other side of Kubla, who stretched out her legs and snuggled in next to her.

"Thank you." Several moments of awkward silence passed, during which both of them looked out to the city. Zander followed her gaze but remained silent.

"I hope I'll remember it forever like this. It may not always be so peaceful."

Zander nodded again to himself. From a distance, everything looked perfect. Only after entering the walls did one discover the reality of city life.

Ymber stretched out her hand and touched Zander's knee. The sensation made him jump, but he liked the warmth from her fingers. "I'm sorry we haven't talked. I need to ask you some questions, if you don't mind. I know you're not the best at communicating, but Silexa assures me you can speak very well, so I hope you can try tonight."

Zander looked up into her face. "O-okay."

"We have been talking, Silexa and I, and have questions about the girl that came to our rescue. Can you tell me about her?"

Zander gulped. "She is . . ." He cleared his throat again. "She was my g-g-guardian."

"What do you mean 'guardian'?"

"She . . . took care of me before . . ." Zander tried again to clear his throat, holding back the emotion that wanted desperately to escape.

"Before you came here?" Ymber finished.

Zander nodded.

"Do you know how she came to us that night?"

Zander just shook his head.

Ymber bit her lip in thought. "Why don't I tell you what I know and then maybe you can help fill in the gaps as we go? Sound all right?"

Zander nodded in agreement.

Ymber suddenly reached for her chest and gasped. The moment seemed frozen in time. She recovered but looked somewhat paler than before.

Zander watched, helpless. Her spells had become more frequent. He only hoped that it wouldn't overtake her.

"I'm dying, Zander."

Zander felt uncomfortable that she could talk about it so casually.

"I won't survive long without my stone," she continued. "We are one. The magic needs to live and breathe. It needs life. I'm dependent on it. It's only fair I should tell you." Ymber became lost in her memories. "My father knew, you see . . ."

Zander leaned forward. "Knew?"

Still catching her breath, she continued in a whisper. "He knew he would be killed. He knew it wasn't his throne they sought. He understood the danger. They wanted the stones."

"Like Silexa's?"

"Yes." Ymber's expression turned grave. "My father thought it a great discovery. He gave each one of his daughters a stone. The bonds were too strong for our youth. Little Ferra was only two." A tear ran down the length of her cheek. "He provided a protector for each one of us, like Silexa's wolf." She scratched the wolf's ear, which twitched wildly. "My protector, Jaxon, is dead." She stopped, composing herself before she continued. "He sacrificed himself to save me from a troll sent to hunt me."

She became very quiet. "Sharrod sent it. He wanted the power, but because I'm not dead, he doesn't have full control." She choked, barely whispering. It took a few seconds to recover.

"I tell you this because that is what I know. That is all I know. I do not know anything of the outside world. Like my sisters, I have been isolated. I have been roaming the western ridge with Jaxon, my only company. I know nothing of friendship or love."

Zander stared in confusion.

"I thought I was dead that day you came and rescued me," Ymber continued. "I was prepared to die. Living a life without love is not worth living. And then I saw a small boy trying to save me. I didn't understand. I still don't. Why you would want to save me?" Tears streamed down her reddened cheeks.

"Then I saw something even more incredible. I saw my mother welcoming me into her heavenly arms. But she went to you. It took a moment for me to realize it wasn't her, but someone else. I didn't understand then, and I still don't. I've never experienced magic that powerful."

"But she's . . ." He gulped. "She's dead."

"Dead?" she shook her head. "No. I've never felt anything so alive. She created a vortex that night and pulled us through it to safety."

Zander's heart began beating very fast. Naomi wasn't dead after all. Relief rushed through every vein.

"What is her name?"

"Naomi," he whispered, almost afraid to speak the word aloud.

"It's time." Silexa approached, accompanied by Bryant. "It is nightfall and we need to move."

Kubla, the lounging wolf, stood as her master spoke.

"Sorry, girl." Silexa ruffled her ears. "It's not safe. I'll call soon."

The wolf shook her fur and turned to run, disappearing with long strides into the shadows.

Silexa turned to Ymber and Zander. "I've spoken with someone who can get us out of the city."

"Who?" Zander asked, suspicious.

"A girl by the name of Giselle."

"But she could be . . .?" Zander wanted to say Audra, but couldn't manage.

Silexa bent over to look into his face. "Everything will be all right, I promise."

Zander nodded, though he didn't like it.

Ymber stopped and sank to the ground, another spell taking her.

Silexa moved to her sister's side to aid her. "Zander, help Bryant."

"Yes, sweet princess," Bryant said as he let Zander move beneath him, using him as a walking stick.

"Giselle will be waiting at the Cat's Tail," Silexa encouraged. "It's not far."

<hr>

The Cat's Tail shop sat on a lonely street with nothing but a sleepy inn as company. In a shady corner stood a figure not much older than Zander. It must be Giselle.

"Hello," she greeted in a whisper. "I can't be gone too long. Mama will worry." She skipped down a dark path behind the shop. Silexa led the way after her.

The city of Southwick felt like a giant maze in the dark, designed to hinder invasions during the years of war. The walls deteriorated and new structures were built in their place, increasing the confusion.

Giselle moved like a cat, slinking from area to area in a way that seemed natural for her frame. "Not much further, ma'am," she said to Silexa.

Helping Bryant along, Zander felt uneasy about the little girl who led them through the city, although he did not quite know why.

They turned down a narrow winding alley of cobblestone and broken rock steps that wound downward in an endless spiral. Carefully, the others worked their way down the dizzying slope. Halfway down, a crooked door hung on broken hinges. Giselle tinkered with the knob until it opened. She went in first and the others followed. The door slammed shut behind them.

Complete darkness surrounded them. Zander stood at the back of the room, petrified to move any further without light.

He heard scuffling and then a gasp. Zander grabbed his little dagger, terror filling his veins.

"Giselle, where are you?" Silexa's voice rang out in an echo, empty and hollow and deep.

"It's no use, friend," a gruff voice answered, hard and unfamiliar. A small match lit a lantern in front of the stranger, his face distorted and twisted, yet vaguely familiar. Half the size a man should be, but with the bulk of a normal adult, he stood in the corner with a pipe in his mouth.

The girl had disappeared.

～❖～

"Hello, your highness."

Bryant squinted in the light cast by a dim lantern. "Matlock?"

"I am not Matlock," the short, scarred man replied through his thick beard. "But I am glad to see that my good relation has brought recognition. My name is Thornock Mullgilly. Matlock was my brother."

He lifted the light, showing two others. Neither of the others bore the scars that Thornock or Matlock displayed like badges of honor, but both wore the stern look of a Mullgilly brother. The one on the right had mousy brown hair and a thick beard. The other was much younger, with lighter brown hair and a baby-face. All three had very prominent noses, the same as Matlock. "These are Hix and Brandell, also my brothers." The two bowed low in respect.

"Where are we?" Bryant asked. "Where has the girl taken us?"

"To a trap," Thornock returned.

Zander felt the sting of the deception.

"Don't worry, my lord. We've taken care of her." Thornock moved the light to show Giselle laying at his feet, out cold, with her hands and feet bound with wire. "If you had continued on, she would have led you through the tunnels and back into the palace. Unfortunately, she is not the girl that she pretended to be."

Zander knew who Thornock meant. "Audra," the word escaped his lips. "Audra found . . ." He couldn't finish, too horrified.

Silexa turned to him. "Zander, tell me what you know."

Zander felt strengthened by Silexa's kindness. "She is a . . . shape-shifter."

Thornock watched, impressed. "Good lad you have, princess."

Silexa turned back to face the dwarf. "Where is Matlock?"

"My lady," he started. "I wish I had time to tell you, but by and by. Right now, we have to get you out of danger. There is a plot to murder you all—that is, all but the boy. I am here to take you to safety."

"Are you taking us to UnderElm?" Bryant asked.

Thornock bowed again. "We dwarves like the life underground. It will be safe for now, but we are in more danger underground then on the surface. I will explain when we reach the tree."

"The tree?" Silexa asked.

"The Elm under the surface that keeps our civilization alive."

Silexa leaned in close to Bryant. "Can we trust them?"

Bryant grabbed her hand. "Trust me," he said tenderly. "I trusted Matlock with my most precious treasure, and I will trust them as well."

Thornock waved them on. "Come, Majesties. We have very little time."

"What of her?" Zander asked, pointing to the heap on the ground.

"When she wakes, she will be rather angry. Best we don't find out. Hix!" Thornock shouted, turning to the others.

"Yes." Hix stepped to the forefront.

"Take the girl to the harbor."

Hix stooped and swung the girl over his shoulder. Zander looked closer at the figure and thought how horrible Audra had used her body.

Hix took up the rear, behind Zander, and Brandell placed himself near the middle.

The brothers ushered the group back through the door to the street and down the stairs. Hix veered right, toward the direction of the sea and out of sight. The others moved with swiftness, ready at any moment to defend and protect. Fortunately, they encountered no such need. They soon located a tunnel beneath an outside alleyway which led to a small, secret door. Thornock moved his fingers over the hidden keyhole and it unlocked.

They entered into complete darkness.

"Follow closely," Thornock said as he lit a small lantern. "The entrance is rather tricky."

The group followed without question, guided only by the lamplight.

The building had a very peculiar odor: the smell of musty dirt and old leatherwork. Although they couldn't see much beyond the light, the travelers felt they were no longer in a room—more like a large rabbit burrow.

~◈~

As they traveled, the burrow got smaller and smaller, with more tunnels splitting off in different directions. Slowly, they moved downward into the earth until they came to a wall made of beautiful, smooth granite, chiseled with great time and effort. It felt out of place there, surrounded as it was by earthen-works.

The outline of a concealed door became visible in the thick rock wall. Thornock placed his hands on it and pushed. It opened easily and he waved the others through, following up in the rear with Brandell, who sealed the door closed behind them.

"Welcome to our home." Thornock gestured broadly before him.

Zander blinked. His eyes had to be fooling him. He had envisioned UnderElm to be dirty underground dwellings with small burrowed homes made of mismatched brick. This place was not at all like that.

UnderElm was a grand sight. The entire city was made of granite— smooth, polished, and intricately carved. Tall structures loomed high in the vast cathedral space. Shops and homes lined the torch-lit streets, as if they were on the surface. At the heart of this city grew a wonderful tree, its branches lit with balls of lights, creating a calming ambience.

"The door is magically sealed." Brandell's voice was higher than the others'. "You will be safe here."

"Come," Thornock ordered, and the group followed him down through the silent streets. They passed the tree on their way, and Zander had to stop and marvel.

The lights of the tree were not lanterns at all. Instead, they were little round-shaped homes.

"What are they?" he whispered.

Hix stopped and gruffly said, "Fairies," then marched on.

How remarkable. Zander stared harder and thought he saw the little wings and bodies—unlike anything he had ever thought possible.

Thornock led them through the streets to a small dwelling. A door carved with a boar's head and winding branches stood at the entrance. The dwarf opened it and they went in.

It was a modest living space: very cozy and warm and comfortably furnished, though everything was proportionately smaller.

The visitors hardly fit. Too tall for the room, Bryant hunched down.

"Please sit." Brandell's manners were cordial and kind, a refreshing change from their recent experiences.

"Thornock?" a voice came from the upstairs of the home.

"Mother, we have returned."

A tiny, squarely built lady descended the stairs to greet them.

"You have them," her little voice crackled. "You are so beautiful." She reached for Silexa's hand, a small tear coming to her eye. "Matlock told me of your beauty."

Silexa bent down and hugged the old woman as if she were her mother. "Thank you. Do you have a place for my sister to stay? She is ill."

The woman looked upon Ymber, barely alert to anything around her and on the verge of collapse.

"Oh, yes, yes." She turned to her sons. "Boys!"

Within seconds, her sons took charge of the fading girl and led her to the upstairs rooms.

After Thornock and the others returned, and Bryant had found a solid wooden chair to sit in, he asked, "You must explain, how did you find us?"

Thornock puffed on his pipe and smiled. "I was in the palace with Matlock. He often returned home. Family's vital to him, but I hadn't seen him in a while. We all knew what he was doing and how important it was. But he said he was nervous about the princess' safety. So, he asked me to help. I was there when he died." The room became solemn and reverent.

Silexa's eyes widened with shock. "Matlock is dead?"

"Oh, yes, princess. My brother was murdered by the same creature who led you away tonight."

"How is that possible?"

"I was in hiding near the secret room. He came to find me. We returned to the room and found the form of a young woman, unconscious. When she began to stir, Matlock shoved me behind some tapestries. I witnessed the entire bloody mess."

Thornock stopped in his telling to collect himself. "So, I followed her. This girl collected blood from him and drank it. Then she did something I have never seen before: she transformed into my brother. Disguised as him, she passed through the security. I kept a watchful eye on her. On the day of the feast, she passed a tall, blond man and persuaded him to follow. Within minutes, I found him dead and his blood collected and used. After that, I lost sight of her."

"But how did you find her again?" Silexa asked.

"I searched for days to find the girl. She could have been anyone. But she made a mistake. I saw the same blond man again. Knowing he was dead, I followed him. He went into what was once the prince's chamber and found a large cloak and some other things. Then I saw him transform again into a teenage girl.

"I had known her for years. Giselle lived among our kind as a child. I knew her and loved her as one of our own. The sight disgusted me—to think that this murderous thing was killing anyone it wanted and using their appearance. It was wrong, and anger filled me. I needed to make it stop. I was the only one who knew, so I followed her. She met with the king, and I listened in on their conversation."

Bryant leaned forward in interest. "But how?"

"I'm very sensitive to rock vibrations, so I listened," Thornock explained. "I heard her plans, so I decided to get there first. I discussed it with my brothers. We decided to stop her, and it's lucky I did. I don't know if she could have gotten into UnderElm disguised as Matlock, but if she had, our world would be in jeopardy."

"Where did you take her?" Silexa's voice quivered with emotion.

"Hix will get her on a ship. That should take her far from here."

"But if she murdered so many, why did you leave her alive?"

Thornock raised his eyebrows, surprised. "I do not kill. We are a peaceful people, and I will not raise my hammer in anger. Do you think me just as her?"

Silexa became silent, looking as though she wished she had never asked.

Thornock puffed on his pipe thoughtfully. "My brother did not share my ideas, so I can't say the outcome would have been the same if I had fallen instead of him."

Bryant rubbed his unshaven chin, curious. "What did my father say—when he was speaking to the Louving assassin?"

Thornock looked to the princess. "That you and all your sisters are in danger. He is hunting for you. Down here, you are safe. The tree protects us. If we could get all your sisters here, they would be safe."

"Not safe enough, I'm afraid," Bryant interjected. "We are too close to the palace. Sharrod is up there right now, scouring the city. We're endangering you as we speak."

Zander listened intently to the conversation and wished he knew somewhere safe they could go.

Thornock held his tongue, seeming to mull the matter over a moment. "What do you propose?"

Silexa exchanged a glance with Bryant, standing up. "There is a place up north I know of that would be far safer than any earthly place. But getting there could be dangerous."

"I am prepared to fight if I have to." Bryant clenched his fist.

Silexa stopped him. "You do not understand me. As a bearer, I am prepared to die—"

"Silexa," Bryant started to protest, but she hushed him with her finger.

"I have known most of my life that it could come to this end. If I call my sisters, they will come. Sharrod cannot have the stones. I must protect them, even if that means I have to die."

Silexa gazed at the people in the room, ending on Zander's face. Her sad smile couldn't hide the reality of what she must do, and it broke his heart to see it.

"I'm not going to let you die." Bryant grabbed her hands. "There has to be another way."

"I am cursed. If there is, I don't know it."

"Let's look for it, then. Do you know where your sisters are?"

Silexa shook her head. "I have not been in contact with any of them for years."

"Would Ymber?"

"I cannot ask her now. I must wait for her to get some rest. But more than likely, she doesn't know either."

The room fell silent for a moment.

". . . I know," Zander spoke up from the corner. He knew things the others didn't. The time had come to share. He fumbled underneath his cloak for his hidden pouch. He pulled out what looked like a wad of brown paper bound together with string. "This is hers."

Silexa seemed to understand. "Naomi?"

"Naomi has . . . a burn mark on her n-neck, like yours. This is hers."

"What is it?"

"Her dream journal. I kept it w-with me ever since the day she dis . . . appeared. It doesn't look im-mportant. No one cared about it."

He handed the manuscript over to Silexa and she thumbed through the pages. It described places Naomi had seen: six young women, all with stones around their necks. On the last page, she told of Ymber and Jaxon, her protector, and the beast that hunted them. It went into frightening detail.

"But, how . . .?" Silexa started. Tears of confusion shimmered in her eyes. "I don't know her."

Zander met her gaze. "I have pieced it together. I think she is . . . your sister."

CHAPTER NINETEEN
THE ECHOES

Taren's world changed when he kissed Naomi. His magic knew where to find the answers, but it wanted more than her touch could give. What he found confirmed his theory. Her magic flowed the same as the medallion. He had never experienced anything so wonderful—but that only made the decision harder.

Frantic to find her, Taren searched the trees and rocks, hacking every vine he saw, without discovering any hint of where she'd gone. He could no longer deny the frustrating conclusion: Naomi must have made it over the river—which meant there must be a way across.

Taren heard rustling behind him to the north and saw two women arguing, both with braids to their waist. *Best avoid detection as much as possible.* Light on his feet, he headed south, staying close to the raging mountain river, all the while looking for any hint of Naomi. The trails looked as though no one had traveled them for years.

Then he stopped. A muddy boot print pressed in the soft grass near the edge of the river. The track looked fresh—a large print made with firm pressure. He could tell a tall man's stride had made this—in a hurry, careless. Taren searched further. Two other prints accompanied the first. Naomi's little bare foot couldn't be found among them.

A small smile crept over his face. These belonged to Landon, Katia, and Micah, moving with haste, desperate to find their friend—a perfect opportunity.

Taren followed the footprints to a drop in the river. Large boulders sat in the middle, providing an excellent route for crossing. With caution, Taren leapt forward across the rocks until he reached the opposite side. The large boot prints picked up again, and he continued to track them over the mountainside.

He noticed one print—Micah's little boot—disappeared from the others. As a ground dweller, had he separated from them to find an alternate entrance into the caves?

Ahead, Taren saw a large cave open up by the edge of the trail. As he crept closer, he heard voices inside, echoing off the walls.

"I don't get it, though," Katia complained. "What did Micah mean about 'The Deceivers'?"

"Someone mentioned them in the inn. What did he call them? Lordings?"

"Laughlings."

"Whatever, but he said they're shape-shifters."

Louvings. Shape-shifters who drank the blood of their victims and could take on their form. The game had just become more interesting. He crouched behind a boulder, waiting for his opportunity.

Landon continued, ". . . and if they can turn into whatever they want, how will we know if anyone is really who they are?"

"Do you think these shape-shifters took Micah?"

"Probably."

"We should come up with some sort of code, right? So that I know it's you and not someone else."

Landon seemed to be suppressing a laugh. "Okay, what's our code?"

"I'll ask you a question that only you will know." Katia paused in thought. "Like, what's my favorite flower?"

"Sunflower?"

"No! Come on. You know."

"Chrysanthemum?"

"Snowdrops," she huffed. "I thought that would be easy."

"How am I supposed to know your favorite flower?"

"Okay, what's my favorite food?"

"I don't know. Ham?"

Katia gagged. "You have to know this. You made fun of me for liking it."

"When?"

"Last year. After Leto ganged up on Micah and me and you slid your foot out to trip him as he left the hall."

"You remember that?"

"I don't forget the good parts, just the bad parts." Her voice fell quiet. "It's peaches, by the way."

"And that was why your hair was that same color."

"Right."

"Okay, then. That will be our code word. Peaches."

Silence fell. Taren thought up a plan of action in the brief quiet, knowing he needed to act soon.

"You know," Landon spoke up, "you complain about me not knowing things I should about you, but you don't know that much about me."

"I know more than you think."

"Okay, amaze me."

"You're smile is crooked when you lie. And you never eat anything that is green."

"I didn't think anyone would know that. I hate leafy green things."

"I know you're in love with Naomi."

"Wait—what?"

Taren sat up. The conversation just became amusing.

"You are. All the guys are. But you especially."

"Wait, Kat—"

"Don't lie to me. I can tell."

"Do I have a crooked smile?"

She paused. "That doesn't matter. I know what I know."

"There is an appeal about Naomi, I won't hide that. But it's not what you think. I want to improve myself when I'm around her. It's like she lights a path when she walks."

Taren understood perfectly. And now, he also knew how to set his plan in motion. Looking around, he found a large enough rock—not too much damage, and he would still have mobility. Plus, a little blood on his face would emphasize his plight.

Taking in a deep breath, Taren smacked his cheek with the jagged-edged rock.

A sharp sting accompanied the fresh blood, swelling, warmth. Taren shook his head, trying to collect his thoughts, as he used his sleeves to smear the blood for more of a dramatic effect. He groaned at the pain.

The cave fell silent.

"Someone's out there," Landon whispered.

Taren just lay there, waiting for them to discover him. It didn't take long.

"Why, you swine," Landon muttered, short sword aimed at Taren's chest. Taren only heaved against the rock. "Did you follow us?"

"Yes," the word escaped Taren's bloody lip.

Landon replaced his sword, grabbing Taren's shoulders and dragging him up. "Where's Naomi?"

"She's not with you? She has to be."

"You took her," Katia accused.

"No." Taren shook his head, sending a streak of blood down his cheek. "Trust me. I watched some people take her. I didn't know who they were, so I followed them."

Landon glared. "Liar. I always knew you would turn on us."

"Two girls. They can change their shapes—I saw them do it."

"Where was this?" Katia demanded.

"Back across the river." Taren resisted the urge to fight Landon's grip. "I tried to stop them, but I couldn't see in the rain."

Landon eyed him skeptically. "Why didn't you use your fire magic?"

"It doesn't work in the rain." He almost had Landon convinced. "I watched them take Micah, too.

"I knew it." Katia shoved at Landon's arms. "Let him go. He's telling the truth."

"Where did you see them take him?" Landon demanded.

"The slope on the western face, not far from the river. I think he tried to climb there."

Landon loosened his grip. "I'll give you a chance. But that's all you get."

Taren couldn't help his smug expression but nodded his head. "Do you have a plan?"

Inside the cave burned a small fire built with sunsparks. Landon scooped up a few embers, then led them deeper into the mountain. Carved into the stone of the cave wall was a star shape with six points, each weaving in a different representation of elemental magic.

"I've seen this before," Katia whispered. "This is the mark on Naomi's neck—the one she hides behind the scarf."

Taren remained silent, thinking.

"I thought I'd seen it before!" Landon raised his fists in the air in triumph. "Her magic—it's in her magic!"

"But that doesn't explain why it's on this wall."

"Does it matter?" Taren interrupted. "This is an entrance to something. I think we need to follow the tunnel."

Landon looked between Taren and Katia. "What do you think, Kat?"

"I hate caves," she shivered. "But I think Taren is right."

"All right, then. Taren, you go first—I like to keep an eye on my enemies."

Taren didn't care. He preferred to be first. With a snap of his fingers, a flame appeared in the palm of his hand. Down they traveled the long tunnel into darkness—deep into the realm of the underworld.

The winding passageways of caves confused the mind, and the stifling air smothered the group as they descended further into the earth. Taren felt the pressure surround him, like a tomb sealing their fate.

Uneasiness crept through him. The tightness of the tunnels constricted his air, the flame losing the oxygen it needed to breathe.

"This is maddening." Katia huffed at the slow pace. "We have been at this for hours."

"If you would like to lead . . ." Taren suggested.

"He's fine, Kat," Landon stated. "Leave him alone."

"I don't think he knows where he's going." Katia's voice became shrill. "Some rescuers we are. First Naomi, now Micah. After everything, we're going to be the ones who need rescue."

Landon shushed her. "These walls carry our voices, you know."

Seeming to realize her mistake, Katia swallowed back a retort.

"I'd appreciate it if you had a little more faith," Landon commented. "I don't usually mind your sarcasm. In fact, sometimes it's cute, but right now I'm sorely tempted to leave you here."

Katia gritted her teeth. "Sorry."

They traveled a great distance in silence. The tunnel continued to wind down and down. Occasionally, they came upon an opening where the path cleared and large catacombs grouped together. The spider webs appeared more frequently, as if no one had entered that part of the cave in years. The sweat on Taren's brow trickled down to his chin.

Then, he turned a corner and found something quite unexpected: the tunnel forked in two directions, while the path before them dropped down into nothingness. Landon halted behind. Without warning, a gust of warm wind blew, extinguishing the light.

Taren snapped his fingers, but his magic wouldn't ignite the torch.

"Where's the light?" Katia asked.

"I'm trying." Taren snapped with no spark.

The suffocating blackness of the cave affected his thoughts. The magic wouldn't come as it always had. He lost control, the anger building again. Remembering the fork in the path, he backed away from the other two and listened.

"What now?" Katia whispered.

"Good question." Landon stumbled somewhere in the dark.

"Can you inch over?"

"Which way? I didn't get a good enough look to be sure where we should go."

Another gust came, stronger than before, and nearly blew them off their feet. Taren pushed his way into a safe crack. He felt someone crouch down and huddle next to the wall. Someone else stumbled, and the sound of rocks slid down the slope, echoing around the cavern.

"Landon?" Katia asked.

"I'm here."

"Don't leave me," she pleaded.

"I don't plan on it," he assured her. "Taren?"

Taren remained silent.

"Taren?"

"He fell," Katia exhaled. "Oh, no! He fell, didn't he?"

"Behind you," Taren called, though he wished he hadn't said anything.

"Oh, good. Everyone be careful."

Taren strained to see. Tiny veins of the faintest blue stretched out before them like tree limbs or roaming ivy. His eyes followed them around the walls and down the pathways.

"Do you see that?" Katia asked.

"Follow it," Landon ordered. "I think it's coming from the walls. Stay close to the rock."

"I can't," Katia cried. "I'll fall."

"Got ya." Taren pulled her to her feet, feeling Landon's eyes following. "Hold on to me. I won't let you fall."

Taren felt along the wall as they moved ever so slowly down the left side of the cavern, following the blue veins. After a time, it appeared as if the veins became brighter, giving more light to the cave. The lines moved under his feet as they wrapped down through the mountain, leading ever closer to what they hoped would be a safer place. As they worked their way down, the bottom of the cavern came into view, fifty feet from the top of the cliff.

Finally, they reached the bottom. This place didn't need light; it would only ruin the beauty of the illuminated atmosphere. From there, the chamber fascinated. The blue lines passed in patterned crisscrosses and patchwork clusters, appearing like heavenly stars. Three-dimensional shapes popped up before his eyes.

"Incredible!" Landon exclaimed.

Katia walked away from Taren. "What is this place?"

"No idea." Taren gazed upward, not realizing that someone was standing before them until he heard a voice from the darkness.

"Are you lost?"

The trio stopped. A man stood before them, transparent as a ghost and broad, purposeful. He wore draped, fine linens, a regal crown sitting prominently atop his head.

Fear raced down Taren's spine. He took a few steps back.

"You must be lost if you made it all the way down here." The man's deep, powerful voice echoed on every side.

"That might be true," Landon remarked. Katia elbowed him in the side. He winced, but recovered. "I mean, don't you think you might be the one who is lost and that we actually know exactly where we are?"

The man chuckled. "Yes. That might be true also, my dear boy. So, if I am the lost one, where am I?"

"Standing before me."

"A smart one, you are." The man walked closer to them. "I do not have visitors down here. I try to keep it that way. But the three of you amuse me."

"So you trapped us like mice?" Landon asked.

"Not like mice, no." He examined them. "More like children, lured in by candy. Just for the company. You made me curious." The man's smile was kind and sincere. "I don't imagine you will be able to get out again without a little help."

"That would be very kind," Katia returned.

"And may we ask to whom we are indebted for this kindness?" Landon asked, turning on the charm.

Standing behind the others, Taren knew who the man could be, or possibly who he had been. He feared the worst.

"I am what remains of the man who was Errenhardt Prolius."

"King Prolius?" An astonished Landon slowly bowed down on one knee, seeming confused at what to do. Katia backed away.

"Please, boy," the king said, "that was a long time ago, and my remains have long since become dust."

"But how is it possible?"

"I am but a Stain," he said. "Those who do not have magic would be unable to sense it. It will fade in time but not for many, many years."

"Well, why stay here?"

"This is where I am most at peace," he smiled. "Believe me, I would love to see the sun again, but I think I am more useful down here. You spoke of a girl with a star on her neck?"

Landon and Katia exchanged a look. "Do you know the significance of the star? The same star pattern reflects on the ceiling."

Prolius stood straighter than before, like a proper king. "It is an elemental marking, the seal of six elements in harmony. It is also a seal of commitment, the branding of a promise."

"Is it you who I can blame for the magic that lives in my veins?" Taren spoke up, addressing the king.

Both Landon and Katia stared at the boldness of Taren and his question.

The king straightened up, looking larger than a man. "That, I cannot tell you. But the blame resides with me always. I am sorry." Prolius gestured to Taren with his palms open. "What can I do to help?"

"Help us find our friends, please," Katia interrupted. "They are missing in this mountain."

"I will do what I can, but I cannot leave. However, there are others that might be able to help."

Prolius looked up toward the heavens. Slowly, streams of blue slid down the walls and gathered themselves into a vapor-like, human-shaped matter, much like their beloved king but ten men strong.

Taren stiffened as the forms took shape and a familiar strong jaw of one of the Stains angled toward him. He knew it had been years, but Taren could never mistake the man his father replaced standing near the dead king.

"Help them as much as you can," Prolius ordered, hailing the familiar Stain to his side. "Cornwallis, a word before you go,"

A strapping ghost stood before the others. "Are you prepared to fight? The Louvings will not give up easily. They are dirty deceivers with a magic of their own. Do not trust them." Prolius faced them again. "Do not fear. Find your friends and find peace."

Landon nodded. "Understood." He turned to Katia. "Right, Kat? Taren?"

Katia also nodded, but Taren stood, white-faced.

"Taren." The Stain next to the king flinched at the name. "Taren Lockwood." The name dripped like poison from his tongue.

Before anyone could react, Taren disappeared from sight.

CHAPTER TWENTY
LOST AND FOUND

Morning came, though Naomi couldn't see outside light through the cracks in the mountain. She hadn't slept well, either. But she woke with hope that her life could have meaning or purpose—a thread to hang on to.

"So glad to see you smiling," a friendly voice called out from the isolated pool. Ferra and Paolo were knee-deep in the crystal blue water, searching for food. "I'd like to get some breakfast into us before we leave. Who knows when we'll get to eat again?"

Naomi froze, the memory of last night coming back to her. "Right. Your father. He's . . . alive?"

Ferra smiled again. "No, silly, he's dead all right. But he made it possible for us to counsel with him if we ever needed to."

Paolo's head shot like a flash into the water and came up with a large fish dangling from his teeth.

"Oh, wonderful, Paolo," Ferra cried in jubilation. She reached up and hugged her bear friend, who growled tenderly. "We will share it."

She was soon preparing the fish in a small fire. Naomi sat down beside her. "I'm curious. How did your father make it possible to communicate from the grave?"

"I couldn't tell you." Ferra moved her hands through the fallen tendrils of her chestnut hair, wrapping them around her fingers as she thought. "Not that I'm bound to secrecy or anything. You'd just have to see."

Ferra filleted the fish and threw the guts, head, and a good portion of the flesh to Paolo, who wolfed them down like a starving dog. As the fish cooked, she talked about her father and the cave—what it looked like and the many illusions it hid.

With her hunger satisfied, Naomi began to feel more comfortable. "Tell me about your sisters?"

Ferra's eyes brightened with the question. "Well, let's see . . . Sera is the oldest. She's a fiery redhead and tough. With all that we've been through, she's always protected us and understood the most.

"Vespa is probably the sister I'm closest to. She is very serious, though. Sometimes she doesn't like my jokes. But her stone is closest to mine. My stone protects living creatures—hers protects earth and everything that grows within it. There are many places in this world that have been poisoned by misused magic and it has been very hard for her.

"Then there's weather; that's Ymber, and she is a sweetheart, but very quiet . . ." Her voice trailed off in thought.

". . . and Silexa protects the minerals and has an adventurous spirit, but is a little rebellious at times. She feels the curse of the stone gets in the way of having a family of her own, but I think the stone is amazing. My life is very fulfilling as it is. Why would I need someone to complicate things?"

Ferra's rambling thoughts tickled Naomi. She sat back against the rock and watched the animated girl continue.

". . . Fontine is slightly older than me, by a year, and she protects the water elements. I argue with her the most. She can be so self-absorbed. She thinks too much of herself and doesn't like my attitude sometimes. I think it comes from jealousy, but not all the time. Once in a while, I find it fun just to see how far I can push her to get a reaction. I'm evil that way. And then there's me." She smiled big and bright.

They ate in silence after that, each lost in their own thoughts.

Once Ferra finished, she stood up. "Let me go grab some provisions, just in case." She winked.

Minutes later, they headed down the steep mountain slope on Paolo's broad back. The heavy clouds lightened, though the sun struggled to penetrate them.

From the mountain peak, they could see across the entire valley, and very far to the south. Naomi looked for the sea but couldn't see it. Ah, the sea. She prayed in her heart for Zander.

About halfway down the mountain, they stopped. The two girls slid off the back of the furry beast.

"Thank you, Paolo," Ferra said, hugging him. "Watch for us here." She turned again and grabbed Naomi's arm. "How are your eyes?"

"I don't know—fine, I guess." She shrugged, not sure where the question led.

"It will be dark once we are in the cave. Can your eyes adjust?"

"I don't know."

"Stay close, then." Ferra turned away from the light and headed toward the darkness.

"Wait." Naomi turned to Paolo and raised her hand to his head. "Thank you from me, as well."

The big bear rumbled something and looked into her eyes. She knew he would protect her, too.

"Come on." Ferra ended the goodbye by dragging Naomi's arm away from the beast. "Paolo will be fine. He's survived much worse. Bye, Paoly!" She yelled like a child leaving its mother.

The cavern got dark quickly. A suffocating thick air smothered them with a stagnant smell. Ferra held one arm, while Naomi used the other to feel the walls for reassurance.

⁓⁓⁓

Although Ferra seemed confident, she stumbled on occasion. Bumps popped up, rocks emerged, but still she led on.

Many times the walls around them would disappear and the high-pitched echoes of bats filled their ears—an uncomfortable sensation, knowing thousands of bats could fly at them at any moment. Just thinking of it, Naomi began to crouch out of pure instinct.

"Stop it," Ferra whispered after a while. "I can't lead you if you bend down like that."

"Sorry," she whispered back.

As Naomi began to stand, a strong wind rushed through the cavern, surprising both of them and sending the bats in their direction, swirling and flapping about their faces and ears.

Naomi squealed, flailing her arms, trying to wave off the flying rodents. She lost her footing and tumbled down the slope. Screaming, she tried to regain her footing. The cry echoed and bounced off the walls. She flailed about, grasping for the least handhold, but her grip failed and she couldn't see anything around her.

"Help me!" she cried, but her voice blended with the squealing of the bats.

"Reach for me!" Ferra cried out.

"I can't see. I'm still slipping!"

Somewhere amongst the noise and scattering of the bats, Naomi could see a floating green light, and her eyes fixed on it. The round orb was the color of snow peas, pretty and light. Within seconds, the bats calmed down, disappearing in a spiral up the cavern. Meanwhile, the light moved closer to her.

It illuminated Ferra's face, guiding her down the slope. She looked beautiful and soft under the dim light, her green eyes reflecting the fire in the stone around her neck. "Grab my hand." She extended her arm. "Are you okay?"

Naomi struggled back to her feet. "I think so. I'm not hurt."

"Good!" Ferra rushed on. "Because we're in danger."

"Why? What happened?"

"I used my magic. Harrow will sense it and know I'm here. We'll need to change our course to keep my father's Stain safe."

Naomi looked around nervously. She hated the caves so far. "Do you know where to go?"

"We're close to the Pit. If we move past the falls and down the Grand Hall, we might be safe."

"What's the Pit?"

"Oh, it's a big hole in the ground that has no conceivable end." Her tone was so calm, it was almost silly. "It was said that the demon Sharrod himself found a way out of the Underworld to the surface through it. Spooky, huh?"

Dumbstruck, Naomi could not comprehend how the girl could talk about something so dangerous as if it were nothing more than a spider crawling up a wall. She must be kidding.

"You took me this way? After you knew what was out here?"

"Yeah, but don't worry. You're with me. I live for this kind of rush. Don't you love it?"

"Are you crazy? I could have fallen to my death."

"Naomi, you have magic. You need to use it to its potential. No mere hole in the ground can stop that."

Naomi still didn't feel very comfortable with her magic. She would rather pretend it didn't exist. She started to object, but Ferra shushed her.

"No fear." She looked deep into her eyes, instilling promise and hope back into Naomi's heart. "Now, come on. The bridge isn't far."

Naomi took Ferra's arm again and moved with her along the cavern walls. She could see a little bit better than before; prominent outlines of rock cliffs and ledges stood out in the darkness.

She thought she saw a sparkle of something ahead of them and heard a small trickle of water. In some ways, she wished she could see it all. But would she really want to see a giant, bottomless hole? Gnomes, bats, other unsavory creatures—they all lived in caves. She didn't like the thought of meeting any of them.

No fear, Naomi thought. How would it be to live a life with no fear? She hardly even knew when it all began. While living with Ferrell, she could never remember really being fearful. She had to be strong for Zander.

Malindra had taught her to live as a free spirit, without fear. It must have begun when she realized her life meant something. But even knowing that, she could hardly decide what she feared the most—the fact that others were willing to risk their lives for her, perhaps?

Yes, she feared most of all for them, not herself. She didn't want anything to happen to the others while they were trying to help her.

How she envied Ferra and her carefree ways. To live a life without fear; to live for the adrenaline and adventure; to use her magic without restraint . . . She wanted that.

"We're near the bridge," Ferra whispered. "There's a way to the Grand Hall behind there. It could be tricky, though. Trollmartins live on the other side and don't like it when people cross. So, when we get there, we'll need to run through the waterfall to lose them. They won't pass the water."

Naomi liked the thought of getting wet. It sounded nice in the muggy cave. But she didn't like the thought of trollmartins—little fiendish rodents with horrible, bulging, white eyes. This whole experience was too similar to the Blackwoods, and she never wanted to relive that again.

"The bridge is not very sturdy, and strong gusts can throw you off, so wrap your hands around the rope as you walk."

This was all starting to feel like a very bad idea. "What rope?"

"It's a rope bridge," Ferra answered back. "Don't worry. It's old, but it will do."

"I can't believe what I've gotten myself into."

"Quiet," Ferra whispered. "They have excellent hearing. And we'll be just fine. If I have to, I'll use my magic again to help calm them down, but let's avoid that if we can. I don't want more attention than we've already attracted."

Ferra went forward and grabbed onto the bridge. It swayed and creaked.

Naomi hated it. In no way did she want to grab on to a moving, creaking, swaying bridge that crossed a fathomless abyss, all in pitch darkness. If it broke, it would send her tumbling to the center of the earth. As Ferra crossed, Naomi lost her presence and felt completely alone. She had no choice. She had to go.

With a huge effort, she touched the rough rope and slid her feet to the rotting boards. The bridge vibrated under her weight.

The steady wind rocked it back and forth. She could only think of getting off, but she slid her foot forward and found another board. Her hands clung tight to the rope. Not wanting to let go at all, her hands groped their way forward in the same way as her feet. The prickly splinters from the aging fibers cut into her hands, but she pressed on.

The process seemed to take hours, but only minutes had passed. Her fear mounted as she edged slowly across. She tried to trick herself, imagining Reynolds alive and waiting for her on the other side. His gentle eyes and strong jaw, his scent sweet as sandalwood warming under the sun. *Keep going.* She imagined his voice.

"Naomi?" Ferra's voice called in a whisper. "Where are you?"

"Here," she returned. "I'm coming."

"I think you'd better hurry. I'm close now and I can see one staring me in the face."

Naomi sank. Her vision of Reynolds vanished and changed into a snarling, hissing creature. She didn't want to move forward, just retreat. "You shouldn't have told me if you want me on that side."

"I'll think before I speak next time."

Naomi pressed on, ever closer to the creatures. "Why don't they attack?"

"They fear the pit," Ferra explained. "I don't blame them. Strange things live down there."

"Will you be quiet! Don't talk about that, either, while I'm dangling for my life."

Ferra snorted. "You know, you were a lot more fun last night."

"You mean, when I was crying?"

Ferra laughed. "Yes, exactly."

A gust came from nowhere and shook the bridge. Naomi went numb. *Just a little more, a little more*, she kept encouraging herself. Her arms began to shake from fatigue and fear. Out of everything she'd faced, that terrified her the most. And then she bumped into Ferra.

"Can you see them?" Ferra asked.

Naomi looked around and saw nothing but the outlines of strange-looking trees. "Not really. I don't know what to look for."

"Do you see the falls?"

Naomi heard the rushing water and knew what direction to turn. A sparkling shimmer glistened on one of the cave walls. "Yes."

"Stay close to me. When I tell you, run toward them. There's a pool at the base. When you hit it, keep going forward until you are behind the falls, understand?"

"Yes." Naomi trusted Ferra, but not her own ability of running in the dark.

A weird snarling sound came from beneath Naomi's feet.

"Run!"

The bridge swayed wildly with the weight of the girls on it. A trollmartin clung to the underside of the boards, keeping pace with them as they tried to escape. Naomi clung to the ropes and pulled herself forward. The trollmartin nipped at her feet and scratched at the boards, trying to get to her.

Others scrambled forward, attempting to nip and slash the two girls.

Naomi tried to stomp on the claws of the animal. The board broke and she fell through, dangling from the fraying rope in her hands.

The trollmartin lost its grip, but swung by its tail around the bridge and scurried to the top.

Naomi felt a hand around hers.

"Grab on!" Ferra yelled. "Hurry!"

Naomi grasped Ferra's hand and felt herself being pulled up the rock face.

But the trollmartins still surrounded her. She kicked and pushed to get away, all the while being whipped by the animals' massive tails. She finally reached the cliff top, but the beasts attacked mercilessly. Their deep bites sank into her flesh.

"Use your magic!" Naomi cried.

"Not yet! Run. I'm right behind you."

Naomi broke away and ran. With darkness surrounding her and a monstrous pit beside her, she had to trust without fear and race toward the sparkling falls.

She plunged directly into the pool of ice-cold water. Her breath froze as she struggled to the top. She gasped before finding her footing.

She could hear the animals behind her. Not knowing if they were following, she swam toward the trickling waterfall. She could see it better than before, a hint of aquamarine reflecting off it. The long stream softly cascaded over the rocks and down into the pool. Naomi heard a splash behind her—and hoped Ferra had found the water.

The falls became ever clearer as she moved forward. A faint, colorful light glowed within the cracks. Her head hit the wall of water and passed through it.

A delicate illumination lit the other side. A ledge stuck out close to the edge. She climbed out, cold, anxious, and apprehensive as she waited for Ferra.

A moment later, a figure emerged from the falls and began to climb out of the pool. A tall shadow crept toward her out of the water. A shadow much taller than Ferra.

~⚜~

A man walked through the waterfall and shook out his hair with his hand. Light from the reflective pool bounced around the cave walls in eerie slices of color, shadowing the figure in silhouette.

"Where are you?" his voice called out in the darkness. "You shouldn't be here."

Naomi kept still, petrified without Ferra near. Her heart beat like a drum, pulse thumping in her ears. She strained her eyes in the darkness, trying to see the man's face.

"Who are you?" she spoke in a whisper, her voice hushed under the rushing of the water. "Where's Ferra?"

"Ferra, is it?" he asked.

"Where is she? What have you done with her?"

"Nothing," he answered, still moving closer, "though I can't speak for the trollmartins. They were sparring for a fight."

"What do you want?" Panic filled her voice as he crept closer.

"What I have always wanted. To be—"

Thwack! He fell unconscious to the ground at Naomi's feet.

Naomi looked over and saw the silhouette of a girl, holding a long board in her slender hand.

"Are you all right?" Ferra spoke in a hurried tone as she bent down toward Naomi's face. She seemed frazzled from the duel with the trollmartins. "Someone else is coming. We've got to go."

Naomi stared in shock at the crumpled man lying unconscious before her. She still could not see his face and bent down to get a better look.

"No, Naomi." Ferra tugged her away. "There's no time. Come on."

At that moment, a second figure emerged from the falls.

Fear flooded Naomi as Ferra pulled her up the tunnel. She looked back at the approaching figure. It looked smaller compared to the first, but Ferra kept moving her forward.

"Naomi!" a cry echoed off the walls. "Naomi, stop! Wait—please!"

The voice sounded sweet and familiar. Naomi looked back.

"It's a trick," Ferra warned. "It's the Louvings. We have to move."

Naomi strained back to look. "But how would any of them know my name?"

Ferra stopped in place. "Good question." She closed her eyes, breathing in deep. "It's not an imposter—at least, I don't think so." She looked a little closer at the individual moving toward them. "This girl is not very careful about hiding her emotions."

Then Naomi knew. Katia.

"Naomi! It's you!" the voice cried again.

No trickery could fool her. Katia stood out, one of a kind. In spite of the wet clothes and dim light reflecting off her hair, Naomi would know her friend anywhere.

She ran forward and embraced her with relief. "What happened to you?"

Katia ruffled her wet hair. "Oh, so much, but I wouldn't know where to start. Where's Landon?"

"Landon?" She looked to the black mass of clothes heaped on the ground. "Oh, no!"

Naomi quickly ran back to the man that Ferra had knocked out with a plank of wood, turning him over to look into his face. *Poor Landon*, she thought. Out cold. A small amount of blood trickled from a cut on his brow. She ripped a piece of cloth from his tunic and spat on it.

"What are you doing?" Katia asked.

Naomi placed the cloth on his cut, wiping gently. "I would do this to heal Zander's bruises. Lytte explained how I had the magic inside to do it. Look."

The cut slowly closed and sealed itself with a tight scab.

She held Landon's face in her hands as her fingers caressed his eyelids and ran down his cheeks. Over and over again, she let her healing touch run through him, soothing and reassuring, until his eyes flickered open.

Landon looked around, groggy from the blow. "Peaches . . ." slipped from his mouth.

Katia smiled to herself. Naomi couldn't help herself; she laughed and hugged him, and he gladly accepted it.

"What? No kiss?" Landon swore, feeling his head. "Ouch! Was that necessary?"

"Absolutely," Ferra defended herself. "How was I supposed to know you didn't want to harm her?"

"You could've asked," he replied, checking his lip for blood.

Naomi broke in. "I don't understand how you found me."

"Well." Landon seemed to mull the events over before speaking. "I don't have time to tell you everything right now. Just know the king sent us this way."

"The king?" Ferra asked. "*My* king?"

"If you mean Prolius, then yes."

Ferra searched his expression. "How did you get there? It is a great secret."

"No time, remember? Some of the Stains were guiding us to where they may be keeping—"

"Micah?" Naomi interrupted.

"Yes, but I'll get to that later. Taren ran off before—"

"Taren's here?" Naomi felt the panic in her chest.

Landon glared. "Let me finish. The Stains sensed the magic and heard the screams. They changed course to find where it came from. I think they recognized your friend, but I recognized you and ran after you."

Ferra seemed very interested. "Where are the Stains now?"

Landon looked at her and rubbed his temple again, mostly for effect, it seemed. "They won't cross the falls. Their leader, a Stain called Cornwallis Fairborne—"

"Fairborne?" Naomi interrupted again. Reynolds' father!

Landon continued, ". . . said they have to travel around the falls—that the falls would make them disappear, or something to that effect."

"Tell me about Taren."

"He ran off when he saw the Stains." Katia spoke up. "I think Cornwallis knew him."

Taren was roaming the tunnels. Naomi needed to be more watchful. "Hurry, let's help you up. Can you stand?"

"I don't know." He looked again at Ferra.

"Oh, come now! You would have done the same for Naomi."

Landon grinned. "You're completely right." He put out his arm, and Ferra pulled him up. "I'm Landon Rhees, by the way, valiant friend of our dear Naomi."

Katia planted herself between the two, her narrowed eyes examining the other girl. "I'm Katia Ravenmoor."

"Yes," Ferra answered. "I heard you before . . . while you were arguing. My bear and I patrol the entrances to the mountain."

Landon's jaw dropped. "Amazing."

Katia elbowed him in the stomach, bringing him back to his senses.

"Micah is being held near the Grand Hall, I think," he said, rubbing his stomach. "That's where we were headed."

"That's not far from here. But we need to be careful. Louvings live in the Hall, and your friend could be in any one of the surrounding rooms. And Harrow is a dangerous man. We need to have a plan before we attack. If we do things right, they might not even know what happened."

Landon leaned in toward Naomi and winked. "Glad to see you know how to choose your friends."

The tunnels wound in twisting patterns like ant burrows, man-made, chiseled, and hewn. Ferra, knowing the caves well, led the group down the paths designed to mislead. As the opening widened, a magnificent sight laid out before them.

They stood on a balcony looking over a huge chasm—the Grand Hall, named so for a reason, but the name seemed insignificant compared to the enormity of its grandeur.

The landing overlooked an enormous geode, more than mere crystal formations; light illuminated every crystal in varying hues, like the colors from the falls. Carvings were scattered in and around the crystals; statues stood inside hollows and out of stalactites and stalagmites. The visual trickery gave the impression of the hall being filled with people. Bridges and catwalks crossed like intricate spider webs, while each light reflected off its neighbor in a dazzling display of sparkling color.

Ferra had warned them not to speak when they reached the hall, but it turned out to be a moot point, since they all fell speechless at the sight. Landon's facial expression said everything as he gawked open-mouthed at the splendor.

In the center of the hall sat a throne of deep blue crystal—a monstrosity out of place beside the intricate workings surrounding it. A man, withered with age—more ancient than the sea or the earth—sat in the chair and wore an encrusted gold crown.

Naomi had revisited the dream so many times in her head that she knew instantly who sat on the throne: Harrow, the ruler of the undermountain. Every hair on her body stood on end. She felt a sudden impulse to disappear, to sink back into the shadows.

Instinctively, she reached beneath the scarf and rubbed the mark on her neck for comfort. She felt exposed and wanted to hide. The treasure Reynolds had guarded so carefully lay around her neck. Harrow would find it and find her. He had set a trap—and Reynolds the bait.

When Ferra caught sight of Harrow, she pushed Naomi back into the shadows, but Naomi resisted.

From the landing, a bridge made of a dark blue crystal, lovely and luminescent, crisscrossed at various points to pathways on the other side, the only way forward. The easiest and best choice would be to travel down the middle and then branch off to the left, heading toward the southeast corner of the hall.

But before anyone could move, a tall man with darkened skin appeared near the doors. A deep growl of a laugh came from the old man. "Well, well, well," he spoke. "One of my most trusted Louvings. You wouldn't come in here, Urick, unless you had something to tell me."

"Yes, Harrow, I do," the man answered. "One of us has gone missing. It is Hughes."

"Missing? One does not simply disappear here. Who was the last with him?"

"Madden. He was near the falls."

Harrow seemed to be digesting the information. "If he fell, all the better for us. Hughes was useless."

"But he had the vial of Reynolds' blood."

Harrow sneered. "All that effort, wasted."

At the mention of Reynolds' name, Naomi took a deep breath to keep herself from succumbing to her sorrow.

"We also found an Arenma climbing outside of the mountain."

A sneer moved across Harrow's lips. "A Shadower?"

"We believe so."

"What an interesting turn of events. A Shadower come home. Does he have information?"

"Yes."

Naomi froze. She glanced at Landon's and Katia's faces and saw the same look of horror in their expressions. They had Micah. She slid back toward the security of the wall, unable to take her eyes off the underlord.

"Bring him forward."

The man snapped his fingers and two other Louvings appeared: one man with a fidgety expression and a girl with long braids of sandy brown, dragging Micah's small form, his white head smeared with blood.

A greedy look crossed Harrow's sallow face. "What is your name, traitor?"

Micah seemed hardly able to speak. "Micah."

"What brings you here, Micah Shadower?" Harrow spit his name out. "The Arenmas banished the Shadowers. You are not allowed to enter. But here you are, my sightless bird. My Louvings guard your precious race. They obey me, as you will, too. Fronzi?"

The girl holding Micah's right arm took out a small, sharpened metal rod and scraped it down his spine.

Micah screamed.

Naomi held her breath.

"Why have you returned?" Harrow demanded.

Micah looked up with a slight smile. "My body longs to be in the earth."

"You lie!" Harrow's fist slammed down on the arm of the throne. "Are you here to steal from me!"

Micah cringed but remained silent.

Naomi couldn't stand to see anyone hurt Micah. He was doing this to protect her. She couldn't watch; she had to do something to stop it.

"Confess it now, or you will die." Harrow stepped forward. "I will have Fronzi take out your heart and drink your blood. Her body will adapt to your delicate image. Spotswood wouldn't even know he had an assassin living with him. Soon all the Shadowers and anyone who crosses her path will find out the painful truth, right before they die."

Micah stayed still as he looked up to meet the underlord's gaze.

"Take him away and be done."

The hall echoed with footsteps as they left. The room returned to dead silence.

Harrow stretched out his arms, his head raised to the ceiling, a small hum on his lips. He snapped his fingers. The sound echoed through the hall and down the tunnels, changing in intensity as it traveled, making a rippling effect as it moved down and down toward the earth's core.

. . . Search . . .

Naomi felt the vibrations surge through her body. The Vivatera became violently hot. She grabbed for it, but it burned her fingers. She wanted to scream, but it would give everything away. She leaned forward in an attempt to draw it away from her skin. Harrow wanted it. He would destroy her to get it.

Ferra saw Naomi struggle and ran to her side.

Harrow stood and turned. He appeared hideous, with pupils completely white and eyes sunken in his bony face. His stringy black hair fell long and matted, and his robes hung loosely on his skeletal frame.

A low, sinister laugh shook from deep in his throat. The laugh ran low and rumbled the very ground.

"I think you have heard enough." Harrow's terrible smile chilled. Speaking rapidly in a language Naomi did not know, he raised his arms high above his head and snapped.

Everything went black.

CHAPTER TWENTY-ONE
FIGHT AND FLIGHT

Wild wind howled from the belly of the cave, and Naomi held on as it whipped about her. Her fingers lost hold and she began to slip. Grabbing onto the rock, she instinctively begged it for help. The rock softened and formed around her hands, gripping her tightly. It seemed impossible, but there it was. The earth had helped her yet again.

Ferra reached out for Naomi as the howling force sought to remove them all from the side of the Grand Hall. Her medallion glowed bright, her magic alight. Naomi felt the Vivatera burning with life, intense with energy.

"Come on!" Ferra yelled through tumult. She grabbed Naomi's hand and pulled her to her feet, trying desperately to find the tunnel.

As the wind died down, arms surrounded them, tugging and pulling, scraping and gnawing, trying to tie them, to bind them.

Ferra lashed out with her staff, determined that whatever it was, it would not get her. She swung out, knocking a few hands free, but more came—many more. She swung again.

"Ow!" Landon grunted, feeling the blow of her staff on his chest.

"What is it!?" Katia's defenses came up and her fingertips began to frost. Naomi felt the cold of the other girl's magic begin to encircle them.

A small, dancing ball of blue light glided toward their struggle. The Arenma, dressed in white cloaks with their dark, beady little faces, surrounded their bound prisoners. Landon struggled and was both tied and gagged. Katia's arms were wrapped tightly against her body. Ferra found herself fastened securely to her staff—all of them strung together in a great train. Naomi stood separate from the others with her hands bound.

In the dim blue light, Harrow's startling outline crossed the catwalks. He moved with fluid grace, as if he weren't solid, his body propelled by his blue-crystal staff—the source of the light. He spoke again in the Arenma language and many scurried away, back into the caves, leaving only a handful to deal with the prisoners.

"This is a welcome surprise." Harrow's voice reflected the darkest tones. "Set a trap and you never know what treasures you will find." He directed his speech toward Ferra, who struggled with her bonds. "But as intriguing as a daughter of Prolius would be, I'm more interested in your companion."

Ferra fought her holdings. "I'm what you want. Take me!"

"In time." Harrow moved his staff toward Naomi. A flash flew out and hit Naomi in the chest, slamming her against the wall.

"No!" both Katia and Landon yelled, yanking at the ropes.

Naomi's head rang with the impact, but the rock sided with her and softened her blow. She sat up, catching her breath.

Harrow sneered at Ferra. "I know why you're here. You're on a rescue mission. How long have you been at Mt. Ibis? I have heard of your coming." His yellow teeth sharpened with his grin. "Effrenus, the stone of the Wild, hangs about your neck, calling for me."

Heat surrounded Naomi as Harrow talked about the stone. Her heartbeat pulsed stronger and louder through her body. Tingling sensations flooded to her fingertips. She didn't know how to react. She'd never experienced anything like it. Fear struck her heart. Losing control of herself, she clung to the Vivatera for help.

Ferra reacted also, feeling the stone lift from her neck. "No!" She struggled, helpless. "You know nothing of this stone. You have no claim on it."

Harrow's smile faded. "You are wrong, sweet princess. I have all claims on it. It is mine. The elements were stolen from me."

"They were never yours!"

Without warning, he slapped her across the face with the back of his hand, slicing open her cheek.

"I'm what you want," Naomi spoke up. "Don't hurt her."

Harrow's head turned toward her, his stare sending chills down her spine. "Your dream-sight is powerful, little bird. Too bad your rescue will fail. Reynolds is no more."

Naomi lost her breath. Her head began to spin. The reality she feared pressed heavy on her chest, crushing her spirit from the outside. Against her heartache, the Vivatera's searing heat felt suddenly, strangely comfortable.

"Stop it!" Katia yelled, then seemed to wish she hadn't as Harrow's glare shifted momentarily toward her, then back to Ferra.

Naomi saw Landon glance down at Katia, seeming to pick up on the rage in her face and the ice forming around her fingers. He tried to inch closer to her through the bindings.

Harrow stroked Ferra's bleeding cut with his hand, his lust apparent. "I haven't seen fresh blood in so long. I will not take it from you. But that doesn't mean that I don't crave it."

Naomi watched Harrow, disgusted. She hadn't notice until then that her ropes had unraveled a fraction. Glancing at Landon, she could tell he had a plan, though not what it was. Landon had almost reached Katia's hand. Maybe he needed a distraction in order for it to work.

Then she had an idea. The Vivatera would help her.

Naomi stood, the ropes falling down around her ankles. The Arenmas around her scattered, sensing her magic. She grabbed the medallion around her neck.

Harrow's attention turned immediately to her. "Where did you get that?" His voice echoed off the crystals.

"I stole it!" Naomi's voice rang just as clear.

The intense hunger made Harrow's white eyes glow.

Landon reacted perfectly. He grabbed Katia's hand, the magic moving quickly through their bodies. Ice moved up their arms to the ropes. Landon moved his wrists and shattered the ropes, pulling the icy gag from his mouth. Still holding onto Katia, he lifted her hand high and forced his magic through her.

An enormous roar echoed through the hall.

Harrow stopped. The remaining Arenmas scattered in alarm.

It emerged slowly, but the form was unmistakable: a large, white, crystallized lion rolled out before them, the mane frost-tipped, the body clear and smooth. He shook out his mane and snow flew all about, blinding and freezing as it fell.

The giant lion reared up, sending shards of ice toward Harrow.

He raised his staff to deflect the icy assault, but the lion's roar continued, crashing against the walls and shaking the earth.

Naomi used the distraction and aimed the Vivatera at the blue crystal. A light shot from the medallion and fractured into a million different rays. Each crystal in the entire hall lit up, a hum of life accompanying the glowing rock.

Harrow, enraged by the onslaught of magic, created a powerful cyclone surrounding him.

Landon lifted his arm forward again, and the lion headed straight for Harrow.

Sparks and shards collided, scattering in a brilliant display, filling the hall with dancing snow and falling ash. Harrow disappeared.

Naomi collapsed, letting go of the Vivatera, which cooled and slid back in place next to her chest.

Pull away from the rock! an inner voice screamed in her ear, reverberating through the stone. She moved her hand away and the vibrations stopped.

Landon let go of Katia's hand. "Come on," he yelled as he ran over to Ferra and untied her.

Naomi moved forward.

"No!" Ferra shouted. "Go back and hide."

"I'm ready to help—"

Ferra cut her off. "He's not gone. He's traveling through the rock, alerting the others. He'll come after you first."

The doors in the large hall swung open, and the sounds of swiftly moving feet approached. The time had come to find out how prepared they really were.

~⟐~

Harrow's voice rang through the hallways and pathways of the cave, the vibrations causing everything to shake. The Louvings immediately went on alert. Three returned from the Hall, two girls hauling their prisoner and a dark Louving standing guard. All stopped dead in their tracks to listen.

Taren also listened. His magic felt the vibrations, hearing the instructions for the Louvings.

He sat, perched on a small ledge in the tunnel leading to the Grand Hall. The small cove gave him a full view of what happened below. He expected to see the Stains from the Echoes, but he hadn't expected to see Micah.

The Louvings dragged the boy back to a holding chamber. Blood smeared his face. Micah might be odd, but he had his uses. Taren couldn't have him die at the hands of such worthless creatures.

At that moment, Micah turned to Taren, communicating through his look. Somehow, suddenly, there was a connection between the two of them. Micah had understood Harrow's message loud and clear: *The trap worked. The girl is here. Kill the intruders! Bring me the stones.*

Taren watched the Louvings carefully, waiting for his opportunity. Tucked deep in his vest pocket rested his knife. The small blade, though inconvenient for swordplay, hid a deadly secret. The metal hilt still bore his family crest, rubbed smooth but legible. It had been used once to kill, but not by him. He had never used it for anything but his own amusement. Tonight, he would use it for more, if needed. The thought turned his insides cold.

"Fronzi?" the one with dark braids asked as the last of the vibrations faded. "What does he mean by the girl? What girl?"

"Reynolds' girl." Fronzi turned her head side to side in order to hear the full message. "Stay here with him, Browneyes, while I go look."

The one called Browneyes rolled her eyes. "I'm not staying here. Urick can stay with him."

"Your captive is coming with us back into the Hall." The dark male referred to as Urick didn't look like the kind of Louving to be ordered around. He pulled out an intimidating sword from his waist. "Something happened in the Hall."

Other Louvings joined the girls, each one arguing about Harrow's message.

"Stop, everyone!" Urick yelled at the others as he raised his hands to calm them. "Stick to the plan. I'll get the girl. Leave no one else. Harrow's orders."

"Does that mean this one?" Fronzi pointed to the roped Micah.

The group of a dozen Louvings now stood near the poor tied-up figure of Micah, their eyes shining with a strange hunger, inhuman and morbid. Urick grinned. "I think he qualifies, don't you?"

Taren's reaction came as impulse. With a swift leap, he landed near Micah. The Louvings barely had time to register what had happened before Taren pulled sharply on the rope, whipping it toward them and sending little Micah flying with it. He felt sorry about using him as a weapon, but surprisingly Micah reacted, coiling himself into a ball as he came toward the others. He hit the Louvings, knocking a few down.

Before they recovered from the surprise, Taren whipped the rope again and again. The rope felt as dry as a grass reed and heated immediately at his touch. As it began to glow, it burned his fingers, but he withstood the relatively small discomfort compared to hungry Louvings.

The fire smoldered down the length of the rope until it singed Micah. He yelped in pain, losing his concentration. Taren yanked the rope again and it snapped, sending them both flying. Micah hit the wall and slid down, dazed. Taren tumbled backward but quickly recovered and jumped to his feet, unharmed.

The Louvings swarmed again, this time in anger. Fronzi looked especially menacing, having been whacked by Micah repeatedly. Taren caught sight of a Louving in the back, not threatening but curiously staring at him. He felt familiar, but in those few calculated seconds, he pushed the feeling aside and stood ready to defend.

Taren felt the magic inside him screaming to get out, ready to destroy the Louvings. His body began to tremble as the rage coursed through his veins. It needed an outlet or it would consume him.

He bent down and grabbed a handful of stones. They instantly burned like lava and he threw them at his attackers.

The rock exploded, popping and sizzling around the Louvings, causing panic and confusion. Some retreated and hid, but others advanced towards him again with fury in their eyes.

Taren headed closer to Micah, protecting him from further harm. "Come on!"

Micah shook himself awake. The faces of the Louvings were coming at them from every direction. Micah rubbed his fingertips. The dust gathered around his hands in rolling whirlwinds, and he blew it at the Louvings, blinding them.

Taren launched another big rock which exploded like fireworks around the dazed Louvings. The distraction worked.

Ducking through the dust, he sprang toward the opening, snagging little Micah under his arms as he went. He ran toward a faint blue light before him. Suddenly, his eyes were dazzled as they entered the splendor of the Grand Hall.

"Micah!" a voice echoed around the hall, coming from above.

Taren looked up, his eyes connecting with Naomi, a look of horror visible on her beautiful face. His magic inside ignited with the hunger once more.

She was hunched down near the rim of a cliff above him. A girl with a long bow staff stood beside her, someone Taren hadn't seen before. They were all in danger. The Louvings wouldn't stop. He had to find a way to her. "They're coming!" he shouted in warning.

The next moment, the Louvings rushed into the hall behind him, swords and other weapons in their hands and bloodlust in their faces. Chaos broke out.

Taren dropped Micah in time to turn and create a wall of dragon fire behind them. The scorching heat deflected some attackers but fueled others. His eyes landed on the one named Browneyes, clearly one of the most dangerous. An inner intensity resonated through her narrow brow.

Browneyes stared Taren down, but something above distracted her. Taren turned his focus up to see Landon and Katia crossing the crystal bridge.

Eyes rolling into the back of her head, Browneyes let out a high-pitched shriek. Everything around the room began to shatter—ornate statues, glass ornaments, stalagmite sculptures.

Cracks began to appear in the blue crystal bridge. Landon and Katia scrambled back, but the bridge shattered under them. The girl near Naomi tried to use her staff to help, but she also slipped, and hung over the edge. Naomi grabbed her hand as the bridge fell. It crashed with the glass onto the polished floor below, taking Landon and Katia with it.

Katia screamed as shards flew about the entire hall, cutting and piercing skin.

Naomi crawled to the edge, attempting to leverage the dangling girl with the staff, but her weight couldn't do it.

The smell of blood filled the air. Like sharks taunted by a fresh kill, the Louvings turned toward the victims of the fall.

His concentration shattered, Taren's heat shield vanished. Three Louvings advanced on him. He cupped his hand over a broken rock, and a fistful of smoldering embers appeared. He blew gently, igniting them, before hurling the fiery rocks at the Louvings. They shouted in pain and slapped at the flames with their arms. The distraction gave Taren enough time to scale up a teetering statue and away from them. From that vantage, he could see the entire room.

Down below, Taren could see a look of panic covering Landon's face. His magical strength—creating confusion, beguilement, and charm—couldn't compete with that type of onslaught. Landon tried to charm them. "Are you sure you want to harm us? We're more of an asset to you than you think."

The Louvings stopped and blinked at him momentarily but then moved forward again.

"Forget it, then." Landon shrugged as he pulled out his sword.

The tall Louving, Urick, advanced with his own sword drawn—a nasty scimitar with a jagged blade which didn't cut, but mangled. The weapon looked intimidating but wasn't created for swordplay—rather, as a clumsy weapon of torture.

The first swing proved it. The Louving swung heavy overhead, like a club. Landon sidestepped it perfectly. The next blow came from the side, which Landon dodged and parried. Then Landon thrust forward, blocked, and sliced. His weapon moved with ease, gliding lightly in the air.

On the other side of the hall, Micah ran toward the Louvings advancing on Landon and Katia. He began rubbing his fingers and talking to the crystal scattered on the ground. Swirls of the shards spun in little cyclones.

"Nice try." Fronzi struck him hard on the head with a rock. He crumpled to the ground.

Taren couldn't allow the Louving to win. He threw a flame burst directly at Fronzi, hitting her on the back of the head. The blow knocked her off her feet and ignited her hair. Her tough façade melted as she screamed, rolling and smothering the flames. The smell of singed hair and flesh filled the humid cave.

Fronzi screamed in horror. Micah forgotten, she turned her spite to Taren. He read her magic: she wanted to cut him, to kill him, to taste him, to be him. She wanted his death. She was no longer playing a game.

Taren moved up the statues, scaling the cave wall like a monkey. Out of the corner of his eye, he saw something move higher up in the cave tunnels. Naomi? He turned quickly to the spot where she had been, but she wasn't there.

The girl Naomi had tried to help had fallen onto the stone floor. She spun around, picking up her broken staff and facing the oncoming Louvings. Using both hands, she thrust the staff side to side, knocking them down one by one.

Taren finally reached the highest ledge and looked back down the dizzying cathedral. He tried to find Naomi, but she had disappeared down the tunnels. Fronzi no longer followed him, heading instead for Micah, who caught her with his cyclone of glass shards. Taren scanned again around the Grand Hall, searching for Naomi. She was too important to lose.

His eyes held on a sleek-haired, violet-eyed Louving, who felt strangely familiar to him. He stood near the entrance of the hall, hidden in shadows, not participating, but watching the entire fight.

Taren blinked, his magic had found something else—a disguise. Without his art in reading magic, he would have missed it, but he had read this one before. There stood an imposter among the Louving.

In all the mayhem, Taren slipped quietly into the outlying tunnels.

The fight continued in the Grand Hall—a perfect distraction. The time had come for the deception to be over, and the sleek, violet-eyed Louving needed to act. Naomi had vanished in the back tunnels and he had to reach her before anyone else. But first, he needed to check on his prisoners.

Past the entrance of the hall lay a tunnel which spiraled downward, wrapping around and down, past empty rooms and hallways. He heard the rushing of water from hidden falls.

Madden reached a room in the middle of the path and opened the door. Inside sat two silhouettes: one small and fidgety, the other hardly responding to his entrance, staring and expressionless. Their hands were tied and their legs bound at the knees—the true Louvings, Hughes and Madden.

Hughes made a strange whimpering sound but hardly moved.

"You won't get away with this," the prisoner Madden said in a voice as smooth as silk.

"I already did."

The prisoner analyzed the disguise. "How dare you pretend to be me?"

The mirror image of the Louving smirked at his clever deception. "It takes a lot more bravery to pretend to be a Louving than to actually be one." The fake Madden ripped a bandage from the man's arm to expose a fresh cut, still bleeding. "I may not need this, but just in case."

The real Madden swore in anger, but returned to his sullen, hate-filled glare as he watched the imposter squeeze a few drops of blood from his arm and place it in a vial around his neck.

"Why do you do this?"

The man disguised as Madden capped the little vial of blood. "Things just got more complicated."

"But why *my* blood?"

"Yours will do."

The Louving's eyes flashed in the dark as Madden's doppelganger sealed their cell.

The Imposter Madden moved down the tunnel toward the sound of the falls. He remembered a secret ladder somewhere nearby and needed to find it before anything happened.

Someone spoke. He stopped and turned, but saw nothing there. It came again, whispering in his ear.

Madden reached for his sword and prepared to face whatever it was.

There was nothing—or was there? He looked hard into the dark tunnel. Mists formed along the pathway, moving about like ghosts.

A form molded and a shape appeared—the shape of a man.

He stood before Madden. His broad chest and shoulders now appeared real, light and transparent, but thick in mass. His face looked careworn, but his expression reflected honor.

Madden froze. He knew this man who stood before him—yet this man had been dead for years. *Cornwallis Fairborne.* Madden lost his breath as he stared at the figure.

Cornwallis looked Madden up and down. "There is one here." Four other apparitions appeared behind him.

"Find where they have hidden the prisoners," Cornwallis commanded. He turned back toward Madden. "Who are you? Why are you here?"

Madden could not speak. He had so wished for the day when he could see this man again. The shock and emotion ran through him like life flooding back into his veins after so many years.

"Answer me or die!" Cornwallis commanded.

Should he tell the truth? If he did, he might die as a consequence.

It didn't matter. He would rather die than live with regret. It was time.

"It's me. Reynolds," he said in a near whisper. "Your son."

Cornwallis stared hard at the Louving. "You lie. How dare you?"

"No! It is me. Believe me." He reached around his neck and pulled the amulet over his head—an amulet that shielded his real appearance. He appeared, unmasked: Reynolds, undisguised, warily met his father's gaze. No tears. He couldn't spare them here.

Cornwallis looked at his son. He eyes shone with pride, and his face with sadness. The two embraced. Reynolds felt the strange, magical imprint—different compared to the warmth of real skin, though his reaction was the same.

The moment ended too soon. Both had to complete what they had come to do.

"We must find the Louvings."

"They are in the Grand Hall," Reynolds answered. "There are also prisoners deep in the outer rooms."

"We will take care of it," Cornwallis assured him. "We heard Harrow's message. He is looking for a girl."

"I'll find her." Reynolds felt the determination stronger than ever. "I promise I'll keep her safe. It's time for me to make things right."

Cornwallis placed a firm grip on his son's shoulder. "You can find me here, if you need me."

Reynolds nodded, and then the Stain vanished. No goodbye, just as before. For a brief moment, Reynolds relived the childhood memories he'd buried in the recesses of his mind: his troubled magic-meddling, his years of loneliness without a father.

His life could have been so different with the continual improvement and guidance provided by a parent. And all those years were lost because of magic. He could find his father here. The hope to make everything right filled his soul with new life.

Naomi, he exhaled inwardly. There was nothing more important than her life—to the world, and to him.

He slipped the amulet back around his neck, and into the appearance of Madden, and went back in search of the ladder behind the falls. The light from the Grand Hall illuminated all the outer tunnels. A rushing wind whipped around, pushing toward the cascading water.

His magic searched out hers and found her like a beacon in the dark. She felt close.

He ran down the path and back into the darkness. The tunnel turned and spiraled, but he didn't care. He ran blindly, feeling his way toward her into the depths of the cave.

From somewhere nearby, Reynolds spotted an eerie luminescence and heard the roar of the falls.

Voices of magic echoed around him; Harrow moved through the rock, taunting Naomi with the inevitable absorption of her magic to his. The desperate thought pushed Reynolds forward.

A scream resounded through the tunnels—Naomi's scream. Harrow had found her.

Reynolds' pace quickened. He had to be close, but he couldn't find the way in. He could hear the conversations passing through the rock. Harrow's ravenous hunger terrified him. A low, throaty laugh sent vibrations through his soul.

Reynolds turned and found himself in a cavernous room, a large pool splashing water from the nearby falls.

Across the water, Naomi leaned against the wall, terror in her eyes. Light shone from her neck as the medallion pulled away from her body—sweet purples and brilliant blues swirling around, breathing her life. Harrow chanted ancient words, coercing it further.

The Vivatera, his precious treasure—held fast around the girl he loved.

Naomi screamed in pain, grabbing at her chest and sinking to the ground. Harrow hovered over her now, consumed with the greed of his years of confinement. Her breath slowly squeezed from her body.

Reynolds ran forward, still disguised. "Enough!" he shouted as he pushed the underlord away from Naomi, standing between the two.

The connection between Harrow and Naomi broke, and her breath evened. She looked at him now, not recognizing the illusion before her eyes.

Harrow spun around in anger, turning his staff toward Reynolds. More incantations flew from his mouth, and bolts of lightning came flashing out of his staff.

Reynolds dodged the blast and whipped out his sword, but Harrow only laughed. "So you want to fight me, Madden? Do you think you can win?"

"You are not going to harm her."

Harrow shot another electric pulse his way. "Louvings only care about money and blood."

Reynolds sprang back. The strike narrowly missed. He steadied himself again. "You don't want her just for power, Harrow. You want revenge."

Harrow's brow rose. "I'm impressed. You have studied, haven't you?"

Another strike grazed his left side, making Reynolds wince in pain. But the blow only made him angrier. He charged his sword at the old man.

Harrow deflected with his staff and countered with a gust of wind from his breath that knocked Reynolds back.

Naomi scurried to her feet, giving Reynolds a puzzled look—or rather, Madden the Louving, who now stood before her as a guardian. "If you want her, you'll have to kill me first, and I'm not that easy to kill."

Harrow laughed. "The Louving with a heart—how noble of you."

Reynolds stood ready for the advance—so focused on Harrow's attack he didn't notice the figure at his side. Suddenly someone hit him square in the jaw. Pain seared through the right side of his face. Shaking his head, disoriented, he looked up to see Taren.

Reynolds recovered in time to defend another blow with his arm, and a third with the hilt of his sword. "What are you doing?"

"Get away from her!" Taren shouted, running right for him, plunging himself full force against Reynolds's chest and pummeling him repeatedly.

"Stop!" Reynolds cried. "Naomi!"

Naomi looked stunned as he shouted her name. A glimmer of recognition filled her eyes.

Harrow laughed more at the two men brawling than anything else. "It seems I have already won." Abruptly, he hurled a powerful shock at Naomi, overwhelming her and dragging her body toward him.

Reynolds finally pulled free from his attacker. "Taren, stop! We have to save her."

"We? That'd be your job." Taren grabbed the amulet and yanked it from Reynolds' neck, severing the illusion and revealing Reynolds' true self. "You're pathetic, hiding like this. I knew it was you."

Reynolds stood before him, exposed. The years of hatred built up between them boiled to the surface. Reynolds pulled back his fist and swung, hitting Taren directly in the jaw. Taren fell to the ground, seeming stunned, then angry as he tackled Reynolds around the knees, and they were at it again.

"Naomi!" Reynolds stretched for her.

In her magical bindings, Naomi gasped. "Reynolds!" she cried out to him for help, struggling more than ever.

Reynolds gave another good punch, this time into Taren's back, which sent him to the floor.

"You!" Harrow shouted as he recognized Reynolds, whom he had undoubtedly thought long dead. He sent out ropes of energy around Naomi, lashing her to himself as she lay on the ground.

Seeing his rage, Reynolds advanced. "Let her go!"

Harrow's face seethed with anger. Bolts shot out of his staff, shaking the ground above them. "You were foolish to trick me! Her death will be the result of your deceit. I rule the Underworld!"

"Then why do you need her magic?"

"Because I am banished here!" Harrow's voice boomed. "She has the power to bring me to the surface. I will break free of the bonds and rule with power above. It is time for me to return to my world. And it is time for you to leave this one." Harrow directed his staff right at Naomi's heart.

Reynolds couldn't think, only react. He lunged for Naomi, shielding her from any assault. He grasped the medallion around her neck. The delicate stones inside revealed the innocence of his youth, the pain and regret, the loneliness and heartbreak—and a small infant, cradled in his arms. Power began to build up, surging to the surface of the stone. Reynolds held it out from her neck and pointed it in the direction of the light.

Streams of magic shot out like piercing darts, striking Harrow in the chest. A sharp ripping tore through his body as he neared the falls, the border of his realm. He grabbed his robes, his head rolling back as his scream echoed, unearthly, rumbling from the depths of hell and pushing upward to the heavens.

His cry of rage filled the mountains with the energy of waking giants. The rock and river sucked the life from the demon of the dark. Harrow had crossed beyond the boundary of his exile. His body went limp and his face fell, mangled and melting as if burned with acid. With the heat of the fierce magic, his reign came to an end, and he disappeared.

The energy around Naomi vanished. She looked up and blinked, confused. Reynolds offered her his hand, and she stood, staring without comprehension. "You're here." She lifted her hand to his face for reassurance.

Reynolds took her in his arms and held her close. Her scared little heart raced next to his body. He no longer cared about her magical hold on him and how it controlled his actions. He wanted this, her near him, safe from the unspeakable horror Harrow would have exposed her to.

Behind them, Taren interrupted the sweet reunion. "I know what you did to her."

Reynolds broke from his embrace and stood, defiant against the accusation. "I just saved her."

"I assumed I had it right, but the magic confirmed it."

Reynolds knew where Taren was trying to lead him, but this wasn't the place for the truth to come out. "I've protected her as no one has."

"Just as you protected me?" Taren walked closer until he stood toe to toe with his former friend, eyes flashing with anger. "Did your protection come from obligation or guilt?"

Reynolds darted a quick glance at Naomi, who didn't seem to understand what Taren was hinting at.

"From sincerity."

"You know nothing of sincerity—"

"You know nothing of love!"

Taren's hatred intensified, his neck turning red from anger. "I understand what you don't." He raised his fist, which gripped a small knife. "It's time to finish the experiment."

Taren moved faster than Reynolds could react. Naomi screamed as Taren's dagger plunged deep into her chest. "So much for your promise."

"Taren . . ." she started, but lost breath. She stumbled back into the wall.

Reynolds rushed to her. "No! Naomi, no, please." He dislodged the knife, which clattered against the stone. The unbelievable truth stabbed at his heart as blood began seeping through her clothes.

Taren stood back, watching without satisfaction—only duty. "It's the only way, Reynolds."

"Naomi? Don't leave. Naomi." Reynolds couldn't control his panic, his heart felt as if ripped from his chest. "Find the magic, please."

Naomi struggled against the pain, blinking and gasping.

Anger coursed through Reynolds' veins as he met Taren's gaze. "How could you do this?"

"I know the rules."

There was no time. Reynolds worked quickly, fastening and ripping. Blood dripped from the corner of Naomi's mouth. "Oh, no, please . . ." He pressed on the wound, mopping up the blood that soaked through her clothing.

"Do you realize what you've done?" Reynolds shouted back at Taren

"No more secrets!" Taren cut him off. "It's time to own your mistakes!" He stared at the mess surrounding Naomi—the blood scarlet next to her snow-white complexion.

Naomi's eyes moved to Taren, briefly connecting. Her breaths came slowly, her face contorting in agony.

"Stay with me, Naomi. Come on. Fight . . . find your strength." Fury raged inside Reynolds, but he was helpless.

She struggled to breathe.

"No, stay with me." Reynolds stroked her neck. His hand grazed against something—a tiny metal chain traced with blood. His hope now lay with something over which he had no control.

Naomi's breath came in short gasps as the pain took over. She closed her eyes, fading away.

"No!" Reynolds gasped. His grief overwhelmed every impulse for control, and the tears he'd held back coursed down his cheeks. His arms curled around her as they had long ago, rocking her as his tiny hope faded.

. . . Light

. . . Warmth

Swirls lifted away from her chest: pink, purple, gold, wrapping and entwining in delicate patterns. Magic, sweet and pure, pushed out, surrounding the precious vessel. Naomi's limp body lifted in the air.

The colors wrapped around her form, tendrils holding her in place. Gold streams circled her heart like a protective mother containing her life force, the innocence and purity quietly sleeping in her blood.

The magic held her taut in the air, exhaling as the last of its life entered to save her. Peace could reside inside her now without the unnatural exposure. The Vivatera had found a way home.

CHAPTER TWENTY-TWO
PARADISE

A glorious sun lit a beautiful meadow. No one could plan a day like this. The sun smiled brilliantly, high above the trees. The grass, long and tender against her toes, tickled the soft pads of her feet.

Naomi could not remember feeling like this. Her arm reached up and fingered through her long golden tresses spiraled across the turf. She lay among the grass and wildflowers and thought of nothing.

She had no recollection of how long she stayed there, silent, listening to the sounds of life. It didn't matter. Freedom filled her. For the first time, she had no worries.

The valley about her smiled. The wind danced lightly above the flower tops and weaved happily in and out of the reeds before breezing by and kissing her nose. A gentle nudging started at her palm, and she glanced down to see a kitten snuggling and purring next to her. *How tender*, she thought, and petted the little thing.

What a wonderful place. She lay back down, closed her eyes, and drifted as the kitten cuddled on her chest.

Time passed, or maybe it didn't—dreamless, still. The wind switched direction, and a familiar smell wafted past. *Sandalwood on a hot day.* She opened her eyes and saw him sitting in the grass next to her.

She remembered him, or did she? The image looked different from any memory she had of him. He didn't look as worn or tan or nearly as tired as she remembered, but his eyes were the same: grey and bright. They transmitted everything: sadness, loss, hope . . . The hope caught her attention. She sat up.

Naomi had forgotten everything while sitting in the meadow, in the glorious sunshine; all the horrors that had befallen her and her friends. She couldn't remember any details, but she remembered the pain—lots of pain in her heart, and a man with a look of guilt and shame in his eyes. *Reynolds.*

She clutched her chest and fell back down.

"No, don't," Reynolds spoke. "Please, stay with me." He reached down and touched her brow. "Come on, where are you? I need you here."

Naomi blinked twice, but his image didn't go away. "I thought I was dreaming again."

"You are."

She sat up again. "Then why are you here?"

"Because you invited me."

Naomi knit her eyebrows. "I'm sick of riddles."

Reynolds smiled a different smile. Not cautious or with hidden affection—genuine, with a glow of its own. He leaned back and rested his hand on his knee. "I'll try. I promise."

"This is my dream, right?" Naomi asked, trying to figure it out. "So, how are we having this conversation?" Then the reality of the situation hit her. The nightmare of her tragic life came back, and she sat straight up. The kitten leapt off her lap and ran away.

"Oh, no! I'm dead! I died! And you died, too!"

Reynolds laughed. "This might be death, but let's say this is a dream. I'm not dead—not quite."

"But how are you here talking with me?"

He started, pulling at the grass. "In reality, Reynolds is sitting right next to you where you lie."

"Well, you're right here."

"No, I'm not right here. I am Reynolds' imprint of magic. I'm communicating magic-to-magic, not face-to-face."

"Oh, I like that." A rare connection to his magic she never saw—she felt privileged. "How long have I been dreaming?"

Reynolds looked up from his grass pulling. "Too long, and it's time to wake up. You wouldn't allow anyone in but me." He winced. "I'm sorry it took me so long. I didn't want to try."

"Why not?"

Reynolds avoided her gaze. "I was afraid of what I'd find. That your mag—well, never mind. The point is, I finally agreed to try, and you let me in."

"You can't 'never mind' in *my* dream."

"I promise we will get to that."

"Why wait? Tell me now. Everything. No secrets."

Reynolds shifted his weight, seeming to think it over for a moment. "I can't tell you everything, but I'll do what I can. My memory begins from when the magic imprinted."

Naomi thought about that. "Magic-to-magic."

Reynolds tilted his head and finally looked at her. His eyes told such a sad story, one she couldn't fathom. He started to speak but shut his mouth again, tripping over his tongue.

"Reynolds, it's okay." She placed her palm over his, reassuring, and redirected her focus. "How about if I ask you questions?"

Reynolds gave a half-smile. "Questions might be a good way to start."

Naomi watched his expression with interest. "How much do you know about me?"

"A lot."

Naomi twirled her finger in the grass, eying him. "Quantify a lot. I know you've kept your eye on me for years, but when did you first know me?"

Something quivered in his throat. "As a baby."

Naomi stopped twirling and sat up. "A baby? Did you know my parents?"

"Yes. Yes, I did. Your mother more than your father."

"You've known this whole time and you never told me?"

"I only thought of your safety." He shifted his position closer to her "It would be dangerous if people knew who you are. I'm sure you understand."

"Well, who am I?"

"Your real name is Redemia, daughter of King Errenhardt Prolius and Queen Andriana Levenmore."

"What?" *That couldn't be true.* But it sounded like such a beautiful idea. She would hate it not to be true. Her tone softened. "Really?"

Reynolds nodded.

A strange burning started in her stomach and ended in her throat. *Parents. A Family.* They existed. She had once belonged to them.

Naomi straightened up. Her hands came to her face. "I have parents. I'm a princess. Oh, Ferra will be so happy."

A sudden thought struck her. "But how does Ferra not know about me?"

"The queen kept it secret, since the unrest in Southwick upset her. I didn't know until that night . . . I lived in the palace. I was nine years old when it happened—the ceremony, the uprising . . . and you. It was around the same time the Pryxian stones were discovered."

"Where did the stones come from? Were they stolen like Harrow said?"

"I don't know. I only have knowledge of them once my father and Lytte got involved, when I got exposed to the magic. Nothing before."

He continued pulling the grass as he spoke. "But my feeling is yes, they were. That's when the world really changed. The stones altered everything. It wasn't done purposefully, it just happened. Concentrated, pure elements that could control . . . everything! Everyone would want that."

Naomi smiled. Truth. What a wonderful thing. She lay on her side, propped up by her elbow. "So, go back to me now."

Reynolds smiled a little. "Not yet, your highness. I think you should know about the stones.

"Prolius liked the discovery and thought he would give them as gifts for his daughters. But the stones were troublesome. They couldn't be shaped like gemstones. They broke the jeweler's instruments.

"That was when my family got involved. My father was a member of the court and grew favor in the army as a strategist, but he'd started out as a forge master. When the stones proved they couldn't be cut, my father suggested an idea."

Reynolds got lost in his telling, in memories. "Sorry." He stopped.

Naomi didn't mind. She liked knowing Reynolds' vulnerability. Seeing the emotion helped her understand him better and respect him more.

After a moment, he continued. "My father suggested making amulets, medallions with the stones in the center. The trick was, the stones weren't round either, but he had a solution. My father brought it to Lytte, the king's healer. Lytte's daughter was my mother. I spent a lot of my time working as his apprentice after my mother died. My father . . . never truly recovered."

Naomi felt ashamed at the talk of Lytte. She turned her head to watch a honey bee buzzing around the wildflowers. "I like that—you working with your grandfather. He must really love you."

"He still does, despite all my mistakes. I helped Lytte shape the stones until they fit. I had the important job of cleaning up the leftover pieces. He ordered me to destroy them, dispose of them properly. But I didn't."

Naomi could tell he had reached the surface of his torment. She reached out and touched his hand that lay in the grass. Reynolds didn't react, but didn't flinch away.

"I couldn't throw away such beautiful magic, so I saved them. I kept each one in a small clay jar and hid them until I knew what to do with them.

"I let some of the boys around the palace have a chance to play with the magic."

"Are you talking about Taren?" Naomi asked as gently as she could.

"No," Reynolds shook his head. "I tried to protect him from it. He was so young. He pestered us to be a part of the secret group, but I told him no. He found us anyway and saw the magic. He promised not to tell, but I didn't know if I could believe him. I had an idea and I needed help . . . so I asked Taren."

Despite Taren's version, Naomi assessed the pain in Reynold's eyes and searched for the whole truth in the telling.

Reynolds took his hand away and stood up. He watched Naomi's expression as he paced the grass.

"I knew what I should do with the pieces. I thought I would make a medallion like the others, not with just one magic but all of them. I couldn't get over the power in my hands. Nothing turned out as I planned, and Taren's magic is a result of it."

"What happened?"

"An explosion. Taren wouldn't stay away from the fire. He got hit by most of the blast. I got hit, but nothing like his injuries. He wasn't the same kid after that."

Naomi looked up. "You created the Vivatera."

"Yes."

"Was it worth it?"

She could tell he wasn't prepared for the question. "Yes, I think so." Reynolds knelt back on the grass near her. "That's not all. I didn't use everything. I still had some magic left and I kept it."

His hands ruffled out his hair, like he often did as he thought of how to tell her things. The long strands fell into his eyes, masking much of his pain.

His gaze lifted, and he smiled at her. "A lot of things happened the week you were born." Glancing around the meadow, he sighed. "The ceremony where the King presented the medallions to his daughters didn't go as planned.

"After the magic fused to them, the king sent them away, fearing for their lives. Greedy men wanted the magic, and the uprising took over the palace. My father was killed protecting the king.

"King Prolius was murdered the very day you were born, and they took your mother into hiding. The shock of learning of her husband's death actually caused your early arrival."

Reynolds stumbled in his telling. "Lytte and I hid in the palace. It's amazing—the depth of the place, with all the old walls of previous palaces standing within. I took him to my secret room. Malindra and Jeanus met us there, being friends of Lytte's. They had the queen, and she hid with us."

A stray tendril of hair whipped over Naomi's face. Without thinking Reynolds reached over and lifted it from her eyes and tucked it behind her ear. "You're much like your mother. She showed such kindness to me. When you were born, you were so small. You should have died."

"But I didn't."

"No. But you lead a cursed life because of it. I thought I could save you. I thought I was doing the right thing. You were dying, but it was more the curiosity of what would happen. That's what stings the most. I'm selfish."

"You were nine—"

"That doesn't mean I didn't know right from wrong. I took the rest of the minerals and I mixed them together, and I fed them to you."

The news shocked her far less than Naomi had imagined. The information only confirmed her suspicions. Strangely, she liked hearing it—finally knowing the truth once and for all. Reynolds' poor face hung low, the guilt of his actions weighing heavily on his shoulders. She didn't know what to say or how to comfort him.

"I promised the queen I would keep you safe." Reynolds lifted his face now, his eyes pained but holding back his emotion. "After Malindra died, I watched you wander. I found a farmer who had just lost his wife and needed help with his son. He agreed to take you in."

Naomi couldn't tear her eyes away from him. His beautiful tale had revealed her identity. She felt whole, complete. No tears came. None were needed. She smiled. "You haven't broken your promise."

"Come back to me." His restless expression filled with sorrow. "Come back."

His voice faded to a whisper, lost in the meadow, echoing around the valley.

Naomi looked around her. For a moment, she sat alone, listening to the far away voices pleading for her return. Then she lay back down in her meadow and smelled the grass, closing her eyes as the pain returned to her heart.

CHAPTER TWENTY-THREE
AWAKENING

Naomi awoke to pain and burning. The pressure in her chest felt unbearable. She tried to take a deep breath, but her lungs couldn't hold it. She coughed, fighting for air.

"She's awake! She's awake!" she heard someone yell.

A person came to her side and put pressure on her chest. Her airways relaxed and her breathing returned.

Naomi had not yet opened her eyes, afraid of what she might see.

"Naomi?" Katia's sweet voice filled her ears. "Naomi? Please wake up. We need you."

She heard little Micah's voice next. "Ah, if feathers had feet, she would run swiftly to the dawn." He was so peculiar.

"That doesn't make any sense," Landon interrupted.

"It's a metaphor, you dolt," Katia returned. "If she could have come quickly, she would have. Let's just hope Reynolds guided her home. That was lovely, Micah."

Naomi could almost see the scowl on Landon's face behind her eyes. She wanted to see it face-to-face. Maybe it wouldn't be so bad to wake up. She stirred, and then slid her eyes open a fraction.

The room looked fuzzy, but the faces came into focus. How did she get here? What had happened? Katia and Micah stood close by, staring down at her.

She moved her head and saw Landon pacing near the back of the room with a tiny man she could only guess was related to Micah—same stature, same skin, and same magnificent eyes.

She looked to the right and saw Reynolds. He held her hand, but dropped it the moment she made eye contact, rising to his feet and looking down at her. His eyes were full of worry, but he didn't speak. Seeing that she was all right, he nodded and walked away without a word.

Naomi's head began to swim again. She lay back on the pillow. "Hi," she uttered in a near whisper.

Katia reached over and held a cup to her lips. Naomi sipped the water. It was cold and tasted wonderful.

"How are you feeling?"

Naomi thought it over. "Pretty much like you would imagine. Where am I?"

"Durundin. My Uncle Spotswood's home." Micah smiled. "He is a gracious and honored host."

The man near Landon bowed gracefully.

"Thank you for your kindness to us," Naomi said.

Spotswood waved off the praise with his hand. "Too kind, too kind."

Naomi tried again to sit up but noticed it was hard to move. She looked down and saw the bandages that bound her tight, wrapping around her body like a mummy. A soft, silk blanket covered her.

"I'm so glad to see you all here with me," Naomi started. "I'm not sure what happened. I don't remember anything."

The room became silent as everyone looked at her solemnly. "We aren't sure, either," Katia answered. "Someone tried to kill you, but Reynolds saved you."

"How did you get out?" Naomi asked. The last time she'd seen them, angry Louvings swarmed, ready to kill them.

Her friends rattled off a story about the fight between the Louvings and the appearance of the Stains coming to their rescue and chasing off the rest of their enemies, including Browneyes and Fronzi.

"After the Louvings ran away, the Stains led us out of the cave. That's when the quake started."

Landon's voice got softer as he talked about the rest—not as excited, more solemn. "The imprints have very strict lines they cannot cross or they will disappear. The rumbling started and the mountain shifted. When we saw the light of day coming from outside, the Stains disappeared."

Naomi fell back in exhaustion. "I need some rest," she muttered, her strength nearly gone. "Where is Ferra?"

"She's not here," Landon answered.

"Why not?"

"She left about three days ago, as a favor to Spotswood, but she'll be back soon." He ushered everyone out. "Come on." Grabbing Katia around the waist, he helped her hobble out of the room. The others followed and shut the door.

Restful quiet returned, and Naomi looked around. The room was pear-shaped, small, and appeared to be made from dirt or clay. Small torchlights hung in clusters around the ceiling. Rope streamers hung down from the torches, attached to different objects: moonstones, cloves, and crystals, each reflecting bits of light. Eerie, rippling, blue rays filtered in through the ceiling. It seemed very odd but warm and comfortable.

She lay quietly in her little bed. Although her mind seemed wide awake, her body felt weak. She wanted to see Reynolds, to talk to him again, like in the meadow. But before Reynolds could be found, she drifted off to sleep.

Naomi woke, alone. She turned over and sat up. She couldn't stay in bed any longer, eager to see the rest of this curious underground dwelling.

Fresh, clean clothes lay at the side of her bed. After she dressed herself, she felt drained. Her lack of activity had caught up with her. She'd lost strength from lying in bed for so long.

Beyond her door, she found a large circular foyer with surrounding rooms but saw no one else. Light filtered in from the ceiling through little side openings, but again, the source remained unclear.

She thought about exploring further, when a door opened and Micah's uncle shuffled into the room, hunched over and using two canes to assist him. He took small steps but at a wicked pace, reminding Naomi of a little creeping spider.

He saw her and made his way to her. "Hello, Blondie. Sleep well?"

"I guess. Where are the others?"

"In good time, good time. Come," he beckoned her. "You are safe here, princess, safe, safe . . . Come, now . . ."

He laughed a silly little laugh to himself and led her into a different room.

The room was very dark. Plants and roots hung from the ceiling, and water pooled inside a hollowed rock. To one side, stood a solid, wooden table with benches on either end.

"Sit," he told her. She complied, and within a minute, he had placed food in front of her. The food was fresh, earthy, and uncooked—assorted beans and something that tasted like a potato, but saltier—she didn't care. It all tasted wonderful.

"Thank you," she said between bites.

He bowed graciously and hobbled to the water hollow, scooping up two cups. He brought them to the table and sat down across from her.

"Food nourishes the soul and brings forth the magic," he said in a hum-de-dum voice.

It was the first time she had really taken a look at him. He tied his streaked gray hair in a knot behind his head, but strands came down into his face. He wore magnificent oval spectacles on his nose, and his startling blue eyes popped out from his dark skin, making him seem even more mystical. He wore silk robes of vivid color, the patterns intricate and unusual, tied in different ways around his skinny frame. She liked it very much.

"Where is Reynolds?"

"In good time, sweet one."

He sipped his water gingerly, then placed his gentle hand across the table. "May I touch the Ever Star?"

"Ever Star?" Naomi wondered how he'd learned what Malindra called her, a nickname only a few knew. She nodded anyway, and he ran his fingers along the top of her hand.

A look of contentment showed on his face. He breathed in deeply, seeming lost in a pleasant memory. Smiling, he returned his hand. "Thank you, sweet."

"What do you mean by 'Ever Star'?"

"The last star, brightest of all, forever. Six in one starlight hold—seven mix young to old. Ever Star."

"How do you know this?"

"Ah." He reached in his pocket and pulled out a scarf, the very one Malindra had given her so long ago.

"How did you get that?"

"There are no two patterns alike. This one is from Malindra, sister of Jeanus, Elemental whirler. I never forget."

"You made this?"

He bowed again. "Shadesilk, with a kiss of Illusion."

"Thank you, it's beautiful." It pleased her to find out a little more about the history of something she treasured. "I've always loved it."

"It is protection. Do not take it off. Reynolds has commissioned a cloak out of it. My worms are working very hard."

Naomi wrapped the scarf around her neck again and felt at home. She had more questions to ask him, but before she said a word, Spotswood spoke.

"There is no need to worry, princess. All will come out right. Reynolds' blame is unfounded, only a tool for the prophecy of old."

"How do you mean?"

Spotswood smiled widely and recited:

"Legends and Secrets in nature's peace
Six will reign down from the east
Elements gathered in beauty and grace

Sharing the secret boldly embraced
Wind and rain, rock and stone
Rivers flowing, earthen grown
Fires kindled, creatures tall
World protected from goodness fall
But secret from guarded truth
A power untempered in unknown proof
Beauty abounding, wholeness and pure
Brings to the ill and infirm—a cure
Blankets of heaven full in the night
Bring daytime to darkness
. . . and shadow to light."

Naomi liked the poem very much. "But what does it mean?"

"You are the key to everything. We must keep you safe and sacred." Smiling faintly, he left the room. All went quiet following the hobbling of canes down the pathways.

Naomi had been so wrapped up in Spotswood's tale, she hadn't heard the footsteps approaching. She turned to see Ferra crossing the large room toward her. Naomi jumped up and ran to her.

Ferra had a tremendous smile on her face. The two embraced and laughed and cried.

Naomi finally broke away and looked at who she knew now as her sister. Dirt covered her and there were more twigs than usual in her hair, but she looked well and very happy to be there.

"Where did you go?"

"To retrieve something that might help. Paolo and I traveled up north. I had to find my mother."

Mother, Naomi repeated the word in her head. She liked the way it sounded. "What did you need to get?"

Ferra pulled an old cloth out from her dirty pocket. She lifted the delicate fabric to reveal a round ball, purple in color, with a gentle glow in the center. Naomi knew this ball. "This is on loan. I promised to return it to Jeanus."

"What is it?"

"This is the Conjectrix, a dream interpreter. Pretty, isn't it?" She raised her eyebrows toward Naomi. "We'll need it with all the plans."

"Plans?"

"Sorry." Ferra wrapped the ball back up. "You'll find out soon enough."

Naomi felt a stab of pain over her chest that sent her in a spell.

"Whoa," Ferra steadied her. "Come on, back to bed."

"I'm sick of bed."

"I'm sure. But we need you healthy."

Landon and Katia entered the room. Seeing Naomi buckle over, Landon ran over, taking her other side. "Hey!"

"I need Reynolds," Naomi strained as she felt another stab.

Landon picked her up in one scoop and carried her back to her room and the safety of her covers.

⁓⟡⁓

A small doorway . . .
   Into a room of no comfort.
      Little light reflected bouncing around the white sheet.

              A girl stood before the room
                   Hesitation,
                   Reveal the truth
                  She did not want to know

A hand in hers,
. . . small and warm.

A boy growing,
but not grown.

Her other hand empty,
But wanted it filled.
. . . By her love.

A gentle woman comes forward.
Small in height, big in heart.
"Come, my sweet.
"It is time to say your goodbyes."

She froze.
The room sat silent . . .
. . . No thrashing
. . . No screaming
All peace and silence.
She gripped the hand and walked forward.
Tears flow freely down her cheek
The boy's eyes dry, but swollen.

Porcelain skin.
Silvery strands flow from the bed.
Touch the hand.
Ice cold

Curse.
Blame.
Anger!
The stone around her neck felt strangling.
Whispers . . .
"Sharrod has won . . .
"He severed the bonds."

Fingers through the strains, still silk and unreal.

"There is no hope, Zander."
Overwhelming despair . . .
The hand squeezes tighter.

The boy helpless to comfort.
A glance at her,
The mark glistening.
His thoughts on her.
If only Naomi could see?

The woman raised the sheet.
. . . one less star to shine . . .
. . . one less stone to protect . . .
. . . one less sister to save . . .

～❈～

The dim light in the room rippled in unusual patterns of the stone. Naomi's eyes watched the light waves until she saw the silhouette outlined next to her.

His head lay on the bed, hidden in his folded arms, his breathing even.

Naomi hardly moved, but still Reynolds lifted his head to check on her. He met her eyes, his expression grieved and worried. But then he smiled, if only faintly.

Worried about disturbing the peace, Naomi spoke in a small whisper. "I think one of my sisters died." The dream rested near in her subconscious. "She couldn't survive without her stone."

Reynolds looked deeply into her eyes. "I'm so sorry. I'm sorry you didn't get a chance to meet her."

In this one moment, Naomi could see the weight he shouldered. One small, almost insignificant decision he had made when he was younger now rippled through time and had set him on a course he did not design.

"Where have you been?"

"Thinking." Reynolds stared at her with those amazing gray eyes and took a few deep breaths. "I don't think I have the answers you want."

"I'm not looking for answers." Naomi moved a small strand of hair that hung in his eyes. "I want to know why you blame yourself for saving my life."

Reynolds sat up. "No. I blame myself for putting you in that situation. I should have never left you there with Taren. I knew better."

Naomi moved to sit up, but the bandages around her dug uncomfortably in her side.

"Don't move—stay still." He grasped both of her hands in his, sending butterflies through her stomach. "Don't go anywhere."

"Okay." Naomi's voice cracked with emotion. "Where is the Vivatera?"

"It has returned home."

He reached to his neck and found the gold chain, pulling it out to show it to her. All that remained was the round, gold casing with the hawk's wings. The stone had disappeared.

"It saved you. I asked it to. The stab wound was deep and deadly. Taren's knife had magic in it, and I couldn't save you." He stopped. "I'll leave so you can remove the bandages. You don't need them anymore, but you will see it there." He stood up to leave.

"Reynolds," Naomi called, without knowing what her next words would be.

Reynolds stopped. "We have a funny history, you and I. I swore to keep you safe, and I will fulfill that promise."

Naomi remained silent, a tear rolling down her cheek.

Reynolds smiled at her tenderly. He placed his hand on her cheek and wiped the tear away.

The gentle action created an unexpected emotion welling up inside her. The overwhelming realization of everything he had done and said found a new home in her heart. She flung herself into his arms and sobbed like a baby, burying her face against his chest as he held her tight and rested his head on hers.

"I won't let anything happen to you," Reynolds whispered.

Naomi lifted her head. "I'm counting on it."

Face to face, eye to eye, there was no one else alive at that moment.

Reynolds leaned in to kiss her, then stopped. He unlocked his gaze and moved his eyes away. "I'm not impervious to your charm."

"Is crying charming?"

Reynolds laughed. "No, but your intense need to make everything better is charming. Right now, I want to save the world for you."

"Please do."

He leaned in and kissed her cheek where her wet tears still lay. "I'll try." He stood and left the room.

Naomi no longer had tears to shed. She no longer felt so hopeless. All the questions running through her brain were now answered with a single act of kindness.

She began removing the bandages, layer upon layer. Stains from dried blood appeared down the center as the cloth became thinner and thinner. Without even removing all of the wrappings, she could see the scar already.

She stopped at the sight of it—strange and beautiful. The Vivatera stone had liquefied itself into her.

The pink, pearl-like color looked odd against her pale skin, but the swirling magic left a shimmering, glittering mark right in the center of her chest over her stab wound, above her heart. Over that, the shape of a circling hawk had formed: the ornate family crest Reynolds crafted with his own hands, the Accipitor.

Happiness filled her soul at the sight. It would be with her always. She sank her head into her pillow, wrapped the scarf around her, and for the first time in a very long time, dreamt peacefully about nothing.

END OF PART ONE

READER'S EDITION

BONUS

MATERIAL

READER QUESTIONS:

1. How do you feel about the magic in the world of Parbraven? What of its relationship between male and female characters?

2. How do you feel about the relationship between the characters? Which one stands apart?

3. In this book you meet a few of the Daughters of Prolius: Ymber, Ferra, and Silexa. What are you predictions for the other sisters? What would you pick as your animal protector?

4. What magic most intrigues you? Which one would you like to master?

5. With the possibility of anyone being anyone, how do you feel about the Louving Shapeshifters? Do you trust them? What of King Harrow and the Echoes?

6. How do you think Reynolds feels about seeing his shade of a father in the Echoes? Is there anyone from your past you would fear meeting as a shade?

7. How do you feel about Taren Lockwood? Do you think he is justified in his action to reunite the magic?

8. The relationship between Naomi and Reynolds happens very quickly. How do you feel about their instant connection?

9. What predictions do you have for Landon and Katia's characters?

READER'S EDITION

ORIGINAL FIRST CHAPTER OF

VIVATERA

UNEDITED

PREFACE

Since my book has been published, I have received several comments that there is not as much information about the magic and that is can sometimes be confusing when rushing into the action, as Naomi does. I thought it would be fun to include my original unedited first chapter that was cut with my original publication, hoping that it might give a few clues into the world of magic, Naomi's relationship with Zander with the abusive danger they are in, and her strange healing that only Lytte understood.

The dream is how I originally presented it to my publisher, as well as Zander's original speech pattern, which I think drove my editors crazy. I also talked with my grandmother, who grew on a pig farm in rural Idaho, about the pig slaughter scene that opens everything. She explained to me that this isn't how pigs are slaughtered, I however never got the opportunity to research it better since it was cut. I do chalk this one up to fantasy with people having a different origin and a different way of slaughtering, probably.

I hope you enjoy it.

Candace

ORIGINAL

CHAPTER I

The noise of the struggle stopped for a moment. Then came the thumps of the axe. It always took a few swings before she heard the thud. It was that sound she waited for - a signal it was clear to enter the room.

The wooden door felt heavy, an effect of the harsh reality she was about to confront. The blood would be splattered about the room; the poor animal's head, frozen in shock still in the bucket underneath the butcher block and bloody drippings covering the canvas beneath the table. The poor creatures never had a voice and all the care she and the boy had put into loving these animals made very little difference.

She knew it happened but struggled with witnessing it. She was grateful the chopping and sectioning took place in the back of the barn because it took everything she had to deal with the brutality.

The protective leather apron, pants, and boots helped keep her dry from pools of blood, but she hated wearing them — the boots bothered her most. She never wore shoes - her feet needed the air. Shoes were just another way to confine her freedom. These thick leather-hide creations affected her balance, making her feel clumsy. But she wasn't clumsy - never had been.

Inside the slaughterhouse the mess was not as bad as she had feared. The blood on the dirt floor soaked easily into the ground and had been raked smooth. The pig's head, thank goodness, had hit the pail in such a way the eyes were not visible. They always looked at her with pleading eyes. She never wanted to look, but sometimes she couldn't help herself - curiosity had always been a flaw.

It was difficult to witness these lovely animals getting slaughtered daily. But this was her life now, helping the widower and his boy in exchange for food, clothes, and warmth. It was the best living an orphan like she was could ask for. Her only belongings consisted of a very small vial of liquid and a silk scarf, which she never took off. The months she had spent on the street were embedded in her mind. This life was not as bad as that - she had the boy and she loved him. The love came naturally. She had only truly loved one other person; Malindra, her beloved guardian. Everything she knew about love had come from Malindra. So she protected the boy and loved him as a mother, a sister, and a friend - all of which she had none.

"Naomi!" a yell came from the drying room of the large, expansive barn. It was Ferrell's. The boy couldn't make that kind of noise if he tried. She hated it when Ferrell yelled. Who knew what kind of a foul temper he had today? All had been quite peaceful, but she should have guessed it wouldn't last.

She walked back to find Ferrell hanging the pig he had just butchered. It was hardly recognizable from the plump thing that had waddled into the barn earlier that morning; the skin peeled off, the hooves cut. Looking at the slab of meat made it possible for her to think it had never lived.

"There you are, you lazy girl," he said. His temper was not at full range, but the day was young. "No need to clean yet. I got two more to slaughter - big day tomorrow in town. Now where's my boy?"

"I'm not sure, sir," she replied, though she had a hunch.

"That boy," Ferrell started muttering. "He better not be day dreamin' again. Nothin' fittin' in that numbskull of his. Well, go get him! I need two more. Have him bring two blacks."

Naomi hated hearing it. Zander would not like this. She nodded and headed off to the pens to tell him the bad news and found him just where she thought he would be - feeding the babies.

"Hey, Na...omi," he stuttered. "Mama here let me feed... her ba...bies." Zander cradled one of the piglets gently with the feeding bottle propped against his arm. He had such a sweet and kind heart. She didn't want to interrupt the moment.

"Great Zan, honest," Naomi spoke. She fumbled with her words. "I'm glad you care about these animals so much, but don't you think it's a bad idea getting so attached?"

Zander shrugged. "I can't help it. Look! They're soo cu..cute." The piglet squealed as it struggled for more milk. He laughed gently at the animal.

"Listen Zander," Naomi spoke up. "I hate this, but your father needs you. He needs two more blacks."

"What?" Zander froze. The piglet squealed. "Why? He got Gert today. Why two more?"

"There is something going on in town tomorrow, I guess - some big celebration."

The boy was instantly in tears. He loved these animals. Week after week he watched his animal friends get slaughtered one by one. Now three would be gone in one day. "N... No..." he stammered, his will weak. "Please, no..." He dropped the piglet and it scampered away. "No more..."

Naomi rushed to him as he crumpled to the ground. The little frame of this twelve-year-old body couldn't deal with the sadness of his life. She stroked his head gently, but with urgency. His father would want the livestock soon and would come hunting for him.

Zander, there is no time," she spoke.

"I ca... can't..t," he struggled with his voice. "Please he...lp... me...."

Naomi thought rationally. "Zan, there is nothing we can do. Ferrell will get his way and we..." she stopped. We will save our lives and stay away from Ferrell's temper, she thought. Naomi understood what would happen if Zander didn't obey. It was one of the reasons that kept her here. The protection of this little soul was the only thing important to her. "We will be fine, promise."

Zander sobbed on her shoulder, shaking his head and mumbling into her clothes. Though a boy of twelve, his body was scrawny and small from poor nutrition. He had not yet hit the growth spurt common to boys his age, and his maturity level had also been slowed. His mother had died years before; how long she wasn't sure, but long enough that Zander couldn't remember being loved by anyone.

Naomi rocked him but worry came over her. Ferrell would soon appear. Then, without warning Zander pulled away from her and stood, staring at her with new powerful determination. Before she knew what he was doing, he turned away and ran.

Naomi was stunned. She watched as the boy headed directly for the pen. It took a moment to realize what was happening. The boy opened the fenced pen and yelled loudly, waving his arms as big as he could.

The pigs fumbled around in an excited frenzy, curious, scared, and stupefied. Some made it to the exit, escaping to freedom.

Naomi ran to the pen just as a large sow moved in a panic to the gate. Naomi's instincts took over and she wrapped her arms around the animal. The smell of filth and muck filled her nostrils and gagged her. She struggled to get control. The animal whipped and squealed. Naomi's light weight could not hold an animal so large. She glanced into the sow's eyes and through them she could feel the danger it felt. But there was also kindness behind the animal's eyes. With a small moment of understanding, the animal quieted. It sunk its head obediently and returned to the far end of the pen. The fear in the animal's eyes disappeared.

Naomi fell to the ground, shock pulsing through her body. But there was no time. Others had escaped. She moved to herd back those that she could and thatched the gate back in place.

Zander sat on his knees sobbing in the mud.

Then the yelling started.

Ferrell's face turned a vivid red, matching the carrot-top color on his head. His arms flailed about like a raging bull and swearing escaped his lips. His path would soon collide with Zander's and she knew what was going to happen.

"Stop!" she yelled, coming to Zander's defense.

"Out of the way!" Ferrell yelled. "I know what he did! There ain't no denying! That numbskull son just near cost me everything! No son of mine acts so stupid! Now out of the way!!"

Zander cowered on the ground, waiting for the beating.

Naomi braced herself between the boy and his father. "It wasn't him. It was me!" she shouted. The mighty paw of the man swiped her light frame like a bear's. She flew to the ground, dirty but unscathed.

Zander took a blow to the cheek which knocked him down into the mud. A few whips across Zander's back with a belt followed before Ferrell felt satisfied.

"I never want a stunt like that again!" he shouted. "Now, go find every one of my pigs or don't bother coming back!" He stormed away.

Naomi watched the brute walk away before she dared move her eyes back to the crumpled little body in the middle of the mud. She rushed over to find Zander swollen and bleeding. His lip was split from the blow, and his back in pain. She lifted his tunic and revealed three large gashes. Blood oozed from the wounds.

"Help, Na…" he tried to say, but failed.

She understood what he needed, but it would have to wait. "Later," she whispered. Together they stood up, Naomi supporting Zander's shaking body. She took him to a dry area by the hay stacks. "Stay here. I need to gather all the pigs. Stay calm. I'll fix you."

It took a good portion of the day, but Naomi did return all the pigs back to the pen. All the animals were receptive to her approach, even though she never had much experience with pigs. That was Zander's job. But she hoped the kindness that he showed them daily had something to do with their behavior toward her.

Zander slept all day. When Naomi returned to him, she found dry mud smeared on his face and clothes. A warm bath was what he needed, but that would have to wait. She still needed to clean the slaughter house or she, too, might suffer Ferrell's wrath.

Hours passed; dinner had come and gone. Ferrell had retired early after butchering two more pigs, leaving Naomi to care for Zander's wounds.

Zander lay on his stomach on a small feather bed. The wounds on his back were still painful and swollen. He was clean, but only barely; just what could to done without scrubbing.

"Oh, Zan…" Naomi said with sad pity. "I tried to help."

Zander nodded in understanding but didn't speak. He just stared out at nothing.

"Are you ready?" she asked.

He heaved his chest in response.

To make it easier she spoke softly to him.

"This is the only thing I have left from Malindra, besides my scarf," she said. She thought fondly of her guardian. She missed her terribly, especially on days like this. "Hold still," she whispered.

Naomi splashed some of the clear liquid from her precious bottle onto Zander's back. It ran down between the swollen welts. Her fingers softly rubbed the liquid onto his back. Her touch was gentle and loving as she moved her hand slowly, spreading the liquid over the open wounds. It took a few minutes of constant attention but within that time, the swelling disappeared, and the wounds miraculously closed.

Zander moved and arched his back, feeling the life return to his body. Without Naomi here he would have died from his injuries long ago. When he was younger his father only pushed or shoved him around. But as the years passed his father's attitude toward him had changed and his new disapproval usually turned to violence. Naomi was a godsend and he loved her deeply; not only for staying with him, but for saving his life.

"I don't know what will happen when this is all gone," she muttered, placing the stopper back in the ancient blue bottle.

"What is it…" Zander mustered.

"I really don't know," Naomi answered. "It doesn't really have an odor that I can identify. Other potions and such I knew. But Malindra never got a chance to tell me about this one; only that it was made special for me and was only to be used in the most urgent circumstances." She reached under her scarf to rub her neck gently, like she often did when she thought of the gypsy.

Zander managed a smile as he rolled over on his back. "Thanks…" he whispered. In just a few minutes he had fallen to sleep.

Naomi waited, watching the boy before she too sank back with her head on a pillow. She pulled the scarf she wore around herself softly and drifted off…

Naomi awoke. Sweat lined her face and seeped into her clothes, making her shiver. She rubbed her head gingerly as memories of her dream enveloped her thoughts. She glanced out her window. There was no trace of rain, not even a cloud.

She double-checked her room. Everything looked the same: still, small, and simple. Zander snoozed peacefully across from her. The thought that she might have awoken him passed along with the anxiety of the dream. Breathing a sigh of relief, Naomi took out her journal and began to write.

Tunneling…

    The feeling of traveling… searching…

        far, far from any town, city, life…

A man in a dark room

    …small, unfamiliar flicking light from a single candle
Worried…

    Confusion…

        Failure…

The woman, unearthly beauty
Long silver hair slivers lie in gentle curls around her heart shaped face

Stirring on the ground… uncomfortable sleep…
She awakes.

"How is the storm?"

> *"It is holding, my lady."*
> *"I do not see the dangers we encountered before."*

"Oh, Jaxon,
I know you will keep me safe."

The woman worries…
Eyes drifted unbelieving…

> *Emptiness…*
>
> *Despair…*

Her hands held a glowing stone
"The others?"

> *"It is too late to contact."*

"How far are the Ibis Mountains?"

> *"But two days, my Lady."*

"And the Echoes?"

> *"At the horn of the mountain."*

Sigh…curling into herself
"I'm scared…" a whisper.

…a low rumble of thunder in the distance…
The midnight blue stone about her neck pulsed with the

> *flash of light*

"We cannot fail."

> *"I will do what I must."*

A crash of lightning!

A dark, monstrous figure silhouetted in the light…

A dream… Another dream.

Naomi couldn't recall a night where she hadn't dreamt in one way or the other; vivid, complicated dreams of wide fantasy, or others of plain simple truths explained. This dream bothered Naomi more than some of the others. This one was different, the urgency was real, the danger gripped around her heart. She never was good at deciphering between reality and fantasy, so Malindra advised her to keep a journal. It didn't look special in any way, just a small insignificant parchment of scribbles. She added to it over the years with scrap pages and spare twine. It really didn't look important to anyone, more like a pile of litter, but she liked it that way; it gave it character.

After scribbling for a moment, Naomi laid her head on her bed in thought. Waking in the middle of the night made her restless, especially after such a bizarre dream. It was hard to shut her brain down again. This dream affected her deeply, but the events of the previous day were still so near the surface of her emotions.

As her thoughts meandered, an idea came to her that she might have dreamt about the silver-haired girl before. She dreamt about a lot of different people, but the silver hair was distinct. She remembered it and quickly thumbed through some of the other pages. She read a few and soon was lost in the words of her journal, forgetting her original quest.

As she reached up to stretch, Naomi rubbed the nape of her neck in habit, massaging her muscles and remembering the odd mark she bore. The star symbol was something she seldom thought about anymore. No questions ever arose about it, thank goodness, since she always hid it behind a scarf; the silken scarf Malindra gave her. She loved the feel of the smooth fabric around her neck. The gypsy gave it to her, trusting she would always wear it. It provided security from her insecurity.

The night rolled on as she lay there in the dark, feeling the warmth of the covers over her feet and the comfort of the pillow beneath her head. But in the end, the brain won. She grabbed her journal and got up.

The moist, cool night air felt good on her face, refreshing with the wonderful fragrance of the earth. The night sky sparkled with the twinkle of the stars. How she loved the heavens and the night sky. She momentarily lost herself in the vast space, but reality soon returned.

A quick glance at the cottage reminded her of the prison her life was. Outdoors felt more like home. Naomi often thought about leaving. She hated living there. She hated the treatment; the wrath, the constant walking on eggshells, the constant demands and ridicule. And she hated Ferrell and hated the beatings. Ferrell had never attacked her, but she wished he would. She could handle it. How she wanted to rip into him every time he threatened Zander. She couldn't even say it was kind of Ferrell to provide a shelter for her. He clearly hated her as much as she disliked him. She detested his lifestyle. She wasn't a butcher - hated the idea entirely. Why did she stay in a place that was so utterly disgusting to her? But the thought always returned. Where would she go? What would she do? And what would happen to Zander if she left? Defeat rushed over her as she realized there was nothing else she could do. Her love for Zander was too great. Even though she felt this was no place for her, she had to protect him. She couldn't leave him helpless and alone in such misery.

The tall grass tickled her legs as she walked in the night air with her feet bare. She preferred to go bare foot everywhere she went. There was never an excuse good enough to make her wear boots. Town was not very far away, and she never ventured anywhere else, so what did it really matter if she wore shoes or not? Ferrell hated it. He said it made her look like a peasant. But that only spurred her on.

At first people questioned his taking in the orphan girl, but he never said much about it and concerns soon went away. Naomi was neither grateful nor angry about his decision to keep her. She cared nothing for the man. To love him was virtually impossible. Zander, however, she did love. There was no denying him the love he looked for in his father. How could she not love the boy? Such a tender creature he was. If it weren't for him, she would have left long ago.

The walk in the cool night air washed new life into her overactive mind. All the disturbing thoughts of her life and dreams seemed to disappear in the crisp air. The heaven of stars sparkled brightly around her, everyone smiling as it twinkled. No other lights disturbed the darkness and solitude of the moment. It was just her, feeling free and alive, away from the harboring troubles that weighed her down.

Was she disappointed with the way her life had turned out? She shouldn't have any complaints. She had a bed, a warm place to stay, and someone she cared about. As a child she had no aspirations, nor any expectations. She was an isolated, peculiar orphan who didn't belong anywhere. Even the gypsy children even had a hard time with her. She was different and strange, and they couldn't relate to her, though she had never done anything to provoke her seclusion. She always wished to be liked but had gotten used to being isolated and it had made her turn inward. She was tough, strong minded, and self-sufficient. She had to be. The world had abandoned her long ago.

The tall oak stood majestically near the river's edge, waiting and welcoming her home like an anxious mother, ready to sweep her child into her arms. The roar of the river made the tree even more inviting. Naomi loved this tree more than any living person should. There was no way to adequately describe her feelings when she climbed high into its branches and looked out at the world with no one knowing she was there. It was her private escape. It felt more like home to her than the cottage, more than the gypsies, even more than Malindra's place.

Naomi smiled as she reached the tree. It had been near two weeks since she had last climbed it. There was a trick to the climb, but she had done it so many times she could swing up easily now. Halfway up the arms of the tree, she found a cradle perfect for her frame. She sank into it and felt the pulse of its life flowing through each branch. She hugged it good morning.

Naomi pulled her homemade journal out from under her arm. Slowly she flipped through the pages, looking at her scribbling and deciphering notes she had written with her hen-scratch on the sides. A sliver of blue crept up the eastern horizon telling of mornings approach. She tugged gently on her scarf, wrapping it about her like a blanket of comfort. Soon she fell asleep.

NAOMI'S ADVENTURE

CONTINUES IN

PART TWO IN THE VIVATERA

SERIES

Available by Shadesilk Press

Acknowledgements

AMAZING THANKS to my original team at Xchyler for introducing me to your world, and my editing team: Elizabeth Gilliland, Heidi Birch, McKenna Gardner, and the wisdom of Penny Freeman.

LOVES to my cheerleaders, especially all my amazing family; Kevin, Mia and Jules, thank you for your patience; Bryon and Susan for letting me live; Becka and Lily—my muses: Beth for inspiration—Anata wa saikoda: Laurieann—my kindred spirit, for your kind instruction; Becky, Wendy, Sarah, and Todd, for waking the writer in me, and Gina for the Count Chocula; the Thursday girls, including Hong Kong Annette; the Blood Bankers, for asking about my book, like you cared; Martin and Benedict, for helping me survive editing; and Mrs. Carol Sawaya, for cultivating the first threads of creativity.

IN THIS EDITION: Oh, how my world has changed since I first released this beautiful book. Thank you to all the crew at Shadesilk Press, the Whiskey Writers, the League of Utah Writers and everyone involved in my authoring process – including the Infinite Monkeys, (the former) SLCC and FanX, LTUE, Fyrecon, and all who have come to my classes, talked with me, believed in me, and made me the writer I am today – THANK YOU.

ABOUT THE AUTHOR

Photo courtesy of Virginia Benincosa

CANDACE J. THOMAS is author of the VIVATERA SERIES, winner of the Diamond Award for Novel of the Year and Silver Quill. She has also penned VAMPIRE-ISH: A HYPOCHONDRIAC'S TALE, THE HAWKEED, and WANDERING BEAUTIFUL: Poetry for Dark Days, acclaimed 2019 Recommended Read by the League of Utah Writers.

Candace is known for her extreme fanatical love for both Count Chocula and smart, witty writing that expands her imagination and makes her wish she had thought of the idea.

Candace lives in Salt Lake City, Utah with her husband, two daughters, and her Siamese Snowshoe.

Follow Candace J. Thomas on:

candacejthomas.com

Facebook.com/candacejthomas.author

Twitter: @cjtwrites

Instagram: @candacejthomas

OTHER BOOKS BY
CANDACE J. THOMAS

Young Adult Fantasy

THE VIVATERA SERIES

VIVATERA

CONJECTRIX

EVERSTAR

Paranormal Satire

VAMPIRE-ISH: A HYPOCHONDRIAC'S TALE

Short Stories/Novellas

THE HAWKWEED

OF SNOW AND MOONLIGHT

Non-Fiction

SIX SIMPLE STEPS: BUILD A WORLD

Poetry

WANDERING BEAUTIFUL: POETRY FOR DARK
DAYS